TRUE
TO YOUR SERVICE

Sandra Antonelli

True to Your Service

For my dear dreadlocked friend Angelo Thompson, whose smile always reaches his eyes.

CHAPTER ONE

A dog and a wife, two things one didn't typically associate with a man in his profession. Married spies in fiction or on screen were few and far between—unless one counted tales of Russian sleeper agents living in plain sight. Married spies with smallish dogs best known for being the favourite companion to noblewomen in the Middle Ages were also an anomaly.

As the dog in the back seat nudged his snout between the headrests, Kitt glanced at the woman driving his car, and joy, unanticipated, vast joy enveloped him. He smiled. The last few months with Mae had been filled with moments of joy, joy that was as unexpected as having a wife and a dog, but with unexpected happiness also came an immeasurable sense of responsibility that stretched beyond his own self-preservation. It was a sober counterbalance to the giddiness of his joy and he frowned until his wife's sniff of disdain brought another smile to his face.

He watched Mae give the Bentley's ash veneer dashboard a once-over full of scorn. At the traffic lights, she looked at him in the passenger seat, picked a wad of fluff from the shoulder of his jacket, her mouth pursing, lips bunching like the white spring clouds over London. "Three months," she said, hazel eyes crinkling at the corners.

"Three months?"

Mae adjusted her grip on the steering wheel and accelerated through the intersection. "Three months is when the restlessness typically begins, when the inactivity of office-based work has burrowed beneath your skin, and it becomes evident, in subtle ways, that you believe the sedentariness of desk work is turning you soft in mind and body. I worked for you long enough to know the pattern. The occasional pulse in your jaw, the long sigh when you finish your scrambled eggs, the tension in your shoulders every time I turn onto the Outer Circle. You've been out of the field and in an office since mid-February. Three months is your limit."

"Valentine's Day to the first week of May is only two months and three weeks, and my mind turned to mush the day I confessed my feelings for you, which was nearly a year ago."

"My, how time flies when you're soft and in love." She gave him a quick, sidelong look and blew a tendril of blonde hair from her eye.

His transition from field agent to station-based intelligence officer had happened a little earlier than he had planned. He had actually been *reassigned* to Section SOST—Special Operations Selection and Training—as a result of breaking protocol in an unauthorised, yet successful action, where he lost bits of two fingers, nearly died, and uncovered ties funding terrorism through the sale of stolen cultural artefacts and counterfeit luxury goods. Most intelligence officers departed the harshest field work at fifty-five, leaving the more hazardous postings to younger women and men. The Consortium viewed all intelligence officers as assets to be utilised, it was 'once a field officer, always a field officer', regardless of age. How very broadminded of them.

The selection and training of new intelligence recruits was a challenge, and not the sort of challenge that stirred more than a generic enthusiasm in him. He lacked the patience for instructing officers who had some experience, yet were basically still novices, like Eaton, his current field trainee. Bryce had suggested his making an application to become head of Section SOST—an attractive prospect if it hadn't been for all the bloody paperwork Section Heads necessitated. At the moment, what he'd envisioned, and what Bryce had suggested, didn't matter, seeing as his reassignment was temporary and held him in limbo at HRM's—or more rightly, Llewelyn's—pleasure. His transition had yet to move from cocoon to chrysalis.

Kitt sighed exactly the way he had when he had finished his scrambled eggs this morning. "I admit I'm a bit bored, a bit impatient. I'll grow accustomed to it, as one does any change, but how do you think I'm soft?"

"Shall I start with this car?"

"You've never liked my car."

"Yes, because it's soft. For example," she gave another disdainful sniff, "it has a heated steering wheel."

"It's designed to warm the hands of a man with a cold heart."

"Your heart's not as cold as you think it is."

"And I'm not as soft as you think I am, but my hands are certainly like ice in winter."

"You could wear gloves when driving in the cold."

"The steering wheel is heated, so there's no need for gloves." A cool nose poked into the side of his neck again, this time, a little tongue licked his ear. Kitt pushed Felix's snout away. The Italian greyhound strained against his harness and set his narrow, ginger head between the front seats again. Somewhat absently, Kitt scratched beneath the dog's white chin.

Mae shook her head and continued her critique, eyes on the

road as she passed York Bridge at the edge of Regent's Park. "There's also the matter of the wooden dash."

"It looks pretty."

"Yes. Your car is very pretty, very *soft* and pretty."

"That little Sunbeam Alpine Julius Taittinger had in New Mexico, the one you said was the perfect car for me, had a walnut dash."

"That car was hot pink."

"Yet you said it was the car I ought to be driving instead of my Bentley."

"Which, I'd like to point out, *you* haven't driven in over a month."

"One must keep up appearances, Mae. That aside, I think, in embracing my soft life, I've come to enjoy your chauffeuring me about."

A loud *ha* burst from her mouth. "Did you learn nothing about how to lie when you were a young lad at spy school?"

"What should I have said?"

"Driving is difficult with my stubby fingerlings, Mae," she said, voice low and plummy.

"Yes, I sound just like that. I am always amazed by your uncanny talent with mimicry."

"And mockery." Eyes on the road, she caught the wiggling of stunted fingers on Kitt's left hand. He'd lost the tops of his fingers in a fight last year, and lived to tell the tale.

"Is there *anything* about this car you like?"

Her mouth pursed again. "It's a nice colour."

"It matches the green in your eyes," Kitt said as Felix licked his ear. Mae laughed and the Bentley skirted Regents Park, along the Outer Circle.

The muscles in his shoulders began to bunch and Kitt forced himself to relax as Mae chuckled. "Oh, stop it," he said, chuckling too. The mobile in his jacket buzzed. He pulled out the device. Morland, his superior's chief assistant, had sent a message—*Review relocated to Gray, 7:30.*

Kitt tapped out a reply: *Received.* He shoved the phone back in his jacket pocket and gazed out the window, watching bright green spring leaves flutter in the breeze, scratching Felix under the chin as Mae turned off the Outer Circle onto Chester Road, the street lined by fresh, new green leaves, an explosion of tulips, and pink cherry blossoms. "There," he said pointing to a parking space that had been vacated. "You can drop me there."

She pulled into the spot not far from the Broad Walk and The Espresso Bar café, shut off the engine, and released her seatbelt. For a moment, she rummaged in the centre console's cubbyhole and drew out the dog's lead. "Not to sound like a wife, but when do you think you'll be home tonight?"

"Not to sound like a husband, but after six." Felix nuzzled into Kitt's neck again. Gently, he pushed the eager-for-a-walk dog back and looked up at the parking signs, unlit streetlamps, and the open iron gate near the corner of the Broad Walk entrance. Yes, a wife and a dog, two things he never thought he'd want or have. "I like when you sound like a wife," he said, his tone idiotically earnest, and not any way corny.

"That's the benefit of being married to you rather than being your employee."

"Yes, I no longer pay you and you *still* care." He turned in his seat to face her. "Have you planned something for this evening?"

"Sean's invited us for dinner. He has something he wants to show us."

"Oh, goody."

"He's trying."

"Yes, you brother is quite trying—and judgemental."

5

"You can't blame him. His baby sister married a spy. He's being protective."

"No, no, he's being judgemental."

"It's taken years for him to step outside his comfort zone and make a change. He's worried about relapsing, slipping into old patterns of thoughts and behaviours. It's a challenge to start again in a new place, away from the support system he had."

"Ah, the cloistered brotherhood of priests keeping each other's secrets."

"You do realise how absurd that is for you to say, don't you?"

"I'm crushed by the irony." He opened the door and paused. "I understand the complexities of combat exposure PTSD, symptoms relapsing, and the previous government's inadequate support of veterans with mental health issues, but sometimes..."

"Sean is just a prick?"

"I was thinking misanthropic arse, but prick works well for Padre Sean Vincenzo."

Mae chuckled and watched a white sedan pass. The dog strained forward between the seats, but the harness he was belted into kept him from getting in front and into anyone's lap. Kitt glanced at the street lights and parking signs again. "Come here to the boot for a minute." He got out of the Bentley and shut the door.

Mae checked that no traffic was coming and climbed out of the car too pretty for an ugly-handsome man like her husband. Felix scampered about in the car, barking at two passing young men playing with a football. Mae went to the rear where the boot sat open, Kitt leaned into the space where she'd put her handbag and he'd tossed his sports bag and a shabby, old leather satchel. Dark, ginger-blond head bent, he stood with his arms inside the grey-lined gap, head hidden by the boot's lid. When he didn't straighten, she said, "What is it, have you become so soft that bending over to fetch your bags has made you slip a disc?"

"Come here."

She moved nearer. "Oh, you *have* hurt your back. Poor diddums."

"*Diddums?*"

"Would you prefer *schnookums?*"

"I would not." He motioned with his chin. "Come closer. I want you to have a look at something." The transit van behind them had its side door open, the driver unloading and stacking boxes onto an upright hand trolley on the footpath at the rear of the Bentley. Across the road, a mud-spattered Land Rover Defender, one that looked like it had come fresh from an expedition in the Amazon, had parked in the front of the bollards.

At his side, Mae bent forward, hands on the rim of the boot as she looked into it. "Yes, I see. You need a new car *and* a new satchel."

"I'd no sooner replace either one of them than I would replace you. Now, look." His eyes darted to the Land Rover and the bollards.

Felix let out a little half-whine of a bark. "What is it you want me to see? Felix is doing his little need-to-pee dance."

Blue-grey eyes met hers and he turned slightly. "Did you notice the street lights and bollards on either side of the Broad Walk?"

She shifted to straighten and look, but his swift hand kept her in place. He smiled softly, his fingers brushing over the top of hers. "The lights are there. Trust me.

"And you're telling me because..."

"There are digital video cameras hidden inside. CCTV cameras in the bollards across the footpath too, and the cameras see everything."

"As one hopes they would."

"One must keep up appearances and away from prying eyes, yet, like most husbands, I'd like to kiss my wife goodbye before I toddle off to work to deal with people and," he winced, "paper-work, but the cameras can see everything, Mae."

"You are ridiculously melodramatic," she said.

"Perhaps." He brushed the two normal-sized fingers of his left hand over his lips then touched them to the hand she'd rested on the inside rim of the boot.

She laughed and straightened, patting the dog's tennis ball bulging the pocket of her sporty pale-blue jacket and pulled at the waistband of cropped, black leggings. She was dressed for a run with the dog. Kitt's eyes travelled over her as she pushed back a strand of silver-shot blonde hair loosened from a ponytail. These days, she seldom wore her old uniform of navy-blue shirt dress and apron, and, unless working on a renovation project, her hair was rarely in a French braid. Kitt looked down at her hot pink joggers. He smiled, chuckling. "I miss your Doc Marten Mary-Janes—and your apron. You don't wear your apron anymore."

"I'll be sure to have it on when you get home." She took his satchel and an umbrella with a curved handle from inside the boot. "Here," she said, thrusting out the black, quintessentially British-looking object.

"It's not raining," he said, casting an eye at the blue sky.

She thrust the brolly closer. "Keeping up appearances?"

"Ah. Yes. The cameras." He took the old briefcase and umbrella.

"I know. You think about my apron and it addles your brain, makes you so sloppy you forget about cameras that see everything."

"You're a nuisance and I love you." He stepped away from the back of the car and their curtailed moment of marital normalcy. The transit van driver came back and shut the rear door, a small group of Lycra-clad men on bicycles hummed by, a woman wheeled along a baby in a pram.

Mae closed the boot and took Felix from the car. He'd pressed his nose and paws all over the rear-side windows, leaving damp smears all over the glass she'd polish clean later. She clipped on his lead, handed it to Kitt, and took his battered briefcase.

Umbrella in one hand, dog's leash in the other, Kitt walked around boxes and the hand trolley. Mae fell into step alongside him on the footpath, Felix sniffing, stopping to pee, prancing along and sniffing again. At the mouth of the Broad Walk, just near The Espresso Bar café, Felix peed on a black bollard and Kitt exhaled in annoyance at the unexpected sight of his colleagues. Three men rose from a table at the café and began to approach. By the time the dog had moved on to the next bollard to continue his business, Bryce had joined them, the others a few steps behind.

"Morning, Kitty," Bryce said brightly. He looked at Mae and peeing Felix.

Kitt wore no expression. "What are you doing here?"

"I've been reassigned from Shaw. I haven't been informed to whom as of yet, but I can guess. I see you brought your entourage."

"Ah, and *you've* brought Morland and Llewelyn."

"They followed me here. Good morning, Mrs Valentine." Bryce gave her a wink before Division Chief Brigadier Roger Llewelyn, and a stout bald man with a round, immobile face arrived to stand beside them. "Morland," Bryce said, "this is Mrs Valentine, Kitty's butler, and his dog, Felix. Morland is the administrative equivalent of you, Mrs Valentine."

"*Ah-huh-huh*," the Brigadier cleared his throat. "A very good morning to you, Mrs Valentine," Llewelyn said, his tone rousingly cheerful.

"Good morning, Brigadier." Mae said, her tone pleasantly professional, "Sergeant Bryce, Mr Morland."

Llewelyn looked like an older version of an actor many saw as a contender to play the 'new James Bond'. He had a rich, melodious voice and he watched Felix trot about on his lead, saying, "*This* is your dog, Major?"

Felix sniffed at his trouser leg.

Llewelyn chortled. "Hm. Not *quite* what I was expecting when Bryce said you had a *sighthound*. Now then, shall we carry on, gentlemen?"

Kitt handed Mae the lead and umbrella, and took his satchel. "Thank you, Valentine. If you get the chance today, Valentine, he needs his nails clipped." He turned away to face his superior, ignoring the stout man beside him.

"Excuse me, sir," Mae said.

Three sets of eyes shifted back to her. "There was a Chelsea bun left from breakfast," she said. "I put it in your satchel. Have a pleasant day at work." She watched Kitt's hard face change from ugly to handsome as he flashed her a smile. She left the four men and took Felix across the inner circle and into Queen Mary's Garden.

It was a lovely spring morning with a soft chill in the air. Green buds and tulips in full bloom showed their vibrant shades against the bright grass. After half an hour's run through verdant, dew-dappled beauty and cascading cherry blossom petals, the dog grew tired and Mae turned about. There were things to tend to at home, errands to run.

She passed by The Espresso Bar café and a strapping man wearing black sunglasses and a grey pork-pie hat too big for his head. He fumbled with a tourist map and muttered in Spanish to his mate in orange sunglasses. His bulky body reminded her of a man she'd come across in Sicily, an Asian man who had been all muscle and no neck. When she reached the car, she wiped the dampness from the dog's paws, shortened the lead of the travel harness, and secured him in the back seat. The Transit van remained in the parking spot behind the Bentley. Cyclists took advantage of the space to cross the street and head into the park.

Mae got in the driver's seat and shut the door. Felix settled down onto the rear seat and sighed.

She started the engine and looked out the windscreen. Up ahead, a small tipper lorry loaded with garden mulch turned onto Chester Road. More bicycles whizzed by alongside cars, cutting in front of the Bentley. On the other side of the road, the man in the orange sunglasses and his mate, the big man in the pork-pie hat asked two women waiting to cross for directions, showing them the map. The blonde in an expensive suit pointed to something, the thin brunette nodded and unbuttoned the front of an ice-blue jacket. Parents rolled along with prams on the footpath. A blur of man and bicycle flew past the dirty Land Rover still parked across the street.

Mae twisted slightly, and reached for the seatbelt. She pulled the metal buckle forward, across her shoulder, and the world exploded in a white-flashing thunderclap.

CHAPTER TWO

A curl of auburn hair spilled across Hilary's forehead as she leaned in between Bryce and Llewelyn to push a plate of biscuits into the centre of the table. She stepped away for a moment and returned with a tray of coffee. The City's Fraud Squad Assistant Commissioner Norman Saltzman cemented his eyes on her rounded arse, doing nothing to hide his lascivious gaze, but he did refrain from slapping or pinching the woman's arse, as he would have, Kitt surmised, had she been a barmaid in a pub and not the Special Operations Division floor manager.

Hilary placed a cup of coffee and a small brown paper packet in front of Brigadier Roger Llewelyn. "I found the chai you like, sir," she said.

He lifted the packet and patted the woman's arm with the affection an elderly uncle gave to a niece. "Why, Hilary, you are thoughtful to remember."

"Oh! It didn't cross my mind." Hilary shook her head. "Would you rather a cup of the chai now instead of coffee?"

"No, no. Don't trouble yourself. The coffee's fine. I prefer the chai in the evening." Llewelyn smiled like a matinee idol from the 40s and lifted the bag of aromatic, Christmas-like scented tea. "Would you be a darling and tuck it inside my case over there?" He glanced at a chair where his briefcase sat.

"Certainly," When she straightened, Hilary gave the Brigadier a wavering and wan smile. The young woman hadn't much cause to smile since her father had died in a shark attack while on holiday in Australia four months ago.

Kitt sat back. His Australian-born half-brother had lost his father in a similar manner, although the shark that killed Simon's dad had—as their mother said—bitten SAS Captain Lancaster Reed right in two when he'd been surfing Bells Beach off the Victorian coast. Hilary's father had been partially-eaten while snorkelling the Great Barrier Reef off the coast of Queensland.

Kitt brushed aside thoughts of fathers and hungry, predatory fish and watched hungry, predatory mammal Saltzman gaze covetously at a Chelsea bun that sat on a paper napkin. Then the man shifted his attention to Hilary tucking Llewelyn's packet of tea into a briefcase. Coffee and tea service complete, she headed for the exit with Saltzman's eyes cemented on her arse. The door sealed behind her with a gentle, audible sucking sound that indicated the room was secure.

The vent above began blowing in climate-controlled air, wafting about the scent of Mae's Chelsea bun, cinnamon, citrus, and a hint of cardamom perfuming the air. Windowless, like much of the Consortium's offices, the Gray Conference room, a space named not for its drab colour, but for Olga Gray, one of England's most successful female intelligence officers in the 1930s, had the most comfortable chairs in the entire building. While spaces void of windows dredged up the occasional memory of how close, not quite six month ago, he'd come to dying in a stifling, darkened shipping container full of counterfeit designer merchandise, forged artwork and dead bodies, the room's luxurious and supportive office chairs gave him a sense of cosy drowsiness and Kitt relaxed into the seat. As Mae suspected, he had deeply embraced the soft life; it was leather upholstered and Chelsea bun-scented.

Kitt strangled off an irritated sigh. Christ, he *was* bored with his work, but he hadn't been completely aware exactly how soft his life had become. It could have been a consequence of age, or maybe it was embracing the soft life with Mae. Most likely the doughiness did come from the mind-numbing restlessness of observing, writing reports, conducting interviews and shuffling papers like his former sergeant and friend Bryce, who now shuffled papers for Shaw, a younger intelligence officer in the field, since Kitt had left active field duty. The words *active field duty* and Bryce working for someone else prodded the low-level, flabby restlessness Kitt pretended not to notice had crept in. He had to get back to sprinting, to having ten-mile runs instead of three because, as he sat at the conference table in a comfy chair, his lethargy was so great he sipped an abominable beverage made from a dreadful machine that extracted the life from what had once been coffee beans, and felt just like the sorry, not quite a cup of coffee in his hand.

It was unusual, the casual milling about, waiting for an intelligence officer, or in this case, intelligence field trainee, to arrive. Eaton was late, something that normally would have reflected poorly on him, on his ability to instruct effectively, but Kitt suspected his trainee's tardiness was by Llewelyn's design. This was more than a performance review for Eaton's progress and Kitt glanced about the room, at the usual team members who sat in on trainee appraisals, and at guest Norman Saltzman.

Saltzman, sitting close to the door, slurped nosily from a mug, dug something from the edge of one nostril, and examined it. Sergeant Morland, Llewelyn's bald, bushy-browed executive, wrinkled his nose in disgust and glanced at Kitt over the rim of a mug, his podgy face a reminder of what a desk job could do to a man.

Llewelyn, Bryce, and Saltzman enthusiastically guzzled the frightful brew that came from a plastic pod. Kitt smiled to himself, aware of an important fact. If anything was truly soft, it was that bloody coffee machine and colleagues who were idiot enough to drink what came from it.

"Something you find amusing, Major Kitt?" An eyebrow arched on Llewelyn's handsome black face. Despite looking like an older version of Idris Elba, and having the stage voice of a Shakespearean thespian, very little actually amused Llewelyn.

Kitt dropped his eyes into his mug, the brew in the restaurant-quality ceramic was nearly as dark as his superior's skin, but not nearly as dark as his heart.

"Kitty's a coffee snob, sir." Bryce chuckled and shook his head, silver glinting in his thick, black hair.

"I am." Kitt lifted his gaze from the shite in his cup. "Yes."

"You could offer to share that Chelsea bun with us," Saltzman said, grey eyes on the sweet scroll Mae had baked that morning. He ogled the bun the same way he'd ogled Hilary.

Kitt hadn't touched the sweet scroll yet. It still sat on a paper napkin, next to the miserable coffee Bryce had made for him. "Yes. I could offer," he said.

"Your delightful housekeeper made that, did she, Major?" Llewelyn leaned forward across the table and inspected the bun that clearly surpassed the plate of biscuits on the table.

"Butler, sir," Bryce said. "Mrs Valentine is Kitty's *butler*."

"Thank you, Sergeant Bryce. I do beg your pardon, Major. I know first-hand that your *butler* is an excellent baker."

"You have a female butler?" Saltzman's upper lip curled, matching his eyebrow.

"They're all the rage this season." Kitt pulled the Chelsea bun closer.

"Butlers are men, women are *housekeepers*. I think the de-gendering of professions has gotten out of hand." Balding Saltzman unbuttoned the front of his chalk-striped jacket.

Kitt hadn't met Fraud Squad's Assistant Commissioner Saltzman until just before this briefing began, but he'd sized-up the man as an old-fashioned, public schoolboy dyed-in-the-wool sexist, misogynist, weaselly prick. Not so different to him really, or how he had been, or could still be on occasion. He looked at Saltzman, lifted the bun, and bit into it.

Llewelyn chose a custard cream from the plate of biscuits. "How's the hand, Major, miss the fingers much?" he said, dunking the biscuit into his coffee. "Your trainee mentioned something about phantom fingers, you finding it hard to scratch an itch, or something."

Four sets of eyes settled on Kitt chewing. He took his time, savouring the delightful cinnamon, raisin, orange peel and a hint of cardamom. Then he washed it down with the black shite in his cup, knowing the taste of the stuff would shock his system from the drowsiness he skirted. "I've adapted. And I know you're busy. Eaton's quite capable, sir—if not prone to inventing stories that are a load of cobblers."

"Rather a handy skill in this line of work. It's good your trainee knows the power of bullshit, the proper channels, the chain of command and such. And yet..." Llewelyn held up his left hand, wiggling five full fingers, and glanced at the tablet screen Morland laid beside his coffee, "despite your efficient training, Eaton is incapable of arriving on time for this meeting, which means we'll get on with it without the Captain. By now, you've probably surmised that this isn't merely a progress review of your trainee, or a learning opportunity your trainee is missing, Major."

"I have, sir."

"Now then, let's get to why. I had a cursory glance at the details so correct me if I miss something. This was brought to Economic Crime Division and the Fraud Squad Asset Recovery Team," Llewelyn orated, his tone stage-like, "after Hedison's auction house noticed an anomaly. Their Product Appraiser alerted Jill Charteris, the company's Research Department Fraud Specialist and Investigator, who uncovered potential fraud that involves the director of Amsterdam's botanical gardens and a ninety-three-year-old, much-lauded Dutch landscape and garden architect. Is that right, Assistant Commissioner Saltzman?"

Saltzman took a Jammie Dodger biscuit. He cleared his throat. "Yes." He bit into the biscuit and spoke with his mouth full, "Hedison's was contracted by Jan Vlaming, who approached a jewellery consignment associate with authorisation to act on the behalf of his Aunt Polly to sell a jewellery collection." He reached for another biscuit before finishing the one in his hand. "In carrying out the inspection of the rather substantial collection, Ignace Yaphet, the Product Appraiser with Hedison's, established that a number of pieces had manufactured gemstones or simply coloured glass. He immediately notified the Fraud Specialist Investigator,"

"Yes, yes. An auction house's case of fraud with imitation jewellery is not our usual fare." Llewelyn sipped his coffee. "Do go on, Assistant Commissioner."

Kitt brushed a speck of bun from his lap and kept his attention on his superior.

"Charteris ascertained that the gemstones had been kept in secure storage within a freeport located in Luxembourg. The nephew and his aunt admit that, in the past, they have used the services of various auction houses, Smythe & Dexter for example, but deny ever approaching Hedison's to sell anything. Which brings us back to Jill Charteris and Hedison's concern of fraud."

Llewelyn held up his empty cup. "Morland, dear boy, more coffee, please."

Casually, Kitt slipped his left hand into the pocket of his trousers, felt the wedding band he couldn't wear mixing with coins, rolled the ring in between the two shortened fingers, and waited as Morland went to the pod machine on a table beneath the painting of HRM. The coffee maker whirred and whined and hissed the way Kitt wanted to.

Llewelyn yawned, his moustache a salt and pepper archway above his open mouth. "Pardon me. Please continue, Assistant Commissioner."

Saltzman took another biscuit. "After several major and well-publicised instances of fraud, the kind that had the auction house making substantial pay-outs, Hedison's is decidedly wary and has doubled down on establishing provenance on every item auctioned," Saltzman said above the droning of the coffee machine. "As I mentioned, the aunt in this, Polly Dankwaerts, has previously engaged the services of other auction houses—Smythe & Dexter and Christie's for some antique gardening hand tools, she's never used Hedison's, and vehemently denies knowing anything about jewellery being up for sale. Her nephew, Jan Vlaming, attests she never directed him to approach Hedison's, which led Charteris to suspect Hedison's had dealings with an imposter."

"So then, this is a matter of identity theft. Again, not exactly our line of work." Bryce shook his head and Morland set a coffee mug in front of Llewelyn. "Does Charteris have any idea who the imposters were?" Bryce asked, a slight tinge of his Welsh heritage coming though. "And why does she believe Dankwaerts was an imposter and not simply a liar?"

Saltzman spoke over Morland's clanging a stainless-steel spoon against ceramic. "When Charteris contacted Jan Vlaming via video chat, Yaphet, the appraiser, said the man looked nothing like the blond Dutchman he'd met. Vlaming immediately went to check on the jewellery collection held in secure storage in the Luxembourg freeport. He discovered that—no surprise here—the Dankwaerts collection of diamonds and sapphire jewellery, in the family for generations, successfully hidden from the Nazis—was missing. Considering freeports and..." he slid his eyes to Kitt, "recent events, a lying nonagenarian who's renowned for her garden tours and garden party seems unlikely."

"Freeports." Llewelyn tapped the table. "There you have it, AC Saltzman. You and the Commissioner were right to believe this matter should occupy Spec-Ops Division and not just Fraud Squad. Although Major Kitt is no longer on active field duty, his recent experience with freeport thefts is why he joins us morning. However, what stands out here most to me isn't merely the Luxembourg freeport, it's the mention of Smythe & Dexter. It seems that case has quite a reach; Geneva, Singapore, and now very likely Luxembourg."

Kitt levelled his solid gaze on Llewelyn. The light brown eyes that looked back were lit with hellfire. "Obviously the Luxembourg freeport makes it noteworthy for us, but you believe the sale of items to Smythe & Dexter is significant, sir?" Kitt said.

"Mm." Llewelyn nodded faintly. "Yesterday, my counterpart in the *Algemene Inlichtingen-en Veiligheidsdienst*—that's AIVD, the Dutch General Intelligence and Security Service, AC Saltzman—mentioned Dutch master forgeries and a few names you'll be familiar with, Major: Julius Taittinger, Smythe & Dexter—as well as their former employee Ruby Bleuville, her partners Milton Foley, and the Consortium's very own dead little rats and associates, Bill Dalton, and Walter Molony."

Taittinger, Bleuville, Foley, Dalton and Molony, those names and 'freeport storage' pointed to a recent, bloody, personally-felt series of events that had nearly killed him, and exposed rot inside the Consortium, rot that, despite being excised, continued to have an impact across all departments within the organisation. Businessman and museum owner Milton Foley had died of a heart attack on his way to court late last month. Julius Taittinger sat awaiting trial at the Santa Fe New Mexico County detention facility. Kitt set his left palm on the table and tapped two stubby fingers missing fingernails and top knuckles. "What did Bleuville have to say about those forgeries?"

"The AIVD is sending someone to the New Mexico Women's Correctional Facility to talk to Bleuville today, Major," Llewelyn said, eyes still blazing. "I know you'd have preferred to have had the chance to speak with her yourself, but seeing as you are no longer an active field agent, that is not an option."

Kitt's head tilted to one side. "One can't always get what one wants," he said and took the tablet Morland handed him. He scanned the AIVD's courtesy report on the screen, found the essential information. "The Americans think this is connected to the Enrico Cartel."

"I understand Bleuville tried to kill you earlier this year, Major," Saltzman said.

Kitt went on reading what was on the screen. "Walter Moloney tried to kill me. Bleuville tried to kill my butler," he said lifting his head from some rather interesting information concerning missing paintings and stolen crocus bulbs.

"How fortunate she failed," Saltzman said. "Would have been a pity it to lose someone who bakes you such delectable-looking Chelsea buns." Grey eyes fixed on Kitt, he tapped the table, the *tik-tik-tik* of one long fingernail a metronome beat. "Yes, this is most certainly your catch, Brigadier. I'll reiterate that to the Commissioner."

"Thank you. Anything else you'd care to add, Major?" Llewelyn sipped his coffee.

Kitt passed the tablet back to Morland. "I see Charteris is set to meet with Jan Vlaming, during his aunt's annual garden party. Meeting Vlaming sooner would be better." Kitt paused for a moment. "Are you considering sending me to The Netherlands with Charteris, sir?"

"I can't send AC Saltzman along with them, now can I, Major? This is a perfect opportunity for you to continue Captain Eaton's training. I've sent Eaton to collect Charteris this morning. They're on their way. Morland's arranged your flights. You leave at one o'clock. Bryce will take over support from here."

Saltzman, clearly believing he'd be part of the action, scowled, which released a hit of dopamine in Kitt's brain. He felt the left corner of his mouth tip upwards. It was only an interview, one that unchained him from a desk and paperwork for a little while.

"A smile, Major?" Llewelyn smoothed his moustache again. "One would think that after almost dying in the line of duty last year, you'd be pleased to be our top instructor, and out of the field."

"Redistributed, shuffled into a new position as an instructor, a consultant, as a reservist asset, or administrator," Kitt angled his head slightly, "no one ever really gets away from or out of this line of work, do they, sir? To be honest, I can't really picture myself as an administrator. That's more for women like SOD Deputy Director Cubby, and men like the Assistant Commissioner and you, sir."

Llewelyn's soft smile was made of spines, the barely visible fine sort one found on Indian figs. "Yes, yes. Off you go to Amsterdam with Eaton and Charteris, Major, as an outside associate investigator for Hedison's. Morland, inform AIVD we're in their garden."

"Everything's in place, sir," raspy-voiced Morland's fingers flew over a tablet screen.

"Splendid." Llewelyn turned to Saltzman. "Many thanks to you and the Fraud Squad for your assistance in bringing this to our attention, Assistant Commis—" Three sharp peals of the crisis buzzer drowned out his words. "There's been an incident," Llewelyn stated the obvious as Morland pushed back his rolling chair and switched on the wall screen. Another tone, one with a higher pitch, sounded, indicating the building was now on immediate lockdown, all operations cancelled.

Morland adjusted the TV's volume, and they watched the BBC's coverage of the carnage on the Broad Walk for nine minutes before Tech Services finally sorted out routing the live feed from the CCTV cameras on Chester Road, footage from the camera closest to the collision nothing but a grey screen.

After twelve seconds of closed-circuit footage, Bryce said, "Is that your car, Kitty?"

"Yes, it is. Will you excuse me, sir?" Kitt rose, eyes on the wall screen zooming in on smashed motor vehicles, paramedics tending to the injured, sheet-covered bodies, a lone hot pink shoe. His fingers closed around the ring in his pocket, a thread of acid burned in his throat. He wanted to blame the sensation on the wretched pretext for a cup of coffee he'd drunk instead of a filament of fear based on a single shoe.

"How fortunate University Hospital is just up the road." Llewelyn reached across the table, snagged the edge of the paper napkin, and slid it along with the half-eaten Chelsea bun. "Morland," he lifted the bun to his mouth, "tell Rattray at the Security Desk to allow Major Kitt and the Assistant Commissioner to pass."

TWO HOURS LATER, the caustic thread was still in his throat when he bypassed the double doors that led to the morgue at University College London Hospital. Kitt walked along the hallway, behind the Forensic Pathologist.

Years of proficient experience nullifying emotion, his brain partitioned action from reaction as if the two things were far removed from ever being whole. There were essential peculiarities that came with his chosen profession. The virtue of patience was necessary to cultivate for intelligence work. Waiting, observing, forbearance were crucial elements for any operation. Being hasty, jumping to conclusions, trying to force a matter were all counter-productive. There were instances where he had to remind himself of all this, to remind himself to be patient, particularly when the passage of time was such an odd thing. The distance between particular moments could seem like minutes or years. The hours since he'd left the Consortium had passed like seconds, but the walk down the corridor behind Dr Marc Phancey lasted seven-hundred years and Kitt tumbled the chunky gold wedding band in his pocket through his fingers.

Dr Phancey pushed a hinged door and ducked into an interior suite. The TV Kitt passed in the family room down the hall broad-cast the media's speculation whether the *major incident* was an unfortunate accident or an act of terrorism. Bystanders and witnesses at the scene who had taken matters into their own hands before police had arrived made the matter even murkier. Confu-sion reigned. Whatever the case, the wounded—and dead—had been brought to this hospital. Kitt followed Dr Phancey into a pale-green room. While he'd expected something clinical, something smelling of antiseptic and hospital, the room was modern, comfort-able—and as windowless as the Gray conference room, the space softly lit up by light boxes showing a lake, green grass, flowers and trees. It was a lifeless view for a lifeless room meant to be soothing about lifelessness. "Why are we in here?" he said.

"We'll have more privacy in the Bereavement Suite than the morgue, where my colleagues are working. We can do this in here with photos on the tablet, exactly the way we would with anyone else." Dr Phancey managed a dry smile. "Are you with SO15 now?"

Another strand of acid laced along his oesophagus. "I'm a bit pressed for time, Marc."

"Of course," he said, folding back the cover on the tablet. "When was the last time we saw each other?"

"Suzuki's wedding."

"That's right. I don't suppose I'll get lunch out of you for this, will I?"

"Not this time." Kitt gave the man a small smile.

He smiled back, head shaking. "You know, I've never been able to find that Lebanese place the four of us went to all those years ago. That was a fun night."

"Simon and Hugo broke up a long time ago, Marc."

"I didn't ask you about your brother. What was the name of that girl you were with all those years ago, after Op Granby, Holly? *Honey*?"

"Honor." Kitt looked out a pretend window.

"Right, how could I forget that stupid 'Honor and off her' joke Simon made? I saw her in Paris last summer. At least, I thought it was her."

Kitt turned about. "Show me what you have, Doc." The burning in his throat intensified and spread into his chest. "Please."

Dr Phancey tucked the tablet against his hip, clearly unsettled by the favour he'd been asked to do. "The bodies haven't been prepared. We don't even know names yet."

"I'm aware of that."

Phancey's mouth flattened. "For fuck's sake, Kitt." He switched on the tablet and handed it over. "If you get queasy, the loo's across the hall," he said, and left.

Regardless of the proficient experience nullifying emotion he'd had, however his brain partitioned action from reaction and kept the two things far removed from ever being whole, a corrosive film scorched his chest and throat. Kitt swiped through the pictures of the dead, who numbered four in total. Broken-bodied, bones exposed, features obliterated by blood, by open wounds and open, sightless gazes, he took it all in until he reached blonde hair muddied and darkened by blood. For a long moment, he stared down and the world, his world, stopped turning. "Jesus Christ," he whispered, every iota of long-practised calm disintegrated as he crumpled, knees hitting carpet, tablet bouncing on the sofa.

CHAPTER THREE

"Excuse me. We're conducting an interview here," bespectacled Inspector Ponsonby said.

"Not anymore. She's being moved to a ward." The Charge Nurse, Gibson, a lean Indian man with curly black hair and muscular arms, slid the cubicle curtain across wider and stepped aside for a young freckled man wearing an orange zip-up vest, *Porter* printed on the back.

"Hold on now, this is important," Police Sergeant Chung put up a hand.

"Then follow us." Gibson turned and the porter began pushing Mae's wheelchair through Accident and Emergency, down a small maze of hallways to a lift, Felix a ginger crescent on her lap, two policemen from Counter Terrorism Command followed along, while Gibson walked alongside the porter and chattered away about the history of the University College Hospital.

Mae looked at the four men accompanying her. It was vests for all in men's fashion choice today; the dog's yellow wraparound,

Gibson's smock-like, the porter's high-visibility orange, Ponsonby and Chung's black—and bulletproof.

Was bulletproof really necessary?

Gibson pushed open a wide door. Impatient, Inspector Ponsonby went into the room, Sergeant Chung two steps behind. The injured witnesses who had been mobile had been moved from A&E and brought up several levels to a wing in one of the old red brick buildings, to a less hectic, quiet ward a world away from the sterile, drab notion conjured by the word *hospital*. With the exception of the standard adjustable hospital bed with side rails, the room was something straight from a country estate, with opulent Victorian furnishings, knick-knacks, and gilt-edged oil paintings of women with bustles and parasols. The sun filtered through filthy, paned glass sash windows that were stuck with pigeon poo, bits of downy feathers, dappling shadows on pink and green floral-patterned wallpaper.

A hospital room with Victorian furniture was not what Mae expected.

"It's where we usually house visiting dignitaries needing medical care." Gibson said, as the porter rolled her into the suite and locked the wheels.

Mae rose from the wheelchair and set Felix on his feet.

Ponsonby smiled pallidly. Well-dressed, his vest hid a slight paunch. Large, white rectangular glasses sat on a hairless face with a solid square jaw sporting a tiny shaving nick on the left side. "Make yourself comfortable."

"I'd be comfortable if we did this after I bathed." The knotted side tie of the pale-blue gown had twisted into her hip while in the wheelchair and Mae rubbed the irritation. Somewhere downstairs, in a different wing, police constables with the Met had collected her bloodied jacket, leggings, and the hot pink joggers she'd worn —or one of them anyway, she'd lost the left shoe. A nurse or doctor had washed her face and hands, but not her hair, and she stank of vomit and sweat and blood that wasn't hers.

The dog's makeshift lead slackened in her grip. She stared out the feather-dotted dirty window. A fat, grey pigeon flapped about on the window ledge. Felix darted to the glass, letting out a small bark. "I had to leave the woman there," she said softly. "I couldn't do anything for her."

"You've been through a lot." Ponsonby looked over his shoulder at the charge nurse. "Gibson, was it?" Ponsonby said.

"Yes."

"Thanks, Gibson," Chung cut his brown eyes to the door and the porter leaving.

Gibson stayed where he was. "She's my patient, she's being observed for concussion, but I'll do my best to stay out of your way, Inspector." Gibson lay a hand on Mae's shoulder. "Your watch and things are in a packet on the bed. We've contacted your brother, Mae."

"Thank you." Mae looked at the nurse's thick knuckles and then up at his moon-shaped face. "I think she choked on her own teeth."

Gibson gave her a pat. "I'll get you some tea and sandwiches. Towels are on the bed and the bed's made up with some rather lovely cotton sheets."

"I don't have to get in bed, do I?"

"No. You just need to relax. I'll get you the tea."

"I don't like tea, but thank you," Mae said.

"You'll have it and a sandwich anyway. I was a Captain and matron in the AMS, with the Queen Alexandra's Nursing Corps, so you'll follow my orders." He turned to Ponsonby, busy on his mobile. "Best you get to it now, Inspector, rather than later." Gibson glanced at Mae. "She'd be better off resting, but I do what I'm told." Frowning deeply, Gibson departed.

Sergeant Chung had busied himself arranging things. Tall, dark-eyed, he swept back a hook of black hair from his forehead and moved a small, square cherry wood table made for playing cards into the sunlight, placing three chairs around it. He gestured to Mae. "Come have a seat."

Mae sat on a straight-backed padded chair. The cushion under her bum was lumpy and needed to be re-stuffed. Felix trotted away from the window, sniffed at Chung's shoes. His paw touched the Sergeant's knee for a moment, as if to latch on and revert to the humping behaviour obedience training had broken, but the dog pranced off and plopped down on a red Persian rug in front of a fireplace. He yawned, mouth wide, tongue curling out and up. How the dog hadn't been hurt was a miracle. She watched Felix settle into a crescent and close his eyes.

Elbow on the table, Mae set her chin in her hand and felt something sticky there. She pulled her palm away, finding flakes of dried blood. This blood was hers; it had flowed from a slice across her ear, from a cut in her scalp, from a blow to her nose to stain her cheeks and sting the burns streaking her neck. The burns, the emergency doctor had explained, were caused by the chemicals that inflated the airbag, and the grimy smears and little cuts on her knees came from kneeling in gravel beside a woman gasping for air, her laboured breathing like pebbles in a Hoover.

Ponsonby pulled out a chair on the opposite side of the table and sat. He lay his mobile on the table and sighed. "Sergeant Chung and I will record this," he said.

"I'm sorry, Mrs Valentine. I know this is unpleasant, but it's necessary" Chung took a seat clearing his throat. "Walk us through it. Where were when you saw the driver being beaten with the cricket bat?"

"I already told you."

The two policemen glanced at each other. "We need you to tell us again, for the recorded statement."

"On the ground beside my employer's car. I'd been inside the car when it was smashed by the tipper lorry."

"Please speak up." Ponsonby pushed the phone closer, sat back, and crossed his arms, yawning.

"I was on the ground beside my employer's Bentley," she said, and glanced down at her wrist to check the time, forgetting her watch, glasses, necklace, and the diamond ring Kitt had given her were in a packet on the bed. She had no idea how much time had passed since the accident—or terror attack—and guessed by now Kitt would have heard the news, despite being shut away training his neophyte little spies or doing the paperwork associated with training neophyte little spies. She laughed, a *pfsst* of air.

Chung slung an arm over the back of his chair and looked over at the sleeping dog. "What do you remember about the tipper driver?"

Early last July, she'd been taken to a police station and questioned about the man she'd killed—in self-defence—in Kitt's kitchen. She'd been on a hit list. Valentine, the name she'd shared with her deceased husband, had been on a list—along with the names Bianco, Man, Torrisi, and Russo. Bianco had actually been the Sicilian town Misterbianco. Man was Li Man, a 'cleaner' for the Gallia Mafia family responsible for the hit list—although *hit or miss list* was more accurate. Torrisi was an immigration lawyer and refugee advocate, who was still alive, Russo had been a baker who lost his hand and his life, while she had been lucky and killed her assassin with a toilet brush. Mae wondered if these two policemen knew about her actions or if some details of the Gallia Mafia family's international money-laundering ring had been covered up or classified by Kitt's employers and the British government. The July interrogation had taken place in a dull grey room, the only window a small square in the door. Those two detectives had been no-nonsense and rude. These two policemen were no-nonsense and guarded.

"What do you remember about the tipper driver?" Chung said again.

"What do I remember?" she said, the top of her head throbbing. "Here's what I remember: the woman pinned between both vehicles, the woman on the ground, the man with the bicycle."

Chung ignored her question. "Go on."

"There was shouting, lots of shouting, and a cricket bat thumping a man on the ground near the tipper. I think it was the driver, but I never saw the person behind the wheel."

"What were you doing in the park?"

Mae laughed. "I dropped off my employer for a meeting and took his dog for a run."

"Can you tell us how many people were beating the driver?"

"No. I remember the cricket bat, not the people carrying out the beating." She looked at Ponsonby again. His spectacles were a throwback to early 70s Elton John, only without diamantes. She snorted, picturing the Inspector wearing a coat made of ostrich plumes and gold sequins. "I'm sorry. I don't mean to laugh. This is rather surreal and I feel as if I'm sleepwalking wide awake."

"Yes. That's totally understandable." Ponsonby inhaled and exhaled. "You're a butler, is that correct?"

"Yes. Inspector, has anyone ever said you remind them of Elton John?" she said.

Chung had a small cough to cover a chuckle before he made a clicking noise with his teeth. "A woman butler. Not something you see every day. Okay, this may be difficult and I'm sorry, but can you walk us through the morning? You dropped off your employer and then... Start with whatever you recall."

"I took the dog for a run. After the run, we went back to the car.

31

I passed a man in lycra whizzing about on his bike and another man in a pork-pie hat. He was built like a rugby player, you know, all muscle and no neck, and the pork-pie hat was too big for his head. He spoke Spanish. The dog and I got in the car to go. Except we didn't go anywhere because the tipper hit the car. I don't remember it actually happening. The next thing I know, I was looking at a woman crushed between the tipper and the car I was in. She was still alive, but choking on something. We were looking at each other. I think I got out of the car—well, I *fell* out of the car, and there was another woman on the ground, a man too. I'd seen him riding a bicycle. They were both dead."

Ponsonby adjusted his glasses and tapped soundless fingers on the table. "Did you see anyone get out of the tipper?"

"No. I was trying to..." Mae heard a sudden, rattling choking sound of the crushed woman's last breaths, "...I was attempting to give first aid to the woman trapped on the bonnet of my employer's car. She died right in front of me. I held her hand. All I could do was hold her hand. I couldn't help her or the other woman or the man. I guess I heard the cricket bat before I saw it.

"Did you see anyone inside the tipper then, or was the driver on the ground then?"

"No, but the door was open. Somebody had already pulled him out."

Ponsonby leaned forward. "How long did you witness the tipper driver being beaten before you tried to stop it?"

Mae squeezed her eyes shut and pinched the bridge of her nose, then wished she hadn't. The flesh was tender. She'd been struck by something that had made her nose bleed. Her head ached, the shell of her ear twinged in time with her heartbeat, the burns on her neck pulsed too, but nothing was broken. The woman crushed between the Bentley and tipper had been broken. The other woman and the man with the bicycle had been broken. The tipper driver, beaten with a cricket bat, had been broken. "A minute, three minutes, an hour, I don't know, he was broken. They were all broken. I couldn't help any of them." She opened her eyes. "Do you have enough? I'd like to bathe."

"Would you recognise any of the people who took a cricket bat to the driver?"

She snorted again. "After everything that happened this morning you could show me a photo of myself and I wouldn't recognise my own face. But I would recognise the cricket bat. It was bright pink."

Chung gave a compassionate nod of understanding, He smiled gently. "Perhaps If you close your eyes again and think ab—"

"When I close my eyes, I see the faces of three dead people, and mob of animals who set upon a man who may or may not have been a terrorist. I'd like to stop now."

"You are remarkably calm." Ponsonby said, glancing at Chung, fingers still tapping without sound.

"Panic in a situation such as this is not productive."

"Productive?" Ponsonby frowned.

"Inspector, do you have preconceived notions of how someone ought to behave when experiencing trauma and its aftermath? Since I'm female, you expect me to be a quivering mess? I assure you, I am bewildered, sickened, by the events of the morning, regardless of how I show it or don't show it."

"You're in shock." Chung said.

She looked at him flatly. "Thank you so much for explaining that to me."

There came a rap at the door, which then opened, a female police constable popping her head around the edge. "Excuse me, Inspector, Sergeant. They're asking for you downstairs."

Chung ceased the recording and stuffed the mobile in his

jacket. He and Ponsonby rose at the same time. "Maybe it's a good idea to take a break. We'll be back in a bit, Mrs Valentine."

A moment later, they were gone and Nurse Gibson returned with a china tea service for two, a selection of small triangle sandwiches, and a jug of water, which he set on the table. "There are some pyjamas in the wardrobe. They may be a little large; I guessed your size." He poured her a cup of tea and handed it to her. "Let me tend to the things in the bathroom. There was such a rush to get you here I didn't have to time to check if it was properly stocked."

For a minute, Mae was alone with Felix. She took off his yellow therapy dog vest and he scampered about before flopping onto to the rug. A crustless triangle sandwich in hand, she left the table and went to the small sitting area where the windows were cleaner, but only marginally. She felt as manky as the windows. Jaysus, how she wanted to scrub the muck off the glass. That sort of activity might scrub the muck and gristly images of death from her flat, impassive mind. Noticing vests, the Inspector's Elton John glasses —and imagining him in a feather outfit—was shock. It would pass. Eventually.

"Bathroom's all ready." Gibson said, coming out of the ensuite. "I've set some baby wash in the shower for you. You'll want to use that; it's milder and won't sting the grazes in your scalp."

The door swung open with a soft hiss. A man clomped into the room. Two bright red blotches stood on her brother's white face, Olivia Newton-John's *If Not for You* audible from his headphones.

Sean. Feck. She'd forgotten. Gibson had contacted her brother. Mae rose, glancing at the nurse.

"Maevy." Sean ignored the dog pawing at him and made a beeline to her. Still built like the middleweight boxer he'd been at twenty, he wrapped her in muscled arms, moaning, "Oh, Maevy. what're ya tryin' to do to me?" he said loudly. "I get a call sayin' you were hurt in that...that... attack in Regent's Park, and I spent an hour runnin' around trying to find ya here. Are ya hurt bad?" He grasped her elbows and held her away, looking her up and down. "Jaysus, look at ya, you're a mess," he half-shouted and let her go, a fist going to his mouth, his breath rushing in and out.

"I'm fine, Sean. I'm fine. I have a little cut on my head, that's all." Mae reached up, took his face between her hands and looked into bright blue eyes full of anxiety that circled close to a black hole of anguish. Then she let him go. He'd been drinking.

With a small sob, he jerked the headphones with one hand and dropped them around his neck. The headphones were a clear indication of the state of his mind; he wore them and listened to Olivia when he was hyper-aroused, when an external force had triggered anxiety that made his heart race, made him remember and relive horrifying memories. Swallowing, Sean leaned forward and pressed his forehead to hers. His skin was sweaty and he smelled of whiskey because self-soothing with music hadn't been enough. "Just one," he said. "Only one swig of the bottle, Mae. Sober for five years until today, and it's that man's fault," he muttered over tinny Olivia. "Everything is his fault, that bloody man ya work for, that bloody man ya ma—"

"Sean," she said, "I'm all right. I'm all right." She patted his chest and drew back. "I just need a shower. Okay?" She glanced at Gibson watching them, the man's face as passive as Sean's was dynamic.

Sean exhaled and nodded. "Okay. Okay." He dropped his eyes, looking at Felix pressing against his leg. "Comin' in here I was nearly brickin' it. You know I hate hospitals. Don't know how I'm managin' to hold in all the shit, but it'll be fallin' from me if I stay much longer. Ya put the heart crossways in me, Mae, and Janey Mack, the stink in here. Gimme the dog. I'll take the little humper home." He rested his hands on her shoulders and stared at her, a deep groove between his brows. "You're, okay, okay?"

"I'm okay. Go home. You can see I'm fine. Go home. Take Felix home for me."

"I just said I would, didn't I, woman?"

Gibson gave a slight cough.

Sean snapped upright, head turning, to eye Gibson testily. "And who might you be?" he blustered.

Mae turned side on and made the introduction. "Sean, this is the charge nurse, Captain Gibson. Captain, this is my brother."

Sean straightened, his disquiet suddenly shifting. "Beg your pardon, Captain. Padre Sean Vincenzo," he said, like the polite former military officer he had once been. Etiquette and formalities, she and Sean had lived their lives wrapped up in professional rituals and routines of one sort or another. Routine was what Sean needed. "Army, navy?"

"I was a matron in the AMS, Queen Alexandra's Nursing Corps, but I'm a clinical nurse specialist now." He held out his hand. "I'm very happy to meet you, Padre." Gibson smiled amiably and glanced at the headphones, then at the slender dog nosing the man's trousers. "That's splendid little dog there. Bet he'd outrun my little rocket Jack Russell."

Sean shook his hand. "Growing up, we had ratters, feisty little things they were—a lot like my sister. This one here's like a skinny little babby, but he'll do." Sean bent and lifted Felix. "He'll do nicely," he said, cuddling the animal close. "You'll excuse me, Captain. I'm not fond of hospitals. I'll take the dog and go now, Mae. You tell me when ya want to come home, and I'll meet ya outside. Unless that man ya," he sniffed derisively, "*work* for will fetch ya."

"As soon as the doctor tells me I can go, I'll let you know."

"Here." Gibson held out a card. "I understand. I know it's a challenge, believe me. I know that every day. Every. Day. If you ever want to talk, have a coffee, give me a ring." When Sean took the card, Gibson handed over the little yellow therapy assistant vest the dog had worn earlier. Mae had left it on the table, "Put this on him," Gibson said. "That way, no one will give you shit for having a dog with you."

Sean wrapped Felix in the vest, gave them both a nod, and the door hissed shut behind him. For a few minutes came a blessed silence. Gibson moved to fuss with pillows on the bed. Mae continued watching pigeons that had faces of the morning's deceased, and wondered if poo glued-on feathers could be removed with soap and water alone. Then there was a soft rap on the door and the hinge *shushhhed.*

"Good afternoon. Are you lost?" Gibson asked.

"I'm here for Valentine," Kitt said, hostility shading his politeness. "Who are you?"

"Mr Gibson is my nurse." Mae went on looking at a pigeon that had the cracked face of a dead woman. "This is Major Kitt, my employer, Mr Gibson. Felix, the dog, belongs to him, as did the car involved in the accident."

"I see."

"How bad is it, Valentine," Kitt said quietly.

"The car undrivable, sir."

"And you, Valentine?"

"I'm fine, sir," she said.

There was a long pause. "Would you mind giving us a moment, Gibson?"

"Certainly. I'm done here for now," Gibson halted at the door. "Please don't stay long. Mrs Valentine needs rest." The hinge *shushed* open and shut.

There was another moment of silence. Kitt looked down at the pattern on the reproduction Persian rug. He exhaled softly. "Are you all right, Mae?"

"I hit my head. How did you know about the car?"

"I saw it on the conference room wall screen, wreckage, paramedics, bodies covered with sheets, your pink shoe live via the CCTV cameras I pointed out to you this morning. Are you really all right?"

"I'm fine. How did you find me?"

"I'm a spy. I have connections."

Mae turned to face him. He looked at her, his face a mask of cool nothing bar the small trickle beneath his runny nose. She shrugged. "I got seven stitches. And this time I didn't need to hold your hand when the doctor sewed me like I did when I got the three in my lip last year."

From the top of her head to the flimsy hospital slippers on her feet, Kitt inspected her, taking in dirt-streaked red burns on her neck, a scabbing slice on her right ear, faintly puffy, pinkish nose, and hazel eyes tinged with half-concealed tension. "Come here," he said, suddenly gravel-voiced, and she came to him, her gait even, her eyes clear. She put her arms about him, her head on his chest, and he held her lightly, instead of crushing her to him and never letting go again. She looked awful, smelled terrible, and he didn't give a damn. His eyes burned and he let them go on burning, tears meandering along his cheek.

Her hands stroked down his back. The woman had been through hell and *she* was comforting *him*. "Don't cry, Hamish," she said.

"This isn't crying, Mae," he sniffled. "This is snivelling. If you want to know about crying, I thought one of those bodies I saw on the CCTV could have been yours. After I got access to the scene, I went to the morgue and looked at photos taken of the victims. The dead had just begun arriving for the coroner. None of the photos were you, and twenty-five minutes ago my relief was so over-whelming I sobbed so hard I couldn't stand."

She reached into his rear pocket, tugged out the neatly folded handkerchief he kept in there, and tucked it in his hand. "Blow your nose."

Kitt let her go and did as he was told.

"Take me home."

"I can't. You're under observation for concussion." He dabbed his eyes. "I spoke with your doctor. You did black out. You were sick. You were a little confused. Those are usually key signs of concussion." He pocketed the handkerchief and started to take her in his arms again, but he knew there was someone—Gibson, most likely—on the other side of the door. "Where were you when it happened?"

"Inside your car," she said.

He lifted her left hand and kissed the inside of her palm, just below her thumb. "Thank Christ for that small favour."

"A woman died right in front of me." She met his eyes. "It's different, Kitt, seeing someone die the shite way those women did, and what those people did to the tipper driver, not being able to do anything... Jaysus, it's all so...so..."

"Senseless."

"Yes."

His eyes wandered over her face, looking at her slightly swollen, pink nose, at the messy state of her hair, darkened with dried blood, at a patch where blue stitching closed a gash just above her hairline, at the dark smears of blood and blotchy red marks on her neck. "I am sorry you were part of it. And I'm sorry I can't stay here long. But I'll come back later and stay here with you, the whole night."

She held his gaze, and asked, almost shyly, "Maybe you could take leave. We could go away somewhere."

"I like that idea. I'd take you to Sicily, to visit with your friend Fiorella. We could eat her delightful food and watch her cheat in another game of Monopoly, but I'm sorry, I can't. As of this morning, I've been reassigned to field duty. I'm off to Amsterdam."

She reached up and touched his cheek. "There is something good that comes from this."

"Good?" He released her hand. "A silver lining in a possible terror attack and our keeping our marriage secret? You're in shock —you know you are—but tell me, where's the good here, Mae?"

"You have a reprieve from paperwork and," her eyes crinkled as she as smiled, her nose pink and slightly puffy, "you're getting a new car."

His mouth quirked and the phone he'd tucked inside his jacket pocket buzz-buzzed. He looked at the message from Bryce. *Eaton. ID confirmed. Level 3, Ward B, 5 minutes. Another change of plans.*

"Back to work?" she sighed.

"Yes. That was Bryce. I suspect he's why you're up here in this room with a private nurse looking after you instead of downstairs. After I looked at the photos in the morgue, I had to call in what I learned. We have confirmation, positive identification on one of two women that weren't you."

Mae went quiet for a moment and looked down at her left hand. "Who were they?"

"One was a fraud specialist investigator from Hedison's, on the way to a meeting with me this morning."

Her head came up, brows arching. "You knew her?"

"I was supposed to meet her this morning."

She bit her lips together for a second, thinking. "Was she the woman with her face crushed or the woman with her torso crushed?"

"Oh, my love."

Mae shrugged. "That's what I keep seeing. What was her name?"

"Jill Charteris."

"And the other woman?"

"Eva Eaton, a junior officer with The Consortium, and my trainee. The three of us were to travel together to Amsterdam."

"I'm sorry. Thank you for telling me." Her expression turned faraway. "I didn't see it, but I think the tipper mounted the footpath and swerved before it hit your car. Maybe the driver was trying to avoid a mother with the pram. Maybe a jogger ran out in front of him. I don't know. I can't figure out how...Jill ended up crushed in between."

The signs of traumatic shock manifested in all sorts of ways. He brushed a strand of hair from her forehead. "Listen. Whether it's a terror attack or dreadful accident, it's different, but it's not different, Mae, and this won't be easy." His blue-grey eyes full of warmth, he leaned in and kissed her, very softly. "I'll come back as soon as I can and we can talk about it. Talk about how to process this. If you want to. I'll have Bryce bring you some clothes." He lifted towels and a dressing gown she hadn't noticed from the bed and put them on the arm of an easy chair. "Go, get cleaned up, and rest like you were told you to. You're safe. That's what matters." He kissed her again, and left.

With a huff of frustration, Mae poured water into a teacup and guzzled it. She drew the curtains closed, turning the light in the room to dusk. Instead of undressing, she sat in the deep, comfortable wing-backed chair with a sprigged, Laura Ashley pattern, and set the empty teacup on the side table next to the chair. Then she shut her eyes, trying to exhale the nightmarish reality of what she'd seen, of what lingered with her eyes open or shut, of the void where emotion ought to have been.

She had lived when others had not. That in itself was disturbing, and not disturbing. It was different. But why was it different? She'd had witnessed death before, had ended the lives of two men, stumbled across bodies recently and not so recently dead. Why was seeing a woman die and the bodies of a nameless dead man and another woman any different? Why was witnessing a man being beaten to death any different? Why was she, as Ponsonby put it, so calm? Had she actually become desensitised to seeing death? Is that why this experience was so much more distorted?

Why was this experience blank and at the same time distorted?

She sat quietly, counting each inhale and exhale, focused, mindful of every breath until the questions ceased and deathly faces faded from view. When she opened her eyes, the mirror in the centre of the antique mahogany wardrobe near the ensuite bathroom returned a distorted reflection. Maybe it was a delayed response to the concussion she'd sustained when the tipper hit the Bentley, the airbag exploded to bloody her nose, the unbuckled seatbelt clasp had sliced her ear and she'd cracked her head on the side window. Last summer she'd had stitches in her lip. Today she'd had stitches in her scalp.

She blinked a few times, but the distortion remained, as did the man sitting in the wing-backed chair opposite hers. Dark-skinned and handsome, the older man smiled at her, and that smile was a distortion of everything a real smile was meant to be.

"Brigadier Llewelyn," she said, her moment of tranquillity giving way to stony antipathy.

CHAPTER FOUR

Llewelyn sighed. "I can't tell you how happy I am that you weren't severely injured, Mrs Valentine."

She stared at him coolly. The man had suspected her of crimes, had used her to ferret out rot within his own government department, had suspected Kitt of being crooked, yet she had a role to play, a husband to protect, a marriage to keep secret. "Thank you," she said.

He glanced at the towels on the arm of the chair. "Are you being well cared for here?

She nodded once and waited, but what she waited for she had no idea. He was here for a reason that would soon show itself. While she doubted it, it was possible he had simply come to pay his respect, to be thoughtful. Blandly, she fixed her gaze on him.

"If there's anything you need tonight, just let Gibson know. He's a fine fellow, Gibson, an excellent nurse. He was in the Army, matron in the AMS, with the Queen Alexandra's Nursing Corps, a captain, I believe."

"Yes, he's quite efficient." Mae went on being courteous like the professional she was. "Do I have you to thank for my lavish surroundings?"

"Consider it a token, a small gift to express my gratitude for your service earlier this year." Beneath a perfectly groomed moustache, Llewelyn smiled his perversion of a smile. There was an envelope tucked between his thigh and armrest. "I know you don't like me. Well, I know I have been a bit ill-mannered, neglecting to say thank you. Rest assured, I was most impressed by your assistance with the counterfeiting business earlier this year, Mrs Valentine. You have the gratitude of the British government...and my gratitude as well."

"Last year, you accused me of murder, money laundering, informed me my husband was a polygamist, and earlier this year you suspected me, and my employer, a man who works for you, of theft and treason. With respect Brigadier, fuck your gratitude," she said most politely.

Chuckling robustly, he motioned to her teacup and the china on the table. "Shall I ring Gibson for some fresh tea?"

"Thank you, I don't care for tea."

He chuckled again. "Just like your employer."

Llewelyn lifted an envelope that he'd tucked beside him on the chair. Well then," the older man said, "perhaps it's best I take my leave as well, and let you rest, Mrs Valentine." He paused, and turned slightly. "Would you mind terribly if I used your lav?"

"Of course not," she gestured to the ensuite, wanting nothing more than to be in that room beneath a spray of scalding water. She moved back to the windows, drawing back the curtain to again stare out glass hazed by bird shit. She was still there when Llewelyn came out of the bathroom.

He said, "Before I go, Mrs Valentine, there is one thing."

Mae turned, toes bunching inside slippers that were too big on her feet. "What do you want, Brigadier?"

"There is something refreshing about getting right to the point."

"Then please get right to yours."

Envelope under his arm, Llewelyn crossed the room and went to the table, pouring himself a cup of the tea Gibson had made. He watched her with devilish, amused eyes and added sugar and milk to his teacup, the spoon a chiming *ting-a-ling* on green and white garland-edged china Kitt would say was Royal Albert or Royal Worcester or Royal Stafford. "It's hard to imagine a man like Major Kitt owning a dog, but there you are, looking after the animal the way you look after him. I do hope the Major appreciates all you do for him, Mae. May I call you Mae, Mrs Valentine?"

"No." Mae touched her head. It had begun to ache and sting. She moved to sit in one of the overstuffed chairs.

"Yes, yes. All right." He sipped his tea, rather daintily. "There is something I am hoping you can help me with."

"Which is?"

He put down the cup, opened the envelope, pulled out a few pages of something, and crossed over to her. "These are some images we were able to isolate from CCTV footage. Do you recognise these men? Do they look like anyone you've seen before, perhaps when you were working for Dr Julius Taittinger earlier this year?" He turned a paper about. The image on it was somewhat grainy, but the colour photo showed two men, one with orange sunglasses and a dark stubble of beard, the other, muscly with no neck, black-framed glasses and a pork-pie hat too big for his head. His features were obscured by the hat and sunglasses

"I don't know who these men are, but I saw them this morning, just before the lorry hit." She released a brittle laugh and pointed. "The man in the hat spoke Spanish. He reminds me of Li Man, the Chinese 'cleaner' who the killed the UN banker, Aurelio Martini, in Sicily last year."

"How interesting" Llewelyn said, as if amused rather than fascinated.

"Did the man in the hat die?"

"No." He shuffled to the next few pages, showing her other images of a brunette woman in ice blue, of men on bicycles, a mother with a pram.

Somehow Mae felt filthier than before. "The woman in blue was dead right beside Major Kitt's car. I don't know who they are. I'm sorry I can't help you more than that."

"Oh, but you can. I once told you your loyalty to your employer was commendable. I understand you're grateful to him for sorting out that trouble with your husband, the money laundering, you killing those two men. You may feel beholden to him for his help with that mess, perhaps you're even in love with him. But we both know what fruitless nonsense that is. We both know his tastes run to women who are, frankly, younger—and disposable. However, he values you and your dedication, your friendship even, and rightly so. Good help is so hard to come by, particularly help you can trust with certain confidences. It hasn't escaped my attention that you're a very capable woman. I've been informed you are quick to think on your feet and take direction well. I need you to do me another favour. Like you did earlier this year."

"I'm a butler, not feckin' Mrs Pollifax."

"And we're not the CIA." He sipped more tea. "You'll simply observe what's going on about you. You are exceptionally well-trained as a butler. Your observation skills are excellent. This suits you perfectly. You'll be briefed beforehand, but the observation is all there is to it. Afterwards, have a little holiday on the British government. I'd say you've earned it." He smiled handsomely. "The Netherlands can be quite pretty in the spring. Your husband was a gardener, wasn't he? Yes, a Master Gardener, if I'm not mistaken. In your short time with Caspar I imagine you learned quite a bit about trees and flowers and grass and such. So then, what do you say?"

"Have a pleasant afternoon."

"Let me think how to rephrase this." He paused, put the photos back in the envelope, returned to the table, and helped himself to a cucumber sandwich.

Mae wondered what the penalty would be for smashing a china teapot over the head of a Brigadier General. She'd had a traumatic experience and concussion, she could say she wasn't right in her head, and that could be used as grounds for defence in breaking vintage crockery and killing Llewelyn.

Llewelyn, brushed crumbs from the lapel of his jacket and moustache. "There are some who were dissatisfied with the Major's conduct in his last two assignments. There were consequences; he's been censured, removed from field duty, and rightly so. There's been a push for a far harsher penalty; he did, after all, break several international laws and treaties that are punishable by imprisonment."

Mae's stomach melted into her feet, taking her liquified heart to the tips of her toes. Her fingers closed around the teacup she'd left on the table beside her chair. "Are you about to extort me, Brigadier?"

"Indeed."

Instead of lobbing china at his handsome face, Mae swore crudely, in English, Italian, and Sicilian, calling him every filthy name she could think of.

Llewelyn smiled again. "How marvellous that you are multilingual, Mrs Valentine."

Mae put a hand to her forehead, teacup hanging from her forefinger. "Jaysus, Jaysus, you people," she muttered. "You won't let go. I've given you no real cause, done everything you've...*asked* me to do, and yet you think I'm hiding something. We both know it is not my antipathy for you."

"To be frank, my dear, I don't trust you."

"Well, we share common ground there. I don't trust you either."

He smiled. "All of our operations require legal authorisation, approval in advance, to avoid political risk. Our political allies don't like it when we shit in their garden. They don't like if we leave shit *in* their garden, and they're especially unhappy if we take shit from their garden, particularly without asking. In the last year, Major Kitt has created quite a shitstorm. One might think the Americans complained the loudest, but the Italians have shouted even louder. Of course, the Major got the job done, he saved lives, including yours, and, to put it bluntly, a fucking load of money. Nonetheless, the Foreign Secretary is being rather vocal about making an example. For some reason, it reminded her of the concealment of sexual abuse and exploitation scandals that took place in Bosnia, the ones that implicated UN personnel, well over twenty years ago. She is adamant that we can't brush things under the rug anymore. Transparency, she believes, is key to international relations."

She wrapped her hand around the cup. "How exactly is extortion, your threatening to imprison Major Kitt if I refuse to cooperate, *transparent*?"

"Major Kitt?" Llewelyn chuckled. "I have no doubt Major Kitt could survive quite well in prison, yet he's better placed, far more suitable where he is. Yes, Kitt would fly through imprisonment, but I'm not so sure about your brother."

"My brother?"

He sipped tea and sighed. "Your brother, Mrs Valentine, he was a Chaplain with UN Peacekeepers in Bosnia all those years ago, wasn't he, with the bunch of chaps who were kidnapped and held? I've been around long enough to recognise PTSD in soldiers. It's insidious how it lingers, how it digs into a man, how it can return.

Anything can trigger it. There are hospitals, you know, institutions that treat that sort of thing. Long-term."

The air rushed from her lungs, her mouth sagged open, and Mae stared at Llewelyn malevolently. Gibson. Fecking Gibson wasn't just a nurse. He was a bloody information-gathering mole for The Consortium.

"Now then, it's quite simple really. I want you to go to The Netherlands and see if you can make an identification. Aside from one or two minor issues to tend to, it's already been authorised. My assistant has already made arrangements." He crossed to her, smiled, leaned over slightly, and held out the envelope. "I certainly hope the Major and your brother appreciate all you do for them."

There came a slight rap and quiet hiss of the door opening. Kitt entered, smiling softly, but his smile widened and the earlier warmth that had shone in in his blue-grey eyes dimmed to ash.

Llewelyn straightened, envelope in hand. "What took you so long, Major Kitt?"

"Excuse me, sir. You said to meet you in Ward B." Kitt said. "This is Ward D."

"Did I? I thought I said *D*. Not to worry, here you are." Llewelyn's tilted his head, his grin self-satisfied. "And here's your delightful housekeeper. Oh, I do beg your pardon. *Butler.*"

Mae's heart beat in her temples while casual, dispassionate, Kitt slid a hand into the pocket of his trousers. "I'm very pleased to see you're not severely injured, Valentine."

"Thank you, sir."

He stopped smiling. "And my dog?"

"Felix is fine. My brother collected him. I am sorry about your Bentley," she said, throat tight. "I'm afraid it's a write-off."

"It's only a car, Valentine."

"Yes, yes, and you are insured, Major." Llewelyn tapped the envelope against his leg. "So, now that you are here, let's get on with it. We take pride in thinking best under pressure. Your meeting with Jan Vlaming has been moved forward to tomorrow. Mrs Valentine will accompany you to Amsterdam."

Any protest Mae had was lost in a freakish little thrill followed by an abrupt paroxysm that rendered her tongue immovable. She watched the dimmed ashes in Kitt's eyes spark to skilfully contained, molten rage. "Valentine will accompany me?" he said, perfectly still, utterly composed, words burning with frostbite.

"Yes."

"Is it your plan that Valentine pose as Jill Charteris?"

"My word, no! Mrs Valentine will simply accompany you."

"Whatever for?"

Mae let out a noisy breath.

Llewelyn shrugged one shoulder offhandedly and ignored the question. "As I said, you will meet with Jan Vlaming. Mrs Valentine will observe."

Mae snorted suddenly, mumbling, *"Jan Vlaming."*

Kitt said nothing for a moment. He glanced at her. She held a teacup in her hand, her top lip in a cynical twist. She didn't look at him, her attention fixed on inspecting the gilt edge of a china cup he automatically identified as Royal Grafton. Oh, Christ.

Llewelyn went on, "Hedison's has agreed for you to stand in for Charteris and meet with Vlaming. Bryce is making the necessary arrangements." He shook the envelope. "Here are the necessaries."

"Sorry. I'm unclear as to the *necessary* purpose of including my Valentine in this action."

"Dear boy." Llewelyn gave a slight sniff. "You've seen the rough CCTV footage Tech's managed to pull, but even before you did, I know you thought this was related to the ghastly business with the freeports that nearly saw you dead last year, and I know you think your Mrs Valentine is in a unique position to identify any player we may have missed."

"I am in exactly the same position," Kitt said bloodlessly. "Send me alone."

"Professor Boothroyd has been invited to the garden party thrown by Polly Dankwaerts, but can't make it. Mrs Valentine will go at his behest."

"Professor Boothroyd? Are you serious, sir?"

"I am. It's all arranged and it's an excellent cover. Mrs Valentine will go about her business, shadow you, and *observe*. You were training Eaton, now you are training Mrs Valentine. Understood?"

Kitt glanced at Mae, reality stinging, tiny poison-tipped darts piercing his heart. "This is impossible," he muttered.

Llewelyn held up the envelope. "If you truly need me to spell it out, the reasoning is all here, along with the 'Professor's' background for Mrs Valentine. Brief her thoroughly."

Mae saw Kitt chew on his superior's explanation and swallow it along with his ire. "She is not a professional," he said, "and she's had head injury. With respect, sir, she's a butler, not an intelligence officer."

"She has proved herself to be excellent in observation, no detail is beyond her scrutiny. As for her injuries, Gibson informed me her scans were clear. She'll be fine after a good night's rest, and come now, she's already participated in two previous actions."

"Her two previous actions were enough. She'll get in my way. I can assure you the woman is a nuisance."

"A nuisance?" Llewelyn half turned, chuckling. "See what he thinks of you, Mrs Valentine?"

"My point is, sir, recruiting, using untrained civilians is criminal."

The corners of Llewelyn's mouth lifted and kissed the edges of his moustache. "Criminal, dear boy? Don't lecture me about what's criminal. Insubordination does not reflect well on your position. I admit I find your sense of chivalry admirable, even if it is exactly what got you stabbed in the back all those years ago. However, I hardly think a woman like Mrs Valentine would see you stepping in as an act of gallantry, when she's perfectly capable of making her own decisions, and she's already decided to assist."

Kitt sustained a mask of nothingness, but his blistering gaze slid to Mae as she set aside the teacup. He stared. Mae looked at the floral wallpaper, at the tea set and lone sandwich on the table, at Llewelyn, at anything but Kitt. She'd been cornered, rendered speechless, someone else had taken control of her life, a life now wholly intertwined, married to someone fascinating and reprehensible who did things fascinating and fiendish. She watched Llewelyn's grin turn smug.

"I object to this." Kitt said. "Untrained civilians are a liability."

"Your objection is noted, Major, but things are settled. So be a good lad and teach the woman. Brief her well." He dropped the envelope on the table beside the tea things, chuckling, and moved to the door "The flight leaves before eight tomorrow morning. It may still be early enough in the season. If the weather's fine, as you fly into the Netherlands, you'll see the fields of tulips in bloom."

Llewelyn crossed the room and left. The door hinge *shushed* open and *hissed* closed, and everything was at once utterly still. Kitt stared at the door. "What have you done?" his words might have been barely above a whisper, but Mae heard them.

CHAPTER FIVE

"I did the only thing I could," she said, rising gingerly, hand to hair darkened by dried blood, and went to pour water into her china teacup.

All the acid that had cooled in his chest and throat had returned to squeeze in around his heart and infuse his muscles. The caustic heat was different now, the sharp sense of this panic— and despite wanting to convince himself otherwise, those moments in the Bereavement Suite had been panic and this was as well, and it was fuelled by self-loathing and swelling antipathy for a man he had respected for years. Except he knew the hatred for Llewelyn was misplaced. The man had always been calculating, and had to be in his position. Kitt knew what was more accurate, what was more abhorrent was that he only had himself to blame for all of this. The shortcomings that put him in this situation, that put Mae in this situation, were entirely his responsibility. "This is impossible," he muttered again, and then swore, vile words strung together nonsensically.

She stared out dirty windows. "Llewelyn made threats," she said.

"Yes. And you know he's a man who follows through, who carries out his threats." He moved behind her.

The too-large slippers she wore tripped her slightly as she turned. "I know you're angry."

"And what are you, Mae?"

"I'm numb, sticky, and I can't think."

"Did you think when you agreed to do him another bloody favour?"

"What would you have me do?"

Full of rage, of fear, Kitt stared at her. "God damn it, Mae. You have not, despite what you may think at the moment, developed a taste for this work. You have not."

"I love you, Hamish. I want to be with you. I had no other choice." She turned about again, watching birds outside dirty windows.

"You're right. I'd say you had a choice," Kitt said stomach twisting with anger and fright, "but he'd have you put in prison just to prove a sodding point."

Mae looked at him over a shoulder. "He never threatened to me put in prison."

Kitt's eye narrowed. "How exactly did Llewelyn threaten you?

Her mouth opened and closed as she squinted back at him. "He didn't threaten *me* at all." She shook her head. "At first, he threatened *you*, he said he'd have you incarcerated, but tha—"

Kitt let out a hard, dry bark of a laugh. "That's what you meant by *the only thing you could*. I would have been fine in prison, Mae."

"Yes, having had the experience of being imprisoned earlier this year, you would be fine, but Sean would not."

"Sean?"

"Llewelyn implied something unseemly happened during

Sean's time in Bosnia with the UN forces, besides his kidnapping, and he made a mention of treating my brother's PTSD—*in an institution*."

Kitt stood very still, maddeningly calm, irritatingly inexpressive. "I'm sorry," he said.

Mae wanted to shout at him, yet her exasperation lay compressed by confusion and desensitising shock. The day had been one different shock after another, nothing lasting long enough to settle into a single comprehensible emotion except for the infuriating scratch of Kitt's composure. With a huff, she went back to looking out the window. "Why does Llewelyn want me to do this?"

"Because it has something to do with freeports and what happened earlier this year. It's tricky to sanction, but it fits, and it's a functional way to get you to The Netherlands. The paperwork's nice and tidy, easy to authorise—since you *volunteered*—and he can justify it by saying 'she had the experience last January, and the man Charteris was set to meet has a connection to theft from the freeport in Luxembourg', or something along that line."

She'd tipped her head, one eye slightly squinted. "Llewelyn's voice is deeper, more Brian Blessed than Patrick Stewart. Freeports as in Julius Taittinger, Ruby Bleuville, Milton Foley stealing artefacts, counterfeiting them, funding terrorism, and you faking your death last Christmas freeports?"

"I did not fake my own death."

She glanced back at him, mouth compressing contritely before she turned and faced the dirty windows. "Forgive me," she said. "I meant freeports as in Julius Taittinger, Ruby Bleuville, Milton Foley stealing artefacts, counterfeiting them, funding terrorism, and *you almost dying in a shipping container last Christmas* freeports?

"Possibly. I think it's related to auction houses, Hedison's, Smythe & Dexter, Ruby Bleuville, maybe Taittinger and the theft of cultural artefacts, but how I don't know. I'm still trying to formulate a theory. I'm hoping to get a better idea once I speak to this man in Amsterdam tomorrow." He fell silent for a moment, watching her watch birds.

She made a sniffing sound. "I'm roped in to this because you died and I volunteered for that mess in New Mexico with Julius Taittinger and Ruby Bleuville last Christmas."

He went on watching her. "There is a way out of this, you know."

Mae spun about. "Are you about to suggest I fake my death like you did, or that I walk away?"

"I did *not* fake my death." He cocked his head. "Head injuries can be sneaky. It's known to happen sometimes, a concussion thought minor turns into a brain bleed. I know someone, a doctor who'd cooperate with the examination. It's not so much fake your death as simulate a debilitating brain injury."

"And then what?"

"You walk away. Far away. You use the passport I got you, the accounts I showed you, and you go to Belize, Tasmania, New Mexico."

"I'm *not* walking away and you're not letting me go. We settled this, remember? That's why we..." Mae exhaled, not trusting his assertion that there was no bug in the room. "So, there it is then. I'm going to Amsterdam with you." A twisting itchiness skittered beneath her skin, the ghastliness of the morning coating her with inexplicable filth that had become thick and heavy and need to be scoured away like the muck on the windows. "Who is Professor Boothroyd?"

"A name, a cover, a backstory for your presence."

She rubbed her arms, her laugh derisive and sibilant. "It's like that Cary Grant film, the one with Mount Rushmore and the nonexistent secret agent. All we need is a statue full of microfilm and a plane to terrorise us in a cornfield."

"This is not a film."

"It certainly feels like one." Mae mumbled and huffed.

"Cover is established as a precaution."

"A safeguard, just like in a film. Was this morning a terror attack or did some poor sod have a medical episode?"

"We don't know yet."

She rubbed her arms harder. "I feel so feckin' dirty." She began trying to unknot the side strings of the hospital gown, the tips of suddenly shaking fingers digging into the cloth.

"Here, let me help." He reached for the gown.

"I don't need your help. I've got it." Mae pulled away and headed for the bathroom.

Kitt crossed the room and locked the door. Miserable and wallowing in it self-indulgently, he plopped into a chair. "What have you done," he muttered between his teeth, watching her push into the ensuite.

Frustrated by the knots, Mae pulled the gown overhead. An array of various sized fluffy, hotel-quality towels hung on hooks beside a thick dressing gown outside the shower. Like a hotel, the lavender and verbena toiletries on offer were from Crabtree & Evelyn, right beside the antibacterial hospital-grade handwash, box of rubber gloves, and yellow sharps container. With a twist of a handle, hot water flowed from a massage shower head above. Although as opulent as the bedroom, the bathroom had also been designed to accommodate a wheelchair, the shower an open space, a curtain in place of a screen or panel.

Perfumed shampoo in hand, Mae pulled the curtain aide, stepped into hot spray, turned, tipped back her head, and let water rain down on her sticky hair. Pain shot deeply across her scalp, water stinging the burns on her neck and slice across her ear, jerking her clear of the last few hours, and the luxury shampoo fell from her grip, her hands smacked wet walls. "Oh, sweet blessed Jaysus!" she hollered, water hammering at her feet.

The shower curtain slid aside. "Mae," Kitt said.

Hair wet, rivulets of pinkish water tricked over her face, her eyes brimming with tears of pain as she looked up at him. "Jaysus."

Kitt toed off his shoes, yanked off his clothes, and got into the shower still wearing socks. He ran a gentle hand down her arm and pulled her from the tiles, pressing his chest to her back. "The water is too hot." Socks sodden, he twisted the mixer to a cooler setting.

She drew his arms around her, one palm flat on her waist, her hand over the top, fingers clawing into his skin, muttering curses.

Kitt held her for a long moment, bending his cheek to hers. "The burns on your neck won't scar, neither will the cut on your ear." He reached above her, to a small wire shelf, pulling out a pale-yellow bottle with a lid he flipped open. "I know the shampoo smells nice, but there's a better way to do this." He showed her the bottle of baby wash. "It's an old spy trick, and the advertising doesn't lie: no more tears. Another thing, you don't want the water to hit so hard that it's like needles on your wounds, you want it to run down, that way it won't sting as much." He guided her forward. "Lean over a little and cover your face. I'll wash your hair."

This time, she didn't pull away when he offered his help. Mae did as she was told, and bent into the edge of the shower spray, flinching and sucking air through her teeth. Then she began to sputter and cry, angrily.

Kitt waited for her tears of pain and anger to explode into tears of fear and the realisation she had survived what had been a lethal morning for others, but her mouth remained fixed with teeth-clenching determination. Carefully, as gently as possible, Kitt began shampooing her hair, the thin baby wash barely foaming as he worked his way from forehead to crown to the base of her skull and nape of her neck, washing away dirt and bloodstains. She sobbed and snorted and swore as he massaged her neck and shoulders, his thumbs sliding over the lumpy scar tissue left behind from the small calibre bullet that had struck her earlier in the year. He kneaded out the tension and her noisy tears of rage began to wane. "There now. There," he said, pushing back wet hair, and, as gently as possible, he moved on to wash the rest of her, his hands soft on her warm, wet skin. "Lift your arms."

Arms raised, she murmured, voice clogged and wavering. "I know this is processing what happened, but I can't stand here in the shower all day and cry."

"Why not?" Kitt soaped beneath one arm and side of her breast. "Crying is a natural release. Women are lucky they can access that release better than men."

"You cry all the time."

"Yes, I've become quite the cry-baby since realising I loved you. I think it's made me a better man."

"And a worse spy."

He gave a soft chuckle and Mae watched his hands move over her left breast. "There's no outcome to crying more. It just gives me a headache different to the one I already have."

"I'm sorry you can't iron."

"I don't want to iron; I want to scrub those filthy pigeon shit-covered windows in the other room."

"I'm sorry you can't do that either."

"What can I do then?"

"Breathe."

"Breathe. Jaysus, that's your answer for everything."

"It works. Focusing on your breathing, on each breath, works."

She looked at his soapy hands swirling around and under her right breast. "Why don't you shag me, Hamish? Turn me about, press me to the tiles, lift my legs around you, and shag me."

"I don't want to shag you."

She nudged her arse into his erection. "Liar."

"There's nothing sexual happening. It's a rudimentary physiological response that happens on its own, nothing more."

"Nothing more?"

He brought his hand to her shoulders. "You don't want to have sex now, Mae."

She spun about, glaring, her wet, clumped eyelashes giving hazel eyes a Kewpie doll look. "Don't fucking tell me what I want and don't want."

"You're right. I apologise. I was out of line, and you're trying to pick a fight."

The flash of her anger snuffed out as she wrapped her arms around herself. "I'm sorry. I am. I made this all about me, not you, not us. I'm angry, but it's misdirected at you."

"I'm angry too."

"Are you angry with me?"

Kitt shut off the water and dragged towels from the hook outside the shower. "Yes. With you. With Llewelyn. With myself. Especially with myself. What have I done to you, to your life? What right did I have to drag you into my wretched, vicious world?" He folded a small towel around her head like a turban and began to pat her dry with a larger one.

"You didn't drag me. There's no need for your sense of guilt. I made a choice. I came into your life willingly. I love you. So here I am."

He stopped drying her for a second. "It's a strange thing, this back and forth between us. One moment you're comforting me as I cry like a little boy, then I'm comforting you as you cry like a little girl, then you're angry with me, and I'm angry with you, angry with myself, and the next thing you're telling me my guilt is rubbish."

"That's love." She pulled the bath towel from him and blotted his skin, the towel dabbing over scars left behind by buckshot, knife fights, beer bottles, wire that had sliced into his skin and she laughed suddenly. "Are you wearing socks?"

Kitt glanced down at his feet. "I was in a hurry to help you, even if you didn't want my help."

She watched him peel off limp, dripping cotton. "I know I can be very obstinate."

"Your tenacity is one of your endearing qualities, but I let you look after me, so sometimes let me look after you." He draped the socks over one shoulder, wrapped the towel around his hips, pulled the dressing gown from the hook outside the shower, and enveloped her with it. "It's what married couples do, look after each other, what a wife does for her husband and a husband does for his wife. And you are *my* wife."

She took the socks from him, wringing water from the soggy cloth. "I never realised how possessive you are. It's bordering on Heathcliff territory."

"After you brushing the edge of death several times in the last year, I've come to understand Heathcliff's obsession for Cathy a little better, despite his sociopathic tendencies, and then there's Rochester's desperate passion for Jane, which now seems utterly sensible."

"How is it we keep coming around to discussing works of the Brontës and comparing their gothic, Romantic stories to us?"

"At the moment, one of us is moody and brooding."

"Exactly what did you study at university, Kitt? That's something I've never asked."

"I took a first in Asian Languages at Cambridge."

"Asian languages? *My hole.*"

The left corner of his mouth rose as he reclaimed his socks, tossed them into the wash basin, and gave her a gentle little push toward the room. "Right then. Off you go, comb your hair, into pyjamas and bed."

"And after that?"

"We try to look at this logically."

She crossed the tiles, tightening the sash of the dressing gown. "There's no bloody logic to the work you do." Mae paused and turned in the doorway. "I think that's why you like it, the lack of logic, the messiness of it, finding the structure. It *is* exciting work. I see that. Maybe we're not so different after all, you're not so different from Caspar. I never realised it, but you both find order in chaos. He did with landscaping, you do with…" She looked down at her bare feet for a moment, then back at him, a rather sheepish look on her face. "Caspar's a point of fact you've always known. I was rather tenacious with his being part of my life. I've always spoken of him to you, but you're my husband and I don't want to be insensitive in making a comparison when you are two vastly different men. I grew so accustomed to your listening that I have taken it for granted, without consideration for your feelings, and I sometimes overlook that you are my husband, not simply my dearest friend. I'm sorry for that. I never thought I'd have a second husband."

Kitt began dressing, pulling on boxer briefs and trousers that were still nested together. "I never thought I'd have a wife, or a dog, or an in-law to dislike, and I expect that you would think and talk about Caspar. He's part of who you are."

"Now you are too. Moody and brooding, yes, I am. It seems we've switched places. I'm Rochester and you're Jane Eyre. I'm riddled with undulating waves of shifting moods and you're the one with the steady soul. Bearing in mind the past year, there's part of me that thinks I ought to have habituated to experiencing trauma, that I'd be better prepared for the lack of emotional control, the sudden slide from tears to anger, the overreacting."

"Perhaps we're both overreacting. It's a weekend. You're there to listen and make arrangements for a man who isn't there. That's all there is."

"You don't believe that for a second, do you?"

"No, but I was hoping maybe you would." He buttoned his shirt.

Mae went into the room wrapped in the dressing gown, and found the pyjamas Gibson mentioned. They were a fine cotton, a Liberty floral print that smelled of lavender, and they were a size too large. She sat on the edge of the bed, the nightclothes on her lap. Right. One of the women who had expired right before her eyes had a name: Had it been Jill Charteris' face—what was left of it—that had become the perpetual camera flash afterburn behind her eyes? What had the woman looked like before her face had smashed? Had she a husband or a family or a brother she wanted to protect? And if she had a husband, a family, a brother, how long would the government keep Jill's name—or her name—from being revealed as a victim of a terrorist attack? All that aside, what the hell kind of sense was she supposed to make of that little thrill she felt, that rush that came from taking a risk, that sense of being alive that cam—

"Stop thinking," Kitt said from the ensuite doorway, jacket over his shoulder. "Put on your pyjamas and I'll tell you how this is going to work."

"Take me home and tell me. Please. I want to sleep in our bed. Or you stay here."

"As much as I want to..."

"One must keep up appearances?"

"Yes."

Swearing, Mae pulled the turban from her hair, disrobed, and slipped the pyjama top over her head. "Why is it some things, regardless of how utterly hare-brained, make sense at a particular moment in time? There's a weird excitement to accompanying you, perhaps a kind of logic behind it, but at the same time it is utterly ridiculous."

"There's a certain level of ridiculousness to this work."

She stood, the top skimming her upper thighs, and she turned, flashing the little Southern Cross constellation of freckles on the inside of one thigh. "It absolutely *is* the sort of ridiculous thing you'd find in a bad spy novel." She pulled on the bottoms. "People make fun of romance novels for being cheesy, but spy novels are where the cheese is; the car chases, the false identities, the gun fights, the gadgets, the villains with scars or weird birthmarks, the dry wisecracking, the expensive car, the wine, the women, the coming back from the dead." She paused and looked at him for a beat. "You've hit every cheesy mark, haven't you?"

"I don't recall ever having a car chase."

"There's still time." She began folding up too-long sleeves.

Kitt slid a hand into his pocket, fingers finding his wedding band. "You know you're going to be fine, don't you? You may have nightmares for a while, but you'll be fine. You're quite resilient."

She stopped folding. "Resilient. How is it two people who are related can be so very different when it comes to trauma and resilience?"

"Do you mean my brother and I, or do you mean your brother's PTSD and your response to trauma, such as your complicated grief with Caspar's death?"

"Sean and I." She dropped her arms, the sleeves falling over her hands. "Are you saying that more than a decade of grieving for the dead husband who turned out to be a polygamist really isn't that different?"

Kitt crossed the room and picked up the envelope from the table where Llewelyn had left it. "If you mean by your intense and persistent longing for Caspar, your detachment and isolation from others, the feeling that life held no meaning or purpose except for your work, then yes."

"Is that what you saw? Is that how I was?"

"Yes. The processing and recovering from trauma depend on many factors; the characteristics of the individual, the characteristics of developmental processes, the meaning of the trauma, and sociocultural factors, the accessibility of support, coping and life skills, the responses of the larger community in which you live." He moved to stand in front of her, envelope in hand. "You've always been independent. Then there's your beliefs, the expectations you have of life, and your sense of hope. You've always had an underlying sense of hope. I believe whatever trauma your brother experienced resulted in his losing his sense of hope, perhaps even his faith in God, and as a result, life holds no purpose, no meaning and he, like you, grieves for a love, or a faith, lost."

She chewed her top lip for a moment. "So we're not so different after all."

"No, you're as different from your brother as I am from mine."

"You and Simon are very different."

"Yes, he sleeps with women and men, says 'please' and 'thank you', and sends rescued Italian greyhounds as gifts to the woman I love."

She gave him that look that said he was full of shite. "Mm-m. Felix is a nuisance, and I see you when you think I'm not looking, I see you coo and cuddle him. I know you love him."

"I love you more." He sat beside her, set the envelope on the bed, and folded up her sleeve, without any protest from her. "We've done this before," he said, moving to the next sleeve.

Mae watched his deft fingers move. "Yes, you did the same thing at the Four Seasons, last year, after I killed Sal Tornatore in your kitchen." Her moment of amusement faded. "I know I've asked you before. I know you don't dwell on it. I know you move on, but how do you move on?"

"I know my purpose and I never had hope or faith in anything except myself. And then you came along and gave me hope and faith, and love and a future I never considered. You really are a nuisance." He gave her finished sleeve a pat. "There you go."

She frowned rather than give him a smile. He'd expected a smile. "How do you process what you do now with this sense of hope and faith and love and a future?" she said.

He tipped his head to the side. "You're not going to like it."

"What are you going to say, *breathe*?"

"Yes. Breathe."

"Oh, for feck's sake."

His smile faint, Kitt reached for the envelope and unwound the old-fashioned string securing it closed. "Let's have a look at the brief on the situation causing me to regulate my breathing so I remain calm and level-headed."

She exhaled, finger combing damp hair. "What should I say to Sean about my leaving?"

"Something like your husband is taking you away for a quiet weekend in the country and would he mind terribly looking after my dog."

CHAPTER SIX

I t was half-past four in the morning and dark when Mae went home in a cab, wearing very nice pyjamas. Daylight wouldn't come for another half an hour. Bypassing her flat on the lower level, she walked around the back of the house and climbed the rear staircase to the home she'd shared with Kitt since February. To keep up appearances, the downstairs flat was still minimally furnished, held clothes and various personal items. Inside, she paused at the butler's pantry, took shoes and the set of work clothes she kept in the small cupboard, and changed out of the pyjamas into a navy shirt dress and navy stockings. As she had for three and a half years, she tied on an apron, went into the kitchen, turned on the light above the cooker, and began preparations for breakfast, taking out eggs to scramble for Kitt's breakfast, setting out the frying pan, butter and jam, readying whole-wheat bread for toasting.

When they'd married, they'd had a long discussion pertaining to the *dos and don'ts of maintaining a secret marriage,* on expectations they had about the institution, and had come to make one very important deal: whichever of them got up first made breakfast for the other. However, whether she scrambled his eggs or he fried hers, Mae always made the coffee. She filled the kettle and readied the Chemex coffee-maker, grinding and spooning out the Tanzanian beans she'd bought the day before yesterday.

The flat was quiet. Felix didn't come to greet her, there'd been no tippy-tapping of his nails on the polished wood floors or kitchen tiles. The kitchen's swinging door into the sitting room stood open. The lamp near the big bay window glowed, which indicated Kitt had likely gone for a pre-dawn a run with the dog. Then again, Kitt might have been at his office, Felix next-door with Sean.

Sean had been more than amenable to keeping Felix for the weekend. Perhaps getting him an actual therapy dog might be better than dog-sitting an Italian Greyhound who wore a borrowed therapy dog vest.

As per years of habit, as the coffee brewed, she laid the little table by the big bay window with pieces of Kitt's gilt-edged blue and white Minton china, then went to the bedroom to make the bed, but the enormous thing hadn't been slept in.

She returned to the sitting room. The first rays of the orange-toned rising sun reflected off the flat next door, shone through the bay window and hit gilt edges of green and white Coalport Green Dragon china pieces on the bookcase. She sat on the cushions in the window seat and picked up the novel she'd been reading, Graham Greene's *Our Man in Havana*.

Kitt laughed about her ongoing appetite for spy fiction, but Greene had been a spy—as had Ian Fleming and John le Carré and, Jaysus, there had to be some measure of truth in the stories they wrote, even if it was simply the lingo they used. *Dead drop, mission, Chief of Station, Honey pot, Asset, Intelligence officer, Backstop, Illegal*. From December to January, Kitt had been *illegal*, working undercover in the US illegally, without any diplomatic cover or overt relationship with the British government, and *that* was an utterly a reflection of the measure of truth in spy fiction.

Other absurdities included the reality that she'd been extorted into a job with Special Operations Division, an intelligence unit within the British government, that she was in love with and secretly, yet not legally, married to an intelligence officer within that government agency. But most ludicrous were the outlandish bubbles of what she could only call excitement floating in her bloodstream—alongside equally bubbly trepidation, anxiety, over-thinking, and ruminating on things such as a dead woman's broken face. All of that, along with Sean's PTSD, did have her wondering about a familial predisposition for mental health issues that affected one's sense of morality.

Maybe brother and sister both needed therapy dogs.

Book in hand, she looked about the flat. The jacket Kitt had worn yesterday hung from the coat rack above the umbrella stand. A piece of luggage stood in front of the chair near the door, ready for the trip to Amsterdam. On the seat of the chair sat a small, black, zippered case she'd seen once before, last July, in Sicily, in the little spartan studio next door to Fiorella's house.

Irritated, frightened, and inexplicably thrilled, Mae swung her feet, heels knocking into the box and moulding below the window-seat. It had *always* been stowed and locked in a combination safe in a space hidden beneath the window-seat. Yet there it was, another piece of spycraft. Or was it *tradecraft*?

She hopped off the cushions, went to the table, and stared down at the canvas or whatever material the damned padded case was made of and traded the book for the case, lifting it to examine the heavy-duty zipper. It had a lock on it.

"Please put that down, Mae." Kitt said from the kitchen doorway.

"Where were you?" She inspected the lock.

"Downstairs, in your pea-sized bed with Felix. I didn't hear you come in the front."

"I came up the back. Shall I scramble your eggs now?"

"Yes, and coffee too, but first, put that down, Mae. Please."

She held on to the case and watched Felix prance over to her. He looked like a tiny high-stepping horse. "Just how frightened should I be about going to Amsterdam?"

"You should always be afraid. There is always is reason to be afraid," he crossed the room, took the case from her, and set it back on the chair, "particularly of this."

"Is your Beretta inside that thing and is it loaded?"

"Yes, the Beretta is in there, no, it's not loaded."

"Why were you in my old bed downstairs?" she said, Felix pawing at her hip.

Kitt slid an arm around her waist. "Last night, the dog and I went downstairs to pack you a bag. Felix hopped onto the bed, burrowed right under the bedclothes. I wound up joining him because I realised that without you, I was all at sea in our large bed, and I forgot about packing my own things. Very careless of me to leave the Beretta out, but then, you know you make me so sloppy. Will the eggs take long? I'm rather hungry."

"M-m. I best get to it. I see the seriousness of the matter of making your breakfast. I know how you get when you miss your breakfast." She put her hand over the top of his and turned around. Kitt started to take her in his arms, but Felix pushed in between them, wanting to share the love. Mae rubbed the dog's slightly floppy ears and looked over to the kitchen door, where Kitt had left her smallest suitcase, the wheels of it touching the edge of the green and cream Persian rug. She looked up at him, at dark, gingery blonde hair sticking up in little tufts, at an ugly-handsome face creased by bedsheets and sleep. "If you didn't hear me come in, perhaps it's time you showed me how to shoot the thing in the case." She turned about and went into the kitchen.

Kitt followed her, stood in the doorway, and watched her cook his eggs in silence. She placed slices of whole-wheat toast on gilt-edged blue and white Minton china plates, and spooned up steaming, pale-yellow clouds of simple, elegant scrambled eggs that were perfect, absolute bites of joy that he always relished eating. Then she waited for him to move out of the way, carried the dishes into the sitting room, and set them on the table she'd laid earlier.

He sat across from her and she ate breakfast while he stared down at his, the simple, elegant, tiny bites of absolute joy before him growing cold.

He'd lost his appetite because he had seen a glimmer in her eyes, an undercurrent of what looked a hell of lot like what he prayed wasn't *eagerness*. Praying. What a joke it was, for him to pray, but he did just that because something about her was different, not unlike lost innocence mixed with a newfound sense of reckless invincibility. He'd caught a glimpse of it yesterday, after he'd helped her wash the blood from her hair, and thought it fleeting, thought it a result of heightened adrenaline and cortisol levels in her bloodstream, but her body's adrenal system remained mobilised, ready for a fight or a flight, releasing the hormones that prepared her, physiologically and psychologically, to deal with a threat. At least, again, he prayed that's what it was. He'd once told her that intelligence work was a game, and now, after one experience as a pawn, another moving across the board, and the fluke of winning like a Grand Champion, she thought she knew the rules of the game. And she was keen to play again, like some goddamned gambling addict.

Christ almighty, wasn't that fundamentally what he was, a gambling addict? What had he done to her? What had he been thinking by believing an ordinary, average, everyday mundane life with her was viable? "This is impossible," he murmured.

She smiled at him softly, absently stroking Felix. "What was that?"

"Did I say something?"

She shrugged. "I'm thinking about doing restoration," she said.

"Sorry?"

"A restoration. I think I'd like the challenge of a restoration. I've done a number of renovations, like this flat, the one downstairs, and two next-door, but I've been looking at a few places. I think I'd like to buy one of them and restore it. Would you like to see some photos? There's a place in Oxfordshire and another in Surrey. Expensive locations, I know, but negotiating a price is a challenge I'm up to. I've had a good deal of experience negotiating."

"Stop it." Kitt stood, moved, and latched onto her elbow. "You have *not* developed a taste for this work, Mae." Suddenly angry, suddenly afraid, suddenly ravenous for the scrambled eggs that gave his life a bizarre sense of normalcy that he'd deeply embraced, suddenly queasy and deadly serious, he drew her to her feet and pulled her so close she had look up to meet his eyes, and he peered down at her, not caring that it was domineering, patriarchal, or bullying. "Now. This is what's going to happen. This what you're going to do. We will not be discussing this in any way. You do as I say, when I say. Am I clear?"

She gazed back at him, irritation and contrariness in her squint. "Eat your scrambled eggs, you bloody big bully."

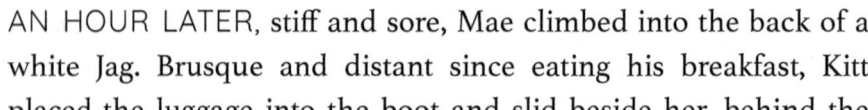

AN HOUR LATER, stiff and sore, Mae climbed into the back of a white Jag. Brusque and distant since eating his breakfast, Kitt placed the luggage into the boot and slid beside her, behind the driver who had crisscrossing red scars running down his hairless head to the back of his neck, an intricate overlay of burns and slices and stitches disappearing into the collar of a black jacket. Half-turning, the driver handed Kitt something from the front seat. "Kitt," he said.

"Connery," Kitt nodded civilly and sat back, a fat folder bound with ribbon on his knees. He took off his ink-blue jacket, tossed it over the seat in front of him. He loosened his sky-blue tie, pulled on his seatbelt, untied the ribbon, and began reading. He glanced at her once, his face devoid of expression.

She took *Our Man in Havana* from her handbag. Book in her lap, she shifted the purse, placing it on the seat, long strap drooping over the edge of the leather upholstery. "Something wrong?" she asked.

"Everything." Stone-faced, Kitt lay his left hand flat beside her right thigh, the two shortened fingers absently caressing as he sifted through pages of documents and photos.

The trip from Maresfield Gardens to City Airport took a little over fifteen minutes. Soon, they were airborne on a small private jet. The flight lasted a little over an hour with no conversation of any sort. His demeanour remained focused, silent, his face a mask of nothingness. Kitt read through the information contained in the files. When he was finished, he dropped the folder into his battered leather satchel and looked out the window beside his wide seat.

After seventy minutes of stony silence, they began flying over patchwork fields of green and tulips, the vivid colours separated by straight lines of waterways and homes. The Dutch landscape was neatly organised, designed to the last detail. In a land so densely populated, this was order in its purest form, and Mae liked the order of the man-made, tidy landscape. She knew the urban districts and traffic plans were organised in a similar, ordered uniformity, the neatly attached brick row houses running along the vast network of canals, broken up by buildings with experimental architectural designs.

The jet touched down at Amsterdam-Schiphol. A humourless, grey-haired female customs agent met them as they disembarked the little jet. Just as humourless, Kitt said, *"Goedemorgen,"* and handed over their passports.

With a grunt, the woman nodded curtly and led them to a golf buggy with a yellow light flashing on the top. They climbed into the rear and the woman drove them across the airport, passing planes, petrol tanks, trolleys full of luggage, heading toward a security booth and a high, razor-wire-topped white wall that butted up against a terminal. She stopped the buggy and jerked her head to the booth.

"Dank u wel," Kitt said, climbing from the rear seat, the officer taking their luggage.

The customs officer grunted again and another customs officer, a thin man with bushy eyebrows, opened the heavy door to the booth, motioning for Kitt and Mae to come inside. The woman rolled the bags across the floor, lifted them onto a conveyor. The man shifted to look at a computer screen, his heavy brows knit together and moved like a millipede above his eyes. He inspected Kitt's little black weapons case, his documentation, Mae's passport, and checked the information on his computer. When he was satisfied, he pointed to a door and pressed a button. There was a buzz and the door slid open, and then they were in a short hallway that ended in a heavy glass door reinforced with steel, a CCTV camera above it. The door rolled open and they exited into the terminal, outside the customs and immigration check.

So, this was how all the cloak and dagger spy shite worked, how diplomats with guns passed through customs. Mae watched Kitt as they headed to the exit. He, quite impassively, watched the people in the terminal, his cold blue-grey eyes shifting, watching, passing over a man or woman here, a group of men there, scanning the crowd, maintaining 'situational awareness.' Watching him watching was the stuff of...well, *spy novels.*

"Wait here, right here. Do not move. Am I clear?" he said.

She nodded once, curtly.

Kitt crossed in front of a woman wheeling a trolley loaded with luggage, walking into the men's lav, probably, she thought, to meet a contact who'd give him an untraceable, disposable satellite-connected mobile or a tiny little camera inside a pair of spectacles. Mae waited. Right. There.

When Kitt came out of the gents', he gave Mae a very faint nod, her cue to walk ahead of him so he could keep an eye on her, but she stood there looking at him, lips pressed together. "You have a bit of sick on your shirt sleeve," she said, reached for her bag, pulled up the handle, and began walking.

Kitt drew out a handkerchief and brushed away the gob of vomit from his pale-blue cuff. "You're a bloody nuisance, Mae," he said, watching her move away.

Outside, it was drizzling and sunny at the same time, the clouds above fat and patchy. Somewhere there'd be a rainbow. Mae buttoned her coat and paused to read the signs leading to P6 overhead, as Kitt had directed her to during part of his dictatorial 'you do exactly as I say' speech earlier in the morning. The silent, need-to-know adherence to protocol, the procedure that informed him of details yet did not disseminate that information to her, and the cloak and dagger shite were equally silly, but she pretended to fuss in her bag for a mint and he passed by. Then he paused, glancing at her, just to let her know she was not to deviate from the course.

It was childish, but Jaysus, she wanted to toss the mint she'd retrieved at him. Instead, she swallowed the juvenile pettiness and continued on, with him following a few paces back, mobile at his ear, his small suitcase rolling along.

"Again, I apologise for inconveniencing you," he said. "Yes, it was fine... I don't see that as a problem... Night Watch at the Rembrantplein... Oh, I see, yes, where the sculptures are... Inside the old bank... Coffee would be most welcome... Thank you. I appreciate you adjusting your schedule to meet with me. I'll see you soon." He finished the call, pocketed the phone, and manoeuvred his suitcase over a bumpy patch of pavement. Moody, brooding, Kitt stayed three steps behind Mae, silent until they reached the edge of the P6 Valet parking area. "Green Jaguar," he said and on cue, a green XJ sedan pulled to the kerbside. The boot lid rose, the driver, a short man in a black cap, got out. "Get in the back," Kitt said, taking her bag. "Sit behind the driver."

Mae pulled the rear door open and climbed into the car while Kitt put the suitcases into the boot. The driver, a different man to the one who had climbed out, got in and gave her a smile. "Hello, Mae." Timothy Bryce said over the driver's seat, his green eyes crinkling beneath an old-school chauffeur's hat.

"What are you doing here?"

"Didn't Kitty tell you?"

"Kitty's told me nothing. He's barely said five words to me since breakfast."

"He gets like that when he's formulating a plan, then it's 'Bryce do this, Bryce get that, Bryce I need'. My job is doing what and going where I'm told, so here I am. He reached for something on the passenger seat. "Here, this is for you." He handed over a small envelope and a little drawstring bag. "Save the envelope for later, open the bag now."

She pulled the strings of the pouch and pulled out a gold necklace dotted with small gold and silver coins strung between fine gold links. "Thank you, Timothy, it's very pretty. Why are you giving me a gift?"

"I'm not. It's not really a present. It's a GPS transmitter *and* a

76

fashion accessory all in one. You can wear your glasses on it too. See that hoop there in the middle? That's for your reading glasses. Oh, and there's another, smaller piece in the bag for you. Did you find it?"

Mae tipped the pouch into her hand. Out spilled a tiny, pinkish-toned item she'd seen several months ago. She rolled the earpiece between her fingers. "Shall I insert this now?"

"No, but I've been instructed to tell you to wear the necklace at all times. How was your flight, did you see all the pretty tulip fields in bloom?"

Before she answered, Kitt slid into the front seat. "Bryce. Drive. The Bank, 9 Utrechtsestraat, the Rembrantplein. It's a café."

"Near the Night Watch statues." Bryce pulled away from the kerbside.

"*Sculptures*," Kitt said, eyes on the side mirror, watching their exit from the valet area. "The Night Watch in the Rembrantplein are bronze-cast sculptures, not statues."

"You're so educational, Kitty." Bryce said. "The hotel master passkey is in the envelope in the console. Are you ready for the current update or is there another tourist fact you think we ought to know?"

"Get on with it, Sergeant."

Bryce chuckled lightly. "Hilary resigned, *sir*."

"Well, we saw that coming. Llewelyn will be put out by losing his 'girl'. And."

"You're not going to like it."

"I don't like any of this. We're going to have to listen to Llewelyn whinge about every 'new Hilary' who tries to fill the floor manager position." Kitt pulled down the sun-visor and flipped up the little vanity mirror and angled it to see Mae, reading glasses on, eyes down as she examined the clasp of the necklace he'd ask Bryce to bring. "Go on."

"One of the CCTV cameras near the Broad Walk was damaged, but the camera across the street from where your Bentley had been parked shows that Charteris and Eaton were pushed backwards, in front of the oncoming vehicle."

"Oh, Jaysus." Mae froze, arms bent, elbows pointed forward, hands tucked behind her neck as she hooked the ends of the necklace clasp.

Kitt met Mae's eyes in the mirror. He watched her drop the necklace and plaster a hand over her mouth. "Suspects?"

"Two men in hats and sunglasses. But there's more," Bryce continued. "The forensic team say the driver was already dead when he was pulled from the lorry and beaten. They believe someone else was in the tipper."

Kitt snapped the visor back into place "Then we can rule out terror."

"Yes, but not officially."

"Where is Vlaming?"

"In his office at The Hortus Botanical Garden. He's scheduled to give a lecture at eleven."

Kitt glanced at his watch. It was nearly ten.

"Now that information is being exchanged, I have a question." Voice thin, Mae leaned forward between the seats, wiping away wetness under her eyes. "Are you joining us on this...whatever it is, Timothy, or are you here to babysit me?"

"While I enjoy your company, I don't *actively* participate in field actions, I merely support Kitty in what he needs, Mae."

Kitt turned about in his seat and looked at her, blankly, silently. His lack of demeanour a clear indication of his seething rage.

She mirrored his lack of expression.

CHAPTER SEVEN

K itt went on being aloof. "I'm a field officer. Bryce is not. Neither are you. I don't want you here, but here you are. I receive authorisation from Llewelyn, who receives authorisation from the Home Office. I have orders. While I follow orders, I am approved to operate on my own terms, make my own decisions, use my own judgement, without needing to check in for permission before I do so. I don't need to clear anything with you or Bryce. Bryce is a support officer, and that's what he does, support me."

"Like a good underwire brassiere," Bryce said.

The conversation ceased, the only sound came from the tyres on pavement, the shifting of papers as Kitt read through them, and the passing of other cars. Mae watched out the window, the Jag travelling along the motorway, passing over a canal, driving by a lake, the landscape changing from semi-rural to the outskirts of Amsterdam. Cosmopolitan, atmospheric, known for being very permissive, Amsterdam was a monumental city full of narrow streets of narrow houses, canals, merchant houses.

The Jag crossed the Amstel, the river that gave the city its name, and another canal. Open green spaces gave way and suburban buildings began to change to narrow, brick structures a few storeys high. The closer they got to the oldest parts of the city, the more the buildings began to resemble picture postcards of skinny, attached row houses and businesses rimmed by trees and canals. Bryce drove by the port, the Amsterdam Centraal train station, and pulled to the front of The Palace Grand Hotel where people whizzed along the street on bicycles.

The façade of the hotel was a modern contrast and juxtaposition to the picturesque, idealised Holland of wooden clogs and tulips, of Rembrandt, Vermeer, van Gogh, of solemn places like the Anne Frank house, of exotic, erotic locations such as de Wallen—the red light district—and sacred places like the *Basiliek van de Heilige Nicolaas*, the Catholic Basilica in the city's old Centre District, right next door to the Palace Grand.

"Follow her in to drop off the bags, Bryce." Kitt said and stayed in the car as Bryce took the baggage inside to the lobby desk, following Mae.

She approached the hotel's reception. "Good morning, how may I help you?' The slender brunette woman behind the desk said, her English coloured with a Spanish accent.

"Good morning. I have a reservation for myself and my employer, Professor Boothroyd."

The desk clerk's fingers *tip-tapped* it over a keyboard. "I must apologise. Your suite is not yet ready. I estimate another ten to fifteen minutes."

A suite. She was booked into a suite, another nicety for her trouble, courtesy of HRM's government. Mae nodded. "Not a worry. I'm aware check-in is after two. May I leave my bags with you and return in a bit?"

"Yes, of course. Your things will be in your suite when you return."

Mae turned to Bryce. "Thank you, driver. You may leave the bags." Bryce nodded and Mae glanced down at the counter, to a gum-edged pad of colourful Amsterdam tourist maps. "May I?" she said

"Please." The clerk peeled off a sheet and handed it over. "You have a reserved space in the car park in the lower level. Will your driver be parking your car now or later?"

"Later." Bryce said.

"Thank you. I'll have Sem collect your bags now."

The clerk said something to a young man who disappeared from the area behind the desk and reappeared at the front to gather the luggage on a trolley.

Then Mae was in the car again with taciturn Kitt, folding the paper map as Bryce drove them along the Prins Hendrikkade. The drizzle had ceased. People whizzed along the street on bicycles. Bryce turned to go one way along a canal, following the trams on Damrak until he stopped near the edge of the Amstel River.

Kitt turned about in his seat, looking between the cream leather headrest. "Remember, Mae," he said. "I'm *Leslie Templar*, and you are here to observe, so sit and watch. Stay out of sight and just watch." He slipped a chunky ring on the third finger of his right hand. Gold, the ring was set with a black onyx cameo. "You can put the earpiece in now."

He watched her stuff a buff-coloured piece of soft plastic into her left ear and motioned for her to lean forward. When she did, he adjusted the coin necklace." You look very pretty."

She looked at him, deadpan. "Don't flatter me, just go on, run through it again like a dress rehearsal. You have the first line. *Listen*," she said, mimicking the intonation he'd used early this morning. "Sit two or three tables away... Take it from there."

"I am so pleased you paid attention and know my lines, Mae. Being well-rehearsed is important. So...listen. Sit two or three tables from us and *listen*. Use your phone..." He went off script and ad-libbed his next line, "I'd prefer if this were something where you could send me a message with cute emojis that express your undying love for me, but you're not the sort to send emojis, and if you were, this morning you'd likely send me the smiling pile of poo. Instead," he picked up where he'd left off, "*listen*, and send me a text if you hear a name, a place, anything that you think might, in any way, however seemingly insignificant, be something you've heard or come across before. Is that clear?"

"Yes, you're right. I'd send you the smiling pile of poo." Mae fiddled with the earpiece.

"That's my girl."

"Your *girl*?" Mae shook her head

"Ah. Yes. Girl. For that I'd get two smiling piles of poo."

Bryce sniffed a chuckle.

Kitt remained blank, unreadable. "Bryce," he said.

Mouth twitching, Bryce got out of the Jag.

"Right then." Dispassionate, Kitt waited.

Mae waited too; the silence marked by the *tock-tock-tock* of the indicator Bryce had left on. "You don't want me here," she said, voice soft as snow and just as icy as his eyes, "and I don't really want to be here, but this was my only option, and you can't keep bullying me."

"I'm not bullying you."

She tipped her head and squinted at him with one eye.

"I'm bullying you." He nodded. "I'm bullying you. I'm sorry. I'm trying like hell to control a situation I have no control over. I want to pretend you're not here. I want to pretend I can do this with you here when the truth is I can't. So I am trying to look past who you are and how I feel about you, to ignore you enough to treat you as I would any novice field officer with barely any experience, but the fact is I should have ignored you the day I met you. Only I didn't. I couldn't. That's my failing. I apologise for bullying you, but mostly I apologise for my shortcomings, for my lack of self-control, for my absolute inability to ensure my work would never again affect your life in this way."

"The self-reproach is a nice touch," she tipped her head, "but I don't want your guilt or an apology. I want you to tell me what you are thinking, what you are planning, and ditch the whole intelligence world need-to-know Junior Secret Agent scenario."

"Junior Intelligence Officer scenario."

Mae looked heavenward for a moment. "I want you to tell me what this is all about. I want to know why a lorry killed three people before smashing into your car. I want to know if this is terrorism or simple, outright murder. I want to know why Llewelyn threatened to put my brother in an asylum if I didn't cooperate. I want to know what he's keeping from me. I want to know what *you're* keeping from me."

"I'm not keeping anything from you. I don't know why he's threatened you. Not yet, anyway."

"But you're going to find out?"

"Yes."

She twisted the coin necklace between her fingers. "In other words, you don't know anything but bullying and bluster, and you going into this blind, or close to it—"

"I often go into an assignment blind or close to it."

"—does not fill me with any confidence. Yet here I am, the pair of us uneven-tempered with each other. Here I am vacillatin' between tellin' myself I can do this and wantin' to light a match and toss it over my shoulder because it's not going to matter what I do or what we do. Here I am, followin' the feckin' instructions you and your employer demanded I follow because I love you, and if I don't feckin' laugh about how absurd this is I'll go bonkers and wind up like Sean. We both know I'm more than halfway there already."

"As am I."

"Why don't you *teach* me what to do, instead of bloody ordering me about?"

"Teach you?"

"Yes."

"Teach you."

"Isn't that what you do now? Isn't that what you were doing with Eaton? Isn't that what Llewelyn wants you to do with me?"

Kitt looked at her, face blank until he took a breath, and she watched the blankness in his eyes cast off sudden sparks of fury, revulsion, recrimination...and tenderness, enough for her to think he was about to say something else, something deeply confessional, heartfelt, and a little on the mushy side, but Kitt got out of the car, the edge of his suit jacket flapping in the breeze.

Bryce climbed back in and resumed driving for another block and a half, taking her past the Rembrantplein, a square filled with life-sized, bronze sculptures of Rembrandt's Night Watch painting. "Here you are," he said, looking at her over the seat's headrest. "I gather early this morning he gave you very strict instructions, like 'keep your ears open and your mouth shut' or something along those lines?"

"Not so much instructions as orders, like I'm his subordinate."

"Technically, *I'm* his subordinate, not you."

"You're also his friend."

"And you're his wife. He's worried about you being here. And he's thinking. He's a very good thinker, a chess player thinking fifty moves ahead kind of thinker, but he's also being a prat. You've never seen him at the very start of an operation, when he's focused on encoding information. It's his SOP."

"SOP?"

"Standard operating—"

"Procedure." Mae hooked her reading glasses through the little hoop on the necklace.

"Yes. You're going to hate me for saying this, but I agree with Llewelyn's logic in having you here. I know Kitty does too, and that's why he's so scared."

"You're a good friend, Timothy."

"I'm also very good at following orders. Out you go. I'll drop the car with the hotel's valet parking. If you need me, I'll be enjoying the two-star comfort of the Hotel Old Amsterdam, a mere one-hundred-fifty metres from the Sexmuseum."

Laughing, Mae climbed out of the back seat and found herself standing in front of an old bank that had been converted into an American chain café with a green mermaid logo.

TRIM, fit, the man was out of breath as he came from the rear of the café, where the toilets were. His eyes darted around nervously, searching the room for someone he was supposed to meet. Early forties, tall and slender, Jan Vlaming jerked his head, flipping back a tuft of straw-coloured hair from his forehead, the movement accentuating a round face, pink cheeks, and large sky-blue eyes that gave him a something of a baby-face and a stereotypical Dutch-boy appearance. He looked to the bustling upper level, up the staircase of what was now a popular American chain coffee house carved out of what had once an old bank and back to baristas busy making coffee at the long bar. As he scanned the café, licking his bottom lip, he leaned against the bar like an old gunslinger in a saloon, trying to be casual in the way his eyes wandered about the space. A barista called out his order and he straightened with a jolt, collecting his iced coffee, whipped cream spilling over the edge.

Kitt decided to put the man out of his misery and gave a little wave. The man came up the staircase. Kitt met him on short landing. "Mr Vlaming?" he said.

"Oh, you must be Mr Templar." With a laugh bordering on reedy, Vlaming shook the hand Kitt offered.

"I have a table up there." Kitt pointed to the table on the mezzanine, where he'd left his jacket and coffee.

The Dutchman's mobile rang. He struggled to get the phone out of his pocket with one hand.

"Let me help you."

"*Dank u.*" Vlaming handed Kitt the large plastic cup with its cinnamon-dusted mountain of cream and retrieved the pealing mobile. "Excuse me," he said, taking the call, moving away a short distance.

Kitt went to the table he'd chosen earlier. He set Vlaming's drink, a fancy, whipped cream-topped concoction, the kind Bryce favoured, on the tabletop and looked across the aisle, where Mae settled into a seat with a fat mug. She opened the little tourist map she'd taken from the hotel.

Damn it. She was too close. "So contrary," he muttered.

She put on her glasses, turned the map one way, then the other, before removing her glasses, fixing her hair, hands passing over her ears in a nonchalant attempt to reposition the earpiece.

Kitt scratched this temple. "Across the aisle is not 'two to three tables away', is it?" he said.

Mae touched the tip of her nose with her middle finger.

He rubbed his top lip to hide the amusement he didn't want her to see. "How very American of you," he said, and picked up his barista-made pour-over sun-dried Uganda Red Cherry.

Green trench coat over the back of a chair, flattish tan handbag on her lap, she removed a small iPad, flipped open the cover and began to type on the tablet. In two seconds the mobile Kitt had on the table buzzed and rattled. He lifted it and found the emoji of a little brown coil of poo on the screen. Mouth pursing to eradicate the twitch of a grin, he placed the phone back on the table and the chair across from his scraped over the floor. The moment of amusement gave way to irritation. The woman distracted him, or rather, he allowed himself to be distracted by her, which is why she was here instead of living the life she'd had before he'd opened his bloody mouth and told her he loved her. Silently, he cursed himself, cursed her dead husband, cursed Llewelyn, and slipped a pleasant expression on his face while picturing the various way he could kill his superior.

Vlaming flicked back his hair and sat. "Apologies, Mr Templar," he said and reached for his beverage, a very faint sheen of sweat shining at his hairline. He had a long, long suck through the green straw, the same kind of plastic straw Mae had shoved into a would-be assassin's ear at the beginning of the year.

"I see you like sweet coffee, Mr Vlaming." Kitt sipped hot brew; the flavour of dark chocolate, strawberry, and Morello cherry rolled over his tongue.

Vlaming shrugged, his blue doll eyes flicking to someone entering the café to his left, a skinny young man with a laptop. "Not usually, but today I need a jolt of caffeine and sugar," he said. "Call me Jan. It's Leslie, right?"

"Yes. Shall we be on our way?"

"If you don't mind, let's sit for a moment. I have an appointment at eleven, and I'll be on my feet all day after." He sucked whipped cream and milky coffee through his straw.

"Whatever makes you comfortable, Jan." Kitt placed his mobile face-down on the table and settled in for the small talk he knew was about to begin. If he'd been a gambler, he would have put money on Vlaming mentioning the weather—and lost.

"First time in Amsterdam?" Vlaming said.

"I've been here a few times."

"For work or as a tourist?"

"Both. Very different place to when I was eighteen."

"Were you like other eighteen-year-old English boys who came here to try weed in coffeeshops and visit deh window girls in De Wallen—deh red-light district?" he said, his Dutch accent softening *th* to *d*.

"No. I went to see the Oude Kerk and Ons' Lieve Heer op Solder."

"Nice Dutch pronunciation."

"I try."

"You went to see deh churches?" Vlaming laughed *tuh-huh-huh*.

"I was after a religious experience."

Vlaming *tuh-huh-huhed* again. "A religious experience *tuh-huh-huh*."

Kitt's mobile buzz-buzzed. "Excuse me," he lifted the phone, turning it to find Mae's *A religious experience? You're really turning into the Roger Moore Bond.*

"Where did you stay when you were eighteen?"

Kitt set the phone screen down. "In a filthy little hostel."

"Where are you staying now?"

"The Palace Grand. I just dropped off my bags."

"Very nice. You know, you should join us tomorrow, for my aunt's garden party. I realise it is probably deh best time for you talk to her. We are eager to get to deh bottom of dis, much like you and Hedison's, as quickly as possible." He said, his accent thickening. "Dis month is deh garden high point of deh year, and it's very busy, but I want to find out how dis happened. I have my own idea, as I said to Jill. I'm sure she told you how we..." He put a hand to his mouth for a moment, solemnness touching his eyes. "I'm sorry we meet under such circumstances. I am sorry to hear about Jill—Ms Charteris' death. Were you friends?"

"We only just started working together."

"It's very sad." Vlaming glanced at his watch, a heavy-looking timepiece with moon phases in the face, and sighed. "Are you in deh same position as Jill, Leslie?"

"Jill was a fraud specialist investigator. I'm an internal investigator."

"Internal investigator?" Vlaming's face lost a little colour.

"It sounds imposing, but it's simply that my scope is a bit broader than Jill's. I'm only here owing to the suddenness of her death. Despite the loss, it's business as usual for Hedison's. We prefer to intervene in a situation like this, and investigate provenance matters, privately, without publicising it. Fraudulent misrepresentation of provenance for private pieces consigned to us is considered an internal matter, yet this particular instance, with some pieces being genuine and some reproduction, and recent events in the auction world, we were, shall I say, concerned for you. Admittedly our first obligation is, typically, to our consigner," Kitt gave a small cough, "or to be completely honest, to our own sales commission. This year's occurrences of art trafficking and fraud has auction houses re-examining their own practice and procedures, as well as their possible complacency with regard to a culture of casual corruption. In spite of the potential fraud here, let me allay any fears you may have. It's not typical for an auction house to disclose the name of a consigner and involving police is, frankly, bad for business."

"You mean Hedison's wants to protect itself?"

"Exactly. We'd like to handle this discreetly. I had hoped Ms Charteris would have explained that to you."

"I see."

"Thank you again for meeting me so early. I know you're very busy with your work and the tour."

"To be honest, our meeting could not have come at a worse

moment, it is deh busiest time of year for me, but my aunt and I do want to find out how we got here."

Kitt had another swallow of coffee and set the cup down. "You went over this with Ms Charteris, and I have her notes, but it would help me if you could take me through the course of what you think happened, and what you found when you went to the freeport in Luxembourg. You can fill in anything I may have missed."

"Where shall I start?"

"With when Ms Charteris notified you." Kitt reached for his coffee again, wrapping his right hand around the paper cup, left hand on the tabletop, the natural curl of his fingers hiding two truncated knuckles.

Mae watched Vlaming toy with his iced whatever it was, turning the plastic cup this way and that, before sucking from a green straw and licking whipped cream stickiness from this thumb. "I was at work last Tuesday," he said, "when I got a call from my aunt. She'd received a call from Jill Charteris with Hedison's Auction House." Vlaming said, his voice clear in Mae's ear. "An hour later my secretary and I were off to my family's unit at Luxembourg Freeport. Sure enough, deh collection was gone. Deh jewels survived Nazi's bombing Rotterdam and now de're gone. *Godzijdank* Hedison's discovered a few pieces were paste and held on to deh collection, otherwise deh jewellery would be lost. We are trying to decide on our next course of action, insurance and so forth, even perhaps suing the Luxembourg Freeport."

"There's much to think about," Kitt said.

"We've been doing a lot of dat, trying to come up with how dis could have happened. I told Jill I believe it started two years ago, at deh Green Tech Global Horticultural Summit. After a session on Nutraceuticals, Edibles, and medicinal crops, deh man beside me struck up a conversation. Even if our discussion wasn't memorable, I remember him for a few reasons: his very pretty girlfriend, his cologne, an overpoweringly sweet scent dat made me sneeze, and his name was Giacomo Negroni—*Negroni*, just like deh cocktail—you know Campari, gin, and red vermouth?"

"Yes, I'm familiar with the drink. Google said your area of interest was in greenhouse management."

"You Googled me? People usually Google my Aunt Polly, but you Googled me." Vlaming chuckled and, listening, Mae took notes, typing on the screen of the tablet as he went on, "As a horticulturalist," he said, "and director of deh Hortus, I'm interested in all aspects of greenhouse management, sustainable agriculture, plant propagation and industry production, greenhouse technology, hydroponics, and nutraceuticals. I find it exciting deh Netherlands are at deh forefront of agricultural innovation, particularly when it comes to sustainable agriculture. Greenhouses are huge, some over a hundred-fifty acres. Dis time of year, I run small tours to some greenhouses, estates and chateaus as a way of raising money to supplement deh upkeep of a few of deh private gardens at dose estates and chateaus, and deh upkeep for deh Hortus as well. Although we receive funding from deh Municipality of Amsterdam, we're an independent organisation, we depend on our income from activities, tours, donations and sponsorship."

"Much like many country homes of the British aristocracy being open to the public for tours," Kitt said, glancing at Mae typing notes on her tablet. "Out of curiosity," he said, "by nutraceuticals, edibles, and medicinal crops, do you mean marijuana?"

Vlaming nodded. "Dat's one example, yes. Medicinal crops—such as marijuana—are a major new industry, with significant opportunities for growers and investors. It's a revolution for growers, home gardeners, and deh horticulture world. At dat summit, I sat at a table with Negroni and his girlfriend, a big Chinese guy from Hong Kong, and a man from Guatemala. We all discussed medicinal crops, deh regulatory side of the industry, as well as deh technology perspectives. I do remember deh Chinese guy and Negroni were quite interested in labour shortages. I came across Negroni and his girlfriend deh next day, on a tour I organised to Chinese gardens at Hortus Haren, to gardens in Menkemaborg near Groningen, and a private chateau northwest of Amsterdam, which is now closed. I forgot deh name of deh company who bought it, it's something Italian. Anyhow, dey moved into experimental greenhouses and interbreeding programs to produce hybrids for edibles, and Negroni found it interesting. He came to deh garden party at my Aunt Polly's. She has a party every year. She thought Negroni was amusing. We got friendly, social. I liked him. His cologne, not so much."

"You recall anything else from that summit?"

"Negroni's very pretty girlfriend. She wasn't interested in horticulture. She was in Amsterdam to buy antiques. Wow, she looked like a porcelain doll with long reddish-blonde hair—what a figure, *een lekker stuk*. I liked her Texan accent."

Mae's fingers froze on her tablet keyboard, she looked across to the two men just as Kitt said, "She was from Texas?"

Vlaming's smile showed one front tooth slightly overlapped the other. "Ja. *Yee-ha!*"

Kitt gave a slight chuckle, glanced over at Mae sitting stiff, immobile, and asked the question they both knew the answer to. "On the off chance, was the girlfriend named Ruby?"

CHAPTER EIGHT

Mouth open, Vlaming's brow arched. "How did you know dat?"

"Some porcelain dolls you don't forget. I've dealt with her as a Fine Art and Collectables Specialist at Smythe & Dexter in Santa Fe."

Vlaming shifted in his seat. "Auction houses must be specialised like horticulture, you get to know old and new players, and move in deh same circles. You know her well?"

"Let's say we were once rivals. Did you spend much time with her?"

"No." Vlaming scratched his neck. "I'm married."

"I mean socially."

"Oh, yes, of course. It was friendly, social. We never got beyond talk about family, travel, exporting flowers, importing and exporting antiques. It took me a while to realise she and Negroni were a couple. My secretary said he's *lekkerding* and I suppose he's very good-looking in dat Italian way women like, early forties, I think. Ruby was a fair bit younger dan him. And me." He smiled sheepishly. "Okay, I admit had a whimsical little dream she might fancy me." He scratched his neck again, his little laugh self-conscious and self-effacing as he looked down at his coffee and shrugged.

"We're all guilty of momentary flights of fancy over an attractive woman. Did you discuss exporting antiques with her?"

Vlaming's head came up.

Kitt sat back, watching the man, letting him talk.

"Not at first. She was interested vintage soil analysis kits, balances for seed, rain gauges—we have a similar small collection of items at de Hortus. And my aunt has a collection of bulb graders, hand tools, gaiters and clogs—yes, I know, how very Dutch, but deh French and Eastern European countries also wore clogs, as did deh Chinese." He exhaled. "Aunt Polly and I talked about it. I invited Negroni and Ruby to have a look at the pieces held by de Hortus, and deh tings in my aunt's collection. It's easy to look back now and see we might have been right about what seemed far-fetched at deh time, and we can't prove what we believe happened, how we truly believe deh jewellery was taken from secure storage." Vlaming glanced at his watch. "Sorry. I need to get back for my lecture. Could we continue as we walk?"

"Of course."

Vlaming grabbed his coffee and rose. "You know, it makes sense to include you as guest for my aunt's garden party tomorrow."

"Yes, it does. Thank you. It would serve as a fine time to meet your aunt." Kitt climbed to his feet, looking for Mae. She was halfway out the door, stuffing her arms into a short, sage-toned trench-coat that matched the green in her eyes. By the time he and Vlaming made it outside she was three metres ahead, map in hand, heading, he knew, for The Hortus Botanicus a few blocks away.

"How is it exactly you think this came to happen?" Kitt walked beside Vlaming on a footpath running alongside tram tracks, shopfronts, and old, narrow brick buildings that had quintessentially Dutch stepped rooflines.

"Deh last time, deh day after deh last garden party, Ruby and Negroni came to my aunt's home again, to see our garden tool collection and stay for lunch. I'm pretty sure Ruby and Negroni did some snooping in Aunt Polly's study—is dat the word, *snooping*? Nothing was missing, but deh room had a lingering scent of sickly-sweet vanilla, like spray to cover smells in deh toilet."

Kitt said nothing for a moment. Then he gave a slight nod. "I think we may have found the connection we've been looking for."

"Negroni?"

"No, Ruby. But I am eager to talk with Mr Negroni."

"You are in luck. He's on deh guest list for my aunt's garden party. I was planning on confronting him. Politely, of course."

"His attendance would certainly make my job easier."

"I wonder if Ruby will still be with him." Vlaming's mouth broke into a smile more sickly than wistful.

"I can tell you she won't be."

"Do you know she's moved on to another man?"

"No. Ruby Bleuville was arrested for murder and a whole rash of other crimes involving the illegal export and import of stolen cultural artefacts."

Vlaming stopped dead, his large eyes grew larger. "*Godverdomme*, you're joking!"

"Sadly, I am not."

He went pale, brushing his flopping lock of hair back slowly. "Are you saying it's Ruby who took advantage of us?"

"I don't know. It's possible. Some of the artefacts she stole were lifted from freeports where she had gained access with a key fob that someone hadn't realised was missing. The authorities still aren't clear on where the key fob originated."

Dumbfounded, Vlaming shuffled a few short paces. "You believe it could be me?" They'd passed modern façades, crossed the Amstel over the Blauwbrug, and were near the Nationale Opera and Ballet. He stared at the curved building and wiped a hand over his mouth. "We have our fob, but...dere was one time... it was after Negroni and Ruby had visited, and my aunt couldn't find it. She swore she'd put it in her handbag, but couldn't find it, and she was angry with me for suggesting she'd become forgetful, for believing a stereotype—you know how some say elderly people are forgetful, but dey are no more forgetful dan younger people who misplace car keys. Naturally, her fob did turn up in her handbag, it was stuck to deh bottom by bit of *drop*. Do you... do you believe... I've seen deh technology, warnings about skimmers on *geldautomaat* and *shimmers* copying credit card information. Do you...maybe...Ruby copied our fob? Is dat even possible?"

Kitt stayed silent. There was no need to say anything since Vlaming was telling him everything, filling in blanks that didn't need filling—and then some. And it was all utter tosh.

"It is all unbelievable," the man said.

"Quite." An idea popped into his mind and Kitt ran with the improvisation. Soberly, he gazed at the man. "There are others, Jan," he said.

"Others?"

"Hedison's has other clients who have been victims of theft from their freeport secure storage, which were all insured with Hedison's. These items may or may not have a connection to the sort of work you do."

"Others..." Vlaming shook his head, hair tumbling back over his forehead.

"One man had a painting taken and replaced with a forgery, another had botanical objects stolen from storage."

"What sort of botanical objects?"

"To be honest, I'm not certain. Seeds, I think. I only skimmed over the notes this morning. It was part of another case Jill was investigating. Are you free for dinner?"

"Dinner?"

"It's still early. I have plans for dinner this evening with two gentlemen whose stories are similar to yours. I have to make an apology to one of them. It makes sense to have you meet, to see if you know any of the same people."

Head still shaking, Vlaming glanced at his watch, his apprehension breaking the surface, tongue passing over his lips, his swallow thick and slow. "Well, I don't know...I'm sorry, I've stuff for tomorrow's garden party to tend to."

"It could be useful."

"Yes. I see. I understand. Let me ask my secretary about my schedule." Vlaming licked his lips, pulled out his mobile, and dialled. "*Hoi, Tanja... Ja...ja... Niet moeilijk... Is de hoofdtuinman er al?... Ik ben uitgenodigd voor het diner met Leslie Templar... Vanavond... Ja, ja, okee...okee...*"

Ahead, on either side of the canal, stood rows of Amsterdam's distinctive, gable-necked, high, slim canal houses. Mae waited, taking a photo of the famous Magere Brug—the skinny bridge in so many tourist photos. She had a nonchalant look at her tourist map as Kitt and Vlaming passed by, and continued following their same cobbled path alongside a canal that skirted the Hermitage Amsterdam.

Soon, the rear of the glass greenhouse structures of The Hortus came into view. Vlaming and Kitt had fallen into trivial conversation about football and English sports hooligans until they reached the front entrance.

Mae went to the ticket counter in the gift shop, and paid the fee. She took the brochure the skinny man behind the cashier's kiosk offered, went inside the gardens and waited for Kitt and Vlaming, still somewhere on the street outside, the Dutchman describing the history of The Hortus Botanical Garden." It's nearly four-hundred years old and relatively small, only one-point-two hectares, but we have over four thousand plant species from around deh world."

With historical narration playing in her ear, Mae moved to where the path opened to a wide expanse. A large tree stood in the centre of a circular area, benches sitting beneath the leafy bright green. To the left stood spring blooms on verdant stalks, white-striped red tulips, pale pink azaleas, purple bell flowers. Brown and yellow-striped bees buzzed about and alighted upon blossoms. A Buxus hedge formed a low semi-circle at the front of the white Orangery and a three-storey red brick building. When Kitt and Vlaming made their way into the garden, she headed for the largest greenhouse.

The sign at the entrance read *Dreiklimatenkas.* Fluency in German allowed her to understand bits and pieces of the Dutch description. The Three-Climate Glasshouse, the newest green-house in The Hortus, held desert, subtropics and tropics under one roof. She passed a Phoenix palm in a large pot and went inside with Vlaming's history lesson continuing in her ear.

"Dat's the original section. Early on it was all about medicinal growth," Vlaming said. "Not so different as with marijuana now, but the Dutch East India Company discovered wealth to be had in trading various plants, coffee and such..."

Mae wandered into the warm, subtropical zone, unbuttoning her pale green trench-coat and removing it, small, flattish handbag slung across her torso. Years ago, she'd come to the Netherlands with Caspar. They'd done a tour of botanic gardens and tulip farms all over the country. She'd learned a lot about the cultivation of tulips on that trip. She'd been here with Caspar too, and he was all around her again, the earthy, humid smell of soil and foliage and mulch and gardening a scent forever attached to him. He'd kissed her on the suspension walkway above the forest canopy, telling her the Latin names of plants of palms and trees below where Mae walked by the spiked leaves of an oversized *Cussonia spicata*, the compacted dirt path taking her deeper into the humid, lush tropical zone, her mind awash with bittersweet memories that came with a very sour tinge. She looked up at the catwalk overhead, the pathway curving as she moved on, shrugging off thoughts of the dishonest man she had loved and the lies he'd told her, thinking instead how the honest man she loved now told lies for a living. It was bizarre she could accept there was such a thing as an honest liar, yet that's what Kitt was. Principled, dedicated, forthright, true, the lies he told were never for personal gain, and that was what made him honest.

At a bend in a pathway heavy with lianas, epiphytes, and plants with elephant-ear-sized leaves, Mae paused beside a large, prehistoric-looking fern and a tall, white, paned-glass case holding small green plants with pretty, heart-shaped leaves. The case was a greenhouse within a greenhouse that felt like a steamy jungle. She bent forward and read the sign in the lower corner pane.

The gympie-gympie (Dendrocnide moroides) is common to rainforest areas of Australia. A member of the nettle family (Urticaceae) this plant has stinging hairs on its leaves and stem. Gympie-gympie is considered the most painful plant in the world. The stinging hairs deliver a toxin called moroidin that causes burning, severe pain, which often lasts for months. The pain has been known to drive men mad or to suicide.

The description of the valentine heart-shaped gympie-gympie's sting sounded similar to the sixteen years she'd spent in agony after

Caspar's death. Those sixteen years of pain had been wiped out in a single afternoon by a professionally dishonest honest man who was currently feigning polite interest in the tour a Dutch horticulturalist gave. "Are these greenhouse frames aluminium?" Kitt said.

"Yes, and here is one of our Crown Jewels," Jan Vlaming said proudly, describing the very greenhouse she stood inside. "*De Dreiklimatenkas* was built in 1993, it encloses tropical, subtropical, and desert climates..."

Mae looked closer at the love-heart leaves and her ear distinguished Italian being spoken. Vlaming's voice became a murmur of description detailing the butterfly house, and she peeked around the gympie-gympie greenhouse case, peering between heavy green fonds, seeing a man just around the next leafy, hidden bend.

Short, built like torpedo made of muscle, the man wore a faded green coverall dusted with soil that also dusted his curly dark hair. "*Si, iddu sa chi devi dire.*" he said. "Yes, he knows what to say."

What pricked Mae's interest wasn't the man's impatience or even that his conversation was in Sicilian, the sort that made him sound like a very old man from a small village, rather it was the part where he mentioned Jan Vlaming. "*Vlaming sa cosa dire,*" he said, "*iddu sa che su cessi sei essi iddu no fa como devi.*" All of which translated to 'Vlaming knows what to say and he knows what will happen if he doesn't do as he is told.'

The man went on. "*Non posso andare per tra mezz'ura... Si, devo incuntrari il quell christiano a Openhartsteeg un naudro ura... Lo stanno pulendu... Unni sei picciridda?... Yo va in campagnia.*" So, he said he couldn't leave for another thirty minutes, they were cleaning something, he wanted to know where the little girl was, he was set to meet 'the guy' in an hour at Openhartsteeg, and then go to the farm. "*Vai, vai, Tanja, yo capicio. Vai a travgire.*"

Mae stood stock still at the front of heart-shaped stinging nettles in a case.

Tanja. The secretary.

The man was telling Vlaming's secretary he understood and she should get back to work. She leaned slightly, peering thought the greenery, lowering her phone to snap a photo of him through the foliage, but he moved about, tucked his mobile in a side pocket, picked up a rake, and begin walking down the partially-obscured wet path, right in Mae's direction.

Quickly, she turned about and headed back through the greenhouse, hurrying along the wet dirt path, making her way from one climate zone to the next where it wasn't as sticky, until she was outdoors in cooler spring air, passing the potted Phoenix palm. Mobile in hand, she sat on a bench beneath the wide, leafy tree, and rattled off a voice-to-text message, sending it to Kitt just as the Sicilian man exited the Three-Climate Greenhouse. Dark-eyed, he was handsome in a short, Roman statue sort of way, nose straight, mouth generous. She watched him go into the red brick building opposite the white building where Vlaming and Kitt stood amid people sipping coffee at green tables, their backs to her.

"Deh Orangery is from 1875. Did I mention it houses deh café and store are—oh, Tanja, my secretary, here at last." He gestured to the attractive woman coming from the café. Striking, mid-twenties, her very fair complexion was offset by straight, glossy black hair that reached her shoulders and kicked out slightly. She dabbed a tissue at a small nose, her wide-set eyes, fringed by black lashes, were an arresting shade of blue. Hand smoothing her hair, she met her boss and candidly regarded Kitt, looking him up and down as Vlaming made the introductions. "Leslie, here is my secretary, Tanja Goedenacht."

"Hello," Kitt smiled. "Leslie Templar."

Vlaming's secretary smiled back and shook the hand Kitt offered. "Good morning, Mr Templar," she said.

"I was just telling Leslie de Hortus is one of deh oldest botanical gardens in deh world."

"Yes," Tanja nodded. "In 1638 it was an herb garden for doctors and apothecaries in the city. The Palm House," she pointed, "is from 1912. It has quite a collection of cycads. The gate you came through was built in the early 1700s. The Orangery dates from 1875."

Vlaming stole a glance at his watch and made a face. "I am so sorry. My lecture is in twenty minutes and I have some papers or to organise. You are welcome to attend, or have a look around De Hortus, go see deh butterflies and greenhouse with tree climates. Whatever you decide, I'll leave you with Tanja to arrange tings for tomorrow."

"Yes, thank you for your time. I'll see you tomorrow."

Vlaming's smile wavered, and he swallowed. "Tomorrow, yes. Dank u." He turned to his assistant. "Tanja, please look after Leslie."

"Of course," she said and then dropped into Dutch. "*Hoe gaat 't?*"

"*Ja, 't gaat goed.*"

"*Je bent pas dinsdag vrij. Ik sprak met tante. Ik zaal met hem gaan eten.*"

The two conversed in Dutch, Kitt fiddled about with his phone to read, Mae suspected, the messages she'd sent him, and she tried to follow the gist of a language she didn't speak, listening to words similar to German or English, picking out good, aunt, dinner, and Tuesday.

"Tanja," Vlaming said, "we're being rude." He turned to Kitt. "Sorry. She tells me dat I am not free for dinner until Tuesday. She will give you details for tomorrow. We have a nice packet of information we give to our tour guests. Perhaps before you go, you can have a look at deh antiques I mentioned." Vlaming smiled amiably.

So did Tanja. "Would you like to follow me, Mr Templar?" she said.

"Yes, I would," Kitt said, rather enthusiastically, pocketing his phone.

The mobile in her lap buzz-buzzed. Mae snorted and watched Ms Goedenacht lead him along a bloom-dotted path that disappeared behind a garden shed. She looked at the reply Kitt had sent. *Ten minutes. Meet me at the corner of the canal beside the Hermitage, the side where there are benches and you can see the Magere Brug.* She shifted her gaze back to Vlaming. He had moved to stand near the café entrance, his eyes had been on the pair and the garden shed. The man blew out a lungful of air, tongue licking at his bottom lip. He rubbed his face, hard. Then he backed up a few steps and went left, heading for the red brick building with the paned-glass sash windows.

Mae went back to her phone and did a search for the odd little plant she'd seen in the big greenhouse.

"That is a rain gauge, this is a barograph, late nineteenth century..." Tanja's voice filtered through Mae's earpiece, "and it's bigger than you thought it would be, isn't it"? Tanja asked.

"Yes, it is," Kitt purred. "Is this oak?"

"It is, and if you ask me, it look a bit like a marital aid," Tanja giggled. "Sorry," she giggled again, nervously. "I know that's inappropriate, but..."

"Goodness me, imagine the splinters...Tell me something, Tanja," Kitt began, but there came a *pop-pop-pop*, and the conversation turned staccato and scratchy with static before a hiss fizzled and silenced the racy conversations.

THE STEMS and leaves of the gympie-gympie are covered with hollow, microscopic spines like a hypodermic loaded with a toxin. Touching or brushing against one leaf, and the miniscule, needle-like spines penetrate the skin, causing unimaginable pain that some describe as being burnt with hot acid and electrocuted at the same time. Even dried leaves can sting...

The mobile vibrated in her hand. Mae swiped away the curious information on her screen's display and read the message from her brother.

Thank you, this is a better idea. A better idea? What the hell?

"As much as I want to pretend you're not here," Kitt said, "I'm so pleased you followed my instructions," Kitt said.

Mae looked up and forgot about trying to make sense of what Sean meant. Kitt had removed his jacket and tie, stuffed both into a cloth bag slung over his shoulder, and folded up his shirtsleeves. He wore a baseball cap, dark aviator sunglasses, and held a red and white paper cone loaded with chips in his left hand. "We're on to disguises now, are we?" she said.

"You don't like my hat?"

"You look better in the cowboy hat you wore on New Year's Eve than in that ugly baseball cap."

"You miss my cowboy hat."

"Go on and think that if it makes you feel better."

"I feel just fine."

"Which is why you took your time getting here."

"I was being thorough."

"Is that what you call chatting up Ms Goedenacht, thorough?"

"She was doing the chatting up. Weren't you listening?"

"No. The earpiece stopped working when the discussion turned to marital aids and splinters."

"Ah, of course it did," Kitt said, lips bunching with a tinge of amusement. "What did you do to it?" he said.

Eyes narrowing, Mae shook her head and looked out over the canal, to all the little flattish boats with glassed-in tourists sightseeing, taking in Amsterdam's charm. "You want to pretend I'm not here. I want to pretend you didn't say that."

"I apologise." He bowed his head in contrition. "Forgive me. Equipment sometimes fails."

She tucked her mobile into her coat pocket. "Are we going to go Openhartsteeg?"

"In a minute." Kitt held the cone of golden-brown chips in front of her, two tiny plastic forks poking out near a yellowish blob of mayonnaise.

"What are we doing now?" She slipped off her coat, the right sleeve dropping over the long-strapped handbag tucked against her hip.

"Thinking," he said, poking a fork into a chip, stuffing it into his mouth, chewing and swallowing, repeating the process.

Mae thought too, only without cramming potatoes into her gob. "Could this have something to do with the cultivation of medical marijuana?"

"You think because Vlaming is involved in horticulture, flower shows, herbology, and has an interest in legal medicinal marijuana that something nefarious is going on?"

"It's possible."

"Possible. Come on. Work with me here."

"I always work with you."

"So what are you suggesting, someone here is trying to develop a new substance that can be used in chemical or biological warfare?"

"That scenario is essentially the plot of—"

He held a chip between his teeth, cigarette-like. "Yes, yes, but in this case, there's no snow-topped mountain lair, no bald villains, no secret agents with a double-oh license to kill, and this is not a film."

"Actually, I was going to say *Wonder Woman*, not the film where Bond's wife dies at the end—and thank you again for that parallel that scares the shite out of you." She laughed suddenly. "We keep coming back to Bond, don't we?"

"I thought we kept coming back to Brontës."

"Them too, but this is about *your* name."

"My name?"

"Hamish."

"Yes, my love?"

"No, *Hamish*. It's the Scottish form of James, and Kitt," she waved her hand, head shaking, "is German."

"I have no German ancestors. I'm missing something here."

"*Der Kitt ist veraltet.*"

"The putty is outdated? Is this your way to remind me you think I've passed my use-by date?"

"I'd never be so cruel."

"Yes, you would, and may I point out that you're older than me and you've yet to retire."

"That's because when I did retire you dragged me back to work for you, *Kitt*, which is German for putty, cement, *bond*. Hamish... James," she drew a little connecting line in the air, "Kitt...Bond, you see?"

He stabbed a potato. "That's quite a stretch, Mae, but as harebrained as your notion may be, there's merit in absurdity. We don't know who's the mastermind behind what are clearly orchestrated events, and these horticulturalists and gardeners may be plotting chemical and or biological warfare."

"I like how you change the subject."

He dipped a chip into curry mayonnaise. "As I was saying, anything is possible. Possible, yet not very likely. However, how about if we work from that ridiculous assumption, disassemble it, and speculate other possibilities?"

"No matter how hare-brained?"

"No matter how ludicrous. The bottom line here is Vlaming's lying."

"The secretary is hiding something too." Mae let her gaze follow the flat-front faces of canal houses with cookie-cutter rooflines, at people crossing the white bridge over the Amstel, the river glittering in the late morning sun. It was warm in the sunshine, but dark clouds hung in the distance. How fitting.

"All right. Tell me. Why do you think Tanja Goedenacht is hiding something?"

"As I said in my message to you, when I was in the greenhouse, I overheard the gardener talking to her in Sicilian. Now, you might say that *Tanja* is a common name in the Netherlands and hearing the gardener talking to someone named Tanja is a coincidence, but how many Tanjas do you think there are working in The Hortus for someone named Vlaming? Then there's what you think about there being no such thing as 'coincidence', as well as what was said to Tanja, which was along the lines of *Vlaming knows what to say and what will happen if he doesn't do as he is told*. Then the gardener went on and told Tanja he would meet a guy in an hour at the place on Openhartsteeg."

Kitt had a seat beside her on the hard, concrete bench, the phone in his pocket buzzing. He handed the cone to her and read Bryce's reply to his request to organise a dinner meeting with an appropriately-briefed 'guest'. *Arrangements underway. Can I come? My hotel's crap.*

Mae took a chip from the cone. "It has now been nine minutes and Openhartsteeg is near the Bloemenmarkt, which is about a twelve-minute walk from here, back past the *sculptures* in Rembrantplein."

Kitt said nothing. He simply pocketed his phone, took back the cone, and gobbled another *patatje joppie*, thinking.

Mae glanced at the cone of fried potatoes and the curry-spiced mayonnaise he'd dipped a chip into. She watched him focus on each bite, tasting, savouring the feel and texture of each delightfully greasy, lusciously fatty mouthful until his mind found a sense of calm, a sense of clarity, and, as it settled over him, she knew he began to make a plan. He became a mindless eater, stabbing his little plastic fork into chip after chip, thinking, thinking, thinking, planning the next step. She chuckled. She'd witnessed that change come over him once before, in Sicily, after they'd found a burnt hand in a bread oven and a dead man in an industrial dough mixer. That day Kitt had eaten cannoli and left a mess of pastry crumbs all over.

Kitt's eyes refocused from internally organising his thoughts to fix on her, sliding his sunglasses down his nose slightly. "You're not eating. Something wrong with the food?"

"I'm not sure. When most people think of spies and food, they see romance, women, caviar, and champagne, not hot chips. You're utterly forsaking the spy legend."

"Few people realise James Bond ate kebabs *and* fried chicken."

"See? There he is again."

"My point is, I have the woman, I'm not fond of champagne, and as for the romance, I refrained from adding onions to the potatoes. Eating onions is poor form when one knows kissing will occur after all the thinking."

"You think there's going to be kissing?"

"I know there's going to be kissing."

"Then thank you for being so considerate."

"I do try."

"Indeed, you are the epitome of romance and fine dining."

"I know it's not fancy, but it is tasty."

She laughed again and reached for a chip. "I don't need fancy."

"No, you just need me." He pushed his sunglasses back into place.

"I've needed you for some time." She bit into a long, golden potato dabbed with yellowish sauce.

"And now you need me like you've never needed me before?"

"I didn't say that."

"But you thought it."

"Did I?"

"You did. It's written all over your face."

"I suspect what you see is actually curry mayonnaise." She licked the corner of her mouth. "I'm glad you're in a better mood. I have a theory about Vlaming—"

"Oh, goody, you have another theory. There goes my better mood."

"—but I'd like to know yours. Please share it with me. Why do you think Vlaming is a liar? My money is on Tanja. His story seems plausible."

"Precisely because it's a plausible *story*, emphasis on that word. It's rubbish any mystery reader could formulate. Ruby Bleuville was identified by name in news stories. It's easy to lay the blame on a woman who made international news for murder, bypassing security measures in freeports, and the theft of cultural artefacts. He told me everything I wanted to know. Everything." His phone buzzed again in his pocket. He ignored it.

"But his story is still something we have to prove is a fabrication."

"*I* have to prove. There is no *we* in this. On the off chance, in the time you worked for him in New Mexico, did Taittinger or any of his wine friends mention the name Negroni or Goedenacht?"

"No, not that I can remember. Do you want to know my theory?"

"I've read the texts you sent me as I walked here and you've recounted what you overheard."

"Yes, but would you like to *hear* my actual theory?"

"My love, I'm aquiver with anticipation."

"Funny, it looks more like you think the curry mayonnaise tastes off."

"No, no," he swept a chip into sauce, "I assure you. I am aquiver."

She watched him and the left side of his mouth curved with humour. "Yes, we both think that everything Vlaming told you is a load of cobblers. He's a pawn," she said, "and he's being black-mailed by Tanja Goedenacht and whoever it is *we* find at Open-hartsteeg."

"She works for him. She was with him when they met Ruby Bleuville. It's not a stretch to think that she would know about the theft of his family's heirloom jewellery." Kitt said, half-eaten curry mayonnaise-dipped chip in one hand, and his expression lost its amusement, hardened to a slab of cold marble, and he spat out masticated potato. "And there is *no* we."

"As much as you want to pretend I'm not here so you can go about your work unencumbered," she looked at him, her expression as colourless and frosty as the bloody truth, "you don't know what the man in the greenhouse looks like."

"You didn't take a picture of him?"

"I didn't quite have the chance, and now that I think about it, it's best that I hadn't because if he'd seen me that would have made it harder for us to follow him."

Kitt swore and got to his feet, tossing the remaining *patatje joppie* into a shiny rubbish bin. Sending her back to the hotel was not an option—yet. "You're a sodding nuisance," he said, looking at her over one shoulder. "Well, come on then, we want to get there before Greenhouse man. Oh, do stop smirking at me." He began to walk away, paused when she didn't follow immediately, and waited without turning about to see if she did.

Mae looped her handbag across her torso, put on her coat, and exhaled. "So much for all the kissing." She followed him over the Blauwbrug, the bridge across the Amstel.

Petulant, saying nothing for the next several blocks until they passed the life-sized Night Watch sculpture, Kitt reached back and took her hand. "You're a nuisance," he said, "but you're *my* nuisance." He ran his thumb over hers and returned to being surly and silent.

CHAPTER NINE

Hand in hand, they reached the edge of the Singel. The innermost canal of Amsterdam's semicircle of canals once served the city as a moat in the Middle Ages. Stretched along a backdrop of narrow, picturesque, quintessentially gabled Dutch houses built during the Golden Age, the modern Singel ran between Koningsplein and Muntplein, where the Bloemenmarkt stood, its flower stalls made of small boats permanently floating in the canal. The north section of the Singel had developed into another well-known red-light district, but this area was popular with tourists. On a mild spring day like this, it was crowded with sightseers—and pickpockets. Illustrated signs warned of the danger.

Mae liked the Dutch word for pickpocket. She read a sign out loud, *"Zakkenrollers winkelen óók."*

"I didn't catch that," Kitt said.

Eyes on a man who could have been, but wasn't the gardener from The Hortus greenhouse, she pointed to a sign with a cartoon of an elderly woman flouncing about carelessly with her handbag. "Beware of *zakkenroller*, pickpockets."

Kitt glanced at the sign and then Mae. "Where's your handbag?"

"Under my coat. Where's your wallet?"

"In my back pocket."

"Your back pocket? Oh, you do live dangerously." She let go of his hand and began walking ahead of him along the Bloemenmarkt, knowing it would annoy him, which in turn annoyed her because it meant she'd become petty. Her pettiness gave way to a sense of remorse that was trounced by urgency, a desire to 'crack this mystery' and get back to the quiet-ish life she and Kitt had begun to lead. In earnest, she scanned the people meandering through the Bloemenmarkt, older-aged folk in a tour group, families with children, stall-keepers, couples, none of them muscly Sicilians built like torpedoes.

Jaysus, who was she trying to fool here? She'd gone into this eyes wide-open, and yet she'd forgotten that they hadn't quite yet succeeded in having a quiet-ish life. A murky, furtive, knuckle-bruising, blood-flowing, people-lying, people-dying life was the sort her husband led, and he believed he made a difference. While she hadn't realised it before, preposterously, she'd begun to believe she could make a difference too, and she laughed at herself.

Arranged in a single row along the canal front, the market stalls were touristy, offering tacky souvenirs of brightly painted clogs, Dutch canal house figurines, spoons, I ♥ Amsterdam mugs, World Cup footballs, loose and packaged bulbs, photos of Queen Maxima and King Willem-Alexander. Across from a brick cheese shop with curved, red-painted shutters stood a stall festooned with packaged flags and tees emblazoned with marijuana leaves. Mae ducked under hanging souvenir tea towels and began looking over a selection of postcards, a rack full of garishly-painted wooden clogs, and another laden with souvenir magnets with photos of topless window girls of De Wallen—Amsterdam's best-known red-light district.

Kitt caught up with her and stood beside her. "Here's a lesson. While some work on their own, most pickpockets are well-dressed males in their thirties who blend in with the crowd. They often work in groups, although it's the innocent-eyed young boys and girls you have to really look out for, the child beggars. Be aware of helpful strangers and helping strangers who drop things in front of you, of people bumping into you, of someone asking for directions, of charity workers with clipboards and coin tins, of touching your wallet or handbag when you see a sign that *says beware of pickpockets.*"

"Thank you." She gave him a syrupy smile. "I have always wanted to learn how to check my six, keep my back to the wall, you know, the finer points of situational awareness. I'm trying to learn, it's OODA, isn't it, Orient, Observe, Decide, Act?"

"This is not a joke."

"Yes, it is. We know this whole thing is a joke. But I have to be honest, I like the fact that you're now the straight man and I'm getting the good lines."

He pulled a floral-painted, bright pink wooden shoe from the rack. "Stick a clog in it, Mae."

"*That's* the best you can do?" She reached into a box filled with loose tulip bulbs, pulling out four from beneath a picture of frilled red and white tulips. "Do you think these would look pretty by the front gate at home?"

He returned the clog to the rack and moved to her side, looking at her coolly, his tone flat, hushed. "Why can't you let me be a brooding, churlish prick for now?"

She shook out a small paper bag, dropped bulbs inside, and folded down the top of the paper packet. "I'll let you in on a secret.

I find your brooding, churlish prickishness strangely charming, but charming, brooding, churlish prickishness doesn't cast light on anything, particularly when I'm feeling churlishly prickish because I'm concerned about my brother. I don't know what's going on, I'm frustrated, and—"

"Frightened and trying to keep sane by defusing the insanity with inane humour."

"Yes." She pressed her lips together for a moment. "You have to teach me how to do this," she said.

Kitt bit his molars together. She saw a muscle in his jaw pulse. Then she moved to the stall assistant. Handbag hanging beneath her coat, she reached into a pocket, handed over a few euro to pay for the bulbs, stepped back out into the Bloemenmarkt, stuffed the packet of bulbs into her pocket. He thought she'd stomp off in a huff, but that's what he wanted to do. She stopped beside a rack of postcards and waited for his childishness to abate.

He coiled up his irritation, dialled back his puerile urge to have a tantrum, roped in his bullying urge to drag her into the little coffeehouse they'd passed, the one near the one *Zakkenrollers* sign, the one he knew sold legal and illicit pharmacological goods, the sort he'd slip into a bottle of water, a cup of coffee, or food, the sort of drug that would incapacitate Mae and remove her from play. Teach her? God damn it, yes, he had to teach her. Thanks to a haze of festering fear and self-loathing, he'd failed to see the bloody writing on the wall. Failure had become his standard practice. Ignoring the feelings he had for her had failed. Protecting her had failed. Attempting to keep his mind focused on his job and not on her safety had failed, jeopardised both their lives, and would continue to jeopardise and interfere in their lives. There was no way out of the life he'd chosen long ago, no way out of the quagmire he'd created for Mae. Whether he stayed or left, whether she stayed or came to her senses, did the practical, safe thing and left him, the future was clear and inescapable. Teaching her was the only real way to try to keep her safe.

He took a breath, then another, and another, each deliberate inhale getting stuck in his chest.

Reality wasn't cold and hard. Reality was hot and softly smothering.

Rather than dwell on his asphyxiating shortcomings, Kitt got on with it. To the left of the boxes of bulbs was a coat rack hung with souvenir tea towels, scarves, and hats. He snatched up a faux silk white scarf dotted with black windmill silhouettes and a red AFC Ajax bucket hat, paid for them and found Mae beside the only stall actually selling fresh flowers. Adjacent lay narrow Openhart-steeg, alley-like and crowded with bicycles. "I got you something," he said, extending the hat and scarf.

She eyeballed the somethings. "Is this a peace offering?"

"No, it's a disguise," he said, his tone brooding, churlish, and prickish.

"Even better."

He cocked his head, his eyes flinty blue-grey. "You know, you'd make this easier on me if you didn't grin like that."

"I'm not ready to make it easier on you, and it's amusingly low tech, unlike the earpiece fiasco."

"Put on the hat and your sunglasses. Keep the scarf in your pocket." He half turned and pretended to peruse bright purple irises, blue hydrangeas, and butter yellow daisies, and dark pink-striped carnations, Mae's favourite flower. When this was over, he'd buy her a bunch of carnations every damned week for the rest of their lives. "See anyone who looks like Greenhouse man?"

Hat and glasses in place, Mae stood beside ready-made bouquets of mixed-colour tulips, people-watching, scanning the crowd, tourists, a man rolling a wheeled platform trolley full of boxes, locals and school children on an excursion passing by,

Mediterranean-looking men approaching the mouth of the canal end of Openhartsteeg. "Not yet."

"Good," he said. "Let's go have a look down there and have a better view of either end of the street." He took her hand again, waited for a Japanese couple to pass and stepped around a father pushing a pram trailing a spent balloon, pulling Mae along into the little side street. Graffiti covered the walls of both sides of the laneway. With the bicycles lined up neatly, it looked like an art installation. Halfway down on the left side was a glass door, the exterior around it painted to look like an open mouth, the two windows above, exaggerated blue eyes surprised at the large, pink dick below moving toward the lips of the door-mouth. The bright colours contrasted with a sky darkening with blue-grey rain clouds.

Kitt looked up at the fat clouds, at the array of bicycles, and back to the tongue-less Rolling Stones-ish icon about to perform fellatio on a spray-art comic book phallus. He grinned. "Since we look like bloody tourists," he said, taking his phone out, "we may as well play that. Move over there," he pointed. "I'm going to take your picture."

"Right in front of the big knob?"

"Yes, a happy snap we can send to your brother to show him what you did on your holiday."

Mae turned away from the bicycles and stepped to the front of the graffiti, snorting, pointing to the lewd artwork. *"Dear Sean, Thinking of you, wish you were here."*

Kitt's eyes cut to the doorway with the exaggerated red lips, where a dark-haired man with a wispy moustache now stood behind the large glass-paned door, peering through, looking for someone. "Ah, here we go," he said, gaze back on her. "Try and keep up with me."

"Don't I always?"

He nodded once. *"Po-russki?"*

"Speak Russian?" Her blink of surprise turned to a squint. "Of course you'd speak Russian, what spy doesn't?" she muttered, squint and disbelief evaporating. "Are we going to speak Russian?"

The wispy moustache man opened the door and stepped out, mobile at his ear, a bucket in hand, the tops of spray bottles, sponges, and rubber gloves poking out of the top.

"We're going to speak Russian," she murmured.

As thin and airy as the hair beneath his nose, the man glanced at them once and tucked his mobile into his orange tracksuit jacket. Kitt cocked his head slightly, saying, *"Lyubov moya, ulybat'sya—* Smile, my love."

Mae smiled wide, the mouth and giant pink cartoony penis behind her as the greenhouse gardener approached from the Bloemenmarkt end of the laneway. He'd changed from his dusty green coverall to stone-washed jeans and a black hoodie with long, black and white-striped sleeves, the double J Juventus Football Club emblem on the chest. It made his body more torpedo-like. He took the rubber gloves from the bucket.

*"Ya lyublyu tebya—*I love you." Kitt smiled. Instead of taking pictures of her, he snapped photos of the two men who met and fell into step alongside each other without speaking.

Mae struck another pose as they began to move off toward the far end of Openhaertsteeg. *"Zaichik—*bunny?" she said, her eyes following the men.

Kitt lowered his mobile and put out his hand. Hands clasped, they followed, lagging a bit behind, watching the two men reach the end of the laneway and make a right. Within a few seconds, Kitt and Mae reached a pizza shop at the corner of Openhartsteeg and Reguliersdwarsstraat, one of Amsterdam's known LGBTQ+ areas for partying and dining. He pulled Mae back slightly, gave the men a bit more distance, and surveyed the brick-paved street lined with cafes, delivery vehicles, gay bars, shops catering to local clientele, and coffeeshops selling legal hash and marijuana.

The men crossed to the left side of the street, passed a café with a lone patron sitting at an outdoor table, and paused at the front of a black brick gabled building with two white-framed, glossy-black front doors, side by side. Single, unconnected to the other, separated by brick and doorframe, the left door led to what appeared to be a residence. The door on the right was a 'pink' business, with a white-framed window display of arty adult books and mannequins dressed in high-end-looking fetish leather and PVC, the name *Erotica* framed by love hearts, written in swirly, unlit red neon above. The gardener pointed to the door on the left. He handed over keys as a delivery van pulled to the side, a logo of lettuce, tomatoes, and carrots bright on the white doors. The two men parted, Mr Thin Moustache moving to the front of the van to talk to whomever sat hidden behind the wheel, the gardener Juventis fan going into the shop, gloves, bucket and cleaning supplies in hand.

On the opposite side of the street, Kitt lowered his sunglasses and scrutinised the two black doors, the white-painted windows above, the step-gabled roofline with the old hoist protruding from the top of the expensive-looking shop front. The windows on the two levels above the shopfront were lined with heavy curtains, the kind that blocked out sunlight and the glare of night-time neon. At present, the building sat in the shadow of the taller structure across the street. Kitt stared at the windows. It took a second before he found it. "What do you see?" he said softly, lifting her hand to his mouth, kissing the middle of her palm.

"Bondage apparel."

He let go of her hand. "I mean above all the pretty leather in the window, in those windows on the two floors above."

"Do you like leather and kink and BDSM? I've never asked you."

"I've never asked you either, but this isn't the time for such a discussion."

"Standing in front of a sex shop is the perfect time for such a discussion."

"This isn't the time for such a discussion. I'm trying to *teach* you. What do you see?"

Mae glanced from the top two windows, then to the ones on the level below and back to the top again. "Windows with the curtains drawn."

"Keep looking."

"Are you really trying to teach me something or avoid my question?"

"What do you notice about the windows?"

"You're avoiding the question." She studied the windows again, head tilting slightly until she realised something about the glass was a little too...precise. "Those aren't curtains at all, are they?"

"Very good. There's a film, a decal stuck to the glass. The two windows on the right have a small strip of heat shrinkage in the bottom corner panes. You noticed the stripe of light from a bulb inside, didn't you?"

"M-m. What does it mean?"

"Something. Nothing. Everything. Hydroponic nutraceuticals and medicinal crops. I have no idea."

"But we're going to find out?"

Expressionless for a long moment, Kitt exhaled audibly and nodded once.

"Oh, off we go," Mae snorted. "Wait here," she said low and plummy, exactly like Kitt speaking with polite, yet tyrannical authority. "Stay here. *Right here.*" She gave him a sideling look, adding, "Please."

"Don't be feckin' daft," eyes narrowed, he imitated her Irish inflection—and the *you are so full of shite* gaze she sometimes gave him. "I'm not leaving you here. However, there's something I need to remind you about, a promise you once made. Do you remember the *second* most important thing I have ever told you?"

"You mean the bit about if I find myself in a situation where someone has a knife or a gun or there is any threat of violence? How I shouldn't throw a punch, a cup of coffee, lash out with a block of cheese, a toilet brush, or a drinking straw but *run*?"

"Ah, you *do* remember. I'm so pleased. Never deviate from that promise." He reached for her hand and paused.

On the other side of the street, the gardener came out of the door on the left with two black men, both thin and dressed in orange-trimmed grey uniforms that hung from their narrow frames. Each man had a bucket, rubber gloves and cleaning products poking out. A man with a potbelly came out behind them, closing the door, locking it, checking that the lock was secure. Cigarette in his mouth, he adjusted large, rectangular wrap-shield sunglasses with orange-red lenses, the sort cyclists wore, banged on the side of the van. An arm, heavy with thick, dark hair, appeared as the double side doors opened. Potbelly got into the van with the two black men, the same hairy arm reaching out to shut the doors behind them. Thin Moustache went around the front and climbed in the passenger side. Then Tanja Goedenacht leaned out of the driver's window and said something to the hoodie-clad gardener.

Kitt pulled the brim of his cap a little lower.

After a nod, the gardener walked into the sex shop next door and the van pulled away.

Kitt clasped Mae's hand again, crossing the street with her, pushing open the entrance to Erotica. Mae looked about the shop. There was no shop clerk. She and Kitt were the only two real people inside.

Two dolls, life-sized and made of silicone, stood beside a white mannequin clad in a black corset and lacy thigh-high stockings. Another mannequin, decked out in a leather face mask and a shiny black strap-on, posed on a table laid with an array of expensive dildos and vibrators, and plugs, all lit by small spotlights. Seventies soft rock played, Toni Tennille asking the Captain to *Do That to Me One More Time*. White and bright inside, laid out like an upmarket clothing boutique, the shop's centre displayed black and red stiletto heels and thigh-high boots on gleaming white tables. To the left, shelves held a variety of luxury bath items, lubricants, oils and lotions. A round table held black and white busts, leather masks full or partially covering the faces, a few masks laid out in a display on the tabletop.

More pleasure toys, his-n-hers, were arranged on an antique-looking sideboard. Lingerie, tees, and other garments hung from racks lining the wall alongside crops, handcuffs, and spiky items that looked like teeth-cleaning chew toys for dogs. Near an alcove where dressing rooms sat at the rear, elaborate attire and equipment for specific sexual tastes was artfully presented: fetish toys, leather hog ties, floggers, collars, shackles, restraints, corsets, and bookcases full of books and DVDs.

"I'm going to go out on a limb and say there's another way out of here." Mae released his hand.

"Probably back there, through the fitting rooms." Kitt marked the shop's security cameras, one trained on the entrance, another above the till, the last pointing towards the rear. There would be an AV screen somewhere near the till, most likely inside the desk it sat upon, and probably another somewhere in the back. From what he saw, he surmised the set-up was a basic DVR device rather than a back-to-base monitored security system. Lucky break. If necessary, he could wipe the recording with the touch of a switch, but still... "Keep your hat and sunglasses on," he said.

The noise of a door opening at the rear of the shop drew Kitt's attention from the cameras. There came the shuffle of heavy-ish items pulled or pushed across the tiled floor, the dull *thud* of a door shutting, the *zzzt* of tape being torn from a roll repeated several times. The behind-the-scenes noises of a functioning sex toy boutique continued, Kitt scanned the space and merchandise, waiting for inspiration to strike, three scenarios coming to mind rather quickly, all involving Mae, all leaving a bitterly sour taste in his mouth. He crossed to her. "Mae," he said quietly, "there might be the need for a bit of improvisation."

"Are we still Russian?"

"I haven't decided yet."

"Did Ms Goedenacht see you?" Mae bent forward, examining something gold and shiny. "Does that really say thirteen-thousand euro?"

"I don't think she paid any mind to us." Kitt leaned over a little to have a look at an information card on the pedestal. "Yes, thirteen-thousand euro, but it's twenty-four carat gold and is, so it claims, the world's most luxurious, exclusive personal massager."

"Jaysus, just call it what it is. Personal massager *my hole*."

"Yes, I suppose you could use it there." He took her hand again, moving closer toward the rear of the shop her until she stopped in front of a lone, absurdly huge, jungle camouflage-adorned dildo perched atop another pedestal.

"You think this a piece of art or is it meant for personal use?" she said, lifting it to examine.

"I think everything in here is meant for personal use." Kitt considered the enormous green silicone phallus. "Is that something you fancy?"

"I'm more a hands-on kind of girl, and the mottled green isn't exactly sexy, unless gangrene is a colour that gets you off."

"You want me to teach you something? Right then. Gangrene,

despite how it sounds descriptive, is brown, purplish-blue, or black, not green."

"Oh, I like learning new things."

"As do I. Tell me. In all your lonely years as a widow, did you own any toys, any personal devices?"

"Five minutes ago, you prudishly told me this was not the time for a discussion about leather and kink and BDSM and now you're asking me if I ever had personal devices."

"Well, did you, do you?"

"As I said, I am, and I have always been, a hands-on kind of girl."

"Were you often hands-on? Are you often hands-on?"

The multi-green monster in her hand, Mae looked up at him with one brow arched. "Is the stuff in here turning you on, Kitt?"

"This is not the time for such a discussion." He pulled her very close. "Not when I said there'd be kissing," he said, mouth hovering over hers.

"*Hoi, kan ik u helpen*?" a man said behind them.

Kitt lifted his head, gave Mae a wink, and turned about as the shop owner, a man, thirty-ish, with a mop of yellow curls and round blue eyes, stood in the rear alcove near the fitting room, a row of shiny PCV tube skirts on hangers dangling from his fingers.

He smiled pleasantly and repeated in English what he'd said in Dutch, "Can I help you?"

"I'd like to try on one of those," Kitt jerked his chin to the mannequin with the corset, his accent pure Dallas, Texas. "Does it come in red?"

"It comes in a selection of colours." The mop-haired blond gestured to the side of the shop where the selection of corsets hung on racks. "Come look," he said, laid the skirts on a table, and led the way to the leather, lace, and rubber.

Mae caught the twitch of Kitt's mouth. She set aside the pricy dildo. He slid his arm about her waist and took her to the garments, running his fingers over them before pulling a few from the rack—blood red, deep purple, and lipstick pink with nipple cut-outs. He handed them to the shopkeeper. "What's your name, son?"

"I'm Gert. Please let me take these to a fitting room for you," he said, his English pronunciation far better than Vlaming's.

They trailed behind the man a few steps, gravel-voiced Rod Stewart singing *Tonight's the Night*. There were three doors in the alcove, all on the left side. The last cubicle stood alongside a large, white-framed mirror and a bookcase display of pastel products aimed at women. Boxes of merchandise had been stacked next to the bookcase; one big carton had smaller boxes of packaged pastel vibrators that looked a bit like Easter rabbits dumped on top. A waist-high table across from the first dressing room displayed more gargantuan, camouflage toys like the ones out front. The curly mop-topped Dutchman unlocked the tiny room across from the dildo table arrangement.

"Will you need my help lacin' up, darlin'?" Mae said, matching Kitt's twang.

Kitt cocked his head ever so slightly and took off his hat and sunglasses, stuffing the shades inside the cap. "I think I can manage, honey-bun."

"Even with those fiddly bits?"

"I forgot how you like the fiddly bits," he said and thought he saw her eyes narrow ever so slightly behind her sunglasses. "Are you with me then, sugar-pie?"

"Aren't I always?" She pursed her lips in a kiss.

Gert twisted a skeleton key in the lock, opened the door, stepped into the fitting room and hung the corsets inside on a hook. As he turned about, Kitt released Mae and blocked the man's exit. "It's sure teeny-weeny in here. Is this the only dressin' room?"

Gert shook his head, curls bouncing. "No, there's the one next door too."

"Is it big enough for us both?"

"Sadly, it's about the same size."

"What about that there one on the end?"

"At the moment it's full of mannequins."

"Where's your stockroom? We could use that."

"The stockroom," his hazel eyes flicked to the large, framed mirror, "is not a fitting room."

Kitt gave Mae a sly, sidelong look. "Maybe you can let us in the stockroom anyway?"

"I don't think so."

"Come on." Kitt pulled a wad of euros from his pocket. "You let the other guy in there." He waved the money in front of Gert.

"What other guy?" Gert said, without so much a glance at the money, his green eyes steady on Kitt.

"The guy who came in here just before we did."

Gert smiled spiritlessly. "No one came in here before you."

"Sure, there was a guy, Italian soccer fan." Kitt added a few more euro to the wad.

Gert went on smiling spiritlessly.

"I see." Kitt stuffed the cash back in his pocket, and smiled broadly at Gert, head down, peering up through his long lashes.

Mae sighed. "Really, honey-bun?"

"Darlin', no need to run off, just step back and let us fellas talk. Go on now. Step back." He slipped off the cloth bag he'd stuffed his jacket into, tossed it into the little room.

Mae took a step back and knocked into the camouflage display, objects on the bookcase wobbling slightly.

Gert's curls bounced as he shook his head and waved a finger in the air. "No, sorry. Nothing's going to happen here in my shop, the fitting rooms, or the stockroom. The places you're looking for are between Zeedjik and Warmosstraat in De Wallen. You'll find they cater to sex acts of all kinds. We don't do that here."

"But we like it here."

"Like someplace else."

Kitt tilted his ball cap, looked Gert up and down, his eyes doing a slow wander before he grinned, and leaned a little closer. "We'd be happy to let you watch."

Gert leaned a little closer. "Get out of my store."

"Come on, sport," Kitt set his left hand on the man's shoulder, "let us in there."

In one move, Gert had Kitt's thumb and he twisted hard, turning him about, forcing him to bend from the waist, baseball cap and sunglasses falling to the tiles. "Time for you two to leave, *sport*," Gert hissed, driving him out of the fitting room and alcove, right past Mae.

Mae snatched very firm, fat, phthalate-free silicone from the bookcase display, and swung the slightly rubbery thing like a club, the adult toy slapping into golden curls and cartilage. In an instant, Gert let go of Kitt. Hand to his ear, shouting, he spun about, fist drawing back, but Mae moved faster and the downward arcing momentum of the larger-than-life camouflage-green imitation dick smashed into very real testicles. Jaw sagging, eyes half rolling into his head, shock and pain froze him in place for a moment. Then, soundlessly, he dropped, his knees hit the shiny tiles and Kitt's fist walloped against jawbone. Gert flopped sideways, back into the fitting room alcove, out cold.

Thumb and wrist smarting, Kitt kicked the man's feet out of the way and faced Mae. "Thank you for taking direction."

She stared at him, at his cold blue-grey eyes, at disconnected, utterly neutral features. "*No need to run off? Take a step back?*" she said. "What happened to *never deviate from the promise I made you,* hmm?"

"I assessed the risk, ascertained there was no need for you to run, and I was better served with you following my lead. I was counting on him doing something," Kitt said, flexing his fingers wide, rotating his thumb, "and I needed to have the upper hand."

She glanced at Gert. "I'd say he had the upper hand."

"Sometimes you need to let your opponent think he has the advantage." Kitt massaged his hand and wrist.

"Is that what you were doing, letting him think had the advantage?"

"Yes. I kept him busy, he couldn't touch you, and I knew you'd hit him with Godzildo."

"Godzildo?"

"It's big and green, isn't it?" His eyes flicked to the monster still in her grip.

"Did you let him do that on purpose? You feckin' *let* him twist your arm? Yes...yes, you did." she said. "You were counting on it." Jaysus, why can't this be easy? Mae dropped the sex toy. It bounced on the tiles a few times and came to rest against the soles of the unconscious man's shoes.

Quickly, Kitt went through Gert's pockets, finding six keys on a ring and a small butterfly knife. After running hands down over chest and flanks, he jerked shirt from trousers, flipped the man over and frisked from thighs to ankles, removing a small, semi-automatic Sig P365 from an ankle holster. "Now why do you have this?" he said, rising, releasing an empty magazine, checking an already empty chamber, and tucking the unloaded weapon into the waistband of his own trousers. "This might just be for show, the kind a shopkeeper has for dealing with unruly customers, or the kind given to an idiot who can't be trusted to not shoot off his own toes. Then again... If he moves, kick him in the yockers."

She took off her sunglasses and shoved them into the pocket with the paper packet of tulip bulbs. "Can I have his knife?"

"Absolutely not." Kitt pocketed the folded, red-handled blade and went to a shelf outside the fitting room alcove. He found leather cuffs with metal rings and tossed them to Mae before he grabbed two other items. A minute and a half later, Gert was bound, hog tied, padded cuffs securing wrists to ankles, the ball gag in his mouth muffling moans as he began to come around. Kitt hauled him into the fitting room and shut the door.

"Now what? I wait here or come with you?"

Kitt swung Gert's keys on one finger. There was a choice to make. Bryce was busy with a task and his escorting her wasn't possible, which meant she would return to the hotel alone, but that option didn't sit right in Kitt's gut. Neither did the alternative of her staying there with him, where he could at least keep an eye on her. Simple decisions were sometimes tiny acorns that burst into giant oaks and he weighed both options; one avoided an argument and was slightly less nausea-inducing that the other, one reminding him that she was his downfall and his love for her would be her undoing as well, a fate she seemed to accept more readily than he could. "Against all better judgement, you come with me. Again. So, safety first. Go back in there," he pointed, "lock the door, turn the shop sign to *closed,* and then stay on other side of this alcove."

"Why can't I help you look?" She picked up his hat and sunglasses and held them out to him.

"I can manage," he said, taking his things and stuffing them into a jacket pocket. "Go on, the other side to the alcove, and stay low, in front of the bookcase with all the tasteful pornography."

"Stay low?"

"I'd rather you didn't get shot."

Her face lost a little colour, there was a little less of an exhilarated glint in her eyes. "And what about you?"

"I'll look after myself. Refresh my memory. What will you do if there's gunfire?"

She exhaled, irritation mixing with apprehension. *"Run,"* she said and went into the shop with him watching her until she slouched in front of the bookcase.

"That's a good love." He twirled the keys on a finger, the Carly Simon song reminding him that *Nobody Does it Better*, and he looked from the final fitting room to the framed mirror, studying. Behind one of the doors would be a passageway to perdition and there were several possibilities that lined the way; illicit drugs, underaged sex workers, or both. "The lady or the tiger," he said softly, and unlocked the last dressing room.

CHAPTER TEN

For his own safety, Kitt stood to the left of the door, took a breath, crouched, and swung it open into the alcove. When no bullets blazed and no one leapt forth with a knife, machete, or baseball bat, he hazarded a look—and found perdition was a space crammed with black and white mannequin segments: torsos, legs, wigs balanced on arms. No lady or tiger behind door number one.

"Kitt?" Mae's low voice held a thread of controlled trepidation.

"Stay where you are," he said evenly, and returned to the first, empty fitting room, pressing against the mirror inside and the rear wall, moved back to the little space where Gert huffed and puffed through his nose like a little piggy, and repeated the process of pressing and pushing walls. Again, no lady, no tiger, just a huffing and puffing tied-up little swine. Kitt shut the door on Gert and returned to the fitting room full of plastic body parts, tossing legs, bent arms, a smooth, black synthetic buttocks, a torso, a few heads, feeling, testing walls, an alarmed Mae shouting over the noise of crashing mannequin bits, again yielding nothing.

"*Hamish!*" Mae hissed, full of fearful exasperation.

"Stay there," he said and kicked the arse he'd thrown aside out of the way and took a breath to moderate his frustration, staring at the mirror. Then he bit off an obscene phrase, pocketed the keys, and ridiculed himself for being a colossal, slipshod, blinded-by-love fool who, until this very point, had neglected to consider the idea that the mirror was not only hinged, but also two way.

Damn it, he'd done everything backwards, and the out-of-order process irritated him, rasped his brain, which fear and love and a sedentary life of deskwork had turned to mush. As he ought to have begun, he went to the mirror, stood in front of it and examined the frame to see if the mirror was hung on the wall or set into it the way windows were. The lights above the mirror were brighter than the ones shining down on the fitting cubicles. He ran the full fingertips of his right hand along the edge of the frame, feeling for a latch or spring, and found nothing, but to be thorough, he pressed against the mirror. No lady, no tiger.

To be vigilant, as he should have been from the start, he cupped his hands around his eyes and looked into the mirror, but saw no light from the other side. Finally, he rapped a knuckle against the glass and when it produced a hollow sound rather than a dull thud, he was certain the mirror was two-way, or more accurately transparent. Instead of jumping to the conclusion that someone was on the other side watching, he said, "You can come in."

Mae was already behind him, stepping around a wig and foot, looking at about the tangle of fibreglass limbs, the thirteen-thousand euro gold personal massager in her hand. "Did you have a little tantrum?"

"Yes."

"Have we made an enormous mistake?" she said glancing at the dressing room where the trussed-up man lay. "Is Gert just a sex shop owner?"

"No. There's another room on the other side of that mirror, but

I'd prefer not to smash it to get inside, as my guess is, it's most likely alarmed." He began to look at the walls of the fitting room, at the seam where wall met ceiling, at the skirting board where floor joined wall.

"Did you look behind those boxes or try to move the bookcase?" she said, pointing the gold massager at the bookcase full of Easter egg-toned vibrators.

"This is not the Anne Frank house," he said gazing at the bookcase and the boxes beside it, at the way they'd been stacked a bit haphazardly, like carefully arranged clutter. "Oh, for God's sake," he said loudly.

When they'd first entered the shop, they'd heard the sound of things being moved about. Kitt looked down at the floor where very faint scuff marks curved across the tiles. He stepped to the side of the bookcase, kneeing boxes aside, and ran his hand behind the shelved unit full of pastel sex toys, and repeated the process on the other side, feeling for hinges, finding nothing. He swore again, pushed against the bookcase, the right side then the edge by the mirror's frame. There was a slight popping *click-click*, and a whole section of wall moved, swivelling like a secret door in a manor house—or the bookcase in the Anne Frank house a few blocks away.

"This is why you should have let me help you look." Mae peered into the dim little space lit only by the light spilling through the doorway, Donna Summer moaning the breathy *Love to Love You Baby*. "Perhaps we're about to step into a world of hydroponic nutraceuticals and medicinal marijuana."

"And perhaps we're not."

She moved to look inside. Kitt grabbed the shoulder of her coat and hauled her back. "Safety first." He tugged the expensive gold vibrator from her, tucked it on the bookcase, and switched on the torch on his phone. "Stay behind me," he said, going into the no-longer hidden room, the mobile's torchlight shining about on two crates with pictures of cabbages on them, passing over the partition hanging above the mirror. The partition, set into runners, gave Kitt a pretty good indication what the room had been used for, and it wasn't hydroponic, nutraceutical, or anything medicinal.

"What's all over the glass on this side?" Mae said.

Kitt shone the torch on the mirror, the small blue-white beam passing over cloudy, smears showing that someone had made a marginal attempt to clean the glass. Given the sort of shop that was on the other side, there was a good chance the dull cloudiness was something he preferred not to get too close to check. "My guess," he said, "is that this little space was once a private booth for watching a live sex show. I'll let you form your own opinion of what may be on the glass."

She made a face. "Oh, that does my head in."

Diagonal from the swivel entrance stood a door without a handle. Kitt crossed the space to have a closer look. While missing a knob, the door did have a light-catching chrome deadbolt cylinder lock, the brand name *Schlege* imprinted across the keyhole. He handed the phone torch to Mae and dug the keys from his pocket. "Shine that over here, please," he said and flipped through the keys on the ring until he found the one stamped *Schlege*.

"At last, something easy," Mae said.

"Easy is seldom a good thing." Kitt gave her a little pat and took back his mobile, shoving it into his pocket. "Keep beside the door. Don't move." He stood sideways, on the opposite side of the door-way. Anyone rushing out of the room would meet him first. He inserted the key, turned the deadbolt, and pushed the door with his forearm. It swung open easily and soundlessly, flat, kissing the wall inside with a soft *pliff*, making it plain no one hid behind the door. Fluorescent light cast a rectangular beam across the floor of the booth. Kitt peered around the edge of the door frame. Again, no hydroponic set-up, no marijuana, but a storeroom full of merchandise one would expect to find in a sex shop: blow-up dolls, racks full of saucy outfits and bondagewear, shelves of gels, lotions, and toys, expensive items like the gold vibrator locked inside a glass-faced cabinet. A rather typical shop stockroom—had it not been for the corrugated foam soundproofing on the walls, the bunk bed with a dangling manacle chained to it, and the dark red drops that trailed across the space, along the wooden floor and into the little viewing booth.

"Right," he said, a bilious flare in his belly. He flipped the switch he'd found just inside the stockroom. A single fluorescent light hummed and flickered to life overhead in the booth, illuminating the dulled colour of the dried smears on the mirror and the red-brown splotches on the dirty, pale grey carpet underfoot. The blood was old, but how old; hours, days, weeks? There was no way to know how long the smears and splotches had been there; the stains had passed from fluid to beyond the gel state, yet the marks lacked the flaking, blackened hue of late-stage evaporation, and evaporation was dependent on size, humidity, temperature, and the climate control system operating in the shop and stockroom. He turned off the light in the booth and pulled the bookcase shut.

A thread of queasiness trickled along the top of his stomach as he took Mae's elbow and stepped into the stockroom. Kitt looked at Mae following the trail of blotches. The room smelled of bathroom cleaner and air-freshener. On the other side of a bed with balled-up dingy bedlinen in the middle, was a kitchen of sorts; a small microwave and electric kettle on a short, stainless worktop surrounded by various cleaning products. Plumped, tied refuse bags sat beside a laundry tub, drying towels pegged on a makeshift line above it. To the right of the tub, a door opened into an orange and pink tiled bathroom, the pink toilet, and black-handled toilet brush beside it framed like a still-life painting. Opposite the lav were two doors; one, a shorter, angled-top often used to access storage under a staircase, the other stood ajar, the imprint of fingers that had gripped the door's edge had left smears of now-dried blood. Kitt considered options again: send her to the hotel alone or soldier on with a woman who had never been a soldier.

Mae took a few steps into the storeroom and froze. The place smelled of bleach and deodorising cleaning products, but the cleaning had been half-arsed. She stared at bloodstains in a back-of-shop flat that housed a bed with cuffs attached to foot posts and a mattress that needed a good boil in a hospital-grade sterilising, sanitising, disinfecting fungicide.

Up to this moment, the play acting had been...fun, but the fight with Gert had been scary—and disquietingly exciting. The exhilaration she felt came from a brush with danger, which Kitt would tell her was perfectly natural human response, yet physiological response aside, she grappled with the thrill, with the morality of the sensation. Was it odd that she preferred clear-cut fear, like the tiny-footed millipede of dread slinking up her spine as she looked at dried blood to gleeful immorality? "As much as I'd prefer to believe that Gert lives here and is an accident-prone, rather half-arsed housekeeper," she said, eyes on the manacle and chain on the bedpost, "but someone's been held here, like as a sexual slave?"

"If I recall correctly, two thirds of the people trafficked every year fall victim to sexual slavery and abuse, but I'm not sure it's only sexual slavery we're looking at here." Kitt gave her a sideways look. "What do you see besides the bed and bits of blood?" he asked.

The question defrosted her frozen feet and shoved aside her immoral tingle, and she began to examine the space again. Amid all the sex merchandise and small bloodstains, there stood an out of place, freestanding metal rack hung with clean, button-front, orange-trimmed grey uniforms, not the kind of uniforms people wore for role-playing sex games, but the kind that housekeeping staff wore in hotels, the sort the two skinny black men they'd seen outside were wearing. "Two men came out of the building next door wearing those uniforms."

"Very good. What else do you see?" He glanced down at the floor, close to the rack of clothes, to where several small, whitish pellets laying in a little puddle of very dark, congealing blood.

She stooped over slightly and straightened immediately. "Are those teeth?"

"They are."

"Something diabolical happened here, didn't it?" she said, shuddering, her breath coming out sharply.

"I believe so, yes."

She hugged herself. And shuddered again. "Does being afraid ever make you need to pee?"

"Are you afraid, Mae?"

"Yes, and I have to pee. Are you scared?"

"Yes, but fear is good. Fear puts you in a heightened state of awareness."

"Are you aware that you have to pee?"

Cool, lacking an expression of any sort, Kitt looked at her, at the door with the dried blood fingerprints, and back to her again. "Pee? No. You being here instead of safe at home has me in a constant state of nausea," he said.

Her laugh was thin. "While it remains flattering that you love me so much it makes you feel sick, I still have to pee."

"Go on then," he said, glanced at the lav with a slight jerk of his chin, and Mae hurried to the dodgy-looking toilet and tried to shut a door that hung crooked on its hinges, a long, narrow gap running down the framing prevented complete privacy. Mindful of the gap and bathroom etiquette, Kitt pulled out his mobile and began taking photos of the storeroom, of the half-opened door that led to a staircase, of the short door under the staircase on the other side of the padded wall, until someone warbling, *"Jamme, jamme 'ncoppa, jamme jà, funiculì, funiculà, funiculì, funiculà,'ncoppa, jamme jà, funiculì, funiculà!"* came from the stairway on the other side.

In a half second, he was in the lav, switching the light off, Mae half-crouched, coat and dress bunched, knickers halfway along her thighs, and his fingers went to her mouth to stifle her protest, a startled look on her face.

Thank the baby Jaysus she'd finished, elsewise there'd be piss all over her legs. Hastily, Mae jerked up her pants and Kitt shut the door on crooked hinges, the gap between the door's edge and frame suddenly seemed wider than she remembered. The shard of light coming from the door gap reflected off a small mirror above the sink, the bathroom very dimly lit by it.

Most Dutch bathrooms had barely enough space to do one's business and turn around. By comparison, this one was a palace—albeit a cosy, colourful tiny palace much cleaner than the living space in the stockroom. The toilet was the typical Dutch sort; a ridged, flat-surfaced bowl with a button for flushing set into the top of the tank. To the right of the toilet, the teeny-tiny sink, and the perpetual birthday calendar that was de rigueur in Dutch lavs, stood a narrow shower stall with an orange and pink floral curtain. The whole tiny room smelled of Domestos and lily of the valley.

Dress and coat semi-tucked into the elastic of her underpants, Kitt backed Mae into the shower, lifting the curtain to not make a sound. "Stay here," he said at her ear and she screwed her eye shut. He drew away and a half-second later was back at her ear, murmuring, "Don't shut your eyes, keep them open—wide open—and whatever happens, don't get any ideas about using that toilet brush there as a weapon." Then, as soundlessly as the curtain falling about her, he stepped out of the shower.

In the dimness, she peered around the edge of pink and orange fabric, watching him lower the lid of the open toilet as someone called out, cautiously, "Gert?"

Seated on the toilet's edge in half-darkness, Kitt, muttered a throaty "*Ja*," and peeked through the little gap in the door at a man in a black and white hoodie, what looked like a fat riding crop under his arm.

The man faced the entrance into the alcove with the mirror and sighed in irritation, shaking his head, hands on his hips. "*Hé klootzak! Deur dicht doen!*"

Kitt's little "Uh..." blended into a small moan of discomfort as he drew the not-quite-useless little gun from his pocket. While he knew the weapon lacked bullets, it could still be used to menace, just like the cattle prod the man had tucked in the crook of his arm. To some, a cattle prod would have seemed a very odd thing to have in a sex shop, yet this shop catered to all tastes and there were those in the BDSM world who got off on electro-torture and elec-tro-stimulation. There was a very real possibility the blood they'd found was related to consensual SM, but Kitt guessed that this had nothing to do with pleasure and everything to do with non-consen-sual pain and fear and domination of another kind.

"*Idioot! Sluit deze deur!*" With a grumble, the man jerked the hood from his dark hair and shut the door into the little alcove.

Not game to make any noise by pulling her dress and coat from her knickers, Mae peeked around the edge of the shower curtain again. Still seated on the toilet, Kitt had a foot planted against the door and Gert's stupid gun—the one without bullets—in hand. She knew guns gave people a false sense of security and power. She knew that most people were injured by their own firearms. She knew that she would rather have that feckin' manky chrome-handled brush next to the base of the toilet than a stupid Walther, Beretta, Sig or whatever pistol Kitt held at the ready. Ever cool, void of expression of any sort, he glanced at her, jerked his chin to indicate she needed to stay behind the curtain, and gave an uncomfortable moan once she'd stopped peeking around the fabric.

The man called out, *"Is er iemand met je, of bij je verstopt?"*

Dutch wasn't too difficult to translate; *open* the same in English, *deur* a cognate to door, the context and the other words like *iemand* and *verstopt* were similar enough to German and English that Mae had no problem interpreting what was being asked: *was someone with him or was he constipated?*

Kitt appeared to understand as well.

In the last few months, it had become evident that he spoke a few more languages than he'd previously mentioned, Russian for example. There was much about her husband she still didn't know, things she hadn't asked because she wasn't sure she wanted to know. Occasionally, she had to remind herself that he was a spy and, regardless of how he liked to disavow the cliché, however much a joke she thought it was, Kitt had the spy skills one read about in novels and saw in films and television series, so it wasn't a surprise that he'd speak Dutch any more than it was that he was a master of improvisation. As he had from the start, he grunted and moaned again, this time with an edge of annoyance and exertion.

"Mincha," the gardener said in Italian. *"Ricordati tirare l'acqua dopo aver cagato!*—Remember to flush after shitting." A sliver-view of black and white moved closer.

"Rot op!" Kitt said gruffly.

"Okay, okay." The hoodie-wearing gardener laughed like Flipper the dolphin, stone-washed jeans and hoodie disappearing from sight.

It went quiet for a moment. Kitt waited, counting to ten, eyes on the crack in the door. Waiting, counting, he got all the way to seven when the gardener hammered on the door and shouted in Italian, *"Ti ha cagato adosso, Gert?"* asking if he'd scared the shit out of Gert.

It went quiet again.

The sudden peace expanded, a few heavy and frightening seconds ticked over to a minute that felt like an hour and Mae's heart thumped faster, the beat droning in her ears. Why the feck did Kitt tell her to hide in here, in this minuscule space where she was utterly cornered with her eyes wide open? She looked about the tiny, bleach-perfumed shower, at the shampoo and bar of soap sitting in a wire rack hung from the neck of the shower spray nozzle. Her hand closed around a tube of blackhead scrub. She wondered how much damage she could inflict with apricot kernel exfoliant and hazarded a peek around the edge of the shower curtain.

One foot jammed against the door almost casually, the gun resting on his knee, Kitt sat on the toilet, perfectly still, unruffled, patient, expressionless, maddeningly detached from the threat as he kept watch through a crack in the doorframe. Jaysus, the man looked...zen and she was trembling, she was sweating, she was dry-mouthed, she was...letting fear get the better of her. She took a long, slow breath and let it out without a sound.

The man outside the bathroom sighed. "Okay, okay, sorry," he said in Italian. "I know you're pissed off. I'll send Luciana to clean. Women clean better than men. Okay?"

"Okay," Kitt muttered, watching through the crack.

"*Allora*." The off-key Pavarotti began singing *Funiculì, Funiculà* again and crossed the storeroom. He paused at the angled under-stairs storage door, waving his cattle prod as if conducting an orchestra, before he left the way he'd arrived, entering the staircase behind him, his footfalls on the treads muffled, his operatic warbling ending abruptly.

Kitt waited another minute before he lifted his cramping foot and pocketed the Sig. "Mae," he said softly, rose, and slid the shower curtain across. A groove of worry fixed between her brows, she stared at him, a tube of something clutched in her fist. He put out his hand. She set the tube into his palm. "You right?" he said.

"If I hadn't taken care of things before you burst in, I surely would have wet myself." She pulled her clothes into place, the paper packet of tulip bulbs in her coat pocket crinkling as she adjusted her little handbag under her coat. "I would have preferred to run rather than stand in here."

"There wasn't time to run. Now," he said, glancing at the facial scrub she'd handed over, "what were you going to do with this?"

"Throw it in his face and kick him in the bollocks."

"You need to get close enough to kick someone in the balls."

"That's why you should have let me have the toilet brush."

With a faint laugh, Kitt tossed the tube in the sink and took her hand, drew her out of the shower. "Stay behind me," he said and opened the ill-fitted door, pausing to look about. "Come on." He led her across the stockroom, past the door to the stairs, heading toward the exit into the little alcove. He pulled Gert's keys from his pocket and had them ready to unlock the deadbolt. Then he turned about. "Hang on a second."

Mae followed him back to the short door with the slanted top. He studied it and she said, "What do you bet that's where they keep the vacuum?"

He pushed against the angled door and, spring-loaded, it popped open to reveal another door, this one with a deadbolt lock like on the other two doors leading into the stockroom. Kitt looked at Gert's keys, chose one and began to slide it into the lock. It did not fit. He chose another, slipped it into the mechanism, which turned freely, and the door opened outwards. "No Goddamned vacuum in here," he said through his teeth.

"Dear Jaysus," Mae murmured, gathering a fistful of the back of Kitt's jacket, a hand going to her mouth and nose to block the pasty, slightly sweet smell of shit and vomit and blood that wafted out.

The body of a Caucasian man dressed in a grey uniform smeared with his own filth and blood lay stiff on the floor, hands bound with fluffy, hot-pink cuffs. Bearded, his split, bloodied face was wrapped tightly in kitchen plastic, disfiguring his features, his open, gasping, scarlet mouth missing teeth. Miraculously, the orange collar of his shirt was pristine.

Revulsion and fright gave way to facts both practical and scientific. Kitt disentangled Mae's hand from his jacket and crouched over the body. The onset of rigor mortis varied from one to six hours after death occurred and lasted, depending on location and circumstances, for a few hours or several days. This man had not been dead long.

"Okay, he's dead. Let's go," she said, digging her fingers into her temples, her breathing sharp, shallow, and noisy with an edge of irritation mixed into her fear.

He rose. "I know it's going to make you cross, but *breathe*."

She yanked off her hat and glared at him.

"Breathe, my love. Breathe and tell me what you see here." He turned her to the dead man.

"I don't want a feckin' lesson in observation right now." She crossed her arms, eyes narrowing, and took a deep, begrudging and slightly sarcastic breath.

"There's my gir—" The sharp, hot shock hit him hard, an electric jolt shooting up his left arm and across his shoulder. Kitt pitched forward with a shout of pain and stumbled over the dead man.

The former opera warbler turned for Mae, cattle prod at the ready. She kept good on her promise to run and darted for the door, but the gardener leapt, caught the lapel of her coat, drove her against the angled doorframe, shoved the cattle prod into her hip with a noisy, electric *tzzzt*, yet she remained standing, hurling abuse. "Get off me, ya bealin' cuntiballs!"

Snarling, the gardener discharged the prod again, electrical current arcing, *tzzzt tzzzt*. Mae hissed Italian obscenities, and a split second before her knee met testicles, the gardener dropped, chin hitting the floor first, the deep pink tip of his tongue a small stone skipping over the grey carpeting, the red butterfly knife Kitt had plunged into the base of his neck protruding like a handle for easy carrying, the smell of scorched fabric and paper in the air.

CHAPTER ELEVEN

One minute she was looking at a dead man whose face was a plastic-wrapped mess of dark beard and pulp, the next she was staring at a red-handled knife stuck in the base of another dead man's skull, and a moment after that she stood in the doorway of a room full of bunkbeds, breathing in the stink of body odour and fish fingers. Where was she now? Where were they?

Everything moved so fast, she moved so fast, Kitt moved so fast, and leaving Erotica became a blur. Shoving the bookcase aside, passing back through the fitting room and shop, walking back along Reguliersdwarsstraat, through the Bloemenmarkt and crowds out for lunch was a smear of colours. Historic canal houses with gabled rooflines, sunlight sparkling on water, the cobbled street beneath her feet, and passing bicycles blended into a single panorama of high-speed multi-hued fuzziness.

Mae shivered even though she wasn't cold. She shoved a hand into a pocket and felt the little hole the cattle prod had burnt into the pale green fabric and the paper packet of bulbs. There was another brown-toasted fissure right where her purse sat beneath her coat. The one impractical thing in her life—besides loving a man who killed for a living—was an indulgence in the occasional vintage garment. How many vintage garments had she had spoiled thanks to feckin' henchmen and thugs? What was it now, three or four dresses, a coat, and a few pairs of shoes?

She looked at Kitt. He tossed his baseball cap into a rubbish bin. He'd put his jacket on the minute they'd rounded the corner from the shop. When had he grabbed the hat, sunglasses and the cloth bag he'd discarded from the floor in the sex shop fitting room?

"Slow down," he said, taking her elbow as they rounded the corner onto Rokin where a tram passed by. "There's no need to break a speed record. A walk will do us both good. We need the fresh air." The bottom edge of his jacket flared out as he fell into step beside her.

"Please don't remind again me to breathe," Mae said and continued her swift pace, yanking off her hat and the cheap wind-mill scarf, squeezing them into a ball, shoving them into her coat pocket with the bulbs, making the green cloth bulge.

"I wouldn't dream of it." Kitt smiled faintly, so faintly Mae barely caught the expression before it vanished into a mask of nothingness.

His nonchalant façade made her want to scream.

He made a blasé call, in English, coolly leaving the address of the place they'd just left, casually mentioning a few other details, like where to find Gert, two dead bodies, offhandedly noting the filth and rubbish of what appeared to have been cramped, recently-vacated living quarters upstairs in the building next door.

There had been handcuffs attached to the beds, and not the fuzzy or padded fun sort that had been for sale in Erotica.

The sunlight shifted as Kitt spoke, moving clouds alternating the bright and dark, bright and dark. Then he tucked his mobile away, and slipped his arm though hers, controlling the speed of their walk.

As swift-footed as she wanted to be, as much as she resented slowing down, the blur of colours began to sharpen. The simple action of walking, of navigating a way through a crowd, loosened her anxiety—but not her annoyance at his detachment. Still, she let Kitt lead her along Rokin and into the historic centre of the city, toward Dam Square and the National Monument.

They passed the Obelisk commemorating Dutch casualties of WWII, the Royal Palace of Amsterdam, and the Nieuwe Kerk, a fifteenth-century church turned exhibition space. At the edge of Dam Square, Kitt turned right, avoiding the crowds and ever-present bicycles. He took her through cobblestoned back streets that became narrower and snaked between brick buildings until all at once they were on a cobbled street alongside a canal lined with small boats, bicycles in racks, trees with branches green with new-budding leaves, and charming red brick canal houses. Again, he reduced their pace, making it more leisurely and lethargic, until he halted next to bicycles racked beside the open-edged canal, and let her go.

Finally. A crack in his armour appeared. Mae had wondered when it would happen, and, rather pettily, she waited for Kitt to move closer to the canal, to bend forward and disgorge his chip lunch into the water.

He didn't move. He stood looking across the canal, blank-faced, maddeningly calm, as if his nausea wasn't there. Instead of moving forward, he stepped sideways and pulled her into his arms, her back to his front. "Have you noticed," he said, hands splayed at her waist, "how some of the houses are crooked?" He nuzzled his cheek to her ear, nudging her to gaze across the water.

Automatically, she looked at the row of gabled houses on the other side of the canal, the skinniest home with the bell-shaped white gable listed to the left, as if sinking into the low Dutch earth. The house to the right just as slanted. Crooked and sinking, that summed up how she felt. She leaned back into Kitt, who was not sinking but was employed in a crooked occupation full of crooked people who did crooked things. She pulled his arms closer about her and pressed into him, squeezing his forearms.

Kitt held her. It was surprisingly quiet where they'd stopped. A soft breeze stirred branches. Sunlight glimmered in and out, changing shadows and colours. Water lapped gently at the sides of a houseboat tied to a short, black post. Kitt watched the boat bob gently. "It's really quite lovely here, isn't it?"

"It's charming, and," Mae made a sound, a half sigh and snort, "I find you so irritating when you are unperturbed, as you are now, which isn't charming."

"I thought you found my ability to disconnect endearing."

"I find your vomiting after a frightening event endearing." She turned in his arms and looked up at him. "Why aren't you hunched over the canal spewing?"

"Because your work here is done. You've managed to uncover a little nest of snakes, just by listening. I have no idea what the nest means yet, but now you can go home and I can get on with hunting reptiles."

"You think Tanja Goedenacht is a snake?"

"She may be a Hydra or a little reptilian hatchling. Either way, that's for me to find out. You've done as you've been...ordered, and," he smiled, "you're going home. Thank Christ."

"But you're not."

He held her a little tighter, her handbag a lump between them. The sun's light disappeared behind cloud, its warmth replaced by Mae. Her hands moved beneath his jacket, fingers slipping over his shirt, gliding over the scorched cloth and small burn he'd plaster over later. He wasn't proud of how he'd killed a man—*another* man—in front of Mae, but he was impressed he'd maintained enough self-control to not take the cattle prod and beat the living hell out of Gert like he'd wanted to. He'd really wanted to.

Her fingers found the hole burnt in his shirt again and felt the spot gingerly. "Why didn't that Taser thing shock me like it did you?"

"The handbag under your coat and the bulbs in your pocket took the current."

It began to rain, a delicate, cool mist. She rested her cheek on his chest. "Did you expect to find hydroponic equipment and plants growing when we got upstairs?"

"Expect, no, hope, yes. I admit I was concerned we'd find young women, girls, and boys."

"Because of the proximity of the sex shop or the manacle on the bed in the stockroom and beds upstairs?"

"You saw them. Very good observation. Sexual exploitation seems likely, but the two men we saw getting into the van outside, the grey uniforms hanging in the storeroom, and the man we found dead in the cupboard don't quite add up. It's not only forced prostitution. The window decals, the mattresses and beds upstairs, say sexual exploitation, but it could also be accommodation for refugees and immigrants trafficked for employment—most likely in the hotel or restaurant industry."

"Restaurants and hotels?"

"The hospitality industry has vulnerabilities that make it ideal for the exploitation of refugees and illegal immigrants, like seasonal tourism, when there's a spike in the need for short-term temporary labour. A trafficker may be a member of hotel management, or a labour recruiter or labour broker, subcontracting with the hotel to provide cheap labour. The subcontractors take advantage of the business and the immigrants." He stroked her hair. "You heard me on the phone. I reported the situation to the local police. The police and the AVIM—The Aliens Police, Identification and Trafficking in Human Beings Department—will deal with this. Should anyone return to the shop, or next door, the police and AVIM will offer them assistance, find them a safe place and not prosecute. But I think the place was in the process of being shut down, cleaned up. I doubt anyone will return."

"Cleaning up. That's why it all smelled of bleach." Mae drew away and looked up at him, brows knit together in bewilderment, a sheen of rain appearing on her cheeks. "What in underfuck does this have to do with Vlaming and his jewellery, if it has anything to do with Vlaming and his jewellery, or if it's all Tanja Goedenacht?"

"Your guess is as good as mine. It's puzzle pieces, Mae. Some fit, some don't fit, some seem to fit, but they're from the wrong box entirely. Whatever the case, one picture is clear: you are going home." Kitt couldn't help himself. He smiled and it began to pour. Despite the rain, there was a spring in his step when he took her hand and headed for the hotel, leading her along pretty, cobbled streets into the now-quiet red-light district, past the empty shopfront windows where sex workers would later sit on display.

HAIR DRIBBLING WATER, Mae's feet ached from walking. A blister had formed on one little toe. She looked down at fashionable taupe kitten-heels not meant for playing tourist, their colour contrasting against the gleaming tiles of the hotel's foyer. Her shoes click-clacked over white tiles and, for a moment, it reminded her of the white kitchen tiles at home, and how they'd once seemed to gleam even brighter when covered with blood. Tiles gleamed brighter when the blood was dried too.

At once, Kitt stopped abruptly beside a tall white pillar and she nearly ran into him. "What a beautiful dog," he said. "I have one just like it at home."

Mae followed his line of sight to a seating area across from the lobby's front desk, where a dreadlocked black man sat on a sofa across from an older, handsomer black man.

Ever so relaxed in an easy chair, Brigadier Roger Llewelyn scratched Felix beneath the chin, the dog's leash loose in one hand.

"What...the...feck," she muttered, heart tumbling into her stomach.

Kitt muttered something obscene. "Take a breath," he said softly. "Take a breath. He is Boothroyd, *Professor* Boothroyd. Count to five, then move.' He began whistling *Always Look on the Bright Side of Life* under his breath, left her standing beside the pillar, and approached the desk to check in.

"Welcome to the Palace Grand," the petite brunette clerk behind the desk said, casting a glance at Mae before giving Kitt a pretty smile.

Breathing in and out, Mae counted to ten and then moved to the front desk, behind Kitt, trying to be nonchalant, pretending not to see the Brigadier, shaking rainwater off her trench coat, the clerk behind the desk acknowledging her with a smile and nod.

"There you are, Mrs Valentine!" Llewelyn boomed like a stage actor.

Hair plastered like a helmet to her head, a trickle of rainwater dribbling down her neck, she muttered, "That diabolical fecker," a little louder than she'd intended. The desk clerk glanced at her and Mae turned around, watching Llewelyn cross the space, smiling cheerfully. The dog pulled on his lead, stretching forward to reach her.

"Oh, my, you're all wet!" Llewelyn stated the bloody obvious. "Did you forget to take an umbrella? It is my experience that Amsterdam is wetter than London. Yes, yes, I'm earlier than you expected, but you are capable and I knew you wouldn't mind. There will be four for dinner tonight, if that's not too much trouble to arrange. By the way, your brother sends his love. I ran into him at Heathrow, on his way to Dublin."

"Dublin?" Mae took another breath, quashing fear that threatened to jerk her over the edge of rationality and into kicking and pummelling Kitt's employer.

"I know you're concerned about him travelling, but you can't hover." Llewelyn chided her with good-natured aplomb that hid a poison sting. "The man has to live his life. He's feeling much better, and he quite enjoyed meeting Gibson."

Kitt looked over his shoulder. Mae's eyes widened for a moment and then collapsed into a very short-lived squint. She blinked once then fell right into the role as a patient butler. "Yes, I'm sure he did. I'll see to dinner, Professor," she said, and Felix began to lick her hand.

Llewelyn held out the dog's lead. "Here, take the little chap. Let me know when you've settled everything upstairs." His eyes cut to the black, dreadlocked gentleman heading off. "I'll be in the bar."

"I ADORE THIS AREA," Llewelyn said melodically, hand sweeping across the view from the balcony. "The Grand Palace is so ideal for its proximity to the Oude Zijde. The oldest side of the city is so very Dutch. Pity you won't have the time to explore it." He crossed to the large sitting room, dumping his ink-blue Burberry car coat on a sofa. "Now then, before you ask, my dear Mrs Valentine," he pulled his shirt cuffs straight in his jacket sleeves, "your brother is fine.

The padre is with his religious compatriots in Dublin. Gibson, you remember him, the nurse? He knew your brother was, shall we say, struggling. Gibson took the liberty of arranging an invitation, and I was more than happy to see to the Major's dog. You know I have two of my own."

"Yes. You did all that out of the goodness of your heart." Damp hair in place, Mae stood at the paned glass balcony doors, staring at the wet view, relieved and seething.

"Why naturally, Mrs Valentine."

Mae went on staring out the balcony doors. The hotel, on Warmoesstraat, was situated a few blocks from the National Monument and Koninklijk Paleis, the Royal Palace. The view from the balcony of the two-bedroom suite looked down over a dead-end canal and the start of De Wallen—the red-light district she and Kitt had walked through a short time ago. The Catholic Basiliek van den Helige Nicholaas, right next door to the hotel, also bordered the dead-end canal and De Wallen. It was a strange juxtaposition of religion and sex that the Irish Catholic in Mae suddenly found rather amusing. Felix nosed his snout into her hand as she gazed down at the canal again and laughed to herself. So, Llewelyn liked this part of Amsterdam. The man probably had a penchant for prostitutes and pot, both of which were readily, and legally, available just on the other side of the canal.

"Is that a smile, Mrs Valentine? You're quite attractive when you smile."

At the bar on a sideboard, Kitt sorted through a disappointing selection of booze on offer. He looked up at her as her smile died. "My hole," she said under her breath, and turned around, slipping on the comfortable mantle of composed professional, her attention on Kitt. "Excuse me, sir, I'd better take Felix out, unless there's something you need."

Kitt shook his head at a bottle of Yellow Label Four Roses. "A better bourbon."

"Of course, sir." Mae gave him an agreeable nod and patted her hip. "Come, Felix."

"Mrs Valentine," Llewelyn said.

Mae faced him, smouldering fractiousness concealed in a fist she held clenched behind her back. Walking the dog and the better bourbon would have to wait. "Brigadier?" she said, watching the dog trot over to the man and latch on to his calf.

With a scowl, Llewelyn pushed the animal away. "I must apologise," he said. "It is unusual for someone in my position to step in to a field action so abruptly, before any real intelligence has been gathered. It's not typica—" Felix wrapped his paws around Llewelyn's knee. "Oh, not again. Get down!" He pushed at the animal and the dog scampered off, leaping upon the sofa. "You need to take this dog to an obedience course, Major."

"Felix tends to do that when he's anxious," Mae cocked her head, "or with people he dislikes."

Kitt chuckled softly and took a glass from a small shelf. "Care for a little bourbon, sir?"

"No thank you, it's a bit early in the day for me." Llewelyn gave his vintage Rolex a glance and smoothed his moustache, eyes shifting to the dog shaking a throw pillow like a rat. "It's not typical for the head of Special Operations Division to step in, Mrs Valentine. I generally leave the relay of information to my assistant. However, Morland's dealing with an internal matter and I'm here because AIVD Director Kurt Albert requested a meeting, Major. Two birds, one stone."

"What is AIVD?" Mae asked.

"The Dutch Secret Service," Kitt said. "What information would I have expected from Morland, sir?" Pillows spilling to the floor, the dog launched off the sofa and rocketed about the room.

"We'll discuss that after Albert liaises with his Croatian counterpart this afternoon."

Kitt poured a splash of amber liquid into the glass. "Another bird, another stone," he said, glancing at Mae straightening cushions and pillows on the long sofa.

"There's an additional circumstance that's rather compelling— if it's true. We'll see if either matter has legs. Albert's reque—Major, you *really* ought to take this silly, bad-mannered dog to obedience training! You'd never find my Bambi and Thumper behaving this way."

Mae refolded a wool throw and looked over her shoulder. Felix had wrapped his white-dipped paws around Llewelyn's leg again, humping energetically as the man shook him off and pushed him away.

Glass of bourbon in hand, the left corner of his mouth lifted with amusement, Kitt said, "Off, Felix!" The dog huffed and plopped onto the carpet, white paws crossing daintily.

"As I was saying," head shaking, Llewelyn brushed tiny ginger hairs from his trousers, "Your need for local assistance, and Albert's request to meet, made it necessary for me to step in as Professor Boothroyd."

Step in. The wily bastard was staying, taking on field work. Kitt swallowed the amber liquid he'd just drawn into his mouth. Christ. He hoped like hell he wouldn't be expected to do the man's paperwork.

"So, your morning with Vlaming," Llewelyn purred. "Tell me about it." He looked at them both, his light brown eyes vulture-like.

Mae glanced at Kitt and had a seat. Felix jumped into the chair with her and settled beside her, head on her lap. She rubbed his ears.

Kitt had a sip of subpar bourbon, put his tumbler on a side table beside a crystal clock, and painted Llewelyn a picture of the meeting with Vlaming, telling him about Mae's chance eavesdropping on his secretary's conversation in the greenhouse, following the gardener to the sex shop, and the locked storeroom, the body, the end of the gardener, the lodgings on the upstairs floor next door, the probability of human exploitation.

A smile, the sort matinee idols of the 1940s had, bloomed on Llewelyn's face. Kitt knew that handsome grin was an I-told-you-so regarding the value of Mae as an asset on this assignment, and the man went on smiling handsomely. "I take it you informed the locals?" he said.

"I have, sir."

"What's the secretary's name?"

"Tanja Goedenacht."

"What a good sturdy Dutch name. It's eyes on her then?"

"It appears so. We've arranged to meet for a drink. She doesn't know she's having dinner with me instead."

"Yes, I know. Bryce advised you needed briefed, local support. However, since Albert is coming for dinner, there's no need to roust Ivar or Tilly. Bring the secretary here, Major, we'll perform a little play in this suite." He turned his attention to Mae. "Mrs Valentine, please see to ordering a *rijsttafel* supper, and whatever other necessary things for breakfast,' he said then paused for a moment, watching her with a wry little smile and careful scrutiny.

She mirrored his expression.

His laugh jolly, his smile even merrier Llewelyn said, "When you unpack, you'll find Morland tucked a delightful packet of chai for me. I believe it's in my smallest bag. I'll take the chai in the evening, but whatever tea you find in the kitchen now would be suitable," he said, brows arched expectantly.

"The Major doesn't drink tea," Mae glanced at Kitt.

Llewelyn sat back, fingers flicking in an insouciant wave. "I'm sure you can scrounge up some coffee for him."

Mae rose, hands behind her back. "If I may, Brigadier, in what capacity am I here, to serve as your butler or as an observer who need not be informed of anything?"

"Oh, dear. I've forgotten myself entirely."

Filthy words hit the tip of Kitt's tongue but remained trapped behind his teeth. Llewelyn never forgot himself.

"I was quite out of line," the older man said. "Forgive me, Mrs Valentine. I am quite capable of looking after myself," he cast a sidelong glance at Kitt, "but yes, let's establish ground rules, shall we? I think it best we maintain our roles and, given your career, you look after me as you would any employer, making tea, unpacking my things, taking that pretty, little, silly dog for his walk and such. Does that clarify things?"

"As you wish, Brigadier." With a nod, her expression dispassionately professional, Mae turned and the dog followed her across the polished wooden floor to the luggage near the door. She took bags into one bedroom and then the other.

Llewelyn had a seat on the dark green sofa, a little blue folder of information on his lap.

Kitt set the empty bourbon glass on an end table and sat on the fat arm of the charcoal grey upholstered club chair had sat in earlier. "My dog, sir?"

"Not *quite* the dog I expected you to have."

"So you've said."

"A dog is not the most practical the thing a man in your profession to have, is it?"

"You have dogs."

"I am not a field officer."

"No, you're not. Why is he here? Why are you here?"

"Careful, Major." Llewelyn shook a finger. "Her brother was struggling and needed support. We support our own, Major. I sent

Gibson to look after the Padre, and having the dog here gets Mrs Valentine out of the way."

"You said her presence here was necessary and now you want her out of the way?"

"Your butler is exactly where she needs to be. It's obvious she's quite fond of you, perhaps even a little in love with you. You have noticed how she looks at you, haven't you?"

CHAPTER TWELVE

God damn it all, what had he done? Why had he ever been such a quixotic fool and given in to foolish emotion and attachment? It all would have been different if Mae were still in love with a dead man, if she'd still clung to that desperate bond to a ghost of a man she never really knew. But no, she'd let go of Caspar and let go of any pretext of professionalism that she'd hidden behind, she'd reached out, opened herself, opened her heart to him, loved *him* and Kitt was lost to her foolishness, to his own foolishness. Here they were, fools in love, fools who loved each other in a foolish profession that was no place for fools.

This job was his for life, he'd known that from day one. Mae understood and accepted that cold fact. The problem was he never expected love would burrow into his life or that he'd love someone the way he loved Mae. He'd never prepared for love, never considered it...necessary. What he had expected was that he'd be dead before he hit fifty, which wasn't that far away, yet he now had a compulsion to stay alive that went far beyond self-preservation. He looked at Mae coming out of the second bedroom wearing a navy-blue shirt dress—and an apron. The woman travelled with her uniform and an apron.

Dog trailing behind, she headed through the dining area and into the small but well-appointed kitchen, the packet of Llewelyn's chai in hand, pushing through a swinging door, and Kitt's insides scrambled, nausea bubbled up hot and acidic to burn his throat. He swallowed back the sick that reached his mouth.

Kitt stared at Llewelyn shuffling papers in the folder, knowing that he had to find a way to get her out, to get Mae away. His immediate thought was to plot Llewelyn's demise. His next thought was equally preposterous, but he glanced down at his left hand anyway, at the missing quarter bits left of his ring finger and pinkie. Losing the rest of his hand might get him out, put him on the second reserve list, but it would do nothing to extricate Mae. "What's obvious to me is that she's loyal and faithful to her husband." Kitt said, matter-of-God-damned fact.

Llewelyn tossed the folder on the coffee table. "As loyal and faithful as you are to me and the Consortium's service. She may be twenty-five years beyond your tastes, but have you slept with her?" He held up a hand. "Oh, I know, it's hardly a gentlemanly question, but you two have been in several stressful situations together, and sex can add a level of trust, a particular intimacy, can make another more agreeable to undertaking something disagreeable. Yes, yes, she might be too old for you, but even if you pretend not to notice, even if you keep the propriety line of employer-employee relations very much in place, *I've* seen how she looks at you and I imagine Mrs Valentine would happily get in your bed. All you need do is ask—if you haven't already. Then again, I could be mistaking her respect for you and gratitude to you for saving her life as love, infatuation, or simple hero worship."

"I assure you," Kitt said, "Valentine fails to see me as heroic."

Llewelyn chuckled. "Good help, as we know, is hard to find. A trustworthy employee is an asset, and taking advantage of that trust might be unseemly, but you've already taken advantage of her, Major. The woman would do, and has done, anything for you."

"I know Valentine well, and she's not doing this for me. I am aware you coerced her to participate by offering an...alternative for her brother's ongoing mental health therapy. While your faith in me has been restored, you don't trust her. Why is that? Why is it not enough that she offered her assistance twice before and exposed true criminals and corruption within our offices?"

Llewelyn smiled faintly. "Two things, really. For a while, someone has wanted to embarrass us, to have it look as if various government departments are entangled in illicit activity, to create scandal, to redirect attention to disguise the actual criminal acts. We suspected this and had eyes on you, Gettler, Springer, and Dalton. If you recall, my money was on you."

"Yes, I recall." Kitt smiled back broadly, looking up through his lashes. "Perhaps someone bears a grudge."

"I know that's not your style, Major. My name being bandied about as the account holder paying off the assassin who tried to kill your butler and you—the one you stuffed into the boot of a VW Beetle in New Mexico, what was his name?"

"Derek."

"Yes, attaching my name to paying off the assassin you killed was a grudge move by Dalton and Molony to discredit me, and had you not succeeded in clearing yourself of suspicion, it would have embroiled me in scandal that ended my career. This is far reaching, stretching much farther than we thought. In our discussion this morning, AIVD Director Albert mentioned something we'd come across before. He'll bring it along this evening. You'll want to have a look at it. The sweeps, surveillance, internal audits and, well, the actual business with the container and smuggling revealed it was Dalton. His activity with Molony proved me wrong about you. I can't tell you how happy that made me, how happy I was that you didn't die last year."

"Is that an apology, sir?"

Llewelyn chuckled aridly. "With Dalton and Molony's demise, we'd believed we'd found the chink in our armour and repaired it. Only the rot is much deeper than we realised, and encompasses so much more. The Americans report that Ruby Bleuville was found dead in her cell this morning. It's early, but a preliminary report suggests suicide."

"Or murder. My money is on the Yeoh Triad, the Enrico Cartel retaliating, or someone covering their tracks. Do you think Ruby's death is most likely related to the Dankwaerts' freeport theft?"

"I don't investigate these things, my boy. You do. Find out what you can from Vlaming's secretary. I'll have Albert's people run a check on her as well." He looked to the left and set the blue folder aside as Mae appeared with a tray laden with a small pot, a plate of biscuits, and a beautiful blue and white Delft cup and saucer. "The tea, oh, splendid! Where's the Major's coffee?"

Mae set the tray on the coffee table, placing a cup and a plate of little spiced biscuits in front of Llewelyn. "The Major would not find the coffee suitable."

Kitt arched an eyebrow. "Instant?"

"Pods, sir."

"Good God, what is the world coming to?"

"Dear boy, you are a snob." Llewelyn poured his own cup of chai.

Mae stepped back. "Will there be anything else, Brigadier?"

Llewelyn looked at the dog poking his long snout forward, cautiously sniffing at the biscuits shaped like windmills. Finding the aroma disagreeable, Felix backed off, plopped down, and gnawed one rear paw. "See to the Major's hound."

Mae ran hands down her hips, smoothing her apron. "Walkies,

Felix," she said and turned, the dog leaping up to scamper alongside.

"Take an umbrella, Mrs Valentine." Llewelyn called out.

Kitt waited until she had crossed the large sitting room and disappeared into the smaller of the suite's two bedrooms. "The second thing, sir?" he said.

"I think your butler is hiding something."

"I'm guessing it's her antipathy for you."

"Don't play with me, Major. You're aware that she is too, but whatever she's concealing, her previous contributions, what she ascertained and experienced in those particular activities make her ideal to join in this action, and despite your reservations and protests, you understand that. You know she is an asset and a liability."

"It's best to keep such people where you can see them."

"Well, it pays to keep tabs on one's best-valued employees."

"As you kept tabs on me."

"For which you are fortunate. You are valued, obviously. I may not say that often, or may not have ever said that at all, but this is, at times, an indecorous business, dear boy. We utilise the talent and resources at our disposal."

The talent and resources at our disposal. God all bloody mighty, Llewelyn would find ways to keep Mae, to use her as an active asset when it suited him because, however much he valued them, that's what he did, use people, and the hypocrisy of *talent and resources at our disposal* wasn't lost on Kitt.

Using people is what he did too.

He looked across the sitting room to the door where the excited ginger dog pranced about after Mae hooked a lead to his harness. He watched the pair exit the suite. "I'll do my best to discover what it is you think she's hiding, sir, any way I can."

"There's a good lad."

Kitt rose. Then he was in the hallway outside the suite, then at the lift where she stood waiting in her still-damp trench coat.

There came a *bong*, double doors parted, and the three of them stepped into a space scented with lemon and lavender. They rode in silence for a floor, then the dog yawned and Kitt sighed. "You have to stop looking at me the way you have been," he said.

"How have I been looking at you?"

"Adoringly, your eyes aglow with warmth."

She arched an eyebrow. "Aglow with warmth?"

A faint smile quirked the left corner of his mouth. "Yes. Llewelyn's noticed. Those were his exact words."

"I shall take care then and gaze at you indignantly, my eyes ablaze with contempt."

"Is that what you feel?"

She paused before she answered. "I am trying very hard to be professional."

"You didn't answer my question."

"I think you're mighty. What the ever lovin' feck is he doing bringing my dog here?"

"*Our dog,* and Llewelyn has his reasons."

"Which he'll share with me if and when he sees fit." She made a noisy, half-grunted *pfft* of irritation. "This business and its ridiculous 'need to know' shite. There aren't dogs in spy stories!"

"He wants to see if he can set you off, disarm you, find out how far he can push you. It's what he does, it's how he sizes up people, but what you really need to know is that the paperwork on this is going to be astounding," he said, exhaling his fractiousness.

She exhaled in a similar manner. "I have only just realised, this being our third go around with working together, that you..."

"We are not working together. You were forced into this, which..."

"...like to have something to complain about. If it's not your access to scrambled eggs, then it's bitching about paperwork—"

"...is an additional level of... I am *not* bitching."

She half turned to look up at him. "The paperwork on this is going to be astounding."

"That's not how I sound. My voice is not high-pitched like that."

"I'm mocking you with more sarcasm than usual because all this time I've been in awe of you how you're able to remain maddeningly calm and see beyond the hell of whatever's happened, but now I know you balance your composure by complaining about the *paperwork*."

"You think you're enjoying this, don't you?"

"You know I relish mocking you."

"I mean you think you like the, for want of a better word, *action* involved in this operation."

"Maybe I do."

He swore. "No. No, you do not."

She looked down at the still damp sleeve of her trench coat, the green cloth made darker by moisture, the deepened colour reminding her of the tropical part of the Three-Climate Greenhouse at The Hortus, reminding her of what she'd overheard and what eavesdropping on a conversation carried out in a Sicilian dialect had led them to. "I'm not trying to be anything other than what I am, and I am afraid, Kitt. The action is better than being at home waiting for you to return, hopefully unscathed, better than being alone with my thoughts of a dying woman's shattered face, better than wondering how the man in the Erotica met his end, and preferable to trying to convince my brother that he's better when he may not actually be, or ever be, better. I don't want to fixate on the fear or mayhem or trip over the edge of the madness of this. I can't help that some of this is so preposterous that I find it absurdly entertaining and startlingly invigorating. But rather than wallow in

fear or helplessness, or wrestle with the depravity and the contra-
dictory emotions over the person I have become, or how the edges
of whatever this is keeps changing, I'd rather focus on how to get
on with it, how I can help, on how one of us, or both of us, can
finish this as quickly as possible and move on, with some of my
morals intact, which is, I have come to suspect, exactly what
you do."

"Well," he said, softly, "I have to say that choice is more
productive."

She met his eyes. "I'm doing the best I can."

"I know you are." He gave her a faint smile. "Would you like
some happy news?"

She shrugged noncommittally.

"Ruby Bleuville is dead."

She winced. "That's hardly news I ought to be happy to hear,"
she exhaled, "but, God forgive me, it does lift my spirit. Did she
succumb to her...injuries from drinking the denture cleaner I gave
her?"

"It's not yet clear how she died, only that she was found dead."

"God forgive me," she said again.

The dog yawned. The lift let out a *bong* and half a second later,
the doors slid open. They walked through the lobby, across black
and white tiles, and out to the front of the hotel to the footpath.
They didn't get far before the sniffing-at-everything dog crouched
to do his business just off the edge of the low footpath. While she
could not curb the dog's predilection for humping, she'd managed
to train him to 'empty out' off the footpath into the kerb. Mae
pulled a dark, biodegradable bag from the pocket of her coat.
Before she moved to pick up the little brown cigarillos, Kitt took
her elbow and slid the plastic from her fingers, popping the thin
bag open, inserting his hand in it. Then he bent and gathered the
poo in a neat and tidy package.

She burst out with a hearty chuckle. "I do love how you can make me laugh."

"I don't like when you're angry."

"How odd. I *love* when you're angry."

The bag of poo swung in his hand. "I apologise. I may be in blind bully mode, but I am not angry with you. So close. You were so bloody close to being out of here and now... It was not and is not my intention to vent my anger toward you. I am...exasperated. Incredibly exasperated and I am not a very adept juggler when it comes to work and husbanding. I lack the experience. I am an experienced intelligence officer paid to do a job, which is what you damn well keep me from accomplishing since I have to pay attention to you, try to keep you and myself safe instead of focussing on finding the information I need to finish my damned job, and this is not at all coming out the way I'd like it to."

"I believe you're trying to tell me you were an utter prick."

"A scared utter prick."

"I'm no picnic either, Kitt. I could whinge less. I've been with you long enough to understand your demeanour is part of the SOP when you start a new operation. Or is it mission? Which is it? You said operation a moment ago."

"Either. SOP? Did you get that from a spy novel or a film?" He glanced at the plastic bag as full of shit as the ideas she had about spycraft.

"Bryce told me."

"Ah, Bryce, generator of paperwork."

"You know, I've been told my paperwork has always been excellent. I'm concise, I paint a clear picture, yet do not waffle on with unnecessary descriptions. I get right to the point. Perhaps I can handle the paperwork on this mission, or whatever you call it, and you can deal with all the shit."

He laughed and then shifted the moment of amusement to a

topic that was foreign, that displayed his lack of experience, and was far, far more unpleasant than paperwork or picking up dog shit. "I'm going to beg for forgiveness in advance," he said, "and then ask for permission."

LESS THAN FIFTY metres from the hotel, the Prins Heerlijk café sat on a three-way intersection of cobbled laneways. The tables out front were empty, the large umbrellas above them folded up in the rain. Kitt sat inside, in the corner. He had a clear view of the three laneways through the front and side window beside his table. Half an hour earlier, he'd gone into In't Aepjen, the bar down the laneway, the place he'd agreed to meet Tanja Goedenacht for a drink. He'd had a look around, found an exit near the lavatory, noted that the bartender kept a large wooden baton behind the bar, and then went across to the little café with the umbrella seating. He waited.

Soon, Tanja Goedenacht hurried along Sint Olofspoort, a gorilla of a man walked alongside, a heavy line of dark chest hair poking out from the top of his zippered knit jacket, a mobile in his big, hairy hand. The pair paused near a wine merchant with red awnings. She glanced at her mobile. The burly man beside her said something and they went into the wine shop.

So, she had a minder or, potentially, a bodyguard. Whichever, Kitt would soon find out.

Having a gorilla with her was fitting, considering where they were meeting for a friendly drink. In't Aepjen was one of the oldest in Amsterdam. During the golden age of seafaring, if one had been short of guilder, the bar accepted sailor's monkeys as payment. A bustling, popular place since 1519, the wooden interior had dark ceiling beams, décor consisting of oil portraits, old posters and carved primates that reflected its past as a precursor to a monkey park that would lead to the establishment of the Artis, Amsterdam's zoo. Kitt let five minutes pass, exited the café, and slowed for a moment to look at the green and brown bottles displayed in the window of the wine shop, making sure they saw him before he headed down Zeedjik, the laneway on the left, and went into the crowded, noisy old bar.

He ordered a lager, paid for it with euro instead of a capuchin or macaque monkey, and found a seat in a corner near a statue of a cigar-smoking chimpanzee. Well-hidden by the heavy decor and a group of boisterous backpackers, their pile of rucksacks, and table full of beer glasses, he had a clear view to the front windows and door, to patrons coming and going, to customers sitting upon red stools at the wooden bar.

When Tanja arrived, the gorilla sat by the door, and rather than wander about searching for the Englishman she'd invited for a drink, she gazed about the people at the bar, at the backpackers, at a group of older men roaring with laughter. She found vacant stools close to the entrance. She removed her black coat, placed it over the back of the stool. Then she straightened a fitted, salmon-pink dress and repositioned the large pendant on a black beaded chain, sitting the heart-shaped bit of sparkle at the vee of her breasts before she perched on the stool, and pretended to peruse the beer menu as she waited for his arrival.

Slouched and obscured by rucksacks, Kitt let another five minutes pass, watching her not order a drink. She sat, eyes on her mobile, occasionally glancing up at the windows. Her attention was on the phone's screen when the glass front door opened and two young men came into the bar. One, in black denim, had a red umbrella that dripped across the floor as he crossed to the far end of the bar and ordered. The other shook rain from his orange track-suit jacket. His damp, bedraggled appearance made him look younger than he had when he'd been waiting for the gardener in the building with the lips and phallus on Openhartsteeg.

Well, well, was this to be a reunion?

The kid's wispy, pubescent moustache wet with rainwater, he looked about, saw the burly monkey-man, and found Tanja perched on a stool at the bar and made a beeline for her, pushing in between her and the seat to her left. Her head came up and he leaned close, saying something. Then her pretty face contorted, the rumple of her top lip remained as the boy went on talking, a little excitedly, Kitt thought. Agitated, Tanja stared at the kid, her jaw jutting forward as she shook her head and began to question him. It wasn't hard to guess that the exchange had something to do with finding Gert bound and gagged and the dead gardener at Erotica.

Nervous, the boy made a stabbing motion and touched the back of his neck, indicating how the gardener had perished. By then, beer in hand, Kitt had reached the bar, stood to her right, and placed his lager on a coaster. "I'm afraid I started without you."

Tanja's attention shifted and the disturbed curl of her lip transformed into a quiver of bogus, exasperated helplessness, her large, imploring eyes glancing at the desperate kid who'd suddenly frozen.

Kitt looked at her, at the boy with the sorry little moustache that would never be anything more than a sorry little moustache, and back at Tanja.

She exhaled and half rolled her eyes.

Kitt settled his gaze on the boy again and jerked his head toward the door.

The kid licked his lips, his eyes flicking from the other end of the bar where his mate in denim stood with his dripping umbrella, to the dark, burly man at the table by the door.

Over the din of bar patrons, Kitt said, "*Rot op*," the words translating literally to *rot off*, more or less, the Dutch equivalent of 'fuck off'.

Still licking his bottom lip, the boy backed off and made his way to the friend who clapped him on the back, laughed, and shoved a beer into his hand. It was a good cover for a sloppy moment.

Kitt slid onto a seat beside Tanja. "I bet that happens to you often," he said loudly.

"What gives you that idea?"

"You're rather attractive." He leaned in close so that he didn't have to shout at her or into the heart-shaped faux jet or onyx pendant he knew was an inexpensive voice-activated recording device anyone could buy off the internet. Who would be listening to the recording?

Tanja gave him a wry smile and moved a little nearer. "Is that your pick-up line?"

"Not at all. I'm here in a professional capacity and you're the one who asked me for a drink, and you don't have a drink. How disappointing."

A whoop of raucous laughter burst the air. Tanja touched her ear, wincing. "I'm sorry I'm late and I'm sorry I thought it would be nice for you to experience something historic and very Dutch. I'd forgotten how noisy this place gets."

"Would you like to go elsewhere?"

She nodded before another crack of ear-splitting laughter thundered. "Do you have the time?"

Kitt glanced at time on his battered Citizen watch. "Barely. There's a quiet bar in my hotel."

Tanja ran a lock of hair through her fingers. "And where's your hotel?"

"Just around the corner."

Her head tilted, brows arching. "You make my boss very

nervous. Jan was upset he couldn't accept your dinner invitation, and he didn't want me to meet you for a drink."

Kitt reached for her coat. "And why is that?"

"I know all about the theft of his..." she giggled... "family jewels."

"Do you now?"

"Yes, but it's also..." she rose and let him help her into her raincoat, "...it's also very silly. Jan thinks you'll try to sleep with me and use me to incriminate him."

"I assure you I have no plans to incriminate Mr Vlaming. Let's forget about the drinks. Join me for dinner?"

CHAPTER THIRTEEN

Two men, wait staff from the Michelin starred restaurant on the ground floor, arrived to move furniture. Mae showed them to the dining room. The shorter, browner-skinned man nodded at her, saying something in another language that might have been Malay or Indonesian to the taller, thinner man with pale brown eyes. The thin man shifted two dining chairs out of the way as Shorty manoeuvred the table apart. Together, they inserted a leaf hidden below into the space. Then they departed after returning the chairs to the table.

Mae shook out the tablecloth and laid the table with Delft plates and silverware for five. Shortly before six, the doorbell rang. Felix barked, ears pricking at the chime. Mae led him to her bedroom, shut him inside, and returned to open the suite's door to two men. One, smartly dressed, mid-sixties, had white-blond hair that set off tanned, somewhat leathery skin and very white, very straight teeth He held a folio case under his arm. The other, a tall and wiry dreadlocked black man, smiled a smile that didn't touch the brown eyes behind small, wire-framed glasses. He wore messenger bag across his chest. He'd been in the lobby earlier this afternoon, sitting near Llewelyn with the messenger bag in his lap.

"Good evening." Mae said.

"*Hoi*, Kurt Albert. Roger Llewelyn is expecting us." He pointed, "This is Hans Weed."

"I'm Valentine. Please come in." Mae said, stepping aside to let them pass. "May I take your coats?"

Albert handed Weed the case and shrugged out of a raincoat as Llewelyn made a stage entrance, sauntering into the sitting room, leaving the door to his bedroom open wide. "Kurt, my God man, don't you age?" he boomed.

"As per our mutual deal with Satan, not any more than you do, Roger," Kurt Albert said with an accent that had mastered the difficult *th* sound of the English language.

The two men laughed and shook hands, Llewelyn saying, "I ordered a *rijsttafel*, you know, 'when in Rome' and all that."

"Brave of you. Some dishes can be devilishly spicy—and I love spicy food!" Albert fanned a hand in front of his mouth and turned to Weed. "My minion."

"If you don't mind, I prefer *demon*, sir," soft-spoken, deep-voiced Weed said, and went on smiling his fixed, flight attendant smile, handing Albert the briefcase and Mae his damp coat. He wore a black roll-neck sweater, a dark grey jacket, an old-fashioned digital watch—the kind with a calculator—and amethyst beads that he pulled down from the right sleeve of his jacket and adjusted on his wrist. His dark eyes remained fastened on her, amiable, phony smile cemented in place. It was unsettling.

With creeping disquiet, Mae returned his ersatz grin with a nod, turned about, set the coats on a chair near Llewelyn's bedroom, and adjusted hair that fell into her eyes. Earlier, she'd tended to her hair quickly when it was damp with rain, but it had dried with a mind of its own. Loose hair was an impractical irritation when working; a guest finding hair in their food or stuck to the side of a glass was a sign of unprofessional carelessness. She knew the state of her hair didn't reflect carelessness as much as it did the havoc of the afternoon. Residual effects of the last two days had left her with a burrowing, dishevelled, utter lack of equilibrium, which cognitively she knew was perfectly normal for the death and shocking inhumanity she had witnessed, for the violence she had experienced. Again.

What was the word Kitt had used? Resilient? Yes, that was it. She was resilient. She bounced back like the lock of the hair curling and spilling over her eye. She paused at the edge of the room, near the swinging door to the small kitchen, pushing back hair, studying the guests, waiting to spring back like a lock of hair, like cake that had baked to perfection. Suddenly feeling under-cooked and gluey instead, she took a breath and seized well-prac-tised activity, clinging to the simple, yet productive, professional task of offering drinks to Llewelyn's guests who weren't really guests, and entered the sitting room. "May I offer you a beverage or cocktail?" she said. "I have several off-dry whites, a rosé, a chilled pinot noir, and a ripe but not overly spirituous Australian shiraz, as well as beer and other spirits."

Weed looked her up and down once more and sank into a roll-armed chair. Albert removed a manila file folder from his case and set it on the coffee table in front of Llewelyn. "This is for you later, Roger," he tapped the folder, "as per our discussion. I believe you've already had a look at the documents Weed delivered earlier. You'll enjoy what he turned up this afternoon, it's tucked in the blue file." He took a seat in the wide armchair, crossing his legs, arm draped casually over the back of the seat. "We're briefed and we're ready."

"Splendid. Any questions about how this will run?" Seated on the sofa, Llewelyn tipped his chin and waited.

"Where is your man?" Weed said quietly, his timbre as low as bassoon, his English tinted by Dutch inflection.

"The Major will be along with the woman shortly. I hope. I am famished." Llewelyn cast his eyes to Mae.

She stood at the end of the sofa, waiting to proceed. Before Arthur and his AIVD team had arrived, she'd been briefed too, her part explained; she was Professor Boothroyd's butler—not much of a stretch, Llewelyn wanted to keep things simple, convincing, as normal as possible for her—while dinner 'guests' Albert and Weed had been, in one way or another, 'victims' of theft from the secure storage facility at the Luxembourg freeport. Everyone had a cover and a story to match. The commonality was that they had, one way or another, met Ruby Bleuville.

"Before we get on with it," Weed sat back and played with the amethyst beads around his wrist, "I believe there was an offer of a drink." The man glanced up at Mae. "Water," he said, smiling, his voice soft, warmth absent from his unsmiling eyes.

"I'll have the pinot noir," Albert nodded politely and Felix began to howl, the noise a muted, ghostly, wavering WooOooooOoo.

Llewelyn subtly cleared his throat. "Mrs Valentine, see to the little man."

"Of course." Mae crossed to her bedroom, where the dog was corralled for the evening. Along with scooping up poo, Kitt had taken it upon himself to pick up a packet of Dent-a-chews bones before they'd returned from walking the dog. She gave Felix a cuddle and a chew stick, and returned to the sitting room. Weed's rich brown eyes followed her as she entered, his gaze boring into her as Llewelyn tidied papers and tucked them into the blue folder on the coffee table. "May I get you a drink, Professor?" she said, the periphery of her vision picking up Weed continuing to study her.

"I'll have my chai, thank you." Llewelyn poked his thumb in the direction of the dining table. "We'll dine as soon as my man arrives."

Weed shifted in his seat, drew a handkerchief from a pocket and sneezed, the sound dampened by the folded wad of cotton.

"Will you excuse me?" Mae headed for the kitchen and organised a tray with a wine glass, a tumbler of water, a Delft tea cup. She a spooned loose, aromatic spiced chai into a small teapot. Once the electric kettle had boiled, she poured water into the teapot and the doorbell chimed, Felix letting out another muffled bark. She went to welcome the last two guests, only to find the two waiters from earlier had returned with the food. Mae led them to the dining room. The short man wheeled the delivery cart across the polished wood and carpet, and placed covered warming dishes from the cart onto the dining table.

As the pair departed with the delivery trolley, Kitt appeared— with Tanja Goedenacht. "It was quite a disaster," he said, his attention fixed on Tanja Goedenacht, his bottom-lip biting expression mirroring hers. Then the woman smiled at him as if he'd shared something a little embarrassing, something a little intimate.

The plan had been for Kitt to meet Ms Goedenacht at a bar near the hotel before bringing her to dinner, and here they were, together, looking a bit beguiled by one another. "Good evening, sir," Mae said, stepping into a momentary time-machine that reacquainted her with the not-so-distant past.

In unison, the pair looked at her, Ms Goedenacht's arm through the crook of his elbow. "Oh, hello," Kitt said. He gave Mae a casual nod of thanks as she ushered them inside and took the young woman's black coat.

"Leslie!" Llewelyn rose and crossed the room, hand extended. "Dear boy, we were about to start dining without you!"

"Professor Boothroyd, good to see you again." Kitt shook his superior's hand. "Sorry to keep you waiting."

Mae stood aside. Rehearsal was over. The play had begun. Weed stopped watching her and turned his heatless, dead-eyed smile to Ms Goedenacht. Jaysus, the soft-spoken, amethyst bead-wearing man was the Dutch version of Kitt.

"Come in, come in." He gestured, to the others, "Gentlemen, this is Leslie Templar, and...well, I think it's safe to say you're *not* Mr Vlaming."

"Mr Vlaming couldn't make it, Professor, this is Tanja Goedenacht." Kitt said.

Tanja released Kitt's arm, gathered her loose dark hair, dropped its long onyx length over the front of her shoulder, and extended her hand. "*Aangenaam.*"

"Tanja, meet Professor Boothroyd."

Llewelyn, now 'Professor Boothroyd', took Tanja's hand and smiled his charming matinee idol smile. "It's *Caratacus*, dear boy, Caratacus. We're all friends here," he said, warmly, gesturing to the sitting room, leading the way, "

Mae turned to Kitt. "Your coat, sir?" she said before mouthing, '*Caratacus?*'

One brow arched, Kitt slid a finger up her wrist as he handed over his coat. He followed Brigadier Professor Caratacus Boothroyd Llewelyn as he ushered Tanja to a sofa and presented her to his other guests. "Let me introduce Kurt Albert and his friend Hans Weed."

"Hi." Weed rose, gave a small wave, and blew his nose.

"*Goedenavond*, Goedenacht!" Kurt stayed seated and bobbed his head, laughing. "That's not the first time you've heard that joke, is it?" he said, grinning.

Smiling, Tanja sat. "No, it's not."

"Did someone tell a joke?" Llewelyn leaned in. "I love a good joke!"

"It's a bad joke, Caratacus," Weed said, "a play on the surname

Goedenacht, which translates to *good night*, Albert said 'goede-navond, goedenacht,' or 'good evening, goodnight.' Not exactly comedy genius."

Kitt swivelled to look at Mae, waiting behind everyone with unobtrusive patience, hands clasped. "Sorry. I didn't get your name," he said just loud enough to be overheard.

"I'm Valentine. The butler, sir." She stepped forward. "May I offer you and Ms Goedenacht a drink?"

"What's everyone else having?" Tanja glanced about at the others.

"Mr Weed is having water, Mr Arthur a bit of red wine, the Professor, chai, but I can offer you white wine, beer, bourbon, Scotch, vodka, gin, and rum."

"Oh, chai, I'd love the chai, please." Tanja crossed her legs and three men watched her wiggle down the salmon-pink dress that had bunched up her thighs. She adjusted a black necklace, pulling a heart-shaped pendant from her bosom.

"I'll take bourbon, thank you," Kitt said, watching Mae watch Tanja and the men. Absently, his wife rolled the necklace he insisted she wear through her fingers, feeling for the diamond ring he'd given her. It was there, hanging between her reading glasses and the largest gold coin. For nearly two decades, she'd worn Caspar's ring the same way, and she fiddled with the platinum and diamond the same way she had her first husband's wedding ring. Her hair, usually so tidy in a French braid or twist, was tousled, loosened strands drooping in the back, a lock over her forehead, but the style held together the way Mae did. She'd dug in, locked herself into being productive, focusing on work she was accustomed to, but locked-in woman and twisted hair would both unravel. The signs were already there. "I'll have bourbon, Mrs Valentine," he said again.

He jarred her back to the moment by his use of *Mrs*, and Mae half-turned to Kitt, dropping the necklace. "Of course, sir. Ice?"

"Yes, thank you." He smiled, held her gaze for a moment, seeing fear, anger, and...contrary determination. With a nod, she moved off to the kitchen.

Mae picked up where she'd left off, making the chai, pouring Yellow Label Two Roses Bourbon over ice, filling a water goblet and a glass with wine. She took the tray of drinks to the sitting room, and served them. "Dinner is ready when you are, Professor," she said, as she poured Tanja and 'Caratacus Boothroyd' milky tea with a Christmas-like scent.

"Thank you, Mrs Valentine," Llewelyn said and Felix let out another ghostly little *WooOooo*.

"Do you have a dog?" Tanja smiled.

"Indeed, I have." Llewelyn grinned back. "Would you like to meet him?" He glanced at Mae.

"Please." Hans lifted his handkerchief, dabbing his nose. "I'm allergic to dogs," he said.

Mae stayed where she was. Allergic? Right. Felix would remain in her room as the show went on, actors playing their roles. Her role was to remain passive and attentive whilst fading into the background.

"You were saying you'd retired, Caratacus?" Albert asked.

"Yes, I was at Wageningen University. And you, Hans?"

Weed went all method, embracing his role and acting the hell out of it, his accent something middle American. "I'm a jazz musician—banjo and clarinet. No, you haven't heard of me. I'm not a front man, but I am, if I can blow my own horn, well-known in the industry. I play," he said with a rumbly, sniffy laugh, "well with others. I also compose music for television in the Benelux."

"He's done the music for *Ongeluk*, a popular series about stupid criminals." Albert smiled. "The British picked up and called it *Bad Luck* and made very serious, but they kept Hans's score."

"Maybe you've you seen *Bad Luck*, Leslie?" Weed said.

"Lots of it."

"It's quite dark." Llewelyn gave a gleeful smile. "But that's what makes it so enjoyable." He put his hands together. "Righty-o. Shall we eat?"

Wine in hand, Arthur got to his feet and made a beeline to the table, choosing a seat, lifting the lids from covered dishes, steam rising from the beef rendang. The others followed suit. Mae moved to the end of the sideboard where the bar had been set up. Kitt put his drink next to a plate, pulled out a chair for Tanja Goedenacht, and took the place beside her.

This *rijsttafel*—a Dutch-Indonesian fusion cuisine—spread many small dishes, from beef rendang, pork babi kecap, vegetable gado gado, to rice, fruit, and egg rolls across the table. Arthur examined everything on offer, and spooned small portions of whatever was savoury onto bone china. He scooted closer to the table, bumping it, shaking it, knocking a hard-boiled egg from a bowl. The egg rolled across the tablecloth and tumbled to the floor.

"I'm kinda curious. How did you meet Leslie, Tanja?" Weed asked, watching Mae pick up the egg and wipe up bits of yolk from carpet with a tea towel.

"We met this morning, actually, at De Hortus—the Botanic garden in Amsterdam. He was interviewing my boss." She gave Kitt a smile.

"Tanja works for Jan Vlaming, a gentleman Hedison's may not have actually dealt with in what appears may be another case of identity fraud."

Tanja's smile wavered. "Is this a business dinner for you, Leslie?"

"Just a little one," Kitt nodded contritely. "These gentlemen have stories that may interest you, and perhaps alleviate Jan's concerns about implicating himself." He looked at Kurt Arthur. "Would you mind telling Tanja what happened?"

"Fraud," Arthur heaved a small huff and licked a reddish sauce from his thumb. "Seems your boss and the Professor and I all have Hedison's and fraud in common. Hans and I met the Professor and Leslie earlier this year to discuss fraud. Two years ago, I sold a painting at auction with Hedison's, only to have Hedison's tell me it was a forgery and then proceed to sue me to repay them the amount of the original sale, plus ten percent interest, as well as the art examiner fees and legal fees."

Tanja's pretty mouth dropped opened, brows arched, serving spoon frozen between the bowl and her plate. Yellow rice fell from the spoon and landed opposite the red hard-boiled egg stains on the tablecloth. "Hedison's is suing you?"

"Hedison's *was* suing Mr Arthur." Kitt said, laying a skewer of satay chicken onto his plate. "Please go on, Mr Arthur."

Forkful of food at his mouth, the AIVD director exhaled, laid his bite aside, and showed his chops as an actor. "Maybe you read about it, or saw news reports on television. The painting, a Judith Leyster, had been in my family for generations, hanging on the dining room wall at my family home. My family home is very old and very expensive to keep. Like many estates in the UK, we run a bed and breakfast and only open it to the public at fixed times during the year, or sometimes by appointment, to help with the costs. Prior to my attempt to sell the painting, we were preparing to undertake extensive restorations to the house and move many things, the painting included, to storage at the Freeport in Luxembourg, but we were able to keep portions of the house open as we made out preparations. During that time, I had a small group come to stay. Among them was an American woman, very pretty. She worked for an auction house in Texas. We chatted. I showed her the painting. We talked about the safety of freeports over the usual climate controlled secure storage facilities. I am fortunate that Hans reads the news often. A few months ago, he came across a story about counterfeit wine, antiquities smuggling, and theft of stealing from freeports by a ring of criminals headed by a woman with a master key fob. I had my solicitor contact Hedison's."

"*Potverdorie*, my boss had jewellery stolen from a facility in Luxembourg," Tanja sipped chai to wash down a bite of gado gado. "*This* is why you wanted me to join you for dinner, Leslie."

"I refuse to answer on the grounds that it may incriminate me." Kitt looked at her and wiped away the tiny sheen of sweat that had sprung up on his top lip. The bebek goring—fried duck with hot and spicy chili paste—packed quite a punch.

Weed must have found the food a bit hot as well. He coughed, had a long gulp of water, and dabbed his upper lip. "You were blinded by a pretty woman, Kurt. Bet your boss was too, Tanja." He had another sip of water and passed the bebek goring to Llewelyn.

"She was a beautiful redhead," Arthur said over the *ting-ting* of Llewelyn tapping a spoon of fried duck onto his plate.

"You do love redheads, Kurt." Weed shook his head and had a rather savage bite of a chicken satay skewer, his eyes sliding to Mae.

Mae filled a water glass on Weed's right and moved along to Albert, making her way around the table.

Tanja gave a wry little smile. "I supposed you could say the woman I remember had hair that was ginger-blonde, but I admit I was paying more attention to the man she was with. He was really good-looking."

"You met the woman we mean?" Weed dabbed his mouth.

The brunette nodded. "I think we did."

"Oh, my, that bebek goring is hot!" The 'Professor' downed his tea and sucked in cooling air. "I met a woman at the Aalsmeer Flower auction, a Texan," Llewelyn said, fully embracing the kindly professor persona. "I do think, as Leslie suggested when he contacted me, we may have been victims of the same woman."

Tanja hesitated slightly when she reached for her tea. "What did you have stolen, Caratacus?" she said, tilting her head in interest.

Mae paused beside Kitt, to his right, bottle of expensive water in hand. He looked up at her, meeting her eyes as she filled his glass. She pressed her lips together when he took the glass from her, his fingertips brushing over hers.

"Saffron crocus corms," Professor Caratacus Boothroyd said, "rather a lot of them."

Arthur gave a quizzical look. "Corms?"

"The bulbs. Saffron is the most expensive spice in the world, next to vanilla," Kitt said, and crunched a prawn cracker.

"Yes," Llewelyn said. "It takes eighty-thousand flowers to harvest a mere five-hundred grams of saffron, hence the exorbitant cost, and I had a few hundred-thousand euros worth of saffron crocus corms ready for sale go missing, taken right out of the climate-controlled storage unit."

Tanja set down her chai.

"What are you a professor of, Professor?" Weed asked. "Spices?"

"Botany—Plant Sciences it's called now. The corms were in temporary storage at the Luxembourg Freeport while I made upgrades to my private..."

Discreetly, Mae went about her duties, refilling wine, water glasses and tea cups, wiping up spilled rice, making more chai, listening to plausible bullshit stories with no one taking mind of her as she moved about. She bit her molars together, the way Kitt sometimes did. Rather than listen to eejit 'Caratacus Boothroyd' spin a bullshit tale of saffron crocus theft at the hands of Ruby Bleuville, Mae proceeded to clear away dirty dishes, knowing that maintaining cover was all about acting, method acting. Intelligence field officers were nothing but method actors, just like conmen and conwomen playing a game. Kitt had told her his work was a game, and it was, a game full of actors, with no glitzy award ceremony beyond surviving to play another day. She knew he listened to it all, intently, seriously, flashing the occasional smile at Tanja, and he was just as embedded in being Leslie Templar as Hans Weed was in being a jazz musician, Arthur the CEO of a human resource consulting firm, and Llewelyn a benign professor of botany.

When Tanja began to tell the story about her boss, Mae paid attention. "We met this woman and her boyfriend," the woman began. Her account included Vlaming, his Aunt Polly Dankwaerts, Giacomo Negroni—like the cocktail—and his sickly-sweet cologne, the Asian man, the man from Guatemala, as well as Ruby Bleuville, the strawberry-haired 'Arts and Collectible Specialist' from Texas. It was tripe, the same utter crap Jan Vlaming had already provided, practically word for word. Mae listened, and the woman, like the story, had been rehearsed. Pretty Ruby Bleuville may have been involved, but a now-dead woman was being scapegoated. The subterfuge by all parties put them no bloody closer to uncovering anything of actual substance—except for the fact that the room was full of BAFTA and Oscar contenders that would never be.

Tanja sighed unhappily. "Like you, Kurt, my boss's family opens its estate gardens to the public. Tomorrow, in fact, is the family's well-known garden party. This woman, Ruby, I invited her to Jan's Aunt Polly's garden gala." Best performance by a lead female actor nominee Tanja Goedenacht wore a troubled expression that made her very blue eyes doll-like. "I am responsible for Jan and his aunt losing family treasures that survived wars and Nazi occupation. I should have said something when we met her, but I didn't. Jan liked her and her boyfriend, but I didn't. There was something about them both, him in particular. Yes, she was beautiful. The boyfriend, Negroni, was very good-looking too, polished, but unpolished, like he was uncomfortable in his own skin and he tried to cover it up with expensive clothes. Did any of you meet him?" Hand shaking, Tanja reached for her teacup and gestured to Mae, holding the empty Delft cup aloft as she looked at the men at the table.

Oh, she was good.

"Vlaming said he hoped to see Negroni tomorrow, at his aunt's garden party," Kitt said. "Do you think you could arrange an invitation for all of us to the afternoon's event?"

Tanja turned to Kitt, her head tipped to one side, her cheeks pink, her mouth a lush, rosy bloom. "That's a very good idea. May I be frank, Leslie?" She put her hand on top of his, the relaxed, natural curl of his fingers hiding the fact that two were shortened.

"By all means."

"Jan is a mess. Such a mess. I don't know how he held it together with you this morning. He's...I'm not sure this is the right expression, *a bundle of nerves*. I gave him half a Xanax this morning, just to meet you. To be honest, I'm not much better. I took half a Xanax this morning too. I feel responsible. So much money. He's lost so much money." Her mouth and brows twisted with frustration, her China-doll face suddenly crumpling.

"You're a very considerate employee," Kitt said, turning his hand to squeeze hers ever so lightly.

Tanja laughed and scooped lustrous black hair over one shoulder. "Thank you for saying that," she said, and Kitt smiled at her, giving her hand a reassuring little squeeze.

Mae filled the young woman's cup with the last of the Christmas-scented milky tea and turned away. Janey Mack, Kitt was the business. It was a form of manipulation she knew, something spies were trained to do. There was probably a handbook for intelligence agents with a title like *Neurolinguistic Programming for Espionage, Deception Detection, and Sales*, covering things such as body language, pupil dilation, vocal inflection. Seeing her husband with a woman, one half his age, smiling at her, was so familiar and so normal, and she looked at them with a detachment that was unexpectedly familiar and normal, which wasn't normal.

She poured fresh chai into Llewelyn's cup and wondered how likely was it that Tanja Goedenacht was married or engaged or in some kind of relationship.

She'd never paid much attention to Kitt's technique in the past, but there was something fascinating and decidedly psychopathic in the way he charmed, persuaded, or manipulated women into joining him for a drink, into joining him for the evening, into sharing his bed for the night.

When the story-telling dinner concluded, Mae served coffee, more Christmas-like scented chai to Llewelyn and Tanja, and offered *speculaas* biscuits around. The outside rain, a soft mist, hit the glass of the sliding balcony doors, distorting the pink, white, and red lights from the sex district on the other side of the canal, five floors below.

"Wow," Weed, said, peering at his digital watch, "It's already nine o'clock." He rose. "We'd better say goodnight, Arthur. We've got an hour's drive back to Leiden."

Kurt Arthur balled up his napkin and tossed it on the table. "I'd like to say it's been a pleasure to meet you Tanja, but...I'd prefer it had been over different circumstances. Come to the house the next time you're in town, Caratacus." He got to his feet.

Llewelyn, Kitt, and Tanja followed suit. As butlers do, Mae led the way to the small foyer, the small group shaking hands, exchanging pleasantries. As butlers do, Mae handed out coats, opened the door for them and wished Arthur and Weed a pleasant night.

A few steps behind, Kitt slid his hand in the small of Tanja's back. "Shall we go to the bar downstairs?" he said, smiling, glancing at Mae, her façade of professional efficiency in place. As butlers do, she helped Tanja into her coat and stepped aside to hold the door open for them, looking at nothing in particular. As butlers do not, she failed to give Kitt his coat. "Good evening, Valentine," he said with a nod.

"Good evening, sir." Mae offered a bland smile and ran her hands over her apron, smoothing it as was her habit. He loved watching that simple action, only this time the movement was slower and had a shade of wiping off something disagreeably sticky. Or perhaps that's how he felt, disagreeably sticky giving his attention to a woman he cared nothing about.

How odd it was, how easy it was to fall into a past behaviour of being attentive to a woman he cared nothing about, right in front of his butler, while his butler went on as reserved and professional as she had always been, as if these last few months hadn't happened. Yet the last few months had happened. His butler was his wife, and his old, cavalier behaviour was like a sticky trap, the glue sort used to catch vermin.

And he felt very much like a rat.

BUSY, but quiet and elegant, the Palace Grand's bar was an intimate setting with low lights, little tables, and small booths in black, grey, and soft burnished gold. The bar itself was round and lit from below. Kitt signalled the barman and led Tanja Goedenacht to a table, a tiny, half-moon booth near a gas-burning fireplace. They slid into seating near the fire and had a sweeping view of the entire bar—and the gorilla trying be inconspicuous in a booth with hanging glass beads that gave the impression of privacy. Over the edge of gold-trimmed drinks menu, the brawny man with hairy hands and knuckles had watched them enter the bar, watched them settle beside each other.

A waiter appeared. "*Een moment*," Tanja said, turning to Kitt. "Do you like Negroni, Leslie?"

"I'm not a huge fan of gin."

"The Nederlands Negroni doesn't use gin, it uses Bols Genever, distilled grains and a botanical mix. Are you game to try?"

"Why not."

Tanja faced the waiter. "*Twee Nederlands Negroni*," she said and turned back to Kitt.

He relaxed in the booth, casually dropping his arm on the back of the crescent-shaped seat. "Tell me something," he said with a smile, "why would you need a bodyguard?"

A flash of surprise flickered on her face before blossoming into a brow rumple and pretty, perplexed little squint. "A bodyguard? What do you mean?"

Kitt flicked his eyes in the man's direction. "That man over there, the one with the all arm and chest hair sticking out from the front of his collar, the one who looks like a big gorilla. He was in In't Aepjen. I think he's watching you. Or watching us."

"I think you might be right." She chuckled. "He's probably a tourist, staying here like you."

"Maybe he's interested in you the way that kid in the orange tracksuit was. The way Jan Vlaming is. This morning, Vlaming could not stop staring at you any more than the gorilla over there can. What is this sway you have over men?"

"You're very flattering." She leaned over and kissed his cheek.

"I'm serious. I could see you how make Vlaming nervous."

"He was anxious about talking to you. He was pretty bad on the phone with your colleague, the woman, but he's worse with you. To be honest, he thinks that, because you're here instead of her, you know something he doesn't about Ruby Bleuville. He's fucked because he met her."

"You think he slept with her?" he said and his phone vibrated against his chest. Llewelyn signalling to come upstairs to the suite.

Tanja sighed. "Do we have to talk about Jan?"

The waiter returned with their cocktails, setting them on the table.

"Shall we run a tab?" Kitt said, reaching into his jacket, moving from the inside pocket, to feeling the outside ones, then on to his trouser pockets.

Tanja watched him pat himself down. "Something wrong?"

"My wallet. It's in my coat and I left my coat upstairs."

She lifted her handbag. "I invited you. I've got it covered. I'll pay, Leslie."

Kitt laughed and touched the back of her hand. "And I won't stop you. But it's not just my wallet, my phone is in my coat. I better retrieve them before the professor goes to bed. Will you excuse me?" He left her at the table, exited the bar, went to the marble-lined lift bay and pressed the call button.

When the doors parted, he found Mae on the other side. She wore her green coat, umbrella in hand, his coat over her arm, the dog beside her. "What are you doing here? Where's Llewelyn?"

She watched Felix stretch up his dainty legs on Kitt's thigh. "Llewelyn's not well; something he ate hasn't agreed with him. He asked me to bring your coat, inform you that once you are," she paused, "finished with Ms Goedenacht, Mr Weed is out front, waiting in his car, and he'd like a word. Then I'm to return upstairs to make another pot of tea." She handed over his coat.

Kitt took his mobile from inside his jacket, and stuffed it into a pocket of his coat. "You're not his bloody butler," he said irritably.

She shrugged. "I am for now, and you need to get back to pumping Ms Goedenacht for information."

The lift doors began to close. He shoved a hand against it. "There's no need to make it sound sordid."

"Did I make it sound sordid?" She pursed her mouth, picked up Felix, and stepped out of the lift. "Is she in your room yet?"

Her question thumped Kitt in the guts. Cuckoldry had never been an issue for him; his affairs with married women had been a tool, a means to an end, a bit of meaningless fun, nothing he'd considered to be distasteful—and something he'd never stopped to consider from the other side. "No, she's still in the bar," he said. Sinfulness and guilt were notions he'd discarded long ago, but his tongue felt devilishly serpentine in his mouth, the sensation of growing scales crept up his back.

"Oh," she said. "Is Weed watching me?" she said. "Or am I imagining that he is?"

Kitt sloughed off the slither of snakeskin and put his mind on a goddamned job more reptilian and less redeeming. "He's watching you. He watched you all through dinner. And there's someone watching me, but he's not on the same team. He's playing for Vlaming or Tanja."

"Why is Weed watching me?"

"I don't know yet, but I'll ask him. Go on upstairs," he said.

She didn't move, she merely looked at him with an odd look of expectancy, her brows arched.

"What?"

"Please move. I need to take the dog to piddle and *then* head back up to make Llewelyn tea. If you're worried about my being alone, Mr Weed is sitting in his car out front. He'll keep an eye on me."

Kitt crowded her backwards into the lift. He poked the first-floor button and turned to her, his head cocked slightly. Mae gave him a flat look and went on giving him a look devoid of a flutter or wave that imparted expression of any sort, while he felt his jaw clench.

"Are we about to bicker?"

When the doors closed, he said, "Let's get this straight."

"We're about to bicker."

"You are not Roger Llewelyn's butler. This is a role you are playing. There is no need to take the role to heart. You are not actually working for him."

The lift began to move. "Why would you think I wouldn't take the role earnestly, Kitt? You maintain the role you play in any assignment you have." She glanced at the rosy-red lipstick he knew stained his cheek in a lip-print scarlet letter. "Why would I not do the same?"

"I am an intelligence officer. You are not." He reached over to scratch Felix under the chin.

"You're right. You're a spy, I'm a butler, and I take that seriously, regardless of the charade surrounding the situation. You clear your mind by running, eating or being sick. I clear my mind by my work, by being productive."

"*Productive*? That's your sodding answer for everything." The dog licked his fingers.

"And *breathe* is yours. So how is it different?"

He pulled a handkerchief from his pocket and wiped dog slobber from his hand. "I've trained for the work."

"As have I."

The lift stopped, an electronic *bing* sounded, and the doors parted. Neither one of them moved. His stubbornness, her obstinacy kept them suspended in a box that smelled of a spicy deodoriser. The door closed.

"Regardless of our shared, ongoing churlish prickishness, I know, deep down, you like this," Mae said.

"Like what?

"Having me here, working this operation with you."

Stone-faced, unblinking, unmoving, churlishly prickish, Kitt said nothing.

"You mentioned training. Now you train others to do what you have for so long," she said. "Does part of your instruction to your trainees include how to work with a partner? Because you like having a partner you can bounce ideas off, you like me giving you feedback. You like that I come up with a theory you never considered. In fact, you like that I can think laterally, outside the box, something I know is important you foster in your trainees. Most of all, you like that I can improvise as well as you."

Kitt poked the ground floor button, turned slightly sideways, maintaining his dispassion. She gave him the look that told him exactly how full of shite she thought he and his dispassion were. He loved that look, loved how it held him accountable, loved that she didn't let him get away with anything, but his lack of expression didn't waver.

"Be as pokerfaced as you want." Mae gave a little snort. "I'm not quite the nuisance you say I am."

The dog-slobbered handkerchief made it halfway back into his trouser pocket. "Has this just turned into a contest or is there something you are trying to prove?" He shoved the square of pale blue cotton into his trousers.

"I have nothing to prove. I am trying," she said putting Felix on his feet, "to keep myself—and you—safe while I look after my dog."

"Our dog."

The doors parted and she moved toward the marbled hallway, half inside the lift, Felix outside. "Yes. Our dog. Now, if you'll excuse me. Our dog needs to pee, my employer needs a cup of tea, and Ms Goedenacht is waiting for you. So do get on with being charming to the woman." Mae stepped out of the lift.

She crossed through the lobby, peeking over her shoulder to the bar where she knew Ms Goedenacht sat waiting for Kitt to return. Outside, the wet weather had turned cold. Felix was reluctant to stay outdoors for longer than necessary. She felt the same way, especially when Weed got out of an orange hatchback, leaned against the side of the car, and watched her intently, his arms crossed.

Once she and the dog were back in the suite, she dried his wet paws, tucked him in a makeshift little bed, left him in her room, and went to make Llewelyn's tea.

The scent of the chai was pleasant; cinnamon, cardamom, peppercorn, ginger all mingling together with warm milk. She set the blue and white Delft cup beside the manila folder, small stack of papers, and blue folder Llewelyn had left on the coffee table. He'd been shuffling through the papers when she and the dog had returned.

He came out of his bedroom, slippers shuffling across the floor, his pace listless and careful, a glass of water in his hand. His dark face had an ashen cast to it, bags prominent under light brown eyes, beads of sweat gleaming on his dark brow. "I'm sorry," he said, sinking to the sofa cushions. "My behaviour toward you has been, shall we say, boorish, but it's necessary for the little game we are playing, and you are being a good sport about it, very professional." He put his water glass on the side table beside the cordless phone and crystal clock, reached for the blue file, and set it in his lap.

"May I get you anything else?"

He opened the folder and grimaced for a moment, pressing fingers into his stomach, before he looked at her, and sighed heavily. "I wouldn't really put your brother away."

"Pardon?"

He lifted saucer and teacup, taking a sip. "I wouldn't do that to a man who served and survived what he did, no matter the outcome of this. My threat to do so, well, it's merely the way things work in this particular world." He put down the tea things. "I know you think little of me. To be blunt, I am unperturbed by that, yet there's part of me that doesn't like that I used your brother as a pawn. He deserves better. As does Major Kitt."

"I'll say goodnight, then." Mae began to turn.

"Mrs Valentine."

She came about, hands clasped behind her back. "Yes?"

"You know, I think he must be in love with you, probably as much as you are with him, and he doesn't even know it. For that, you'll be the death of him. Or he'll be the death of you." He glanced down at his hands, at the papers beneath them, a short, low chuckle rumbling. "I do hope it's not true, for his sake. I am, whether you believe it or not, fond of him." He smiled handsomely. "I'm fond of you too."

Unperturbed by his provocation, hands behind her back she said, "You're not well, Brigadier."

"You are correct. I feel absolutely foul. Clearly something from the *rijsttafel* has upset my stomach." He set the cup back on the table beside the folder and papers and smiled, despite his abdominal discomfort. "May I be honest, Mrs Valentine?"

"I don't care for what you call honesty, Brigadier."

He kept smiling. "When all this is over, if it turns out to be nothing of any substance, you and the Major should be paired for field duty. My successor will tell you the same thing."

"Your successor?"

"Yes, can you keep a secret?"

She looked at him flatly.

"Yes, what a silly question. Of course you can. Well, then, here it is. I'm going to retire. Then someone we both know will step into the role rather than retire."

"No." Mae shook her head. "No one in your work ever retires."

He chuckled for a moment before his amusement abruptly changed to swallowing. "Thank you for the tea," he said, stacking the papers into the folder, dropping it on the coffee table, and rising. "I don't think it's much help." He hurried to his bathroom, with alacrity.

KITT SET his empty glass on the table, the ice in the tumbler tinkling. They were being playful, flirty, the prospect for more than flirting was there. The flirting and superficiality of the last forty minutes chafed, reminding him of a superficial past, empty of the joy he'd come to know. He'd thought a profession of self-sacrifice for the greater good of mankind held meaning, and, idiotically, he thought he made a difference. Also idiotically was how he still thought work for the Consortium made a difference to humanity, when what made a real difference was, quite sappily, love. Kitt shoved aside the niggling chafe of self-awareness and personal joy and got back to work.

When he'd returned to the table, she'd pulled her necklace from the vee of her neckline. Earlier, the heart-shaped polished jet pendant had fallen half-inside. The sound quality would have been subpar in its previous position. During his short absence, Gorilla boy had probably told her to move the pendant before he returned to pretending to read while sipping red wine.

Kitt looked at Tanja's breasts, at her cleavage, and then averted his eyes when she noticed, pretending to be ashamed for being so blatantly desirous. The conversation Mae had overheard in the greenhouse, and seeing Tanja in the delivery van before what had transpired in the sex shop storeroom was circumstantial. Yet Tanja's nearly precise description of how Vlaming had met Ruby Bleuville and her companion Negroni was suspicious. Her participation in whatever this was appeared obvious, but all possibilities needed to be covered. One was, or both of them were, being extorted. One was, or both of them were, being manipulated by a puppet master.

One was, or both of them were, innocent—or involved right up their heart-shaped pendant recording device. "All right," he said. "I'll come clean. What you said about Vlaming, Tanja, he has good cause to be wary of me."

"He does?"

"None of this makes good sense. The red-headed woman, the theft from freeports. It was all in the news, across the world. It's too convenient and easy to make up. I don't want you to be hurt in this. Are you fond of Vlaming?"

"Jan's been good to me."

"I think Jan is hiding something and you might be too."

Her hand splayed on her chest, just below her throat. "Why would I have anything to hide?"

"You're fond of him. You feel guilty about inviting Ruby and her boyfriend to the Dankwaerts' last garden party." The way the next ten minutes or so unfolded meant he had to dangle enough rope for Tanja to save herself or hang herself. "I have to ask. Are you trying to protect him? Is your boss is being blackmailed?"

"Why would you think that?"

"It's just how my mind works."

"And you're working right now?"

"Haven't you noticed? I'm working all the time. Vlaming couldn't make it. I blindsided you a little, but I thought it would be advantageous for one of you to meet Albert and the Professor, and since you said you're familiar with the..." he winked, "...family jewels, I thought comparing stories might offer some kind of clue that's been overlooked. My coming to Amsterdam was a bit last minute. I'm working from my colleague's notes, which aren't as detailed as mine would be—different note-taking styles. I can't ask her for clarification as, quite sadly, she died rather suddenly." Kitt shook his head the way one did when discussing an unexpected death. "Poor woman."

Tanja echoed his sorrowful gesture and sighed. "I think Jan said she was hit by a car."

Kitt gave her a tiny, melancholy smile to shroud a flare of anger. No, Jan did not say Jill Charteris had been hit by a car, as Jan had no way of knowing how the woman had died since the names of the dead had not yet been disclosed to the public. The rope was forming a loop. "Yes," Kitt kept the sad smile in place, "she was struck by a car. Left behind a husband and a small son."

A hand went to her mouth for a moment and she shook her head again. "Oh. Were you close?"

"I was just getting to know her. As a result, I'm rushing things a little, being impatient when I should take my time and not get carried away with you. I'm afraid I'm being rather careless and unprofessional."

"And a little drunk too." she waved a finger at the five empty rocks glasses on the table, orange slices tinted a little brown by the Dutch Negroni that had once filled the tumbler. She'd had two and he was finishing his third.

"Yes, a little drunk too."

"Would you like to get out of here?"

And there it was, the suggestion that needed to be made. Kitt was very happy that Tanja had been the one to make it. "And go where?" he said.

She ran fingers beneath the edges of his jacket lapel. "You are staying at this hotel, aren't you?"

Kitt gave a sniffy little chuckle. "You want me to add *inappropriate* to the list with careless and unprofessional?"

Tanja laughed. "Yes. And let's not forget *unethical*. Oh, those Negroni were strong. They've made you silly and me lightheaded. Very lightheaded. This little room is almost spinning. I think I even feel a little queasy."

He let a smile tilt up the corners of his mouth. "Let me get the bill."

"I told you I'd take care of it, and I already have." She got to her feet and pulled him to his.

The black pendant on her neck swung as she reached for her handbag. He gathered their coats. Her arm through his, they crossed the bar in ten seconds, the hairy-armed gorilla in a short-sleeved polo shirt watching them, peeking around the edge of the bead curtain. They rode the lift to the fourth floor in silence, eyes locking now and again. Then he swiped the master passkey Bryce had given him earlier in the day and they were in a room that wasn't his, the light low.

He tossed the coats onto a chair. She slid her arm from his elbow, wandered ahead and gazed about, laying her handbag on the bedside table and having a seat on the bed. "Nice room," she said.

"It'll do for what I have in mind." Kitt pocketed the passkey, switched on the electric 'Do Not Disturb' sign, and stood in front of the door.

"What do you have in mind?"

He sighed softly. "Work. How long have you been sleeping with Vlaming?"

Tanja burst out laughing. "You're one of those people who lose their filter when they're drunk, aren't you?"

"Possibly."

Laughing, she crossed the room, moving toward him, sweeping hair over a shoulder, smiling seductively. "Why would you ask if I'm sleeping with Jan?"

"I'm trying to maintain some professionalism so you don't feel I'm using you to get what I want."

"I'd say I'm using you, but we're both adults. We know what we want." She crept closer. "You do make me feel lightheaded."

"You make me feel guilty for being here with you."

"That's why I plied you with alcohol."

"Yes, three Negroni, like the name of the man you and Jan said was with Ruby Bleuville. That was cute." Kitt leaned his back against the door and heaved a little sigh. It was time to end the cuteness. "Take off your clothes."

"Not yet." She played with her hair.

"I'll get back to work then with the tired clichés about naughty secretaries and their naughty bosses." Kitt sighed again. "Was it just the once, or did you sleep with Vlaming several times to get what you wanted? What did you want, anyway, his jewellery?"

"You're having fun, aren't you?"

Kitt shrugged, smirking.

"Jan's married."

"Married people have affairs. Bosses have affairs with their assistants all the time. The hanky-panky usually ends with both parties feeling guilty or one of them engaged in blackmail."

"Jan's middle-aged."

"So am I."

She looked him up and down and bit her bottom lip, coming closer. "Yes, but you're good middle-aged, 'silver fox' middle-aged, like George Clooney. Jan's just...middle-aged."

"Did you steal the Dankwaerts jewels or are you working for someone who did? Perhaps you're working for the gorilla downstairs?"

Tanja closed the space between them to stand a hand's length away. "You're all work and no play, Leslie, and I want to play."

"I can see that." He touched the heart-shaped pendant with a finger, lifting the thumb-sized ornament that doubled as a simple voice-activated recording device.

Tanja grasped the lapels of his jacket and pulled him near,

breasts mashing into his chest, and pressed her cheek to his, arms going around him. "I don't care if you're middle-aged."

"I need to be honest, Tanja," he said, mouth near her ear.

"There's no reason to feel guilty. We haven't done anything. Yet."

"We're just getting started," he said, then whispered three little words that weren't 'I love you' or 'I am married', and prepared for the result.

She went stiff for a moment. Her arms fell away and she stepped back, pushing him, her large, blinking blue eyes grew very round, her nose wrinkled and her mouth twisted from disgust to confusion, and then horror as she was suddenly, and rather voluminously, sick, the abrupt mess of it spattering her shoes. Shock returned for a very brief moment. She looked down at the mess, up at him, and clapped a hand over her mouth as she heaved.

"That's not quite the reaction I expected," Kitt said. He grabbed her by the elbow the way one does a ten-year-old who's been caught shoplifting, and hauled her into the bathroom. The lid of the toilet banged against the tank when he lifted it and she sank to her knees in front of white bowl, the black heart pendant knocking into porcelain. She was sick again, retching hard.

"Why don't you give me that necklace. Get it out of the way."

With a nod, a swallow, and a little groan, she removed the chain and traded it for the damp face washer he held out.

Kitt dropped the jewellery with its bauble to the tiled floor and brought his foot down hard, crushing the pendant beneath the heel of his shoe. "There. Now that's done, you can take off the rest of your clothes and we'll get on with it."

Tanja gripped the edge of the toilet bowl, glared up at him and swore in Dutch. "*Mierenneuker!* You're kidding, right?"

"Goodness, no! I never joke when I'm working. And I am working, Tanja. I want you to take off your clothes. Then we can have a real chat without you recording me the way I'm thinking you probably recorded Jan Vlaming. This is how professional extortion works, Tanja. A word of advice; if you're going to blackmail someone, you need to invest in a better device than that cheap little trinket you had." He glanced down at the tiles and bits of black plastic heart meant to look like cut and polished jet.

Wide-eyed, pale-faced, Tanja swallowed convulsively and stared at him.

"The gorilla, the hairy man downstairs, what's his name?"

Tanja shuddered.

For a moment, Kitt wasn't sure if it was because she was about to be ill again or if she finally understood. He lowered his head and smiled, looking up through his lashes. "The gorilla downstairs, Tanja."

"Don't hit me." Tanja gripped the edge of the toilet. "Please. Don't hit me."

"Hit you? There's no need for brutality, Tanja. We can be civilised about this. Shall I help you take off your clothes before you soil them?" he said.

A minute and a half later, she was naked, they began having a conversation, and she was sick several more times. The process lacked all sense of decorum and privacy, the sort most people desired. It was cruel to not allow her a simple dignity, but he didn't care. He gathered information until it became evident that she needed a chance to catch her breath. He handed her a face washer and let her clean herself in the tub.

"Looks like you're in this for the long-haul, Tanja. You need fluids. I'll get you some ice chips and an electrolyte drink," he said. Then he collected her garments, the used and dry bath towels, as well as two dressing gowns hanging on the back of the door, and left her to protest, vomit, and shit again, as he shut the bathroom door.

He tossed the linens on the bed. He found her mobile and read her emails and texts. The most recent messages to someone named Bianco, were in Italian—and Sicilian. Bianco, the Italian word for *white,* or as Kitt preferred to think, the thickset gorilla downstairs. Tanja had sent Bianco a photo of him. He'd missed her taking it. How very sloppy of him.

He read through the message trail: *This was easier than I thought... The men at dinner had met Ruby... This should have started with Vlaming, not the Hedison's woman... I'll bring him to the country greenhouse and meet you there... I'll see Vlaming later.* There was something about Negroni and someone named Picciridda. He missed a bit, some of it in the Sicilian dialect, but Tanja's comments were far more detailed than Bianco's *OK,* or *Aggiornare,* the request for an update. She had responded to that with *Saró unpo di tempo*— she'd be a while—and the final text stated that she'd let him know when she was about to come downstairs.

Kitt put the phone in his pocket, found her coat and handbag, and added them to the mix on the bed. Then he looked for a fork and a spoon amid the crockery above the minibar. He bent the tines of the fork, returned to the bathroom door, opened it slightly, and jammed the fork just below the latch in the frame so that the straight tines poked out when he shut the door. He slid the spoon's handle between the tines. It was a crude, but quite effective lock. There were little chocolate mints beside the bed. He ate one, letting the dark cocoa and peppermint melt over his tongue as he stripped the bed, bunched the towels and clothes into the mix, and stuffed it all into two pillow slips. He didn't have to worry about taking any curtains or drapes. The balcony door and window had roll-down shades. If Tanja managed to get out of the bathroom and out of the room, she'd do so in the nude.

"I'll be back soon, Tanja," he called out. Then he exited the room with the linens and rode the lift up three levels. He walked to

SANDRA ANTONELLI

the end of the hallway. This level of the hotel was limited to suites. Llewelyn's was the only suite occupied. Kitt dropped both pillow-cases, took the master swipe-card passkey from his pocket and went into the suite next door, dragging the hotel linens and clothes into the room.

CHAPTER FOURTEEN

Mae slipped the dressing gown on and walked into the bedroom, over wooden floorboards and a sandy-hued rug that felt like silk beneath the soles of her bathwater-pruned feet. Felix lay in in a ginger curl on the cushioned blue chair beside the desk, his narrow snout upon a beige throw pillow. He lifted his head, looked at her, and yawned before burrowing his nose head beneath the pillow.

Mae pulled the towel from her hair, dropped it on the bedside table, and climbed into bed. She wished she could sleep or relax as easily as Felix, but she was no more relaxed than before having a warm bath. Sleep was not going to come. Her mind would not stop churning and whirling and thinking about sex shops, broken bodies, stinging tropical plants.

Irritated, she got out of bed, put on the dressing gown, had a seat at the desk, pulled her tablet from her handbag. She began typing another journal entry, her fingers flying over the little screen as she recounted events, her reaction to them, her thoughts about them, setting out the who, what, and where in vivid etched-into-her-psyche detail that she would never forget because she had an excellent memory, an eye for every tiny detail.

The journal had become more of a book, an adventure story of sorts, an implausible spy story with a dose of mystery and an unlikely romance between two middle-aged leads. It had become easier to write as a narrative, to step away from the reality that she had lived these experiences and think of them as something unreal enough to be fiction. She wrote and wrote, turning those memories into words, into an intense, sometimes lurid, bloody and violent tale that gave her a chill, the sort that made her shudder slightly and prickled her skin. The room grew cooler, a draft wafting over her bare feet and up her spine.

"The dog has the right idea," Kitt said.

Mae turned with a small start. A breeze billowed rain and sheer curtain around him as he stepped inside, shut the skinny glass door, and shook off rainwater. "You think I'd be used to you suddenly showing up when you're supposed to be someplace else —or dead. Good thing for you I'm not a screamer," she said, closing the journal entry she'd send later, shutting the tablet's cover.

"You're not glad to see me?" Raindrops sparkled on his cheeks. He took off his rain-speckled jacket, water droplets making the dark blue even darker, giving it a shake before he dropped it in a chair near the window.

Mae moved to the bed and sat on the edge. Her hair, still in its French braid, had loosened even more, damp, dark blonde tendrils touched her shoulders. She tossed him the towel on the bedside table.

Kitt patted his face and moved to stand in front of her, beside the Dutch Colonial-inspired bedside table, sooty marks on the towel.

"Your shirt is dirty,' she said.

He looked at the grime on his sleeves and the dog hopped from a chair and wandered over to stretch up and plant two paws onto his thigh. Kitt gave the dog a scratch.

"How did you get in here, climb across the balcony next door?"

"Yes. You're not happy to see me?"

She scooted to the very edge of the mattress, setting herself closer to him, her feet on the floor. Then she leaned forward and rested her forehead against his abdomen. "Jaysus, you climbed over the balcony."

Absently, Kitt smoothed her messy, slightly damp braid. "It was the best way to bypass Llewelyn's room."

"We're five storeys up. You could have fallen."

"Yes," he cast a glance over his shoulder, "right into the canal below."

"As if that makes a difference from this height," she said and made a noise, a nasal huff of irritation.

"You sound like my mother."

"No, I sound like your wife." Softly, Kitt stroked her hair and looked about her room, His accommodation for the night was the sitting room sofa in Llewelyn's suite. There were two queen beds in Mae's room. The bed on the right lay untouched, the white coverlet smooth, pillows artfully arranged. The bed she sat upon had its linen folded back on one side, extra pillows and decorative throw cushions from the chair in the room's corner lined up like a barricade, separating the bed into two tidy sections, leaving the bedclothes on the right side of the pillow fortification pristine, unrumpled.

Dividing the bed was a curious custom Mae had developed when she slept alone in a large bed. For sixteen years she'd slept in a single bed, a habit that stretched back to when she'd lost her first husband. After Caspar had died in a multi-vehicle smash one foggy morning on the Autostrada outside Padua, Mae found sleeping alone in a double, queen, or king-sized bed a painful reminder of her loss. Kitt remembered the day that had changed. Last summer, when homicidal bankers and the Mafia had tried to kill her, they'd begun to share a bed; then, just before Christmas, she'd fallen back into her single bed habit because his remains had been found in a shipping container in Singapore. He'd been pronounced dead, and she faced another painful reminder of love lost.

Love lost. Kitt had come to understand her reasoning about the bed. Love lost, love found, love...it was a strange thing to find flattering, but there was something gratifying, something immensely ego-stroking to know she hated sleeping without him—as much as he hated sleeping without her. Love. It was love, love alive, love present, love simple and necessary and entire. "I see you've made yourself a peapod to sleep in," he chuckled.

"Yes," she said, not at all amused. "I'm ready to climb into my peapod, except you climbed over the balcony. What do you want?"

He smiled softly, remorsefully. "I want to apologise about the girl."

Maw sniffed and shrugged. "You did ask for permission."

"I thought I'd be done by now, but the girl is sick, like Llewelyn. I suspect food poisoning. We all ate the same food, but the level of bacteria ingested varies person by person. I don't feel queasy at all."

"You look like you feel queasy."

"Only because I climbed across a dirty balcony five storeys above a canal for you."

"I'd better notify the hotel manager food from the restaurant has made two people ill," she said, still unamused, but made no effort to reach for the phone beside the bed. "How old is Ms Goedenacht anyway, twenty-two, twenty-three?"

"Ah, there it is. You're angry, and it's justified. You know it means nothing, Mae, it was nothing, it's the ac—"

Mae waved a dismissive hand. "Oh, it's all right."

"All right?"

She shrugged. "I know you're working. It's part of your job. It's all for queen and country. It's whatever means necessary to gain a source's trust and spies sleep with an *asset* to gather information an—"

"I keep telling you, you read too many spy novels."

Her sudden, high-pitched and breathy laugh was full of resignation. "I knew what I was getting into. It's all right." She mashed her face into his stomach, shuddering with a sudden, noisy sob.

He stared down at her, aghast. Love was never what he expected. *She* was never what he expected, which made him love her all the more, and he did love her, wildly, wholly, the way sappy songs and poetry and every worn-out cliché known to humankind exalted. His feelings for her were uproarious and profound, and his heart, the thing he'd once thought had been solidified into something diamond hard, damned him. Could she really believe that he'd go to bed with Tanja? Yes, yes, she could, and did, believe. Christ.

Kitt exhaled harshly. "All right? It's not *all right*. I know your previous husband was a polygamist and that might colour your thinking, and my history combined with that, well, my history is just that, history, not current practice."

"Current...p-practice?" She gasped for air, juddering, her shoulders shaking.

He watched her shake and gasp. Wrong. This was wrong. All so Goddamned wrong in a multitude of ways, everything about this moment was off, and the fault was entirely his. He had misread her, had neglected to see what was really happening. Kitt swore under his breath. He'd become wrapped up in emotion. He'd been wrapped up in concern. He'd been thinking like a husband, which was a good, yet thoroughly horrifying thing because it made him overlook possibilities, miss cues, misread body language, and it made him look foolish, but foolishness was the only part of missing the small clues embedded in her body language that he didn't mind. He was appropriately, and simultaneously, impressed and mortified with himself, but he was doubly impressed and mortified by her and how she'd fooled him. The bloody woman was playing him and doing a remarkable job. Mae wasn't clutching at him and blubbing. She was laughing at him.

He swore again, loudly this time, a long, drawn-out, harsh-sounding word hissing though his teeth that drew the dog's attention. Felix hopped off the chair and came to sniff at his legs, jump up on the bed, and mess up all her carefully laid pillows, and then Kitt laughed.

Mae's head came away and she wiped tears of mirth from her eyes. "It's farcical," she sniffled and giggled, "pathetic, to watch a man flirt with a woman more than half his age."

He stepped back, her arms sliding away. "*Farcical*, is that how you saw me when you worked for me?"

"You were my employer. It was never my place to judge you for your endless string of usually married young women," she chuckled, hands in her lap.

"For which you openly mocked me."

"I mocked you, but I never judged you."

"Because you saw me as farcical."

She touched the tip of her tongue to her top lip and cut her eyes to the ceiling. "Next time, I'll excuse myself so I won't have to watch the farce."

"I didn't sleep with her, and there won't be a next time."

"You mean there will be no next time until Llewelyn finds another way to extort me into working for The Consortium and minding *our* dog?" She glanced at Felix in a tiny pillow fortress.

"This will never happen again. I'll find a way."

"Whether you find a way or not, we both know you, and now I, will never be able to retire or walk away from this work. The positions are ours for life; it's a different, strange sort of secret marriage, a different death us do part."

"Cynic."

"You're the romantic one here."

"Hell or high water I will find a way."

She looked across to the desk for a moment, to where her iPad lay, and back at him. "What if I find a way? What if I have a way? Why is it up to you to find a way?"

"Because I got you into this the day I rented your flat and you showed up at my door with Chelsea buns and then made me scrambled eggs. This will not happen again."

"Ah, memories." She smiled. "So, Tanja's quite an actor, isn't she?"

"Yes, she's very good. But so am I. So are you."

Mae tucked a lock of hair behind an ear. "I've found the key to keeping sane in this is to fake it, pretend everything is normal and just get on with it. Speaking of getting on with it, how did you get out of sleeping with her?"

"I told her I had herpes."

Mae snorted. "And how did that go over"

"She vomited on my shoes."

This time Mae laughed. "And what did you do?"

"We had a little talk. I told her I'd get her some ice chips and an electrolyte drink, then I came here. She thought we were doing a little role playing, but realised otherwise after she got sick and I kept on asking questions. And I left no doubt that I was serious when I locked her in the bathroom."

"Why did you lock her in the bathroom?"

"It was kinder option than tying her to the toilet and threatening to give her a thump."

"I would have given her a thump."

"Yes, I know you would have. I'm far too tender-hearted these days to smack someone about. You, on the other hand, would punch a kitten." Kitt slid his hand into his right pocket, feeling for the wedding band mixed in with the coins. "You were right. Tanja's blackmailing Vlaming. He's been raiding his Aunt Polly's jewellery, having pieces authenticated, then replacing the gems with manufactured stones, and selling the genuine. Mae," he took his hand from his pocket, "Tanja mentioned the name Aurelio Martini."

"*Aurelio Martini?* The dead banker from last summer in Sicily, the man who half drowned you in a tank with a fish named Shirley Bassey?"

"Yes. Apparently, he and Vlaming's Uncle Peter, his Aunt Polly's husband, were old friends, served as board members for the UN Credit Union."

Mae shook her head in disbelief. "Giacomo Negroni and Ruby Bleuville, what does this have to do with them?"

"That's not quite clear yet. Tanja's been communicating with a man downstairs in the bar. His name's Bianco. I think he may have been in the vegetable delivery van we saw in front of Erotica. I read through all the messages they sent each other—all in Italian with, I'm guessing, a little Sicilian tossed in, but it was something about Negroni, and someone named Picciridda. Tanja planned on taking me to the country greenhouse and seeing Vlaming later."

"What does this have to do with the sex shop?

"We didn't get very far into those intricacies."

"Then you need to get back to her then and find out. *Picciridda*, by the way, is Sicilian for *little girl*."

"Yes, I'll get back to Tanja," he said, and didn't move. "Hell or high water, Mae, I will find a way. This will not happen again."

"All right. Find a way." She grabbed the flanks of his shirt, pulled him forward, set her chin into his diaphragm and looked up at him, her eyes positively aglow with warmth. "But first, do what you've come here to do, Hamish. Say goodnight and feck off."

His hand came out of his pocket and Kitt crouched slightly, cupping her face as he kissed her slowly, thoroughly, savouring the feel of her mouth, the taste of her mixed with toothpaste and the same lavender and verbena bath gel she'd tried to use in hospital a day ago. Had that only been yesterday? He drew away. "Good night, my love."

"*Mmm*," she said. "That was heaven."

"You didn't like it?"

"I was trying to be romantic."

"With the dog watching us," he cut his eyes to Felix half-hidden by a nest of pillows, "and Llewelyn on the other side of that door?"

"Yes," she slid her calves about him, locked her ankles around his arse, and lay back on the bed, drawing him forward, his kneecaps hitting the edge of the mattress, "he's right out there in the sitting room—or puking in his bathroom." She unlocked her legs, slipped them down until he stood between her thighs.

"My love," he said gently, "we have no time for this."

Her you-are-so-full-of-shite expression appeared. "All spies have time for this. There's always a scene where the spy hero beds the heroine who sighs, 'Oh, *hero's name*'. It's always after a car chase, a fight on a moving train, or being half-drowned in a tank with a shark or a fish named after singing Dames of the British Empire. The lull in the action calls for it."

"And you think this is a lull in the action?"

"Yes."

"And I'm the hero?"

"A role I know you like enormously."

"You watch too many spy films."

"You're right. I do. Go tend to Tanja Goedenacht. Maybe she'd like more of Llewelyn's tea. The ginger in it may soothe her stomach." Mae drew up her knees, tucking the dressing gown to preserve her modesty.

Kitt spat out a filthy word.

Mae laughed, shaking her head. "Stop looking and start thinking."

"I am thinking." Kitt leaned over her and untied the sash of her dressing gown, flipping the nubby fabric aside, pulling apart the lapels, exposing her nakedness, smiling, pleased with himself, pleased that she wasn't wearing those ghastly big cotton knickers she favoured. "It's like unwrapping a Christmas present when I was a podgy little boy." His hands were filthy from climbing, but he ran roughened fingertips from her lips, down her chin and throat, between her breasts, over her abdomen and navel and watched her shiver.

"Did you receive many naked women as Christmas presents when you were a fat little boy?"

"There was the year Simon gave me a stack of girlie magazines."

"For educational purposes?"

"Of course."

"And what did your sister give you that year?"

"A fat lip. And why are we talking about Kate?"

"Would you rather talk about Charmaine and Miles?"

"The mention of my parents sucks the sexiness right out of this moment."

"My parents had children late in life. I was nineteen when my father died, twenty when my mother died. Sometimes I miss having a mother. My friend Fiorella is the closest thing I have to a mother."

"Mentioning Fiorella also dampens the mood—and she cheats at Monopoly."

"I'm a little envious."

"Of Fiorella's Monopoly cheating skills?"

"No, that you still have your parents, that I want to know about them so I can know you better. You can't blame me for being curious about every facet of you."

"As long as you stay curious about me and my...*facet*."

"That's dreadful," she said, and he looked down at her, at pale-pinkish bare flesh, at the puckered scar a bullet had made in her shoulder, at the slight scar at the left corner of her lip where she'd had stitches after being mugged, at tiny reddish splash-burns made by chemicals exploding from an airbag, at a purplish bruise and blue stitches half-hidden by her hairline, at green-flecked hazel eyes. And at once he was overwhelmed by the bottomless depth of a singular emotion, at a loss for words until she laughed, and then he stood still, so still, looking at her. "Christ, I love you," he said.

"Yes, isn't it glorious?" She sat up, scooted to the edge of the mattress and pulled the front of his shirt from his trousers, undoing the line of buttons until she'd reached the ones already unbut-toned at the top of the pale blue fabric. She moved on to his belt and the waistband, tugged trousers and boxer briefs down his thighs, leaning forward to kiss his chest, to kiss the burn mark a cattle prod had left at his waist, setting her chin into his breast-bone, looking up at him, dressing gown slipping off one shoulder.

Kitt pushed her back, slowly, resting atop her, his weight on his forearms, his dirty hands framing her face, his trousers and boxers bunched around the shoes he tried to toe off. He kissed her again, opening his mouth to her tongue.

Mint. He tasted like mint, the chocolate kind the hotel placed on the bedside table. Mae chuckled into his mouth because he'd taken the time to freshen his breath before he'd climbed across a balcony five storeys up to come to her. She slid her hands under his open shirt and up his back, her fingers tracing over the lumpy scar he'd had since his early twenties, when a woman he thought he'd loved had stabbed him. Kitt began to kiss her throat and neck until he reached that little spot that made her breath catch and prickles rose on her skin. Her hands went to his head. "Your hair's damp," she said.

"So's yours." He moved down to kiss a nipple and bite it, softly. He worked his way down her torso, kissing and nipping, scooting back until he was on his knees between her thighs. He kissed the freckly Southern Cross constellation and moved inward, kissing and sucking and tasting, shoving dirty, rough, scraped hands under her arse, lifting her closer her to his mouth, and she made a sharp, hissing noise that sounded like *Jaysus, Hamish*, and he lifted his head, a finger to his lips. "*Shh!* Llewelyn might hear you."

Mae sat up, shook free from the dressing gown, and grabbed him by his ears. Kitt rose, quickly, and stretched out, half atop her, between her thighs, kicking off shoes, trousers, boxers and one sock as she shifted to her side, dropped a leg over his thigh and pressed into his erection. He had one grimy, rough hand on her arse and she scooted closer, closer, until he was inside her. "*Jaysus Mae*," he said, the sound of it deep, low, and slightly sibilant.

He moved slowly at first, rocking up and back, creating a gentle rhythm, watching her fall into the tempo, her eyes on his, pleasure and pressure building. Then she ground into him, both hands pulling his hips and he began thrusting deep, deep, deeper, her breathing quickening, their rhythm quickening as he grunted, and the dog, in his mounded, slightly squashed citadel of pillows, watched, judging him. "Get off," he said.

"I'm trying," she half-laughed.

"Not you, Felix," he said rather breathlessly, the dog jumping off the bed, then Mae twisted and shoved him to the mattress, driving him higher into her. Hands on his chest, fingertips in his hair, she swayed and rose and fell, rose and fell, his goddamned mobile *buzz-buzz-buzzing* in his jacket on the chair. She met his eyes and her head dropped back and she rose, fell, rose fell, her breath catching. He touched her throat, slid his scratchy hands to her breasts and she leaned over, found his mouth, her damp hair tickling his cheek.

Tongues twisting together, Kitt sat up, kissing her, biting her neck, panting, grunting, moaning while she rocked, delight intensifying, and he turned their bodies, her back to the mattress, her knees bent, She wrapped one calf over his back and he slowed, plunging deep and hard, driving the breath from her with every thrust, until she gripped his arse and the tempo shifted faster. Breasts to chest, gasping and grinding against him, she inhaled sharply, shuddering, head falling back, and ripples of carnal pleasure spread up his spine, exploded, and he cried out.

"*Shhh,*" she hissed breathlessly, "Llewelyn might hear you."

Kitt sagged on top of her, crushing her, his heart pounding, his mind awash with delight and astonishing, profound emotion that always arose whether they were making love or outright hedonistically fucking. There, exactly as they were, sweaty, messy, tangled and joined together, he could die a happy man.

"Hamish," Mae wheezed.

"I like when you call me Hamish," he said and shifted his weight sideways, gathering her close, kissing her ear. She reached about for the dressing gown and pulled it over them, covering the chill she felt, his heart still pounding in his chest, in his ears. She trailed fingers through the hair on his chest. They lay holding one another, catching their breath, his nose in her still-damp hair, his mobile *buzz-buzz-buzzing.*

CHAPTER FIFTEEN

Rather than climb back over the balcony and cross through the empty suite next door, Kitt gave up stealth and exited Mae's room via the door. He immediately regretted his choice.

"I didn't hear you come in." Llewelyn said from the sitting room. "What were you doing in there, taking my advice?" Chuckling like a dirty old man, he set a teacup on the coffee table beside a blue file folder.

"I got your message." Kitt crossed the room and sat in a cushioned chair opposite Llewelyn, the coffee table between them. "Valentine said you were ill. You look terrible."

"I feel terrible. Did you get what you needed from Tanja Goedenacht?"

"We're well on our way. Seems a portion of the Dankwaerts jewellery is imitation. Jan Vlaming has been selling off his aunt's family gemstones over the years, piece by piece, and replacing genuine stones with manufactured ones. He's amassed a small fortune Tanja says is held in Panama. He managed to keep his little endeavour quiet from his Aunt Polly until someone approached

Hedison's and tried to sell the Dankwaerts collection. Tanja said the man who stole the aunt's freeport key was an old family friend."

"Is the friend the elusive Giacomo Negroni?"

"No, she said the friend was Aurelio Martini."

"The dead Sicilian banker from the Mafia money laundering fiasco your butler was involved in last year?"

"Yes."

"Fascinating how the dead keep being responsible for this escapade."

"Yes. I think so too. As for the incident at the sex shop, we didn't get that far. Tanja became unwell," he looked at Llewelyn's dull, greyish cast, "perhaps more so than you. It's going to be a long night. I borrowed a book from Valentine." Kitt turned about the paperback in his hand, showing the cover of *Our Man in Havana*.

"Then you've moved from lover to nursemaid. That works. I have to say I'm glad Ms Goedenacht is feeling it too. I wondered if I was the only one with food poisoning. I'm pleased someone else is sharing the misery." Llewelyn pressed fingers into his stomach, grunting softly. "I'll have Mrs Valentine notify the hotel manager."

"She already has."

"How efficient." Llewelyn had a sip of tea and made a face, wrinkling his nose.

"Yes, she is. Why is Weed watching Valentine, sir?"

"You noticed."

"I did, yes." Weed's dark eyes had followed Mae all evening; it was something meant to be noticed. "Any idea why he wants to speak with me?"

"We'll get to Mr Weed in a moment."

"Something is wrong—besides how you feel."

"Several things are wrong, Major. Hilary resigned, and if it's not dire enough that my floor manager decided to leave, Night Duty notified me Morland had a massive stroke on his way home from impromptu farewell drinks for Hilary."

"Good God."

He put the tea aside and reached for the blue folder on the coffee table. "Desmond Wishaw said Morland left the party early complaining of a headache that made his eyes hurt. The man was forty-two. He'd only been with me for three years, and wasn't particularly likable, Kitty, but he was damned good at his job, damned good, and now he's... My Lord, *forty-two*. You're not much older."

"I'm very sorry, sir."

Llewelyn exhaled, the sound sorrowful and settled, the business of Morland concluding and being shoved into the past. "Yes. It's a pity about Hilary. An efficient floor manager is valuable, a loyal chief assistant like Morland even more so, but life does go on. Things move on. I'll find another temporary chief assistant, you perhaps, or your Mrs Valentine. But then, as I said earlier, she's worked for you longer than Morland worked for me; the woman would do, and has done anything for you. Or perhaps that is not really the case." With sigh, he opened the folder and sifted through a few pages. "As for Mr Weed...We had one of these," and held out two sheets, "Arthur sent Mr Weed with the photos this morning. Then, this afternoon, Mr Weed found this one. I wasn't certain I wanted to show it to you considering your...respect and obvious affection for your employee, yet Arthur convinced me I should. Major, a loyal assistant is valuable, but dear boy, do you *really* need a butler?"

Kitt crossed the soft carpeting, took the pages offered, and looked down at a colour photographs of a woman and a man, at copies of two passports. The images were an instant anaesthetic, the kind that killed all sensation, yet left him wholly conscious, his brain wide-awake and utterly cognisant of what the travel documents meant. "If you had this, why did you threaten to institution-alise her brother?" he said, dispassionately.

"She is an asset and a liability."

"And it's best to keep such people where you can see them." He cocked his head.

"Yes." Llewelyn pressed a fist into his sternum and swallowed the way one did when one had a bad taste in one's mouth.

Kitt again looked at the photocopies in his hand.

"You don't seem surprised."

"There was always a chance. Where did you get it?"

"The brother had it. Hired someone who's clearly done a better job than us. Regardless of the concealment, her previous contributions, what she ascertained and experienced in those activities last year and early this year make her ideal to join in this action, and despite your reservations and protests, you under-stand that."

Kitt shook his head ever so slightly. "Everyone is a resource, a means to an end, and use whomever you must to reach that end," he said, hating that he *still* held the same ideology.

"You do know your job well. I'm very glad to see that, Kitty."

Kitty. Llewelyn's odd moment of affection struck the numbness, catapulting it from his chest. Kitt barely refrained from biting his molars together and kept hostility, horror, pain, and disbelief buried. "Thank you, sir," he said as his brain tripped over dismay to land on cold fact. "Then it's what, Direzione Investigativa Antimafia or Agenzia Informazioni e Sicurezza Esterna or the Guarda di Finanzia?"

"Yes, the AISE, but the DIA has a renewed interest since this has come to light." Llewelyn glanced at the photocopy images. "We passed along our information to Croatia's USKOK, Malta's Central Immigration Office in Valetta, and Italy's new Minister of Economy and Finance. Interesting you've uncovered a connection to Aurelio

Martini, especially since the Italians have asked us to sit on our hands for a bit."

"You mean Ministra Seraffimo's asked that *I* sit on my hands."

"Yes. They've asked the Dutch as well. Is that request clear, Major?"

"It is."

"Whether it genuinely comes to anything is another matter. In the meantime, your butler is here where we can see her, she's familiar with the players, so let the game continue."

Let the game continue... Dear God, what had he done? Confessed everything, given in to emotion, succumbed to a disadvantage that exposed far too much, surrendered to a basic human need he never wanted to need because he understood the responsibility, knew the cost. Rankled, Kitt turned, headed for door. "Excuse me, sir. I've kept Weed waiting quite a while," he said, and clenched his back molars together.

"Do you think the secretary will pan out, Kitty?"

"I'll let you know in the morning." Kitt looked over his shoulder at the older man who was cold analysis, calculation, strategy, all traits he'd once admired. He curbed the desire to rush the man, to throttle his superior and toss him through the open balcony door, making sure to miss the canal below, and went with the only option he had: pettiness. "You look peaked, your skin's a bit ashy, bags under your eyes. You know you're not a young man. Perhaps it's best you lay off the spicy food and st—"

"Oh, *do* stop your whining, Major. You can always find another butler. You've done it before. Perhaps you can persuade your Scotsman to come back." Llewelyn dropped the open folder onto the coffee table, sat on the sofa and reached for his cup of tea. "Go on back to Ms Goedenacht. We'll discuss this again in the morning, say...seven sharp. You can join me for breakfast. I hear your butler makes excellent scrambled eggs."

Two minutes later, Kitt was outside. He walked past an orange Renault hatchback parked in a commercial zone, a delivery van with a logo of lettuce, tomatoes, and carrots on its white doors in the space ahead of it. He went to the corner, turned left at the wine shop, and followed the cobbled laneway to the canal beside the hotel, just where the red-light district began. He waited ten seconds, looking at tourists and drunks in football jerseys gaping at the scantily clad window girls, before Hans Weed stopped beside him.

"Last year," Weed said, "British football hooligans smashed a few of the windows you see there. A number of girls were injured, which prompted the mayor to make plans to close down De Wallen and the Singel permanently. She says the injury and humiliation of sex workers by tourists is unacceptable."

"It's a dangerous profession. What do you want, Hans? I need to get back upstairs and finish what I started."

In a long and rambling answer that covered international laws, local customs, and criminal prosecution, Weed outlined what he wanted. "You see the sense in it, don't you? Even if it's only for a short time."

Kitt very nearly shoved the man into the canal. "I think it's best that we discuss what you're suggesting with Llewelyn. Right now," he said, giving Hans a broad, deadly smile.

CHAPTER SIXTEEN

Writing more in her not-quite-a-journal hadn't helped. The sex hadn't helped. The dog beside her and pillows shrinking the width of the bed didn't help either. Mae couldn't sleep. She'd close her eyes and see the face of a woman whose name was Eva Eaton or Jill Charteris. She'd close her eyes and see a man whose bearded face was bloodied and distorted by the plastic wrapped around his head, the way supermarkets that weren't eco-smart wrapped a head of lettuce. She'd close her eyes and see a man with a knife protruding from his neck, another with a knife in his throat and strands of spaghetti stuck to his cheek, and one more man, Russell Grant, a butler like her, lying in the snow, a bloody hole where his nose should have been. She'd close her eyes and see and blood bubbling from the mouth of a Sicilian banker named Martini.

When she didn't close her eyes, her mind led her on a convoluted path of the past year's events, from almost being murdered in her employer's kitchen, to a bloody hand roasting in an oven, Kitt's confession of his love for her, followed by his 'death' and resurrection in blood-soaked, snowy New Mexico.

If Kitt had been there, they would have talked, they would have argued, they would have laughed and held each other, and her anxiety would have settled, but he was carrying on with an activity characteristic of his occupation. She knew how to get bloodstains out of fabric, off wool carpets, off skin, and out of hair, but there was no way to remove bloodstains from her memory. The only method she had to calm her mind was to carry out an activity characteristic of her occupation, a methodical task—like scrub bloodstains from a carpet, or iron, or bake Chelsea buns for tomorrow morning's breakfast.

Mae sat up and reached for the phone beside the bed. She rang the front desk, and made arrangements to have yeast, flour, butter, sugar, dried fruit and spices sent up to the suite. Then she climbed out of bed and tied an apron over her dressing gown.

With Felix tagging along, she left her room and headed for the suite's small but well-appointed kitchen, passing through the sitting room where the teapot and saucer sat on the coffee table, the teacup atop papers and a blue folder. The dog hopped onto the sofa, his tail knocking against an empty water glass and crystal clock on the side table. He pushed throw pillows with his snout and curled into a ball beneath one.

In the kitchen, Mae filled the sink with soapy water. She found a baking tray, mixing bowls, and a rolling pin in a cupboard, along with a wooden tea tray. Tray in hand, she returned to the sitting room to collect the tea things, taking the water glass from the side table with the clock and phone, putting it on the tray with the teapot and saucer. As she lifted the teacup from the coffee table, she saw the photos spread across the blue folder, and her hand sagged. Lukewarm, sweetly spiced chai spilled over colour photocopies, over two people, a man and a woman, seated in an outdoor café in Sicily, volcanic ash dusting the tables. First bewildered, then angry she put the tray and tea service on a chair, leaving the tray's edge sticking out. She lifted the pages, shook tea from the dappled paper, and then looked at images, at passport photos discoloured by tawny, sweet-smelling milk. "Skawly *feckin'* bastards!" she mumbled.

"Did you really think you could keep this from us, Mrs Valentine?" Llewelyn said, his voice a luscious, Shakespearian baritone.

Startled, she jerked around to find the wretched man looking haggard, ashen-faced. "You people stop at nothing," she said, tossing the photocopies and pictures onto the coffee table, the paper absorbing chai from a puddle, further discolouring the photos.

"This is not nothing." He moved closer to her, an arm's length away, his tone honey, the smell of sick on his breath. "This is everything. How long have you two been hiding things, how many years? You almost, *almost* had me believing your stories." He sighed, head shaking. "I told you I wouldn't follow through with your brother; an innocent, broken man like him deserves so much better, far better than a sister like you, but I have no qualms over prosecuting you or a man like your..." he smiled, Cheshire Cat-like, all teeth and cleverness, "...husband." He took a step toward her, doing his best to be intimidating.

Mae crossed her arms and glared at him, doing her best to not be intimidated by the mouldy fecker, doing her best not to slap the shite hawk smirk from his dark, ashen face.

Llewelyn went on smiling. "And there are so many charges that could be laid, against you, against him—especially against him; murder and conspiracy are just the start. If you think you're protecting him you're not," he said, pressing a fist into his breastbone, "you're making it worse, worse for yourself and worse for him. So stop protecting him. There's no need. We know everything about the two of you." His crafty grin altered to a sudden moment's puzzlement, his brows arching, and he gave a thin laugh of disbelief, saying, "Oh, Mrs Valentine."

Then, deadweight, the Brigadier hit the floor, his forehead knocking the edge of the coffee table, bright red dappling the pinkish Turkish rug when his cheek kissed the floor.

Startled, the dog popped up from beneath the pillows and barked, while Mae stared at a man who orchestrated lies for a living. Half on his side, a thin trickle of blood seeped from his dark head, his eyes open and unfocused. Had he fainted, was he stunned, or was he dead? The man coordinated swindles, traded and risked the lives of others, played games, played dead. She didn't trust him. She watched him, watched his chest rise and fall, watched him gasp and gurgle. If wasn't playing, he was dying, and if he died... Llewelyn's eyelids fluttered and closed.

Mae went on staring and Llewelyn became a woman crushed between the Bentley and the front of a tipper and there came the sound of her laboured final breaths, the rattling sound like teeth in a Hoover. Helpless. She and the woman smashed between two vehicles had both been helpless. The woman could not be helped, Mae could not help her, things followed a natural consequence. She'd been powerless to stop the outcome, but now... The thought drifted in seductively. Her mind turned over the unfathomable, pondering the value of letting nature take its course again, of removing what stood in the way for her and Kitt and threatened their life together.

"Jaysus," she whispered. "Oh Jaysus." Mae dropped to her knees beside Llewelyn. "Brigadier, can you hear me?" she said loudly, placing the teacup on the coffee table to shake his shoulder hard. "Brigadier—*Roger*, can you hear me?" She felt his skull, fingertips passing through blood from the slice where his forehead had smacked the coffee table. She rolled him onto his back, tilted his head, put an ear to his mouth, and listened, looking down along his chest for any rise or fall.

He'd stopped breathing.

She swept a finger into his mouth and found it clear of obstructions. She placed her fingers on his neck, into a trickle of blood that had come from his head.

He had no pulse.

The suite's phone sat beside the crystal clock on the side table at the other end of the sofa. She lunged for the cordless receiver, poked a finger on the speaker, and dialled the front desk, dropping the handset beside Llewelyn. She jerked open his heavy dressing gown, his cotton pyjama top, and started chest compressions before the clerk at reception answered with, "Good evening, Professor Boothroyd, this is Kerim, how may I be of assistance?"

"Kerim, the Professor has collapsed, he isn't breathing, his heart has stopped, and he and needs medical attention, urgently." Mae said loudly, and rather soullessly, she thought.

Kerim's voice cracked as he said something about sending up a doctor, ringing an ambulance, a staff member trained with a portable defibrillator would be on the way.

Thirty compressions, two breaths, thirty compressions, two breaths. When was the last time she updated her first-aid certificate? Was it still thirty compressions, two breaths, repeat until... until... until...? Mae kept going, counting, performing CPR, counting, breathing, sweating, swearing at the man who smelled of vomit and holiday spice. "Roger, come on! Ya conniving bastard, come on!"

She looked at the clock. Three minutes passed, four minutes, Llewelyn didn't stir, hadn't begun to breathe on his own, and she kept going, counting to thirty, trying to keep a steady rhythm, forcing back the devil's voice inside her head that wanted to convince her not to keep going.

Where the hell was the hotel staff member with the defibrillator the clerk? Where was the bloody paramedic and EMT? "Wake up, ya big warped plonker!"

The doorbell chimed. Felix let out an *arf!* Mae shouted "Come in!" Sweat ran between her breasts.

The door swung open. The dining trolley loaded with the items she'd ordered for baking Chelsea buns bumped against the door. The same pale brown-eyed man who had delivered the *rijsttafel* earlier moved into the suite and stopped dead, trolley blocking the door open, his mouth agape.

"Do you have the defibrillator?" she asked.

The waiter went on staring with his gob hanging open.

"Help! Ambulance, doctor!" she shouted, assuming the words were similar in Dutch. The man stood there and blinked. "Hey!" she bellowed and Felix popped up from his pillow burrow, leapt off the sofa and sped about barking, barking, barking.

Then Kitt appeared, his jaw set, blue-grey gaze blistering with menace, Weed a step behind. They pushed the waiter out of the way and Kitt swore.

"*Ja. Er is niks aan de hand*, Kitt—there is nothing unusual going on," Weed said as Kitt shoved past him, gently nudging the dog away.

Mae glared at the dreadlocked man and kept going, her neck slick with perspiration, loose hair plastered to her cheek, counting to thirty, trying to keep a steady rhythm that matched, as a first-aid instructor had suggested, a Bee Gees disco hit with a ludicrously apropos title. "Don't stand there gawking like the waiter, Mr Weed, find out where the ambulance is, thank you!"

"*Tot Uw dienst*—At your service," Weed made a slight bow and tuned about, the waiter following.

She bent over, realigned Llewelyn's head, and blew two breaths into his mouth as, coolly, the dog pawing at him, Kitt knelt beside her, felt his superior's carotid for a pulse. His eyes locked with Mae's, her expression one of grim determination. He shook his head, she gritted her teeth, breathing hard, air hissing in and out, and went on trying to revive the man. "Move, my love," he said softly.

"No. I can't stop. If I stop, he'll die, and he can't die. I have to help him. I couldn't help Eaton or Charteris. I have to help him. I *have* to."

"Mae, you're tired. Let me help him." Kitt pulled her hands away and took over chest compressions. "How long?"

Mae sat back on the floor, panting, one leg splayed out, pushing wet tendrils of blonde hair from her forehead. "I don't know," she said breathlessly, and looked at the crystal clock on the side table. Six minutes had elapsed since she'd rung the front desk. "Six minutes. It's been six minutes. Jaysus."

"You did well to keep it up for that long. What happened?"

Felix trotted to her, sniffing, nosing her ear. "We were talking... and he..." she swallowed, took a deep breath, and exhaled hard, "... he collapsed, hit his head on the way down, but it's just a cut, and not very deep. I rang for assistance, which you see hasn't arrived. Why hasn't it arrived?"

"Take my phone, it's in my pocket. Ring Bryce," he said, performing an action he'd carried out more times than he cared to recall, pressing down and up with mechanical, ruthless force. "Tell him to get over here. Say, 'Flag is down'. Have you got that? *Flag is down.* He'll hang up straightaway. Then take Felix into your room. Weed will be back with paramedics and the dog will get in their way."

"Oh, God, Kitt."

"I've got this."

Mae put her arms around the dog, still catching her breath.

"Don't stop," she said, rising, holding the dog. "Keep going. Don't stop."

"Why would I stop?"

She looked at him, rattled, almost shamefaced, and her gaze swept to Llewelyn's dark, ashen face, she bit her lips together and looked away, shuddering. "I...I... didn't th..." Head shaking, her eyes cut back to his. "Don't stop. Just, don't stop." Mae hurried off to her room, carrying Felix.

Kitt watched her shut the dog away and shifted his position, lifting Llewelyn's head. *"Goddamn it, Roger,"* he said, and covered the man's mouth with his, filling lungs that refused to do their job, pumping an equally unobliging heart. The thought struck him when he moved to give another kiss of life, and he almost hesitated. He glanced at his watch. Eight minutes. He'd once kept a man's heart going for forty minutes. He'd despised the man, a racist, misogynist, known double agent, yet, as their position was shelled and strafed, in those long, terrifying, gruelling moments before a medic and evac team arrived, he never hesitated, he never *almost* hesitated or even thought of his own welfare. He didn't consider his own welfare now, but his mind was not set on Llewelyn's either. He was not, as Mae may have believed, cold-blooded, but Christ, it would have been easy, it would have made life simpler, and she knew. 'Don't stop,' she'd said. *She knew*, Mae knew he'd consider, however fleetingly, the option, the out that would free them both.

Except there was no out, there was no free. Everything, *everything*, had changed. "God *damn you*, Roger," he muttered and continued pumping an unobliging heart.

Mae came out of her room, hurrying back to Kitt. He carried out CPR with mechanical efficiency, expressionless, detached from the process. She realised she was detached too, from what was occurring before her. It was as if watching a performance on stage, from the front row where one was part of the audience, yet nearly part of the production.

Noise travelled up the hallway and into the suite. She watched Weed enter the stage, giving orders in Dutch, the thumping of foot-falls behind him dulled by carpeting, and the clatter of a gurney smacking into the cloth-covered trolley that held the door open. The hotel manager rushed into the scene ahead of a lean, short man in spandex bike shorts and cleated shoes, a doctor's bag in hand. Two paramedics, both women, one blonde, one redhead, rolled in the gurney and dropped their gear beside Llewelyn, oppo-site Kitt. For a moment, all the players stopped moving and the action became a tableau by a modern Dutch master. Then, in slow motion, medical professionals took over, and Kitt rolled back and sat on his haunches, still maddeningly detached.

How had he not broken a sweat?

He looked at her, distant, elsewhere, frozen somewhere inside himself.

Weed parked his arse on the edge of the food trolley, arms crossed, and Mae knew his eyes were on her too as she untied the apron over her dressing gown. There was smear of blood on the white strings. She moved to the sitting room, sank onto the sofa, apron bunched in a fist, watching the two women and the athletic doctor work trying save the life of a man she'd wanted to die.

And when he did, she felt nothing.

CHAPTER SEVENTEEN

Grim-faced, Bryce stood near the door with the three police officers attending the scene. For now, local precedent overrode diplomatic precedent. When the doctor in lycra bike shorts explained the legal protocol to Bryce, saying something about natural causes, inquiries if foul play is suspected, death certificates, burial permits, and the worst food poisoning he'd ever experienced, Kitt made his way to the sitting room. He pulled a beige woollen throw from a chair and draped it over Mae's shoulders.

"I'm sorry," she said, playing with the strings of the apron on her lap. "Are you all right?"

"I admit I'm bit shocked."

"I'm sorry."

"You tried. We both tried." He sat beside her, elbows on his knees, the fingers of his right hand feeling what remained of the two shortened fingers on his left hand. He let his eyes follow the swirl pattern on the Turkish rug, numbness swirling through him in a similar manner.

Mae scooted to the edge of the couch and sat the same way. She lay her hand on his arm. "I didn't try hard enough. I'm sorry. I'm sorry for your loss. I'm so sorry."

"People die. Mae."

"Yes, but I wanted him to die," she whispered, and pulled her hand away.

"So did I," he murmured, lifted his head and met her eyes. She made a sound, a low tremor of air, and held his gaze until he looked away. Tea, now half-dried, marred the papers and blue file folder that lay in the open on the coffee table. Despite being stained, rumpled and scented by a merry spice cocktail, the colour passport photocopies remained legible, the images on them clear, if not a tad sepia-toned. Kitt gathered the papers together.

"Oh," she said and the word, so small, was extraordinarily heavy.

He slid the pictures into the blue file.

"This is all so unreal," she said, laying aside the soiled apron that had been in her lap, draping it over the arm of the sofa.

Kitt didn't say anything. He placed the folder back on the coffee table, out of the way of a wet patch of tea.

Mae watched a muscle pulse in his jaw. "Hamish," she said softly, "Were yo—"

"Kitty, "Bryce said, coming toward them, "the doctor, Weed, and I are going down with the crew. You two okay?"

"Yes," Kitt eyes slid to the paramedics wheeling out Llewelyn's sheet-covered body on the ambulance gurney, "we're okay for now."

"Mm-hm. Right." Bryce looked from one to the other. "You're both shell-shocked. I know I sure as shit am. I'll see if I can find a good bottle of bourbon in the bar downstairs. The one in here is crap."

"Are you coming, Mr Bryce?" Weed called out.

"What an arse," Bryce muttered. "Back soon."

"Can't wait," Kitt said watching him leave, watching him usher out Brigadier Sir Roger Niven Llewelyn. When the door closed, he was left looking at a cloth-covered dining trolley a nervous-looking waiter had left behind.

This was wrong. It didn't gel. Nothing about it was logical. Llewelyn was an older man, but he was healthy. He had to be healthy to maintain his position, and unlike some of his junior officers, the man did not indulge in any vice; he wasn't a smoker, he didn't drink or use recreational drugs, frequent brothels, or drive fast. But neither had Morland, and he was dead too.

"We were talking, before he dropped dead," Mae said beside him. "He was insisting that... The file, the pictures you just put away, they are the reason I'm here, isn't it?"

Kitt stopped denying one reality and desperately wanted to deny another. Llewelyn had died, and the pictures, Christ, she'd seen the damned pictures. He went on staring at the trolley. "Yes."

"Were you going to tell me about them?"

"This is impossible," he murmured. Never in his life had he felt so small, so powerless, so inept.

Mae exhaled and shrugged off the woollen throw, tossing it on the back of the sofa. "So you knew. Were ya goin' to tell me or not?" she said, Irish intoned, and lifted the folder, taking out the images, fanning them out on the table.

He looked at her then. And said nothing.

She was tired, she was angry and spoke in a flat, hushed tone that told him just how deep her fury went. "Is it habit because secrecy has been such a necessary part of your job you just fell into automatically? Are we back to that place where keepin' secrets is all about my safety or..." she paused and chewed her top lip for a moment, "...do ya think..." she swallowed, looked at the papers and spilled tea on the coffee table and swallowed again, "...*do* ya believe the same thing Llewelyn does...did, that I've been protec—"

"God damn Llewelyn! God damn Weed!" Kitt snatched up the photocopies, crumpled them into a ball, and pitched it on the table into a puddle of chai, the perfume of which would forever be associated with the death of a man he admired, hated...and loved. "No. *No.* I didn't think that. Yes, it's habit, long-practised bloody habit and I've been weighing up the options, considering reasons, considering the necessity, considering the meaning, wondering if there was any merit, any bloody point in telling you, wondering if it's true, and if it is true, knowing what it means for us."

"What are ya suggesting by *what it means for us*? This is more Llewelyn bullshit."

"Mae," he said, tongue thick in his throat.

A groove formed between her brows. "Oh Lord, ya think they're real!"

Yes, they were real, and she believed they were fake like so much of his life with her had been for far too long. "Two years ago, your brother," he said bloodlessly, "hired an investigator who found things."

She looked at the balled-up photocopies on the table. "Why would Sean not tell me that?"

"I don't know. Perhaps he was prepared to. Perhaps something made him change his mind. Perhaps it was for the same reason I didn't tell you the things I knew about Caspar and his other wives until my hand was forced. I didn't want to break your heart more than it had already been broken. But that was then."

"And this is now. When did my brother tell you he'd hired an investigator?"

"He didn't. Llewelyn did."

"Of course he did." She reached out and grabbed out the crumpled, tea-stained papers opened them, opening the ball, stretching out the photos. "Who made them then, where did these come from?" She waved the creased papers.

He pointed. "That one was found in a drawer in Sean's flat, your former home. The other is from Llewelyn's counterpart in the AVID, who, like Llewelyn got them from the Materials Tech officer."

"How did a Materials Tech officer get copies?"

"Most likely when a sweep was made of your brother's flat."

Mae rose with an irritated snort. "A sweep of... You're telling me someone went *into* Sean's home?

"Yes. All new residents in the area, all your neighbours and tenants, from Masterton to Stephens to your brother, are or have been vetted. It's standard, ongoing practice for the safety of any intelligence officer. You know that."

"I didn't realise being vetted meant a Materials Tech team broke in, poked about homes, and planted crap when it suits The Consortium."

"No one breaks in. They are very careful and very thorough, and finding that information in your brother's flat, a flat that belongs to you, a flat you lived in, added to the suspicions Llewelyn maintained about you. He believed you were hiding something, protecting someone."

"I was. *You.* He never trusted me, he even told me as much. Is that why he had this planted this in Sean's flat?"

There was no way to explain this softly, no way that would not sting, no way that would make sense and he did not want to explain what would destroy them. "Mat Tech didn't plant anything. That passport photo," he pointed, "was in Sean's flat, and this one," he pointed again, "along with the photo of the café in Sicily, was uncovered by Weed. That is why he's been staring at you. Do you see? Do you understand why this is impossible, Mae?"

"No. When did you find out all of this?"

"About an hour ago." For a long moment, Kitt said nothing, the more than a scrap of soul he had twisted, his heart, squeezing it, forcing it into his throat, crowding the words, he couldn't bring himself to say them because he didn't want to believe what was true anymore than she did.

Mae stared at him until what he'd left unsaid broke through and she blinked and squeezed her eyes shut and pressed her hands against her shaking head. "Photos can be doctored; people, faces can be inserted into any setting. That is not Fiorella in that picture."

"Images can be modified," Kitt said, hating himself, "but these have been verified by the Italians. Maltese and Croatian governments confirm that they issued the passports. There's a Dutch passport too, Weed showed me." He said the names on the passports, "Bruno Sciacca, Stefan Fedelio, Wilem Plender, they are all the same man."

"No, no. He is *not* alive. Caspar is *not* alive!" Her hands came away from her skull. Mae sat, and slowly, all the air was sucked from Kitt's body, leaving a hollowness breathing didn't fill.

THERE WAS NO TIME. There was no time for shock. There was no time for mourning. There was no time for panic. The only thing to do was get on with it. The only thing to do was get up and move. The only thing to do was think, but to think there had to be something she could focus on and the only thing Mae could focus on were those fucking photos.

"I don't know about you, but I could use a drink," Weed said as he and Bryce returned to the room. He crossed the room to the little bar on the sideboard, grabbed a tumbler, and poured in a healthy shot of Bols Genever. "Anyone else?" he said, glancing over his shoulder.

No one replied.

Glass in hand, Weed sauntered to the sitting room, gathered his dreadlocks in one hand and let them spill down his back. He lifted the tea tray from the chair where Mae had left it and dropped it on the coffee table, china rattling.

The clattering of the tea service snapped Mae to sit up.

Weed put his drink on the tray beside the teapot and poked the rumpled photocopies before he had a seat. "I take it you had a little discussion with your butler, Kitt?" he said, with the lightest Dutch inflection, all trace of his American accent gone.

Bryce stood on the edge of the pretty, pinkish Turkish rug that was stained with Llewelyn's blood. "A little discussion about what?" he said, eyes on the crimson marks.

"The butler's," Weed smirked, "husband."

"What?" Bryce looked at Kitt sitting on the sofa's edge, elbows on his knees, while Mae stared at the tea tray on the coffee table, her expression leaden, dressing gown dotted with blood and open on a generous amount of thigh. "Kitt?" Bryce said.

"Didn't you know, Timothy?" Mae said without looking at him. "My dead, polygamist husband is alive."

"Shit," Bryce muttered and moved to plop into a vacant chair that wasn't as comfortable as the one Weed had chosen. "Is there any tea left in that pot?"

Mae got to her feet, adjusted her dressing gown, and began to tidy the coffee table, dabbing the remains of spilled chai with the soiled apron she'd pulled from the sofa's arm. "I don't know. If there is, it's stone cold."

"Not at all like your not-dead husband," Weed said, sipping his Bols. "What did you think of the passports and the photo of your friend? That little old lady looks like quite a character."

Kitt let out a quiet breath. It was odd how a catastrophic moment could trigger a chain reaction that piled one disaster on top of another tragedy, on top of another calamity, until it squeezed out a solution—or potential solution—to a final dire situation. It wasn't thinking outside the box as much as letting oneself be crushed by the box and the crawling out from under the rubble. "If there something you want to say, *Hans*, then say it. I don't have time for this." He watched Mae shift gears, saw her set aside her fear, her rage, her disbelief. She grabbed hold of routine, of the familiar, she slid into being *productive* and began collecting the tea things, placing them on the tray.

"I'll make a fresh pot of tea, Timothy," she said.

"No, you won't," Weed said. "You're not going anywhere." Light gleamed off the amethyst on his wrist.

"Sod off, Mr Weed." Tray in hand, Mae turned for the kitchen.

Weed's hand shot out and grabbed her arm, unbalancing the tray she quickly levelled before any china slid off. "I said you are not going anywhere. We're going to have discussion and you're going to sit there and listen."

"Let her go, Hans," Kitt sighed, "or I promise you, you will lose teeth."

"Lose teeth." Weed chuckled at the threat, releasing her, sipping again from his tumbler. "You know, *Major* Kitt. Maybe Llewelyn and Arthur believe your record and commendations mean something, and maybe they once did, but when I look at you, I am not impressed by past accolades."

"I'm heartsick about that."

Head shaking, Weed inspected Kitt for a moment, turning the glass in his hand. "I see a sloppy, unprofessional intelligence officer with missing fingers. Perhaps careless is a better word than sloppy. You'll have to forgive me. English is not my first language." He glanced at Mae standing with the tray.

So did Kitt. Mae stared at the bespectacled Dutchman, the corners of her mouth curved in a tiny smile, the sort, Kitt knew, meant she was contemplating lobbing the tea tray and all its contents at the man.

Weed continued. "I understand this woman saved your brother's life. It's natural you'd be grateful for that, it's even natural you and she share some kind of connection, that you'd feel some sense of responsibility for her, I probably would too, but to miss this, overlook this on purpose or merely be blind to it means you're past your prime, well past. But don't feel bad, Major, it happens to us all. I'll be you one day."

"You'll never be like Major Kitt, Mr Weed." Mae set the tea tray back on the coffee table.

"Oh, yes," Weed said, laughing again, "He saved your life as well. How could I forget. Forgetting, now *that's* sloppy, but I see. Major Kitt's your hero."

She shook her head, squinting. "No. He's not my hero; everything you say about him is true. He's sloppy, he's blind, sometimes acts without regard, he's prone to moodiness, he's missing parts of his fingers, he ought to be put out to pasture."

Kitt looked at her, one brow arched. "I love you too, Valentine."

"Thank you, sir," Mae said, her attention on the wiry, dreadlocked Dutchman. What is it you want to discuss, Mr Weed?"

"Yes," Kitt said. "You've done your part; AIDV has made its contribution on the matter of Valentine's not-deceased spouse. The Italians have asked us to step aside on that matter for now. They've asked you to step aside on the matter as well. As of this moment, it's no longer in our hands. Your responsibility is to assist with the investigation of Jan Vlaming and the theft of goods from freeports, which includes this morning's incident at the sex shop Erotica, for which we, that is, Valentine and I, will cooperate. As for my government, our responsibilities are twofold: continue to investigate Vlaming, and follow protocol with regard to Llewelyn's death. That's why Sergeant Bryce is here. So unless you want to discuss the transportation of the Brigadier's body back to England, or funeral arrangements, or how the British government is going to deal with Valentine, what is it you want to talk about, Hans?"

Weed gestured. "Her husband, of course."

"Ah, yes, her husband," Kitt said sitting up. "As I said, that matter no longer concerns us, Hans. Yet I was wondering something about the polygamist and the older Sicilian woman he's with in that photo too. What's your friend's name, Mae, Fiorella...?"

Mae clasped her hands behind her back. "Gullo. Fiorella Gullo."

"Gullo, thank you. Now, bear with me, Hans. Perhaps, as a gesture of friendship and collaboration between our countries and intelligence organisations, you'd like you to hear what I'm wondering."

"You're very funny, Kitt. Isn't he funny?"

"I know he certainly likes to think he is." Bryce snorted.

Weed shook a finger. "Careful. You're disrespecting a senior officer, Sergeant."

"Indeed I am." Bryce nodded. "I fully expect to be court-martialled. What is your point, Major Kitt?"

"Are you interested in knowing, Hans?"

"*Luł*," Weed muttered. "Get on with it."

Kitt patted the empty spot beside him on the sofa. "Please sit, Valentine. I'd like to ask you a few questions."

Mae sat, wishing she hadn't dumped her apron on the coffee table because she wanted something to squeeze so her hands would stop shaking. She shoved her fingers under her thighs. "I don't know why my friend Fiorella is in the photo, sir."

"Yes. It's a shock, and I know you're tired," Kitt said, his knee touching hers because he couldn't hold her hand. "I know you're upset. I know this is difficult. I know things look," the left edge of his mouth twitched, "a bit shite for ya. But would you say your husband is good-looking?"

She smiled so very faintly and fleetingly. "I don't care to talk about my husband."

"I understand, it may be nothing, just your opinion, just something I'm wondering about. Please. This may seem silly, but bear with me. Men and women make different value judgements about what is and isn't good-looking or beautiful. Attraction is one thing, beauty or good looks are another. Saying someone is attractive is different to saying they are beautiful or drop-dead gorgeous. If you ask me, I'd say Bryce over there is quite handsome."

"It's my green eyes," Bryce said, smiling.

"You're not wrong, Sergeant," Kitt nodded. "Valentine, would you say Caspar was attractive, nice-looking, good-looking, or *very* good-looking?"

Weed shook his head and removed his wire-framed glasses, inspecting them for grime. "This is fascinating, Major."

Kitt ignored the man. "Valentine?"

Mae looked at him sideways. She had no idea where he was going with this mad improvisational song and dance. "I thought he was very good-looking. Why is that important?"

"I'm not sure it is, but thank you." Kitt gave her hand a small squeeze and rose. "If you'll excuse me." He stood. "I've left Ms Goedenacht a bit too long. I only meant to give her twenty minutes, but it's been nearly an hour. I expect she'll be rather cross with me."

"Hang on. Wait." Weed put his glasses back on. "What the hell was this nonsense for?"

"I think there's a possible connection."

"A connection to what?"

Kitt pointed to himself, "Between my case," he pointed at Weed, "and yours, the one the Italians have asked us to step away from for now."

"How?"

"Ah." Kitt made a chiding sound, "*Tst-tst-tst*, you didn't listen very well at dinner. You were busy openly and obviously surveilling my butler because of Llewelyn's tenacious suspicion of her. I hate to say this, but you could use a refresher on carrying out open surveillance. That aside, maybe you don't have all the facts. You were focused on the one task you were assigned to carry out. I'll review things for you. You're here because my boss asked your boss to look into my butler's past again. I'm here looking into the theft and counterfeiting of luxury items from freeports because of a previous action, one that involved the theft and counterfeiting from freeports, me and, by the design of my now-deceased boss, my butler, as well as Ruby Bleuville, a dead woman whose name was bandied about over dinner."

Weed shifted in his seat, exhaling impatiently. "Yeah, so?"

"This morning, I met with Jan Vlaming Director of The Hortus and victim of possible fraud and theft from freeport storage. He mentioned meeting Ruby Bleuville and her very good-looking boyfriend Giacomo Negroni, Negroni like the cocktail. This evening, Tanja Goedenacht recounted the same story, practically verbatim, right down to Ruby Bleuville and her very good-looking boyfriend, Negroni, like the cocktail. There's a thing or two my butler and I stumbled upon this morning, but at the moment, what's important is this:" Kitt stood and put a hand in his pocket, feeling through the coins for his wedding ring, "I'll be honest, Hans. I'm not fond of the Negroni made with that Genever you're not drinking," he said, knowing Mae was staring at him.

"I don't quite follow." Weed shook his head.

Bryce leaned forward and lifted the teapot from the tray, swirling it about to check if there was anything left inside. Satisfied there was, he took the empty teacup Llewelyn had used and poured in cold chai. He brought the cup to his mouth, had a sniff, set down the teacup, and wiped away what had touched his lips with the back of his hand. "Well, that's foul. Maybe it's what killed Llewelyn."

"Oh, Timothy," Mae said.

"Too soon?" Bryce made a face.

Kitt cast his eyes over the disarray on the coffee table and picked up the crumpled passport photos. He looked at Bryce mumbling about 'too soon' and the tea being horrible, at Mae softly swearing in Sicilian, at frowning Weed knocking back the last of his drink. "Shall we see if I'm right?"

"Right about what?"

Mae rose. "Jaysus, how'd you make it out of spy training, Mr Weed? He's saying Bruno Sciacca, Stefan Fedelio, Wilem Plender— whatever he calls himself, Caspar, the very good-looking polygamist ghost is posing as Giacomo Negroni."

"I am, yes. And we have someone downstairs who could corroborate that."

"Who?"

"To start, there's the gorilla of a man who accompanied her here. His name's Bianco, and he's camped out in the bar, waiting for her. I noticed his delivery van parked in the 'commercial vehicle' spot in front, not far from your little Renault hatchback, Hans. Valentine and I saw the van earlier today outside a sex shop— where we found a body tucked away inside a little hidden room, and notified local police to deal with it. Rather than start with Bianco, I think we best begin with Tanja."

Weed removed his glasses and tucked into his jacket pocket. "How is this *stepping aside*, Kitt?"

"Think of this as a courtesy. I told Tanja I'd come back, and, if what I think turns out to be true, you and I both have somewhere to pick up once the Italians are done, or someone to hand over to them now."

Weed looked at Mae, his smile almost mercenary.

Mae had had enough of the mystery novel reveal improvisation. She started for the door. Kitt put a hand on her arm. "If you don't mind, Valentine, stay here. Look after Llewelyn's dog. Please."

Weed got to his feet with haste, fat locks of hair swinging over his chest. "No, I don't think so. The dog stays in the other room. She's coming with us, otherwise she might take off."

"I trust her not to." Kitt said.

"I don't, and," Weed gathered errant dreadlocks and tossed them over his shoulder, "I don't trust you either."

Bryce snorted and headed for the door. "Spoken like the spirit of Llewelyn," he said, shoving the dining trolley out into the hallway.

After Kitt pulled the woollen throw from the sofa's back, the four of them rode the lift down three floors. They entered the room and heard the sound of water running in the bathroom.

Kitt held out the throw. "I think it best if you go in and see to her first, Mae."

"Why me?" Mae's brows arched.

"Yes, Why her, because she's a woman?"

"No, because Tanja's not wearing anything and most women don't typically appreciate having strange men see them naked."

"True," Mae said.

"Why is she not wearing anything? "Weed frowned. "Oh. You... all part of the seduction, I see."

"No. No seduction." Kitt knelt in front of the bathroom door lock. "I just took her clothes."

"Why did you take her clothes?"

"To make it difficult for her to leave," Bryce said.

"I wouldn't have thought to do that."

"How long have you been in active field intelligence, Hans?" Kitt pulled out the spoon, and began to work the fork out of the lock. He'd jammed it in a little too well. "Is this your first solo op?"

"Yes. It is. Obviously." Weed put both hands in his trouser pockets and leaned against a chest of drawers, watching Kitt fiddle with the fork. "I owe you an apology, Kitt. Ageism flows in both directions. You think I'm too young and inexperienced for this work. I think you're too old, worn out, and need to move aside to let the young and inexperienced gain some experience. I could learn a lot from you, and you me, if we didn't let our egos get in the way. I have been a bit...overeager, and I'm sorry."

"If you're trying to get on his good side," Bryce chuckled, "he doesn't have one."

With a self-effacing laugh, Weed put on his glasses. "I can see that."

The fork came away from the lock. "Valentine," Kitt said.

Mae opened the door, woollen throw in hand. "Ms Goedenacht," she said over the noise of water rushing into the bath, "It's Valentine, the butler from dinner." She went into the L-shaped marble-tiled room that smelled of vomit and shit. For a long, long moment, she looked at the dark-haired blue,-eyed beauty, and turned around on gelatinous legs that took her back to the door. Her mouth had gone dry. "Well," she said from the threshold, tongue a shrivelled sea sponge, "there's sick all over the floor and I'm pretty sure she's dead."

CHAPTER EIGHTEEN

K itt moved Mae out of the doorway and went into the ensuite, stepping over spew, going around the corner shower to the bath where Tanja lay half in, half out of the tub, her cheek mashed against the floor, vomit in her hair. Christ, he'd left her for too long. He'd tried to be kind when he should have been ruthless, offered respite when he should have just gotten on with it and done his goddamned job. Hans Weed had been correct. The woman was dead because he'd been utterly sloppy and careless, selfish in a way he'd never been before, his focus on his own life, on Mae, when he should have been focused on his goddamned job. If anything told him he was finished, it was this. It was, without a doubt, time to get out. All the way out.

And he had no clue how to do that.

He reached over her and shut off the water.

Bryce entered, then Weed, slipping across the tiles, hand at his nose, saying, "*Och, 't Is geen zuivere koffie.*" He crouched and touched Tanja's neck. "She hasn't been dead long. She's still warm," he said, rising.

When Kitt came out of the bathroom, Mae sat on the stripped bed. She held up the throw. "Remember when I said I was getting used to finding dead people?" she said. "I lied. I'm not."

Kitt ran the back of one finger down her cheek. "I know," he said, and slipped the throw around her.

She shook her head and drew off the wool. "No, put it on her. Give her some dignity."

"We need to leave her as she is," Bryce had a seat beside her.

"Exactly as she is." Kitt went to the balcony's door and opened it. Fresh air rushed in to clear the heavy smell of sick and human waste that had drifted from the bathroom.

Weed stood at the ensuite threshold. He rubbed his chin and noticed a sticky glob of sick on the sleeve of his jacket. He took off the garment, crossed to the bed where Bryce and Mae sat to snatch a tissue from the box on the bedside table, rubbing the smelly goop from the fabric.

"Blot, don't rub," Mae said.

Weed stopped rubbing and dropped his jacket on the bed. "We were at the same table, all ate the same things: the satay chicken, the rice, the beef randang, the gado gado. We all ate the same things, except for you, Bryce."

"That's because I wasn't invited," Bryce said with a peevish little huff.

"And you, Mrs Valentine, because you were serving dinner. I don't feel ill, do you, Kitt?"

"I'm beginning to," Kitt muttered as he pushed the balcony door open wider. "I'm fine. Bacteria-borne food poisoning is not an equal-opportunity food poisoning, not everyone is infected or affected, and we don't know if Tanja or Llewelyn had an underlying medical condition."

"M-m, yes," Weed nodded, "yes, that's true, but what did they have from the *rijsttafel* that we didn't?"

"The tea," Mae said, rising, her eyes widening as she looked at Kitt.

Kitt felt his own eyes widen. He took a breath.

"The tea?" Weed twisted to face her.

"The chai," she said. "They both drank the chai."

"I knew that stuff was poison," Bryce said, climbing to his feet.

"Oh, God." Mae put a hand to her forehead. "I made the chai and served it."

"Yes, you did." Pleased with himself, Weed smiled the way an infant with gas smiled. "And earlier this year you nearly killed a woman with poison—Ruby Bleuville, in fact—by giving her a glass of denture cleaner to drink. I've read all about you, Mrs Valentine. Obviously, you know something about toxic substances."

"Goodness me," Kitt said, "that's exactly what happened."

"I'm sorry, Kitt," Weed pulled out a mobile. "I know the Italians have asked we withdraw for the moment, and this is a less than ideal situation, one that is awkward for you, but you see the *connection*." His smile widened and he began to scroll though his contacts.

"I understand." Kitt massaged his temples, moving to join his colleague and Mae where they stood beside Weed and the stripped bed. "I understand completely. Bryce, you're going to have to put this baby to sleep. It's clear I am not in the position to do it."

"Honestly, Kitty?"

"Just look at me. You can see the present circumstance. It's about to go over the edge."

Phone in hand, Weed's eyes shifted from the mobile's screen and up to Kitt. Mae looked at him too. Kitt looked at Bryce, and Bryce smashed his fist into Weed's jaw. Stupefied, the man staggered, the phone tumbled from his grip, Mae caught it, Kitt caught the man before he hit the floor, Bryce grabbed his feet.

Dumbfounded, Mae watched them carry Weed onto the balcony. It had stopped raining.

"Come here and see if you can find his wallet and keys, Mae," Kitt said sharply.

She took one faltering step then hurried to the balcony, quickly patting Weed's side and back trouser pockets, finding nothing but a money clip and change. "I'll try his jacket. She darted inside.

"You know," Bryce said, "it might kill him."

"Yes. It might. I understand if you want to step away, Sergeant."

"The things I do for you, sir. He's coming around."

Kitt adjusted his grip. "Thank you, Bryce. On three?" he said, swinging a moaning Weed.

"One..." Bryce said, swinging a groaning Weed.

"Two..."

Mae rushed forward, a set of keys and small wallet in hand. "I found his—what the hell are..."

"Three," Kitt said and off Weed went over the edge of the balcony.

"...you *doing*?" Mae looked at them, aghast, as the man fell two storeys, the sound of a splash emanating from the canal below. She shot to the railing and, for a half-second, looked down to the water and people hurrying to the canal's edge before Kitt dragged her into the room.

"Mind telling me why we abandoned courtesy protocol?" Bryce shook and flexed and massaged his right hand, knuckles red.

"First of all, he wanted to take Mae and hold her in detention until he sorted out whether not Caspar is still alive. And just now he was accusing you of murdering Llewelyn and Tanja Goedenacht."

"*What*?" Mae said, mouth falling open again.

"Oh," Bryce nodded, "that's what he was going on about."

"How long have you been in active field duty, Bryce?"

"Me? I'm not a field officer, I'm in support."

"Exactly like a good brassiere."

"Speaking of good support," Bryce examined his sore knuckles and frowned, black brows knitting over his bright green eyes, "did you hear Morland died?"

"Yes." Kitt grabbed his colleague's hand and examined it. "You need ice," he said.

"Yes, ice. Right. Llewelyn died, the woman in the bathroom died, Ruby Bleuville died, Jill Charteris and Eaton died. Do we need to be concerned about Morland?"

Kitt dropped Bryce's hand and swore. "What in hell is going on?"

"You're the field officer. I'm just support and I'll support you any way you need, Kitt."

"Okay," Mae said, voice pitched high; her long moment of speechless shock had worn off, and she looked from one man to the other, shaking the keys at them. "Okay, okay, first, that man wanted to have me detained, he was accusing me of poisoning two people, and you couldn't just lock him in the bathroom with Ms Goedenacht?"

"Well," Bryce shrugged. "It *was* only two floors down."

"Two floors..." Mae sank onto the edge of the bed. "How could I forget what warped, feckin' lunatics ya are? Now I find out that, on top of Llewelyn, Tanja Goedenacht, and Ruby Bleuville, Llewelyn's Moneypenny is dead as well?"

"I hate to break it to you, Mae," Bryce compressed his mouth for a moment, making the cleft in his chin more prominent. "I never told you Milton Foley is dead too, but your one-time employer, Julius Taittinger, as far as I know, is still breathing in his cell at the Santa Fe County detention facility."

Mae's face sagged.

"Ruby. It comes back to Ruby." Kitt tapped his left thumb against tips of two shortened fingers. "She's got to be the cornerstone to this. The Yeoh Triad, the Enrico Cartel, one of them, both of them, it's been well-organised, perfectly executed."

"Don't use that word," Mae said.

Kitt grabbed the beige throw, shoved it into Mae's arms, and took her elbow, pulling her to her feet. He led her to the door while she looked at him dumbly. "Go up to the suite," he said. "Get dressed. Grab whatever you think you *need*, and go into the suite next door. Here's the passkey card that'll get you in. We're leaving when I get upstairs. I'll ring the bell once and knock twice."

"Leaving? W-what about the dog?"

Kitt looked at Bryce. "You like dogs, don't you Bryce?"

"Yes, especially the ones that like to hump. I'll see to my drunken friend in the canal."

The dregs of shock gave way to irritation. Hands on her hips, she squinted. "And what are you going to do while I'm upstairs in the three minutes it'll take me to pack a bag, Kitt?"

"Think," he said, and grabbed Weed's jacket, tossing it to Bryce, who hurried to the door.

Mae was right behind the tall Welshman, he held the door for her, but she paused and turned around, one eye squinting this time. "*Put this baby to sleep*—Did you really say that?"

KITT RANG the bell and knocked twice. He only waited a moment before Mae opened the door and turned about. He followed her. The dining trolley that Bryce had pushed into the hallway after Llewelyn died stood against the wall. Felix trotted beside her as she moved past it, went through the sitting room that was a mirror image of the suite next door. No matter how they disagreed, Kitt knew the dog was hers, and the both of them trailed after her to the dining room where a familiar, comforting, buttery scent filled the air.

Her small iPad with the folio keyboard open sat on the dining table that had gone from six to four seats. Beside the tablet was a plate, a napkin, silverware, and a large, covered dish. "What are you doing, Mae?"

"Looking at one of the places I'm thinking of buying to restore rather than renovate—if we get through this."

Kitt had a look at the screen. "That's what one calls a ramshackle cottage."

"Mm-hm, a cottage on a ramshackle estate in need of restoration, but look, the cottage has a stone fence, and an apple orchard right out the front."

"All that's missing is the dog."

"No, he's right there." She looked over at Felix who sat watching them, hoping, she knew, for a nibble of what lay under the stainless-steel cover. "You took too long. I couldn't stand the waiting and all the thinking that comes with waiting alone, so I made breakfast. She tipped her head to the Delft china place setting, complete with a Chemex coffee maker.

"You made real coffee too?"

"Yes. Eat."

"It's the middle of the night."

"It's two a.m., Kitt. Good morning. Breakfast is served." She closed the iPad's cover.

"We don't have time for this. Sunrise is in a little more than two hours."

"I've looked outside. I went out on the balcony. There are men in the suite next door. I saw the police down at the canal, more police running toward the hotel. I heard a siren. And then another siren. The canals in Amsterdam aren't very deep, only two or three metres. I think the canal below was only two metres.

Mr Weed broke something. We can wait a while until it dies down."

Maddeningly cool, Kitt slipped a hand into a pocket of his dark trousers. "Listen, in the past, under more usual work circumstances, I would have locked Weed in the bathroom, but this is not a usual work circumstance. A usual work circumstance does not involve you. Do you know I how sodding much I wanted to miss the canal?"

She replicated his cool, maddening nonchalance. "Yes, I do. Sit down. Eat your eggs. I have something to say."

He gave her hard, cold look. "You can reprimand me and tell me how appalling I am when we're in a car driving away from here."

Mae cocked her head.

Kitt pulled a chair from the dining table and sat. "Bloody hell, woman."

She leaned forward and lifted the stainless cover from the serving dish and began to scoop scrambled eggs onto the plate in front of him. "The Caspar I loved is not real," she said. "That man was not real. He was a façade. That man was nothing but lie upon lie upon lie. I was stupid. I was feckin' stupid. I never noticed, never considered he could be lying to me—why would I? He was my husband. I trusted him. I trusted him blindly because I loved him, and he lied. He lied to me and to two other women. Two other women who are dead. He made my life a lie and he's made me a fraud, made me culpable for the sort of deception Llewelyn believed I was guilty of; I am accountable by association. What sort of man lies to a woman he claims to love? I'm sorry there's no toast."

"Mae," he said.

She held up her hand, palm out. "They sent up white bread for Llewelyn and I know you dislike white bread. I was going to make

Chelsea buns." She went around the small table, dragged a chair out, and sat across from him. "You asked me that once. You wanted to know how a husband could hide things from the wife he loved, how a husband could hide thirty-seven million pounds from the woman he loved and—why are you crying?"

"Because you're not." Kitt's hands, flattened on the table's top, curled into fists, and he looked up at Mae through wet, clumped lashes. "I'm going to kill him, Mae. This is not hyperbole. If he's alive, if we find him, I am going to kill Caspar."

Her mouth flattened. "No, you're not."

Damp eyes hard and icy, he said, "How can you be so forgiving?"

"Forgiving?" She sniffed. "What was there to forgive when I thought he was dead? What was the point of being angry with the sins of a man I believed was dead?"

"I meant you're forgiving of me, of things I've kept from you. I've lied to you. I pretended to be dead. We're no different."

"Yes. You have, you did, but you're not the same."

"We're both liars, that makes us the same."

She reached across the table, picked a puff of egg from his plate and ate it. "You were honest about yourself from the moment we met. You told me there were things you would not and could not discuss, awful things, secret things. And then, when it became necessary, you shared your secrets with me, you were honest about the life you lead."

"I live a life of lies. My God, you should've walked away. Look at the horror and misery I've brought you." Kitt gave his running nose a savage wipe.

"You *do* have a napkin," she said.

Kitt lifted the folded cloth beside his uneaten eggs and blew his nose. "You should walk away now. You know the account codes, where the safe house is. Walk away."

"So you live a life of lies. I knew what you were from the start."
Mae sat back. "I knew you had dubious morals. You're a charlatan,
a liar, and I chose to live the life and the lies *with* you. I knew the
options; I saw them clearly: walk away and be sensible. I chose to
share your life of lies. *I chose.* Now Caspar's made my choice a lie
for you and me, made our marriage a lie."

Kitt smiled gently. "My love, our marriage isn't legal."

"Yes, for my own protection and yours, but legal or not, it's a
marriage to us both. I know that scrap of legal paperwork doesn't
matter to you any more than it matters to me. You haven't changed
your mind about your vow to me. We *are* married."

Kitt looked down at the beautiful scrambled eggs his wife had
made for him. If he put the tiniest bite of pillowy, pale yellow in his
mouth the eggs would taste like red wine or mushrooms or something detestable, and he was loath to sully a memory of something
that had always been perfect. He raised his head. "Caspar's reap-
pearance challenges the registration of his death, meaning legally,
he's still your husband. The British and Italian government will
want answers, the insurance company who paid out after the crash
nearly seventeen years ago will want to retrieve assets they paid
out, there may even be petitions filed in probate for relatives of his
other wives."

"Yes," she nodded, "I imagine the paperwork will most likely be
enormous."

"If I kill him there won't be any paperwork." He looked at her,
blue-grey eyes burning like frostbite, and he said it very softly, "If
this is true, I will kill your husband, Mae."

"*You* are my husband," Mae said and was silent for a very long
moment, staring at his right hand, which had clenched around a
cloth napkin. Then she cast her gaze to the floor to stare, saying,
very quietly, "How would you kill him?"

"I'd drown him in a canal," he said and she lifted her head, her mouth curved into a tiny smile that she knew horrified him.

"I know," she nodded again. "I see you're thinking *Dear God, what have I done to her?* I know you are. You school your thoughts so well, but sometimes, like now, I can see what you're thinking, I see your concern. I don't really want you to kill him."

"You don't?" he said, his look quizzical.

"No," she said, her little smile remaining in place. "It's not so much a matter of what he's done to me as much as it is what he's done to you, how this hurts you, and I want to kill him for that. *I want to drown him in a canal.* I want that so much and I can't reconcile that desire with what I know is very plainly wrong. I have lost all sense of morality. And I'm reconciled to that."

"It's revenge."

She laughed softly. "That basic human need."

"The thing of it is, Mae," he said, his hands disappearing beneath the table, "we don't know if Caspar's actually alive. Or if this is an ongoing case of identity theft, as we thought it was with his personal information being used to open a trust to launder money. Maybe you're right about the photo of Caspar with Fiorella being photoshopped. Maybe the photo is fake. Maybe the passports are forgeries."

"Do you believe any of that?"

His hands reappeared. "I want to believe all of it," he said, slipping a plain gold wedding band on the stumpy remains of the third finger on his left hand.

"Eat your eggs, Hamish. Then tell me what we're going to do next."

CHAPTER NINETEEN

It was creased from being crushed in a ball of bedlinens, but Tanja Goedenacht's dress fit fine, despite being a little snug across Mae's bust. The dead woman's shoes were a size and a half bigger than hers too, and tissues stuffed into the pointed toes would not solve the issue of walking without the shoes flopping off.

Kitt stood back and looked her up and down. "Mm. The shoes aside, the outfit suits you better than it did her. That's really your shade of pink."

"Liar. I look awful in this colour. It's almost as dreadful on me as that stretchy, yellow dress Fiorella's goddaughter lent me last summer."

The left side of his mouth rose and stayed that way. "Tell me something, is wearing another woman's dress better or worse than wearing another woman's dress *and* fishnet knickers? As you did in Sicily last July."

"You would bring up those bloody knickers. Fiorella's goddaughter had appalling fashion sense and probably still does."

"Well, which is it?"

"I prefer my own knickers and clothes."

He kept grinning with amusement. "Where's the scarf I gave you this morning?"

"In *my* coat pocket."

He went over to the small bag she'd left by the door, rifled through it, finding her coat at the bottom. He dug into the pocket, tossed aside a packet of tulip bulbs, and jerked out the faux silk white scarf dotted with black windmill silhouettes. He brought it to her. "Put this on, Grace Kelly-like. Tanja's coat and sunglasses too."

"Sunglasses? It's night time."

"They're to hide that your eyes are the wrong colour."

"And how do I hide a three-inch height difference?"

"Play it drunk and lean on me." He cocked his head. "Are you ready?"

"Almost. Can you explain a few things?"

"What?"

"I'm a little confused by something. When I was in hospital, after the accident, or the hit—it was a hit, wasn't it, not a terror attack of some kind?"

"Yes. Charteris, Ruby Bleuville, Llewelyn, probably Milton Foley and Morland too, they were assassinations. My best guess is the Enrico Cartel, Yeoh Triad, or Gallia Family. Eaton, on her way to work, was collateral damage."

Her lips parted. She crossed her arms, the scarf trailing down like a flag that very plainly did not signify surrender as much as it did vexation hiding beneath the surface of silky, spun polyester. "How did Morland die?"

"Morland had a stroke."

"What do you bet Weed will try to pin that on me too?" She uncrossed her arms, her irritation remaining.

"There's something else?"

"I find it odd how you were visibly put off by the possibility of Llewelyn suggesting I pose as Jill Charteris, but you're fine with me posing as Tanja Goedenacht. What's the difference?"

"You posing as Tanja is a temporary distraction to get us both the hell out of here."

"Okay. Why aren't you bullying me into staying with Bryce or having him take me to a safe house?"

"Once Weed's stabilised and the police realise he's not a raving, suicidal drunk spewing gibberish, but an officer with AIVD, he will try to pin Morland's death on you, along with the murders of Tanja and Llewelyn and possibly even Ruby Bleuville. At this point, you're safer being unsafe with me more than you are in any unsafe holding cell where someone can get to you the way they got to Ruby, Foley and Llewelyn."

"In other words, you're not letting me out of your sight."

"Exactly. Are you ready, my love?"

"Did you send the message to Bianco the gorilla?"

"Yes."

"Then I'm ready, Diddums."

Kitt's mouth quirked. He powered off Tanja's mobile and slid the phone into the pocket of the black coat he helped Mae into. Then the bell rang, followed by two short knocks and a sharp bark from Felix. Bryce was here. Kitt went to the door and opened it. "Any trouble?" he said.

Bryce winced, teeth showing. "Well, water was a bit shallow. Weed has a hip dislocation."

"Ah." Kitt shook his head. "I'll send him a nice cane to assist his recovery. I've a lovely silver-tipped one at home. It is still in the umbrella stand under the coat rack, isn't it, Mae?"

"Yes." Mae let out a noisy huff of astonishment and moved to the entrance so she didn't have to shout across the room. The dog hopped off the chair where he'd been curled up and followed her to sniff Bryce's shoes and then latch on to his knee. "You naughty boy!" Mae said, tugging the anxious humper away from the man's leg. "Sit." The dog sat. She picked him up and gave him a cuddle, clucking at him gently.

"Oh, my sainted aunt," Kitt muttered.

Mae ignored him. "You'll look after the furry little man, won't you, Timothy?"

Bryce chuckled and gathered the small bag and handbag she'd packed. "I'll take the furry little man next door to hump Ivar—one of our Station NL locals, Mae. He's been tasked with wrangling the Amsterdam police, which is what he's tending to at this moment next door. He's also handling the local arrangements for Llewelyn. Everything is under the orders of Spec Ops Deputy Director Cubby. SODD Cubby has authorised your field extension, Kitt, but the lady is unhappy about how you've treated our Dutch friends. She assumes there will be reprisals, which you'll be made to face, if indeed Arthur—or Weed—choose to exercise a claim. I'm to tell you Cubby expects a full report outlining your actions. She wants it in writing, Kitty, *in writing.*"

Kitt smiled. "Have I mentioned how very happy I am to have you supporting me again, Bryce?"

"While I am pleased you missed me, I'm not writing your report, Kitty, not when I have my own paperwork to do."

Mae pinched her thumbs to her fingertips, gesturing like an Italian mama who grew up in Dublin. "You joke about pitchin' a man off a building and sending him a cane, but ya eejits eff and blind about paperwork. *I'll* do your paperwork just to shut ya up about how bleedin' diabolical it is."

Simultaneously, the two men turned to look at her and burst out laughing.

"Right. Right." She nodded rapidly. "Just remember, ingrates, I *offered.*"

"I'll take these things down and put them in the boot," Bryce said, still chortling. "The car will be out front in five minutes, standard field kit inside. I'll play valet and will hand over the keys. Ivar tagged the delivery van earlier. Hairy knuckles is sitting in it, waiting for you. I'll follow him, you follow me. Once we establish where he's going, I'll head back here for the furry little man and take him to my pet-friendly hovel near the Sexmuseum, to monitor things, and do my paperwork."

She put a hand to her forehead for a moment. "Let me know if you change your mind, about the paperwork, Timothy."

Bryce touched her shoulder. "I appreciate the offer, Mae."

Mae stood on her toes and kissed Bryce's cheek. "Thank you. Again. Please look after my dog."

"I'll keep the furry little man at my side." Bryce smiled handsomely.

When the Welshman left, Mae shook out the cheap souvenir scarf, wrapped it around her head, put on Tanja's sunglasses, and turned to face Kitt. He'd moved to look out the window, down to the canal below. "Feeling a little remorse?" she said, joining him.

"No."

"Right then. Have you had a pee? Have you cleaned your teeth? Have you said your prayers? Are you ready to go? And if you are, please have a really good, action hero film-worthy line to say so."

Any sense of humour, any playfulness he'd displayed in the last ten minutes vanished. Kitt spat out a string of four-letter words, a series of vulgarities, and a very solid expletive "How's that?"

"Not very catchy or cinematic," Mae adjusted her sunglasses, "but the creative use of obscenities was impressive."

"I thought so too." Kitt took her hand and led her across the sitting room.

He held the door open and she stepped into the hallway, barefoot, Tanja Goedenacht's high heels hooked on two fingers over her shoulder. They climbed into the lift. The doors slid shut. Mae stood on her toes, looped an arm around his neck, and kissed him long and slow and deep, and she was childhood Christmas, springtime rain, and so much fire, an astonishing flash fire that seared and cleansed and healed, his undoing, his remaking. When she let him go, he peered down into hazel eyes that had a wild edge to them. He cupped her cheek. "My love," he said.

"Why," she said, "am I suddenly not scared?"

"You're not scared?"

"No, I'm actually a bit...giddy."

"You're giddy and I'm terrified enough for the both of us."

They reached the ground floor and crossed the black and white tiled lobby, moving by pillars to the front of the Palace Grand Hotel, Mae leaning on him, giggling drunkenly, hand on his arse. The white van with its vegetable logo on the side stood across from the porte-cochère, the hotel's narrow carport where Bryce got out of the car, which was not the Jag from earlier in the day, but a pale green Aston Martin coupé.

An absurd giggle rolled from Mae's nose.

"Your giddiness," Kitt said glancing at her, "part of it is adrenaline. It makes you feel *alive*. The other part is because your safety is off. Events you keep surviving have switched it off. Eventually, it will wear off, it will catch up to you, and I'll be there for you when you crash, but right now, you're high on it. The problem is, with your safety off, you don't examine any decision or choice, you just dive right in, without thought."

"Just like you." She let out merry whoop when he lifted her, slung her over his shoulder, and took the key fob valet Bryce handed over for the green DB11 Volante. Bryce went to the other side of the car and opened the passenger door. Kitt deposited Mae in the seat, handed the Bryce some Euro, and saw the interior of the white delivery van illuminate, Bianco the gorilla waiting behind the wheel lighting a cigarette.

Bryce went back inside the hotel. Kitt got in the DBɪɪ, started the engine. "No, not just like me." He dropped his mobile in her lap, the screen lit. He caught sight of a billow of smoke spewing from the driver's side window of the white van as it pulled out onto the short, one-way laneway, rolled past the closed shops, cafés on the inner Prins Hendrikkade, north toward the IJ waterfront before turning west. Ivar had placed a strip of black gaffer tape running horizontally across one rectangular taillight. It would be easy to distinguish the van from others in the dark.

"We need to talk about safety." Kitt leaned across the console and Mae, grabbed the seatbelt, and buckled her in.

"I am perfectly capable of putting on my own seatbelt."

"I am only looking after you the way any decent husband looks after the wife he loves and cherishes."

"You do know there is nothing you have to prove to me."

"Perhaps I have something to prove to myself."

"Prove what, that you are a better husband than Caspar was, or that this isn't *impossible*?" She rubbed two fingers over her bottom lip and watched him frown. "Because I know you still see this, see *us*, as impossible."

"I do not."

She smiled softly. "Then why do you mumble 'This is impossible' every so often?"

"Do I?"

She looked at him, her expression telling him exactly how full of shite she thought he was.

"I do," he said and looked out the windscreen, watching for Bryce.

"Why is it impossible?"

High beams flashed ahead, just where the van had turned west.

Kitt pulled away from the cover of the hotel's small porte-cochère. "You, *we* will never be free of the life that I chose for myself, and it's not the life I wish for you. Can you navigate?" He tipped his head to the mobile in her lap.

Mae lifted the phone. "Do I simply follow the moving red dot?"

"Yes."

"Then I can navigate. But before I do, put on your feckin' seatbelt," she sniffed. "You say my safety's off, but you're the one driving without a seatbelt."

Kitt pulled on his seatbelt.

She found her glasses in the coat pocket, put them on, and looked at the red dot on the screen. "I noticed this months ago," she said, the dot moving along a little map. "Your life is part Agatha Christie, part Robert Ludlum spy thriller."

"Ludlum, not Ian Fleming?"

"No, no you don't have the gadgets. Of course, that's the *film* James Bond. Book Bond wasn't nearly as gadgety."

"That little dot you're watching move is a gadget. So is one of the coins on your necklace. You are still wearing it under that dress, aren't you?"

"Yes, I'm still wearing the necklace under this ugly pink dress," she said, then she went quiet, her knee bouncing with pent-up energy and impatience.

Kitt followed the same route the van had taken, Bryce ahead in Weed's orange hatchback. The route took them in the direction of the interchange for the A5 and the A10 motorways. After five or six minutes, instead of turning west on the A5, which would take them to the Dankwaerts Estate in the Bollenstreek—the bulb region of South Holland—the van, and Bryce, took the ramp onto the A10, and went north. They travelled over a bridge across the IJ, and swung northwest on another motorway, the A8, where Bryce peeled off and left them, the city lights on the left, dark countryside on the right.

Mae shifted in her seat, her coat—Tanja's coat—*shushing* almost as noisily as her frustrated huff. She pulled off the scarf and shoved it in a pocket.

The mobile continued to pick up the van's tracking signal, the altered taillight visible in the distance. Kitt wanted a better idea of what was ahead. He touched the media screen. A map appeared, their location showing as near Zaandam. "Is there anything noteworthy in Zaandam?"

Mae had a look at the dashboard's display before she did a quick search on the phone. "Windmills," she said, and switched between watching the little dot move on the mobile's screen and watching the little dot that was the Astin Martin moving on the dash's display. "Windmills," she muttered, fidgeting, yawning, sighing.

They passed over cloverleaf exits, crossed another bridge and river, town lights on the left, dark fields on the right. Kitt slowed, dropping back, letting the van gain more distance.

Mae watched the dot move on the mobile. "I said you'd hit every cheesy hallmark of a spy film except for the car chase, and here we are, chasing a van in the morning twilight. I thought a car chase would be more exciting than this."

"This is not a chase. We are not chasing."

"Forgive me. I thought tailing someone would be more exciting." She yawned again.

"It's called *physical surveillance*. Why don't you try to sleep?"

"I'm navigating." Mae touched the map on the car's dash, widening the geographic view of the motorway and land. "He's either going to peel off up here and go northeast to Purmerend," she slid fingers across the screen, "or continue to Assendelft. Then, when he gets to the next motorway interchange, perhaps he'll take the A9 and drop into Alkmaar. I read there's a huge cheese market there. Jaysus, this is the worst car chase—excuse me—this is the most useless *physical surveillance* ever. Perhaps you speed up and run him off the road or something."

"Mae, you're whinging. Stop it."

"I know." She nodded dropping the phone into her lap. "I'm sorry. I have this inexplicable exhilaration and screaming impatience coursing through me." She shifted in her seat again as if it were studded with dull spikes. "How do you teach your trainee spies to be patient, Kitt? What practice do you advocate—yoga, mindfulness, guided imagery?"

He reached across, took her hand, and squeezed it, his fingers tickling her palm. "You already know the answer."

Mae laughed and then groaned and then took a deep breath.

They continued following the van northwest, the countryside backlit by a dim near-light of pre-dawn sun, colours from greyscale to purple and deep blue.

"New day, same shite," she said, rubbing her shoulder. Any pain she had from where a bullet had struck her last January was minor, a sort of itching throb of irritation. The bullet had missed bone and a major artery, but it had taken a chunk of flesh and left a scar bigger than the shrapnel scar Kitt had on his shoulder. She wondered if his scar ever itched or throbbed or irritated him, because the itching and throbbing and irritation was much the same as the itching, throbbing, irritating, sodding *physical surveillance*. "What is it we're doing again, Kitt? Why are we following the van? Tell me again why didn't you grab Bianco or head to the Dankwaerts Estate, or have Vlaming arrested?"

"Vlaming is guilty of fraud and theft from his own family, but he's a victim of extortion as well, and in Tanja's messages to Mr Bianco, she indicated she'd take me to the country greenhouse, which is clearly not on the Dankwaerts Estate. So here we are, heading northwest instead of southwest to Lisse, Leiden, or the Bollenstreek where the tulips grow."

"Maybe we're following Bianco to that farm where a family of seven had locked themselves in a basement, waiting for the end of time. Did you hear that news story?"

"That was northwest, in a town called Ruinerwold."

"Ruin-er-wold—sounds like a fitting name for a place to live when you're waiting for the world to end, don't you think? I wonder if the basement was beneath a greenhouse."

"I don't think that's how it's pronounced." Kitt gave a soft laugh. "You talk such nonsense when you're tired."

"Yes, I'm tired and fidgety and frustrated." She squirmed on padded, luxury leather. "Nonsense breaks the tension, smooths over the absurdity of where I find myself, offsets the absolute outlandishness and unbelievability of the events that have put me here. I am married to a spy and, even when one suspends belief, it's all so...so...so implausible, even for a work of fiction, even if there have been married fictional spies, like Ethan Hunt for example."

"Ah," Kitt said, eyes on the van's taillight. "Here we go. Who is Ethan Hunt?"

"The spy in the *Mission Impossible* films."

"I've only ever seen the television series."

"What century are you living in?"

"I've been too busy being a spy to see many films. Ethan Hawke?"

"Ethan *Hunt*. He was married, but couldn't stay with his wife. It's not really clear if they divorced or if she," Mae gave a sniff of a laugh, "*walked away* for her own safety, of course. She does come back—fleetingly in one film, and then more substantially in another, but by then she's with another man, meaning she and Ethan had divorced, which isn't something we have to worry about on any legal level, and Ethan Hunt was a bad example after all."

Kitt stared ahead, at the road and the van up ahead. He said nothing for two full minutes, reading the road signs and mileage markers, mulling over impossibility and her irrational sense of realism and spies and fiction and the faith she had in him, the faith she had in them. "Perhaps," he said, "the spy we should be focusing on is Matt Helm."

She let out a groan. "Matt Helm is the forerunner of Austin Powers. Have you seen *Austin Powers*?"

"Yeah, baby, yeah." He looked at her and sniffed disdainfully. "I cannot believe I have found a hole in your fictional spy research. Have you never read the Matt Helm books?"

"No. I was put off by the excessive 60s kitsch and camp of *The Silencers* and *The Wrecking Crew*, by Dean Martin's boozy Dean Martin persona and Dean Martin songs. Those movies are spoofs, parodies of Bond and a major inspiration for Austin Powers. And you are none of the three. Except for maybe the boozy part."

"My love," he said as a Porsche whizzed by, "your education is lacking. In Donald Hamilton's book series, Matt Helm is a serious, former World War II assassin recruited by the US government. He's *married*, has children, is middle-aged. In fact, aside from his being overweight and having children, he's rather like me. Matt Helm kept everything secret from his wife. She thought he was an author, not a spy."

"I thought you were a retired Army Major turned Risk Assessment Specialist."

"I am a Risk Assessment Specialist, and Helm was an author and a spy who wrote westerns about cowboys, not spies."

"Whereas you're a spy who once wore a cowboy hat."

"You miss that hat, don't you?"

"As much as you do. What's your point?

Kitt watched a lorry begin to overtake the DB11. "The point is, unlike me, Helm looked his wife in the eye and lied to her every day. She knew nothing about his past, about who he was and still was."

"How is it you know so much about him?"

"Perhaps I don't see many films, but people often leave books behind when they travel. I've read a lot of discarded spy and romance novels. You and so many authors are seriously misguided about how spies actually work in the world."

She inhaled and exhaled noisily. "You want me to believe the Matt Helm books are an accurate representation of the world of espionage?"

"No, I'm reminding you to stop mixing up fact and fiction."

"I will when you stop trying to be a hero. A lot of good it does me to have you step into danger and then get sent to prison, or step into danger and die. So shut your gob about whose safety is off and who's being reckless."

He ground his teeth together and looked at her. "*God damn it,* you frustrate the living hell out of me."

"Good." She smiled.

Her smile tempered his tetchiness and he laughed. "Why can't we argue about the usual things couples argue about, like sex and money?"

"Because we have enough of both."

"Do we?"

"I haven't heard you complain." She lowered her glasses and looked at him in the dim light of the dash dials.

His mouth pursed ever so slightly.

"Do you want more money, more sex, or both?"

His head tipped. "The sex has been a little light this week."

"Do you want to pull the car over so we can climb in the back seat?"

"Not in the middle of a car chase."

Her chuckle was light. "I'll have you know, money and sex are not the only things couples argue about."

"Hm, you've experienced a committed relationship before, and I haven't so, what do they argue about?"

"This is hardly fair. You know all about my marriage and I know nothing of your—"

"Dalliances?"

"I was going to go with *liaisons*, but I like dalliances better. What was it that would trigger you to depart from a dalliance?"

"Complaining."

"About what?"

"Cold-hearted husbands."

"All this time I thought it was because they got serious and you preferred distant, cold passion to heated, messy disentanglement."

"There is that, but mostly I didn't want to be a shameful hypocrite. I never wanted the weight of expectations, which is what I think most arguments are about, unspoken expectations."

She found the control to recline the seat and settled back into it. "You could be right. Besides money and sex, there's the division of household labour, children, communication, priorities, and the in-laws. We have no real reason to argue about money, sex, the division of household labour, or," she shook her head with a sniff, "children, but you do realise we have been at cross purposes about communication, priorities, and our in-laws."

"You like my brother."

"But you don't like mine, and I've yet to meet your sister *or* your parents."

"I don't dislike your brother."

"Do you smell smoke?" she patted her hip, extinguishing imaginary flames.

Kitt glanced at another car in the side mirror. "There's a difference between liking and disliking," he said as a boxy Volvo passed by. "Do you need me to exp...I think we may be headed for Castricum."

Mae sat up. "Why would you think that?"

"Our hairy primate friend Bianco is indicating he's about to exit and the signs point to Castricum." He watched the altered taillights slip out of sight as the van moved off the motorway ramp. A moment later, Kitt took the same exit and stopped at the cross-roads, letting the Aston Martin idle.

"Why are we waiting?" Mae said.

"Look out the window and tell me what you see."

"Dark fields."

"Yes, and dark fields mean if we were to follow Bianco now, our headlamps would give us away. We'll let him get along a bit and then go."

She pushed her glasses up and looked down at the phone in her lap, the little red dot on the mobile's map travelling closer to the town of Castricum. Mae searched for information on the place and didn't find much. "Castricum is known for its vicinity to the beach and its sand dunes. A botanist from Castricum works at the Royal Botanic Gardens at Kew. His name is Henk. He's the author of *Dendrocnide of Australasia*. Do you think that's why Bianco is going, to meet Henk?

"We'll find out." Kitt turned left and drove into flat, dark farm-land, the early twilight sun casting the eastern sky a cool, purplish blue, the road narrow and empty. The route took them alongside a canal and then to the fringe of town, skirting the edge of Castricum until suddenly turning south, back though flat, dark farmland, the sky purply with a pale grey tinge. A pink glow in fields cast upwards onto moving clouds. Trailing the van's course brought them to a clump of thick pines where they turned right onto a dirt and gravel surface, the scant morning light disappearing in the dark of poplar trees and a long, high hemlock hedge.

The little red dot that was the van quit moving. "Bianco's stopped," Mae said.

Kitt slowed, the DB11 creeping along until the road ended at a stone wall and an open iron gate with two signs. One said *Chateau Sicilië* the other *Gesloten*. He let the engine idle and stared at the placards and hedges on either side of the gates. "Do you remember Vlaming saying where he took people on garden tours?"

"Yes, I think he said something about Chinese gardens at Hortus Haren, near Groningen, and a private chateau north of Amsterdam."

"Do you think this might be the private chateau?"

"We are north of Amsterdam."

"Yes, we are."

She handed him the mobile that had been in her lap, pointing out the stationary red dot on the screen. "Okay, he's not moving at the moment, so what do we do now? Do I sit here while you go off and do lone commando stuff?"

"I'm not foolish enough to believe you'd stay here while I do lone commando stuff." Kitt set the phone on the console between the seats. Then he swiped fingers over the dash screen, toggling the image from map view to satellite, and zoomed in on their location, which, if the imagery was up-to-date, put them on the edge of an estate with gardens, barns and outbuildings, a canal-side windmill, and fields of cultivated flowers that were most likely tulips. He looked out the windscreen into the not even half-light of a Tuesday or Wednesday morning, he didn't know which, his eyes on the open gate. "I am, however, foolish enough to ask if you are up for a sunrise walk in the chateau gardens."

"A walk through a garden sounds romantic."

"I hope that's all it is, romantic." Kitt continued to look at the gate that one could view as an invitation to enter or leave freely. Open gates were more frightening than gates that were chained and locked. Chained and locked gates put out a very clear message that one ought to keep away from whatever sat on the other side, while wide open gates, like the one in front of them, were a Venus Flytrap.

And he and Mae seemed very much like curious flies.

CHAPTER TWENTY

He reversed the car along the shadowy little avenue, tucking it in behind a fat pine and low-hanging branches of a tree with little blossoms that immediately dusted the windscreen. He shut off the engine and killed the headlights.

Mae glanced at Kitt, his eyes fixed on the sudden dark, and he breathed in and out with conditioned deliberation, clearing his head, finding inner peace, thinking, thinking, thinking—or possibly all three. He was still, so very still, and a juxtaposed exhilarating disquiet twisted around her spine, threaded into her stomach, pushed up into her throat and sinuses, and scratched inside the top of her skull.

She set her attention on the glovebox in front of her knees and opened it. Inside was a little black zippered case very much like the one Kitt had at home, the case he kept in a lockbox beneath the window seat, the case that held a Walther-Beretta-Smith & Wesson compact 9mm pistol. There'd been a case like that with a pistol in inside it in the glovebox of a silly-looking Volkswagen Beetle Bryce had arranged for them to drive in Sicily last July.

Thrilling uneasiness itched under her skin. She shut the glovebox, looked at the swirling pattern of the surface, and began breathing in and out, focusing on each breath, waiting to feel a sense of calm, but what came over her wasn't a sense of calm or clarity. What rolled over her and popped into her mind's eye her was simply another wave of absurdity. Like Kitt's written-off Bentley, the silly luxury car they sat now in also had a wooden dash—burr walnut —and probably a heated steering wheel too. "What do think of this car?" she said, not at all apropos of where they found themselves.

"I've been waiting for you to say something." He shifted his gaze to where she sat in the dimness, "At the moment," he said, feeling about under the seat and finding what he was after, "I love this car because it's got what I hope I don't need. Do you think the car suits me?"

She snorted. "It lacks an ejector seat."

"It's equipped with other things." He put something on his thigh, reached for her hand and lifted it to his mouth, kissing the middle of her palm. He got out of the car and went to the boot, removing his jacket and pale blue shirt, exchanging both for a dark blue polar neck and brown zippered jacket he tossed on the roof of the car.

For a moment, in the side mirror, the boot's light cast a glow and Mae watched Kitt change clothes at the rear of the car. She unlatched her seatbelt, pocketed her glasses, got onto her knees on the seat, and reached into the rear where Bryce had put her small bag, rummaging about in it until she found her Doc Marten Mary-Janes. She opened the door and swung her legs outside.

Kitt adjusted the roll neck of his shirt and watched her slip her feet into iconic British shoes that were originally German. She buttoned up Tanja's black coat, quite deliberately ignoring him, putting on the shoulder harness he'd found under the driver's seat.

She was out of the car before he'd slid the little Walther into place and shut the boot.

There was a chill to the damp spring air, and it would get colder just after the sun rose. He locked the car, took Mae's hand again, and they walked away from the car and through the open gates, ignoring the sign that said, like so many other shops and businesses would at this time of day, *gesloten*, closed. The dirt and gravel crunched softly under their feet as they travelled up a drive lined with poplars that soon gave way to vast, open fields of flowers. In the sun, the fields beside them would be a carpet of vibrant colour as far as the eye could see. Now all the tulips were shades of grey.

Across the expanse of blooms, a kilometre perhaps, stood barns and a windmill, its silhouette like the design on the scarf Mae had tucked around her neck. Headlamps twinkled on moving farm machinery, light glowed beyond the windmill and barns. Kitt remembered the satellite images he'd seen on the car's GPS. The road they were on led to the chateau and then around to the other buildings. It would be quicker to reach the big house if they went across the tulip fields rather than stay on the drive. In the dim purple, blue and pinkish light of early dawn, the field he took Mae into was a foreboding black. They walked in a dirt track alongside thigh-high tulip rows, quickly covering ground. As the sky grew lighter, they reached the end of the foreboding black field that began to turn blood red, the earth clear of flora, but uneven with ruts made by tractors—like the green John Deere 6R heading into the field flowers ahead of them. Headlights on the giant, modified mower began beheading the blooms, leaving dark stems standing while the petals spilled into a neat row alongside.

Kitt grabbed Mae's hand and jerked her into a run toward dark blooms, to the dirt between the green stalks. "This is wrong," she said. "This should be a field full of corn, not tulips, and we should be running from a biplane, not a tractor lopping off the heads of flowers."

"At least there's no one shooting at us." He let go of her hand. "Run."

She ran. Her bare knees slapped against stalks and fat flowers that might have been pink or white, she stumbled over clumps of dirt, knocking an elbow into Kitt's side.

"Stop, stop!" he said yanking her coat.

She was slightly ahead of him and then she was suddenly beneath him, in the dirt, her cheek pressed into tyre tracks and old tulip stalks.

"Sorry," he said in her ear. "There's another tractor coming this way, but don't worry, it doesn't have the blade attachments. It does, however, have headlights that would have shone on us if I hadn't tackled you. Are you okay?"

She spat out dust. "I'm grand."

The tractor rattled and hummed past the end of the row, a few metres away. When it had reached a distance he thought was reasonable, Kitt got to his feet and helped her up. "This is obviously a working farm. We'll head for the windmill, past those sheds, and stay in the shadows along the buildings."

"And then what?" She dusted off.

"Why do you always think I have a plan? You asked me to teach you and I've tried to teach you that this is always about improvisation. My, how I have failed."

"Yes, yes, you're a terrible spy *and* a terrible teacher. Whatever will you do when you get back to The Consortium?"

"Did I not just say this work is always about improvisation? Stay close and learn, Mae." He took her hand again, hurrying through the tulips, an eye on the tractor, the barns and sheds, the windmill, and the glow behind it, the sleepy rising sun. "There's something that hasn't been sitting well with me, something I neglected to mention."

"I know. *Run*. Turn tail and run my arse off. To where, I don't know, but I'll feckin' run if the need arises."

"Mm," he said, reaching into a pocket. "You have a point. If you have to run, run to the car." He handed her the key fob for the Aston Martin. "Get in and drive. Drive your arse off, Mae.

"And leave you behind."

"Yes."

"Right. Should I know how to unlock the weapons case in the glovebox?"

"Not at all. A weapon is safer in the glovebox than it is in your hand for someone to take from you and shoot you with. I cannot abide the thought of you being shot. Again." He glanced at her shoulder. "Damn. The thought of you being shot again is far worse than the nonsense that was playing on my mind before."

"What was bothering you before?"

"How I never mentioned that Matt Helm's wife divorced him."

With a sudden laugh, she stopped walking for a step. "Jaysus," she snorted. "Divorce. Have some faith in me. I know what you are. I know what you do, and I am aware, as entirely preposterous as it is to say out loud, you believe what you do, the contribution you make, much like firefighters and police, makes a difference, and we need people like you to save us at certain times, in emergencies, from threats we may not even be aware exist. It's assumed people who do the work you do must come from broken homes or they are orphans, psychopaths, or have some sort of death wish. But this isn't something you merely choose to do, it is something you *have* to do. Divorce," she snorted. "I *know* the only way you are going to leave me is when you die."

"Goodness me, you said that with a straight face. You *still* think I'm going to die?

"We are all going to die."

"But not today. Not tomorrow. Not the day after tomorrow or next week or the week after that or the month after that or the year after that."

She gave him a squint. "I think *your* safety is off."

The smell met them before they reached the first shed, a green-painted steel structure. Mae pinched her nose and breathed through her mouth. The shed appeared tidy on the outside, the paint fresh and neat, but the tidy appearance did nothing to disguise the rank odour of human waste or that the left side was an open, outdoor shower that offered no privacy. Facing the shower were two old motorhomes that had been set onto blocks. They stood across from each other, dark, mottled shade-cloth stretched between them, a plastic table and ancient garden chairs in the middle. About the size of a shipping container, the old vehicles once meant for touring holidays had been modified in a number of ways beyond having the wheels removed. The driver and passenger doors had been welded shut, the tall side doors had padlocks.

Kitt drew Mae away from the stink and moved along the exterior of the closest motorhome. Light inside shone from two, small windows that hadn't been papered over. There were bars welded on the outside of both. Kitt peeked in one side of the window, certain of what he would find. He counted twelve men, African, Middle-Eastern, Asian, Caucasian, crammed inside. "Have a look," he said quietly. "What do you see?"

Mae stood on her toes and peered inside. "Dirty men in dirty clothes."

"What do you notice about the dirty clothes?"

She had another peek. "They look like uniforms, the grey sort with the orange trim we saw in the back room of Erotica."

"If you have to run, don't touch the goddamned weapon in the glovebox, Mae."

She looked at the tractor heading away, at a small lorry travelling on the winding drive where the gate stood, at the human forms that had begun to appear in the pale dawn sun. Workers began emerging from two smaller sheds opposite the windmill, heading into the tulip fields. They were all dressed in grey uniforms with orange collars. "You know you've never perfected being able to see the future," she said.

"And neither have you. I'm quite certain your brother has lost his faith, that's what he struggles with, it's part of his PTSD, but I'm very surprised to see that you've lost your faith as well, especially your faith in me."

"Perhaps God, Jesus, Mother Mary and I aren't seein' eye to eye on a few things, but I have faith in you. I still believe that you're a terrible spy."

"Mock, mock, mock."

"You're not as bad a spy as Mr Weed."

"That's the loveliest thing you've ever said to me." He smiled. "Come on." Quickly, still in shadows, he led her toward the big windmill. Hand in hand, they walked close to the old brick building, the white-painted sails spinning in a slow circle, as the pair of them moved around the edge of the old red-roofed building. They came to the front, outdoor lights sparkled on the canal that irrigated the fields behind them. A little footbridge crossed over the water to a smaller field of tulips that stood between the chateau and the road that stretched from the glowing greenhouse sprawling out on the right, winding back to the gates. To the left, half-hidden by the windmill, by lovely purple lilac bushes, flowering trees and tall cypress pines, stood another motorhome and a shipping container with an open door.

He knew the container housed the amenities block, but, automatically, Kitt glanced at his watch and waited for his world to shift to last November, when he'd nearly died shut up in a stifling shipping container. He waited to hear his former colleague Bill Dalton to ask 'What time is it?' Kitt waited to feel a heavy sheen of near-equatorial sweat, waited to hear the scream of a woman, waited to see the young man on work experience fall dead without making a sound, but the phantom voice of a dead man asking the time didn't eventuate.

This was not Singapore, he was not inside a stifling shipping container filled with counterfeit merchandise, stolen antiquities, rank, dead bodies, or traitorous co-workers who had tried to have him killed.

Instead of letting not so distant horrors envelop him, he thought about his home, his dog, his wife, his new life, and took a long, deep breath before he looked across to the windmill, at the enormous, glowing greenhouse, at the chateau in the distance and back to the last motorhome and container that he guessed had once served as housing for itinerant farmhands. While one might argue the motorhomes were reasonable accommodation for travelling, seasonal workers, the padlocks stated otherwise, and like the container that had very nearly been his end, Kitt had no doubt the men in the cramped, brutal conditions faced a hopeless living hell of slave labour.

"Kitt," Mae said sharply, tugging his hand, jerking her chin to a flare of flame lighting a cigarette.

An approaching voice chattered in Italian, a man grumbling to himself, "Non me ne frega un cazzo! Non me ne frega un cazzo. Porco miseria!"

Kitt hurried her into the cover of lilac bushes at the rear of the motorhome. He pulled her into the lilacs, took a long, slow breath that tickled her neck when he exhaled.

He watched over her back, peering through bunches of sweet-smelling lilacs, as a pot-bellied man with a clipboard arrived to unlock the motorhome, cigarette hanging from his bottom lip, a chrome whistle swinging over his man-boobs. Padlock in hand, a cloud of smoke puffing from his mouth, he stood aside and thirteen men shuffled out of their lodging into the grey-blue and pink dawn light. They began to make their way to the big greenhouse. The man with the clipboard blew out another cloud of smoke, scurried up two steps made of a cinderblock and a few loose bricks, and went inside the motorhome.

"Stay here," Kitt said at her ear and pushed her deeper into the lilacs.

Surrounded by fragrant blooms that did little to mask the stench of the shipping container latrine, Mae watched him walk to the motorhome, lift a loose brick, and stand at the top of the makeshift stairs, his jacket obscuring the brick at his side. Her mouth went dry.

"*Scusa. Sono mi perso. Dov´é Signor Bianco?*—Excuse me. I'm lost. Where is Mr Bianco?" Kitt said loudly, in Italian.

A high squeal of surprise and a short, "*Minchia!*" brought the man's potbelly into view, wraparound sunglasses perched on his head, clipboard under his arm. He had been outside Erotica, shepherding two black men in grey uniforms into the white van with vegetables on the side door. He had been in a photo Llewelyn had shown her yesterday. "*Che sei, che fai qui*—who are you, what are you doing here?" he said, his accent Sicilian.

"*Cerchi Bianco*—Looking for Bianco. *Dov´é lui*—where is he?"

"*La piccolo serra crocodrillo, a giardino del castello*—The little crocodile greenhouse in the chateau garden. *Che sei?*" Potbelly said again.

"*Come si va da qui alla serra del crocodrillo*—How do I get to the crocodile greenhouse?"

"*Attraversa la piccoo serra a le grande serra, la prima uschita a sinestra*—go through the little greenhouse and the big greenhouse, first exit on the left."

"*Da dov' é vengono quegli uomini?*—Where are those men from?" He jerked a thumb over his shoulder to the group heading toward a greenhouse.

"*Dal mio culo*—from my arse." With a laugh, he tossed away the cigarette. "*Buggiardu*—liar," he said, lifting the whistle to his lips.

The brick, hidden by the edge of Kitt's jacket, swung and smashed into the podgy man's jaw with a *thunk*. The motorhome shook as he fell backwards, legs dangling over the cinderblocks. Kitt dragged him back indoors.

Mae counted to fifteen and left the camouflage of the lilacs. Kitt exited onto the improvised steps and padlocked the door shut. He had the clipboard in one hand, a biro behind his ear, a pair of sunglasses resting on his head. "Is he dead?" she said.

"Do you care?"

"No." She squinted one eye. "Do you?"

"Not so much, no."

He glanced at the motorhome, at the stinking shipping container amenities block. "Shall we drop in at the greenhouse where the men were heading?"

"All right." She looked at him for a moment, the sun rising higher, the grey-blue and purple sliding to orange and pink. "You have the gun. Why didn't you shoot him?"

"Shooting him would have drawn attention, like his whistle. The brick worked just fine." He stuck out his elbow and she looped her arm through it. "Put your scarf over your hair."

She pulled the windmill-printed fabric from beneath the collar of her coat. "Do you want it to wipe the bit of blood from your cheek first?"

Kitt dabbed away the dark drops from his skin using the sleeve of his jacket.

She wrapped the cloth over her hair and secured the ends

around her throat. "What do we do once we get to the greenhouse?"

"Blend in long enough to get a look." He held up the clipboard. "All we need to do is look official. You can get far with a clipboard and a pen."

Abandoning stealth, following the same trail the group of men in dirty, orange-trimmed grey uniforms had, they went to the wide doorway of a greenhouse full of tulips. In seconds, without question, they wandered about freely, as Kitt said they would. He'd glance at the clipboard, flip through the papers on it, and nod now and again. The occasional worker looked up from feeding tulips with attached dirt and bulbs into a machine.

"A clipboard and a pen." Mae snorted. "No one's paid us any mind."

"One simply has to look as if one belongs. It works with a doctor's coat, a nametag on a lanyard, keys as well. Then, of course, there's the sorry reality of white man's privilege." Kitt watched blank-faced men place bunches of uniformly cut long-stemmed budding tulips onto a wooden-sided cart that was rolled into cold storage units at either side of the greenhouse.

"Improvising, faking it, is everything. Except," Mae crossed her arms to dampen the urge to shudder, "no one in here is faking anything. The men in here are working hard. Years ago, when I came to Amsterdam with Caspar, we went on a tour of a tulip farm, a friend of a friend of a friend owned it. Because of that tour, I know bulbs are harvested from the fields—that's what why the machines lop off the heads, for the bulbs. Tulips for flower shops are grown in greenhouses, like this one, not in the fields. This greenhouse is about the same size as the one I visited before. During the cut flower season, something like eighty to one hundred thousand tulip stems are cut *per day*. The tulip farm I went to had a machine like that one over there." She tipped her head in the direction of a conveyer running along the entire length of the glasshouse. "But that doesn't pick the flowers, it removes bulbs without damaging the stem or the flowers. The harvesting is done by hand. Workers pull the flowers with the bulbs attached, sort them into bunches, and feed them into the machine. They are all men in here. There are no women. Why is that?" She looked over the men, maybe twenty-five or thirty of them, and back to the open exit where Kitt stood, waiting for her. The sun had risen above the horizon, light streamed in from above and across the concrete floor. "Why are there no women?"

"I don't know." Kitt glanced at the clipboard, pretended to scribble something with the biro he'd tucked behind his ear, and exited the glassed-in flower processing warehouse where workers in dull grey uniforms tended to the rows and rows of tulips that had budded but not bloomed. Mae followed him out to the morning sunshine, across a laneway, where, halfway down, stood a lorry with its rear container opened. Men, different colours and ethnicities, climbed from between boxes in the container, hopping to the ground to look about dazed, two men in hardhats directing them to move.

Angry, sickened, Kitt pulled Mae into the massive greenhouse. For a while, neither one of them spoke. There was far too much to take in. The tulip greenhouse was average-sized by farm standards, while this greenhouse was gargantuan. Seeing it from the front had given no indication of the how vast the space was. Plants grew as far as the eye could see. Sunlight, supplemented by LED light, streamed in, shining on flora, on workers tending to vegetables. Indoor farming provided the optimal growing conditions, from sowing to harvesting, and men of all colours and ethnic backgrounds, men in grey uniforms harvested tomatoes from row after row after row of plants under a single roof.

Other vegetables and herbs had been cultivated, onions,

lettuce, and cannabis with its distinctive, serrated blade leaves. What was once farmed outdoors—or hydroponically—was now planted indoors, with the use of pesticide eliminated, disease kept to a minimum, no nitrates leached to the soil. The sowing and growing had become automated, harvesting done in climate-controlled comfort, at a height that necessitated no back-breaking bending or lifting. It was sustainable, space and waste saving, it increased agricultural yield, could stave off catastrophic famine. Yet, despite the climate control and a more comfortable height, gaunt, somnolent, workers moved about like automatons in dull grey, orange-trimmed uniforms, picking tomatoes from rows and rows and rows. Crops were still harvested by human hands.

And some human hands were cruel and greedy.

Mae stopped for a moment, right in front of small, healthy-looking plants that would be left to grow for a few more weeks. "Is this..."

"Yes, it is." Softly, Kitt tapped the clipboard against her shoulder. "Let's keep moving."

"It's legal here, isn't?" she said, falling into step beside him.

"Yes and no." He said quietly, handing her the clipboard as they passed an Asian man and a skinny, young Middle Eastern man clipping bunches of cherry tomatoes. "Coffeeshops selling cannabis is perfectly legal in the Netherlands, but merchants growing and producing the cannabis products for sale is not. Shop-keepers who attempt to grow their own cannabis and sell it are punished with high fines. Growers are still forced underground, which first, makes it rather difficult for authorities to monitor the quality of products that coffeeshops sell to consumers, and second, the growers who supply the products frequently have links to orga-nized crime. The Netherlands' record for organised crime is poor, it's always been a hub for illicit drug trade with an underground economy supported by cannabis. Organised crime funnels profits into their own networks, trafficking harder drugs. So, there is a push to have approved growers, a push to monitor the growth, a push to monitor and provide labels that accurately test the levels of THC in the cannabis and display it on packaging. The approved grower-merchant model is being tested in smaller cities, like Groningen—that's another location on the garden tour circuit— but legal producers are still fronts for organised criminal activity, like human trafficking and forced labour."

"The men in the back of the lorry, the, the men in the motorhomes."

"Yes."

Mae glanced at the clipboard. "That's why you do it, isn't it? For people like the men here. They have no voice, they're invisible, working right in front of us, providing the food we eat, the food we complain about being too expensive. Why don't they run away?" She looked up at Kitt.

"And go where?" he said. "These people have nothing. No home, no money, no passports, no support. So often, too often, when they go to the police, they're treated like criminals, viewed as illegal immigrants, incarcerated again and held for deportation. When the actual perpetrators are caught, they're rarely prosecuted, and even fewer are convicted."

She screwed her eyes shut, clenched her teeth, saying. "From stolen jewellery that's actually fake, a dead man in a sex shop, your employer dropping dead, men living locked in little motorhomes being forced to harvest lettuce tomatoes and marijuana, the men in the lorry, what in underfuck is this about?"

"At some point this will all come together and make sense."

Mae opened her eyes and handed over the clipboard. "Do you believe that?"

"Wholeheartedly."

"Liar."

"Yes." Kitt refrained from taking Mae's hand and hurrying her out of the great glasshouse. She yawned and rolled her head on her neck. Yesterday, yes, it had been *yesterday*, in the rooms behind the sex shop front, they'd stumbled on what could have been interpreted as living quarters for sexual slaves. He wasn't so sure forced prostitution was part of the human trafficking and forced labour ring they witnessed here. Either way, sexual exploitation or labour exploitation, it was modern slavery, and it was the fastest growing area of organised crime.

Wearily, the lack of sleep scratching, but not yet clawing at him, Kitt walked on, Mae beside him. She looked tired, but adrenaline kept her going. He was glad she'd made him breakfast. The food in his belly provided energy that slightly dulled the need for sleep. They progressed through the huge greenhouse, unnoticed, and when they finally reached the first side exit, they took it, moving onto a laneway where three delivery white vans and a lorry were being packed with lettuce from another section of the immense greenhouse, a bright logo of lettuce, tomatoes, and carrots on the side of each vehicle.

The narrow road between the two greenhouses ran all the way to the chateau. Silently, the greenhouses and windmill behind them on the right, they followed the gravel surface and soon skirted the edge of red-tipped yellow tulips bright and cheery in the morning sun, a tractor moving along a row, beheading the blooms.

Kitt flung the clipboard into a row of headless flowers. "I think can we say, without any doubt, that this isn't a merely a flower farm. It's hectares of large-scale produce production under one mammoth roof, the sort of thing Vlaming mentioned. He said the Netherlands are at the forefront of agricultural innovation, that may include cannabis edibles and nutraceuticals. This farm may be an approved grower, part of the country's experiment to monitor, test, and regulate cannabis, to move production above ground, so to speak, and out of the hands of criminals, but I doubt it. This *is* sustainable agriculture, the growing time is reduced, the plants get the nutrients they need, and food production is doubled with half the resources. It's year-round, high volume, high-quality produce farming that is run by big business, companies who, despite their crowing about how they're saving the planet, are using forced labour to cuts costs."

Mae glanced back to the goliath greenhouse and pretty wind-mill against the blue morning sky. It was so picturesque. "In Italy, there's been a surge of illegal agricultural workers. A part of it comes from the collapse of traditional family-run farms, the sort once predominant in Italy. Large industrial farms, like this one, are taking over from the old family farms. Migrants have often worked for very little on the big farms, but *in the olden days*, as Fiorella would say, the farmers fed them well, gave them a decent place to live. That's changed. Now it's all about cost—cost to the consumer, what the consumer will pay, what's cheap. Famers have to find a way to make a profit. Italians call it *caporalato*; it's organised crime taking advantage of desperate refugees, illegal migrants, whatever they happen to be called, it's illegal hiring and exploitation of farm workers, trapping them for little or no pay."

The pen he'd had behind his ear went sailing into the tulips next. "There's a surge of *caporalato* throughout Europe. I think it's what we've found here. Criminal gangs rent out migrants, and deduct services like transportation, accommodation, food and water from whatever meagre pay they receive. This gives farmers— and agricultural companies—an opportunity to avoid payroll taxes and avoid taking any responsibility for the hiring of illegal workers. It's modern-day slavery. We went through just one part of this farm. I counted nine motorhomes. I'm sure there are more. If twelve or thirteen men are in each motorhome that's nearly one hundred and twenty people existing in those cramped, unhygienic conditions. And on a farm this size there may be more men, more motorhomes or camps or lorries we didn't see. We need to find our hairy gorilla friend, Mr Bianco."

"The man you met back at the motorhome said we'd find him in the crocodile greenhouse in the chateau gardens."

"And that is where we are heading."

"Do you think we'll find any crocodiles?"

CHAPTER TWENTY-ONE

Chateau Sicilië stood at the far end of a sculpted, low maze and garden paths bursting with spring colour. A gravel pathway lined with the last of the spring daffodils, hyacinth, muscari, and fritillaria opened to a curving fresh-mown lawn and a small amphitheatre, a fountain of the water nymph Galatea in the centre. Statues of Proserpina, her mother Ceres, and the Four Seasons were interspersed amid topiaries and water features that ran along the paved walk that led to the rear terrace of the chateau. At the start of the path, opposite the maze, a tall yew hedge rose up high, its top perfectly manicured, an old black weathervane, a Trinacria—the gorgon-headed, three-legged symbol of Sicily— barely visible on the other side.

Instead of moving to the house, Kitt backtracked and followed the hedge until he found a slightly overgrown archway where a carved Medusa sat upon a pedestal. Behind the serpentine head, offset from centre, stood another not-so-overgrown archway cut into the hedge, a narrow chain across it. Kitt removed the chain and Mae went through an arch of thick greenery. The hedge, pink blooms of a saucer magnolia and the white blossoms of surrounding dogwood trees kept the greenhouse well-hidden, as it was meant to.

Unlike the gigantic greenhouse near the windmill, this glasshouse was a scaled-down version similar to the Three-Climate Greenhouse at The Hortus. Late Victorian, slightly Edwardian, the base of each of the three structures stone, the framework white aluminium set with glass. It was rather picturesque.

Kitt ignored the *Toegang verboden* sign with the red circle safety symbols, pulled the door open, and stepped into a little foyer where air blasted from vents above with a *wooooosh*. When the rushing gust ended, he opened another door and stepped into a very warm, very humid greenhouse lush with flora and a wet smell one usually came across at a zoo.

Mae pulled off the windmill scarf and shoved it in the coat's pocket alongside Tanja's mobile. She slid off the coat and draped it over an arm. To the right of the entrance stood a rack hung with small gardening secateurs, gloves, brushes, and a long handled microfibre duster for cleaning off plants, keeping cobwebs at bay, and encouraging photosynthesis. A gardening trolley stood beside a wide sink that was framed by old-style apothecary shop shelves holding large, labelled glass jars full of dried leaves. Some jars had little skulls and crossbones pictures on them. Beneath louvre vents and a large fan regulating the climate was a low table holding a box of surgical face masks and thick rubber gloves, the sort scientists wore when handling dangerous chemicals. Strings from surgical masks waved about in the fan's breeze.

For a few moments, they wandered around and Mae re-braided her hair. The glasshouse was arranged and displayed in the style of a Victorian conservatory on a grand estate garden, crossed with small areas that stuck to the usual layout of plants set in rows, some low to the ground, some on benches about a metre high. Green seedlings grew in shelving high along the front of the glass. A centre path made of brick and lined on either side with gravel that allowed for drainage ran between rows filled with pink rhododendron, blue hydrangea, tall, white narcissus, equally tall pink and purple bell blossoms of foxglove, as well as deep purple larkspur, bright red poinsettia, and pointy-edged mistletoe. A large red and white plastic bag labelled *Kippenmest Gedroogd* sat atop another stainless-steel garden trolley, which stood at the front of a cannabis plant and a trellis trussed with a spill of vivid purple clematis.

Kitt started forward. Mae tugged at his sleeve. "Vlaming mentioned edibles and nutraceuticals, didn't he?"

"Yes."

"Clearly this is the chateau Bianco and Tanja discussed, but do you remember Vlaming also mentioned there was a chateau on a garden tour he ran, one that closed to the public to run experimental greenhouses and interbreeding programs to produce hybrids? Do you think *this* is that chateau?"

"Yes, I think this is that chateau. And I see where you are going."

"That's good you do because I don't. I have no idea what kind of hybrids they think they're making because this looks like, and I am not joking, a poison garden, like the one at Alnwick, in Northumberland. Alnwick is outdoors." She moved to the right, inspecting the tall, red-centred amaryllis on the right, then went left to inspect violet-stalked rhubarb. "You say I read too much spy fiction. You say I confuse fact with fiction. Here's a fictional fact that's not fiction at all. There's a garden like this one in a Bond novel. Of course, that garden is stocked with nasty poison plants, venomous snakes, piranha, and a pond of bubbling lava—yes, *lava*—this garden just has the nasty poison plants. Don't touch *anything* in here, don't smell anything in here."

"Interesting."

"Interesting how?"

A muscle in Kitt's jaw pulsed, his smile sardonic. "Like Vincent Weed, I believe Llewelyn and Tanja Goedenacht were poisoned. I wouldn't be surprised if whatever it was that killed them came from this garden."

Mae exhaled, frustration colouring the sound. "Yes. Whatever it was, was in the chai, and Mr Weed was right. I learned a few things about common house and garden plants from Caspar. Whether or not I was interested, whether or not I wanted to know, I learned things because he talked about gardening and horticulture and his knowledge rubbed off. I know Narcissus," she pointed, "mistletoe, foxglove and clematis are all pretty garden plants that are deadly. I'm surprised there's no oleander—oh, wait it's over there, just about to flower," she gestured to a spot across a path. "Oleander will stop your heart."

"It's a cardiac glycoside, like foxglove."

"Do you think foxglove or oleander or lily of the valley was put into the chai?"

"I..." Kitt went still. The humid air suddenly arid, the unexpected dryness clearing away the fog of his weariness and fear and fury. He knew. He knew who, he knew *exactly who* had tainted Llewelyn's Christmas-scented tea with poison. But he didn't know why. "May I have my mobile?" he said. "I need to ring Bryce and we need to check if Mr Bianco is still here."

"I don't have your mobile."

He spat out a coarse word. "I left it on the console between the seats."

"I have Tanja's phone."

"This is why I love you."

"Shall I send Mr Bianco a message?"

"Yes. I think we ought to send Mr Bianco a message."

Mae shifted the coat on her arm, dug her glasses out of one

pocket and Tanja's phone out of the other. The mobile had been switched off. She rubbed her eyes before she slipped on the readers. "I'm tired. I'm so tired."

"So am I."

"What time did we leave yesterday? I think I've been awake for thirty hours. That's like a flight from Australia to London. What if we just leave all this here, go find a hotel and sleep for a few hours, then come back. I'll send Bianco a message that says, *'please join me for afternoon tea at the crocodile greenhouse.'*" She pressed the side switch to turn on the mobile, her thumbs hovering above the screen, and she chuckled, then her mouth sagged and her chuckle turned into a wheeze. Bianco. That name, it had been on a list. Bianco, Man, Torrisi, Russo, Valentine all names that had been on a Gallia Mafia family hit list. Torrisi was a brand of Italian coffee, Russo was a very common Sicilian name, Valentine was the name she shared with Caspar. Man was Li Man, a 'cleaner' for the Gallia Mafia family. Bianco was the Sicilian town Misterbianco.

Only maybe it wasn't.

She looked down at the mobile's screen powering up, then up at Kitt, "Bianco," she said. "We were wrong. Bianco is *Mister* Bianco, not *Misterbianco*. It was *never* Misterbianco."

"What?"

"Last year, with the thirty-seven million pounds in the secret trust account set up in Caspar's name, the money laundering, the Mafia, the list of names, the *hit list* I saw in your kitchen before I killed the man Vivi Gallia had sent to kill me, Bianco was a name on the list that the family's banker Ernst Largo had. You, Vitali with the Direzione Investigativa Antimafia—the DIA—and I thought Bianco was the town Misterbianco, because the cleaner Li Man had a villa there. We were wrong. The Bianco now is Mister Bianco then."

"That's ridiculous. And not ridiculous. What if you're wrong again?"

"But what if I'm right?"

"It could be a coincidence. Bianco is a common Italian name."

"I know I'm tired. I know you're tired, but I also know you don't believe in coincidence. Perhaps it's why the Italian asked you to step away." Fatigued and more than a little dazed, Mae yanked off her glasses and gazed about the toxic garden, eyes wandering over an exit sign suspended from the glass ceiling, over pink hydrangea, orange angel's trumpet, dark berried belladonna, and monkshood, also known as wolfsbane—every bloody part of wolfsbane could kill you.

Then another plant caught her attention. She moved across the gravel path to a single, very healthy green plant with heart-shaped leaves the size of a hand. It was displayed on a tall, square stand beneath a large glass bell cover with a hook on the top. A chain, running from the hook to a pulley above, was attached to a reel with a crank handle. The plant was bigger than the ones she had seen in The Hortus Three-Climate Greenhouse. She shoved her glasses into a pocket.

Kitt had followed her. He slid a hand about her waist. "I don't believe in coincidence," he said, tugging the phone from her grip, finding a string of messages from Bianco waiting. He ignored them and sent a message to Bryce: *Follow Mae's necklace.*

She exhaled. "It's all parasitic and poisonous. Everything, from last July to now, is nothing but a creeping, strangling plant with poisonous roots, leaves and flowers. The plant in front of us is a gympie-gympie, a stinging nettle from the rainforests of Australia. This one is quite large. In the Alnwick Poison Garden, the most dangerous plants are kept in cages. Some of the plants in here you don't have to worry about unless you eat them or get the sap on your skin, but this one... If you touch a leaf or even brush against it, tiny silica hairs break off and act like micro-hypodermic needles injecting a neurotoxin into your skin." She shook her head with more than a little disbelief.

"Did Caspar teach you this?" He pocketed Tanja's phone.

She looked at him and slipped away, taking his hand, heading back to where they had stood before. "No. Any reasonable, safety-conscious gardener ought to know about foxglove, mistletoe, and oleander, but that plant there is not a common garden variety. I saw gympie-gympie specimens inside a glass case at The Hortus. I read the little greenhouse information placard there, then read a bit more about it on the internet as I sat there listening to you and Tanja Goedenacht make suggestive comments about a wooden marital aid."

"I don't remember making any sort of suggestive comm—"

A loud *whooshing* came from the doorway at the far side of the greenhouse, air blasting from a system that regulated the climate, keeping moisture and temperature levels constant. There was movement between rows, the shape of a man passed in the shadowed hollows of foliage. Late twenties, he wore thick rubber gloves, white safety coveralls, and rubber boots. A mask hung beneath his neck, it swayed as he started wheeling the trolley that had been near the trellis with the purple clematis, the bag of *Kippenmest* sitting upright atop of the trolley, a yellow, cartoon chicken smiling from the red plastic. He saw them, stopped, and locked the trolley's wheels with a foot pedal. "*Kunje neit lezen? Deze broeikast is dicht voor 't publiek!*"

Kitt turned to Mae. "Did you get that? I don't speak Dutch."

She frowned. "You spoke it at the airport and the sex shop yesterday."

"Yes, I said, *please, thank you, good morning,* and *fuck off*—the essentials that get you far in any language."

"Perhaps you should have kept the clipboard."

"Yes." He swivelled about to the man, mouth curved into a broad smile as he gave a rousing Texas, "Howdy!"

"You really miss that feckin' cowboy hat, don't you?" Mae muttered.

The man rolled his eyes and huffed. "You're American. Okay. Fair enough. Deh sign on deh door, it says no trespassing—in Dutch. This *oranje*, greenhouse, is not open to deh public. You have come too far from deh big house. Chateau Sicilië does not do weddings or functions anymore. Turn around and go back. Now."

Mae put a hand to her heart and a Texas twang in her voice. "Sorry. We stopped to look at the gardens and saw the sign on the gate, the one that said the chateau was closed, but we let m'dog out to pee before we turned around, and he plum ran off. Have yew seen him?" Mae bit her lower lip for a second. "A small, skinny dog that runs very fast. I left my cell phone in the car, so we came in there to see if maybe there was a phone so I could check with my brother to see if Felix had come back to the gate. My brother is at the car."

"I said turn around and go back."

"Can yew help find m'dog?"

He half turned, smiling, and Mae saw him take something from his pocket. "I fed your dog to deh crocodile," he said. "Now, turn around and go back." With the jerk of his hand, a blade opened.

"Are you threatening my wife?"

"No." He looked Mae up and down. "Your wife is a little old, but we'll still use her, You, we have no use for, so I am threatening you."

When the boxcutter slashed through air, Kitt was ready. So was Mae. She whipped her coat in the man's face. Kitt stepped sideways and the man's momentum took him straight into the potting bench.

Before the man whirled and slashed again, Mae had snatched the red plastic bag with the smiling chicken. The razor's edge sank into the wrapping and split as she drove forward, five kilos bursting with a pungent stench, thrusting him backward, the plastic split-ting apart as he struck the stainless-steel edge of the potting bench.

And then Kitt was on him, and the man fell, a putrid mixture of cow manure and compost raining down on them both. The man lashed upwards, spitting, gagging.

Mae caught the look on her husband's face, which wasn't any look at all, and his cool dispassion stayed with her as she spun about and ran for the entrance, for the way they'd come in, and there came a sharp, abrupt scream, then a *whoosh* from the front door.

She twisted about and shot between rows of lethal garden plants, heading for the green exit sign she'd seen suspended from the ceiling, to another door somewhere in a poison garden. She hit a dead end of wolfsbane, backtracked, rounded a curve, and found herself back where Kitt still fought, but not the man she'd left him with. That man was on the ground, blood pooled under his head, shit all over him. This man was sinewy and hopping up and down like a lunatic kickboxer or mixed martial artist in rubber boots and white protective coveralls.

Stupidly, she hesitated, watching Kickboxer's knee shoot up like a piston and Kitt twisted as a kneecap slammed into his ribs instead of stomach. He sucked a painful breath through his teeth and jabbed out with a hard left, his fist meeting chin, the man's head snapping right, arms flapping. Kitt grabbed a fluttering, gloved wrist, jerked the arm behind the man's back, high between his shoulder blades, and in two steps, drove the man face-first into the garden trolley and held him there, glancing back at her, jaw set, mouth ruthless, his eyes a chilling, stony blue-grey.

Mae's stomach turned as she whirled and took off again, running, only to stop abruptly, skidding on wet gravel to stare, not at more irritating or toxic plants, or the brightly hued butterflies flitting past in a hothouse that was a scaled down version of the tropical green house at The Hortus, but at what sat in the centre of the tropical hothouse garden. The gravel path of green jungle rattan palms, bright red and green bromeliads, rubber trees, orchids, bamboo, and bougainvillea with fat spines that circled around a pond filled with water lilies—and a greenish-brown reptile.

The zoo scent strong here, the tip of a long, flattish snout showed just below the water line, ridged eyes watched her from the other side of a hip-high glass wall smeared with blood and chicken feathers. "Go on outta that!" she muttered, then gravel crunched behind her and she whirled, right fist smacking Kitt's blood-speckled shoulder.

"God damn it, Mae!" Kitt rolled his shoulder, pitched aside the scarlet-stained garden dibber he'd driven into the man's artery, and spat out a mouthful of bloody saliva, all his teeth still in place, the cut inside his cheek. "*Run* means bloody *run away*, not run further into the sodding greenhouse and stop!" He grabbed her hand and jerked her forward, stomping along the gravel pathway, through the poisoned rainforest, toward the exit she should have already used to escape.

"There's a crocodile." She thumbed behind them. "A *crocodile*, Kitt.'

"Alligator. That's an alligator."

"What's feckin' next, a box of spiders?"

The front entrance *wooshed* again. Kitt wanted to yank her off the gravel path, but everything off the path was potentially harmful or lethal. He peeked through foliage, back in the direction where two dead men lay. He drew the gun from the holster beneath his blood-dappled, chicken-shit-dusted jacket, removed the clip, cleared the chamber, pocketed the bullet, set the safety.

"Tanja!" a gruff voice called out, feet moving on gravel.

"Oh, goody. There's your box of spiders, Mae," Kitt whispered at her ear, pulling the windmill scarf from her coat pocket, handing the fabric to her.

"You stink," she whispered back, tying the cheap polyester about her fair hair.

"Take off your shoes, leave your coat, and play along, *Tanja*. I'm sorry if I'm rough." He looked at her, his breath suddenly catching. "Christ, I don't want to hurt, you, but I might."

Mae glanced at his weapon. "It's okay. It's okay. Just don't shoot me." She let her coat fall to the ground and toed off her Mary-Janes. "Bianco!" she shouted.

"*Tanja, unni sei?*" he said urgently, in Sicilian.

Kitt grasped her wrist, pulled her forward to his chest, kissed her gently, took a breath, wrapped an arm around her neck, and pressed the muzzle of his Beretta against her head, just below her ear.

Mae stumbled backwards over gravel, the little pebbles hurting bare feet. "*Ca sugnu!*" she said loudly, the sharp grit underfoot and gun at her head added a note of realism to her acting.

Kitt shoved Mae into the open part of the path, just behind where two men lay dead and the hairy-armed gorilla of a man stood looking down at them, one hand on his hip. Bianco was unarmed. Others who would be armed would soon arrive. Kitt adjusted his arm around Mae's neck. "You move and I'll shoot you," he said.

Bianco turned slightly, holding a rectangular yellow first-aid kit about the size of a loaf of sliced bread, a green marijuana leaf sticker covering over the red cross. He wore long rubber gloves, white coveralls, and knee-high rubber garden boots. "*Che cazzu fai?*"

With a grunt, Mae leaned into Kitt more. "*Che cazzu pensi chi facciu?*"

"Do you speak English?" Kitt said, irritated.

"*Parra sicilianu*?" Bianco said, matching his inflection, shaking his head, looking up from the bodies. "No. You don't speak Sicilian. What do you want, Mr Leslie Templar, Hedison's Auction House Superhero Investigator?

"I want you to stop wasting my time. Who are you?"

"I am Bianco," he said, pronouncing it *Biancu*.

"Are you the *cappu*? I want to speak to the *cappu*."

"*Cappu*! Oh, you *do* speak Sicilian!" He shook his darkly stubbled face. "I could be the boss, I could be the big boss or the little boss. It depends on how you look at it. What do you want, besides me to not waste your time?"

"I'll be honest. You've spooked me."

"What is *spook*?" Bianco frowned.

Kitt pushed the gun muzzle, moving Mae's head. "I'm sorry. You've made me a little nervous. A friend of mine died last night. He was poisoned, he drank poisoned tea, and now I find myself here, in this little greenhouse full of poison where two men wanted to kill me, just like they killed my colleague in London. Perhaps it wasn't these exact men who killed Jill Charteris, but I know what I'm up against. See? I'm spooked." He lifted the gun, waved it, and set it back beneath Mae's ear.

"*Jesu*," she gasped appropriately.

Kitt went on performing, "You've got me spooked. So, before you ask, let me tell you what I know. Vlaming has been secretly selling off his family's jewels and hiding money in an offshore account. You're blackmailing him because he's exposed you or made you vulnerable somehow. I think it has something to do with the men working in your jumbo greenhouse. You'd kill Vlaming, but you need him for some reason. I'm hoping you'll need me too because I know all kinds of people, people with money. If you think the work Ruby Bleuville did was lucrative and impressive, wait 'til you see what I can bring to the table."

"Ruby Bleuville was caught. She was very sloppy and made some people very unhappy."

"Which is why she's dead now." Kitt smiled, baring his bottom teeth. "Ruby wasn't working with the right people."

"Who are the right people—" The phone that bulged in Bianco's front pocket began to play AC/DC's *Dirty Deeds Done Dirt Cheap*. "*Scusa, scusa.* May I?" he said.

Kitt jerked his chin. "Make it quick."

Bianco tucked the first aid kit under an elbow and burrowed furry fingers into trousers that were a little too tight. "*Pronto?*" he said, mobile at his ear. "*Ca sugnu e serra... Si, lavuri in corsu...*

"Really?" Mae whispered. "You're having a monologue moment?"

"I need information," Kitt murmured. "I want you to get his phone."

"Take it, you have the gun."

"Did you not see me remove the bullets?" Kitt began walking, moving Mae backwards until they were a metre and a half's length from Bianco. "That's enough now," he said.

The man's eyes grew large in his dark face when the gun shifted from Mae to level with his chest. He ended the call.

"Toss the phone on the ground." Kitt said, tipping his head.

The mobile hit the gravel and so did Mae when Kitt let her go, the scarf slipping from her head to droop around her neck. She rose and picked sharp pebbles from her kneecaps.

"You are not Tanja!" Bianco's mouth hung open.

"No, I am not Tanja," she said flicking away a red-stained stone.

"Oh, ouch," Kitt said, looking at Mae, at the grazes on her knees and the scarlet trickle down the front of her legs. "I am sorry," he said. "I do hate the sight of your blood."

"You've had worse. I've had worse," she said.

"You are not Tanja," Bianco said again. Where is Tanja?"

305

Kitt tipped his head to one side. "Your little girlfriend is dead, poisoned, probably from something that came from this very greenhouse."

Bianco swore in Sicilian.

"That's not a very nice thing to say," Mae said.

"Was that," Kitt squinted one eye, "was something about my mother and the size of my cock?"

Bianco swore again and threw down the first aid box. It made a *thud* and he gestured, extending his index and little finger, making the sign of the cuckold as he stomped angry feet, kicking the kit in his tantrum.

Kitt had had enough. He took three steps and gave the man a solid clout, the Beretta making a wooden sounding *clunk* as it hit his skull. Bianco collapsed sideways in a heap.

"You know, the only time I have ever seen you use that thing is to hit someone with it. You have never fired it as intended," she said, hands on her hips.

Kitt bent and picked up the phone, tossing it to Mae. "Let's see to your knees, my love," he said, reached for the first aid kit, and opened it. The dried marijuana partially obscured the saline wash, antibacterial wipes, and bandages inside. He brushed away the cannabis the with the stubby little finger on his left hand, looking for tweezers, grey-green dusting his pared-down pinkie. The pain hit in less than the blink of an eye.

The box fell, spilling the contents across the ground and Kitt rose swearing, shaking his hand to get rid of a surging, super-heated electric sting. In another heartbeat, the pain intensified, his finger had turned bright red. He wiped the finger on his jacket and searing, stinging, electrified pain exploded, taking his breath away, the fiery detonation repeating and repeating and repeating.

Nose streaming, eyes coursing with tears, his mind ran through a list of nerve agents and blistering agents, for half a second, then the blistering heat and stinging power current deepened and hammered him with a surge of dizzy nausea. He caught Mae's horrified expression and she moved toward him, dropping Bianco's phone, her hand stretching out. *"Don't touch me!"* he shouted, *"Don't touch me!"*

In incomprehensible, boiling, caustic, electrocuting, insect-stinging agony, he staggered to the front entrance, gasping, tripping around two dead men. With one hand, he yanked off his belt, and looped it over his forearm, tightening it, idiotically thinking a tourniquet might slow the spread of the toxin and diminish the pain. It did not. Hunched over, he retched, staggered to his feet and reeled to the wide sink near the door, thumping on the faucet, shoving his boiling, caustic, electrocuting, insect-stinging hand beneath the flowing liquid that only made the boiling, caustic, electrocuting, insect stinging increase. Kitt screamed and screamed.

Desperate, panting, swearing, his nose running into a flood of tears, he pawed at the secateurs he saw hanging beside a microfibre duster, his left hand in a vat of acid, jolting with electric current, and unremitting excruciating bee, hornet and wasp stings. He held his wet, dripping hand on the edge of the sink. "Mae," he sobbed. "Mae..." He looked at the secateurs and back to her. *"Cut it off!"*

"Are you mad?"

"Take it off! Take it off!"

Wide-eyed, Mae grabbed the little garden cutters and set them into place. "Oh, God. Oh, Jaysus. Oh, Hamish." She squeezed the handles together, severing what remained of his already truncated left pinkie. It was like cutting through a lilac branch.

Kitt's relief was instant, a rushing moment of short-lived euphoria trounced by shock a split-second later. He tried to breathe through the churning howl in his ears, tried to blink away vision that warped and began swimming. He looked at a distorted, tunnelling image of Mae, the front of her salmon pink dress spotted with crimson. "I'm sorry," he said in a faraway voice. And fainted.

Dumbly, blankly unmoving, Mae stared at Kitt, blood pooling under his hand, spreading across and soaking into gravel. Each breath she took offered a choice: panic or act. Panic or act. Panic or act. Vacant of any sensation, Mae dropped to her knees and felt for a pulse. His heartbeat was strong, steady. She looked about for something to wrap about his hand to stop the bleeding, scanning the rubber gloves, the surgical masks, the other gardening tools, the rack of jars with their dried leaves. She yanked the windmill scarf from her neck and wrapped it around Kitt's hand to try to staunch the flow of blood. Then she got to her feet.

And ran.

Barefoot, Mae shoved through the door, into the *wooshing* foyer and rushed outside, trying to remember the route that would take her to the huge greenhouse, the windmill, the field of beheaded tulips, and back to the car. She kicked through the little chain across the entrance, and darted though the arched hedge of toxic yew. She ran along a path opposite the maze, and past statues of Proserpina, her mother Ceres, and the Four Seasons, to a gravel pathway lined with the last of the spring daffodils, hyacinth, muscari, and fritillaria. She rounded the curving, fresh-mown lawn and small amphitheatre, a fountain of the water nymph Galatea in the centre and stopped dead at the passenger side of a black Mercedes van with tinted windows. She jerked open the door. *"Help me! Help me!"*

A man with a shiny bald head and heavy black brows peered up at her, Felix on his lap. Then the very handsome man in the driver's seat leaned over and smiled, his heavy, vanilla-based cologne wafted out, assailing her nostrils. It was a perfume she had smelled before when she'd been drugged and held upright in a hot car travelling on a winding road to the cemetery in Linguaglossa, where her husband Caspar had been buried.

"*Buongiorno, Signora Valentine,*" Giacomo Negroni said.

The side door slid open and Mae stumbled backwards, tripping over daffodils, falling on her arse.

CHAPTER TWENTY-TWO

M ae stared at the black van, stunned, shaking, wanting to be sick. Then Felix was on her lap licking her ear, her face, her neck. Her arms went around the dog and she held him close as Bryce and a man with a crooked nose pulled her to her feet as an ambulance rolled up behind the van, tyres noisy on gravel.

"Hey," Bryce said holding her elbow, "Hey, look at me. Look at me. Where's Kitty? Where's Kitty, Mae?"

"H-he's in a greenhouse on the other side of the hedge, and he's hurt. The place is full of poisonous things, the greenhouse is full poison. He-he..." Mae cut her eyes to the other man holding her up. His name was Vitali. Last July, he had worked undercover for the Italian government as part of an operation to infiltrate the Gallia Family. He'd split her lip open and Kitt had broken his nose. "Timothy? What...is..." Her gaze shot to the other man, the perfumed handsome one, and she watched Giacomo Negroni jerk his head at a tall, bald man and two paramedics who were pulling on hazard gear before they headed off in the direction she'd indicated. They already knew about the toxic little greenhouse.

"This is *not* what you think, Mae," Bryce said.

"How would you know what I think, Timothy? This man hit me," she scowled at Vitali, "and that other man kidnapped me last year. He sat with me in the back of a stinking hot car when I was drugged. We rode to a cemetery where I thought I was going to be entombed alive. He wore a horrid cologne to mask the scent of his sweat."

Bryce's hand went to her shoulder, his green eyes peering down at her as the dog licked him. "You heard Kitt say the Italians asked us to step away from the event. This is why. The DIA and AISE have been carrying out investigations. Negroni has been working undercover, just like Vitali was last year with Vivi Gallia, Ernst Largo, and Aurelio Martini in Sicily."

Vitali nodded. "This is true." His grip on her slid away.

"Hey!" Negroni called out and three heads turned in his direction.

Bryce blew out a breath. "It's okay. It's okay," he said. "There's Kitty now, walking on his own two feet." He let out another huff of relief. "You two have me wanting to change my pants, Mae." He let her go.

Mae turned for Kitt as well taking a single step before Vitali grabbed her elbow. She looked down at his hand and glowered at him, the dog squirming in her arms. "I thought by now you'd have had your nose fixed," she said, trying to jerk away as he held fast.

"I see you have not forgiven me for striking you last summer," he said. "Please know, I am not proud of what I did to you, and it pains me—" Suddenly Vitali was on his arse, in the daffodils, blood spilling from his lips. He swore in Italian and spat out a tooth.

"I did warn you last year, Vitali." Kitt said, gravelly-voiced, stone-faced, a bloodied, black-dotted, once-white scarf wrapped about his hand. He turned to Mae and smiled. "You ran," he said. "I'm so proud of you. I told you I'd be right behind you."

MAE SAT inside the ambulance beside Kitt. He lay on a little bed, the rear door open, as a paramedic with light brown hair and half-moon reading glasses checked the level of the painkiller in the hypodermic.

Kitt reached for Mae's hand and squeezed it as he received his injection. The blood of his injury rinsed away, his knuckles were red and bruised from the fight he'd had with the men in the Croc-odile—*Alligator*—greenhouse, and from the thump he'd given Vitali ten minutes ago.

The battle with the men in the greenhouse didn't irritate her the way the belting of Vitali did. She knew it was incongruous, but it was the closest, most normal thing she could latch onto, and, Jaysus, that wallop really pissed her off. "You seem to be working under the mistaken impression I am a dainty little thing that must be wrapped in cotton wool and held close to your chest."

"I like holding you close to my chest."

"Do you think that's the first time I've ever been menaced or harassed by a man? Jaysus, what woman by the age of fifty hasn't been pursued, teased, bullied, or hassled half a dozen times in her life?"

The paramedic glanced at her, then at Kitt again. "Perhaps this is not a time for a domestic argument," she said, in a motherly tone.

Kitt ignored her.

So did Mae. She squeezed his hand harder. "I am quite capable of taking care of myself, Hamish."

"Yes, I know you are capable," he said, her fingernails digging into the back of sore knuckles. "But my mind goes to the evening you were mugged on Kensington Park Road, the morning when Sal and the banker Largo tried to murder you in my kitchen, the after-noon when the Italian DIA drugged you and kidnapped you and took you to a different location. Vitali and Negroni *are* the bloody DIA. There's also the fun night this past New Year's day, when the fancy-pants hitman tried to shoot you, as well as the following morning with the El Salvadoran football fan, the one who tried to crush your larynx, not to mention the petite *woman* who put a bullet through your shoulder, but those instances aside, yes, I know how adept you are taking care of yourself, especially with cleaning products, I know you have always been able to take care of yourself. But you have *not* been trained for this line of work."

The paramedic rolled off her rubber gloves and shoved them in a yellow bin. "I'll leave you two to rest."

"I do not need *training* to tell Vitali to go to hell. I know how to hit a man in the balls. I did not need you to rescue me, you sodding bully!"

"*Bully*? He had his hands on you, Mae."

"He had helped me stand."

"He touched you. I am a man of my word. I once told him if he ever touched you again, he would lose teeth. I'm a bit miffed I only knocked out one."

"That's your standard threat to men who dare lay a hand on me. 'You will lose teeth.' Jaysus."

Bryce poked his head in the open door. "How are we in here? Painkiller kick in yet?"

Mae burst into tears.

DRUGS WERE A WONDERFUL INVENTION. Kitt was in no pain. With the dog between them, he sat with Mae, half inside the van, on the open edge of the sliding door, listening, his left hand bandaged and in a short sling across his chest.

"Since last year," Vitali said, cold pack on his jaw, "we have been investigating Aurelio Martini for collusion with UNFed Credit Union clients to conceal undeclared 'black' accounts for heirs to some of Europe's biggest fortunes. I had been assigned to Martini, undercover for some time. I acted as bodyguard and driver. Several times during my investigation, I travelled to London with Martini and a woman named Vivienne Gallia. Do you remember Vivi Gallia, Mae?"

"Yes," she said wearily, and yawned.

Vitali went on. "Yes, yes. You would." He looked over at Negroni. "I am certain you remember Giacomo from the day in the orchard and the ride to the cemetery in Linguaglossa?"

Mae snorted, absently stroking Felix, the dog's head on her lap. "How could I forget a man who smells like a giant vanilla-patchouli scented candle people burn in bathrooms to cover the stink of shit?"

Negroni blinked. "That is not very nice. You still have a very cruel tongue."

"She is right, Negroni." Vitali jut his chin forward and nodded, "You wear too much *porfumo. Fa feddo.*" He laughed. "*Allora.* While I had been assigned to Martini, pretty Negroni had an assignment that put him with pretty women."

Negroni dropped his cigarette and crushed it under his foot, "I was engaged undercover to investigate the Orion Foundation, a charitable organisation for refugees and victims of human trafficking." He shoved his hands in his pockets and walked back and forth as he spoke. "Human trafficking is a high-profit low-risk crime. Forced labour is more frequent in Africa and the Middle East, South and East Asia, and the Pacific. Trafficked women and girls frequently wind up in the sex trade while men are forced into construction work or farming. Edibles, nutraceuticals, greenhouse farming are a burgeoning field."

"That's very punny," Mae snorted.

"It's very what?" Negroni's brow rumpled with puzzlement.

"Go on," Kitt said. Mae was punchy, verging on exhausted silliness. The faster they got through this the better.

Negroni continued. "Agricultural workers are often subcontracted, as are many working in hospitality—hotel housekeeping staff and in restaurants. There are drug trafficking groups, such as the Enrico Cartel, the Yeoh Triad, and Mafia families, like the Gallia Family, who have combined or switched their business practices and cargo from drugs to human beings. Trafficking for sexual exploitation is the most prevalent. Trafficking for forced labour is rising. We believe, to cut costs, these groups have all combined their business activities and formed a syndicate."

"They're working together?" Kitt said.

"*Si,*" Vitali adjusted the cold pack against his skin. "Quite often, even if they are caught, few traffickers are convicted. The work the victims do is often legal—like farm work and hotel housekeeping. There are no standards for screening processes. Poverty, discrimination against women, government corruption, the reach of transnational organised crime, trafficking victims are threatened by immigration officials, arrested and placed into detention centres, or deported; the system works against victims. Victims are seldom brought into the justice process as witnesses, and—forgive me for the statistic—there is a conviction rate that barely surpasses one point five out of one-hundred thousand. It is not a surprise that victims are reluctant to come forward."

"We have the information," Negroni said, "we have witnesses, but we have not been able to convince anyone to come forward to testify."

Kitt got to his feet and resettled his hand in the sling. "What is the connection to Jan Vlaming and his stolen family jewellery? Is Vlaming trafficking human beings or is he simply being blackmailed by the Gallia Family?"

Vitali shook his head. "We do not know who stole the jewellery from the Luxembourg freeport and tried to sell it to Hedison's, that is still your case. You believe it is blackmail, and perhaps it is, but we believe the connection to Vlaming and human trafficking is through his deceased uncle, Peter Dankwaerts. Peter was once on the board of the UN Credit Union. Vlaming's Aunt Polly, once a war refugee, is the chair of The Orion Foundation, the charitable organisation for refugees. This only matters because Aurelio Martini once served on the board of the UNCU, alongside Peter Dankwaerts. They remained friends until Peter died early last year, of natural causes. He was an old man, ninety-two. If you remember, Martini's best friend was Pippino Torrisi, a well-known Sicilian immigration lawyer and advocate for refugee rights—his name was on that hit list alongside yours last July, Mrs Valentine."

Hands still in his pockets, Negroni stopped pacing. "We have discovered several things about Vivi Gallia and Martini and how they exploited many, many people using the Orion Foundation as cover. They operated under the façade of that charity, preyed upon desperate people who believed the charity would assist them. Of course, it did not."

Vitali shifted the cold pack and gingerly prodded his jaw. "Their exploits included several names you will both know; Ernst Largo, Milton Foley, Walter Molony, and Ruby Bleuville."

"Ruby Bleuville is dead," Mae said.

"Yes, we heard." Negroni shook his head. "I befriended Ruby, got close to her. I observed her work, watched her plan, research, and set up a mark, like Julius Taittinger and Jan Vlaming. I watched how operations went with the movement of goods and people in shipping containers, on boats, in trucks, using the routes established by the Yeoh Triad and Enrico Cartel. We believe the Triad or the Cartel are both responsible for the deaths of Bleuville and Foley. They are killing anyone and everyone who was connected to their operation, no matter how small, to ensure no further information is revealed about their operations, and the Gallia Family has been obliging. Things changed yesterday."

Kitt turned to look at Mae, her head resting against the door-frame, fingers moving over the dog. She looked like she could sleep for fifteen years. "Who decided they wanted out?"

A fat grin bloomed under Vitali's crooked nose. "The head of the Gallia Family has arranged a meeting this morning."

"I'm knackered, but," Mae pulled herself to her feet, the dog hopping out of the van beside her, "are you saying Vivi Gallia was *not* the head of the Gallia Family?"

"No." Negroni said. "We think now she was number two or number three. Now Bianco is number two or number three. We will know more when we analyse the data on his phone."

Mae lifted Felix into her arms and held him close, for comfort, for security, for the thing Kitt couldn't give her with these men watching. "Who *is* the head of the Gallia family?"

Negroni pulled his hands from his pockets. "*Ascoulta*, listen. My government asked that your government step away from this investigation because we were concerned the Gallia Family would get, as Americans say, spooked, and not come in. We have used you as bait, again, Mrs Valentine, to draw out the head of the Gallia Family. The DIA asked your government to include you, to draw the fire, so to speak. We don't know quite yet who the head is, but they have asked to see you, Mrs Valentine. They will be at the Dankwaerts Estate garden party with Jan Vlaming and his Aunt Polly."

TEN MINUTES LATER, the van was on its way to the Dankwaerts Estate. Mae sat beside Negroni, the dog between them. The man's vanilla-patchouli scented cologne may have been heavy, he may have worn too much, but at least this time the pungency of his sweaty summer body odour wasn't part of the bouquet. Kitt lay across the rear seat, asleep. How she envied him. It was such a godless thing to be exhausted and utterly unable to sleep. Any time she shut her eyes she saw the unimaginable, and it wasn't the face of a dead woman crushed between cars. She saw Caspar, his bearded face, his brown eyes, and wondered, in spite of all that had transpired, how he would look after sixteen years. That in itself was awful, but worse was the idea rolling like a marble in her head.

She stared over the seat at Kitt. He was shattered.

He opened his eyes. "Do you want to come back here with me?" he said.

"I think you need the space."

He smiled very softly. "Shut your eyes."

"I don't like what I see when I do."

"You still see Jill Charteris?"

"Yes," she lied. "Who do you think killed her, who do you think killed Llewelyn and Tanja?"

"Our recent investigations led to significant financial losses for the Yeoh Triad and Enrico Cartel. I am certain that The Consortium's floor manager, a woman named Hilary, was compromised, extorted into giving Llewelyn tainted tea. I was in the room when she handed him the packet of chai. I believe the Yeoh Triad or the Enrico Cartel are responsible for the deaths of Jill Charteris, my trainee Eva Eaton, Llewelyn, his assistant Morland, and quite possibly Hilary, as she resigned and no one seems to know where she is. The Cartel and Triad are seeking payback for exposing their trafficking and smuggling operations. And they've asked the Gallia Family for their assistance to get it."

"So, it's revenge?"

"That most human need."

"Yes."

"Kitt, do you think..." she shuddered and shut her eyes for a moment, which only made things worse, so she opened them again.

"Do I think what, my love?" Kitt said, his cool, blue-grey eyes filled with warmth and kindness, and love.

Mae shuddered and whimpered and the dog sat up to nuzzle her neck, which only made her whimper more.

Kitt sat up. "Tell me."

Her eyes sparkled with ballooning tears. "Do you think Caspar is the head of the Gallia family?"

CHAPTER TWENTY-THREE

Split into three sections, the Dankwaerts Gardens surrounded the brick country house, a scaled down version of Het Loo Palace built by King William III and his English wife Mary Stuart. Classic formal English, French, and Japanese gardens were blended with the casual asymmetry of naturally shaped plants and beds mimicking nature. Somewhere on the grounds, amid the party guests and roaming wait staff, they would find the little windmill, the host of the garden party, Polly Dankwaerts, and the head of the Gallia Family.

She stopped him near a massive, hot-pink azalea. "What if he's here? What do I do? What do we do?" she said, voice high and tight.

"Don't do that," he said. "Breathe, Mae."

"*I am feckin' breathing!*" she said through her teeth.

"Look at me." He took her hand and laid it flat on his chest, over his heart. "Whatever we find, whomever we find, this, here," he put his hand atop hers. "This bears all, believes all, hopes all, endures all."

Her expression transformed from wide-eyed to an out of breath, head-shaking, you-are-full-of-shite squint. "You think quoting St Paul will calm me?"

"Is it working?"

"Possibly. I find I want to poke you in the eye less."

"Good. So, listen. My life, the one I had before you, without love, made me something of a resounding gong or a clanging cymbal."

Mae waggled her index finger. "My hole. A clashing knife or a roaring gunshot is probably a better description of your Old Testament existence."

His mouth quirked. "The Old Testament is a better, more exciting read, I'll give you that, but the New Testament does have its moments. Why do you look surprised to know I've read the Bible?"

"Perhaps it's how I've witnessed your former Sodom and Gomorrah Old Testament lifestyle."

"Point taken. But just so you know, I've read the Quran, the Torah, the Bible, the Sutras, the Vedas, the Book of Mormon. There isn't always much to do when travelling or much to read, so one makes do with what one finds. I prefer romance novels. And why are you so bloody cynical?"

"Guess."

"If I guess correctly, will you poke me in the eye?"

"Is that a chance you're willing to take?"

He squeezed her hand. "It is. Here's what I think. When you spend nearly twenty years loving someone who isn't there, and then find out things about that person, that the man wasn't who you thought he was, that you aren't who you thought you were, and you realise what you loved, what you thought you had, what you thought you were, was a fantasy, you become a bit cynical and unsentimental. Is that about right?"

"One might think that a man who does what you do would be

the malcontent misanthrope, but I'm the jaded cynic, which isn't very fair to you." She said, holding his gaze. "It's important you articulate what and how you feel. I know it's what you need. Expressing emotion, telling me how you feel about me, reminding me, is as much for yourself as it is for me, despite how I mock you for it. Regardless of my unromantic cynicism, I love you. Very much. It's not impassioned, flowery, or poetic, but it's simple. To the point."

"It's perfectly distilled."

"Is that enough for you, Hamish, those three little words?"

"Yes."

"I'll take care to tell you more often."

"Thank you."

Mae placed her other hand on his cheek and whispered. "I like what you say, your declarations, your lovely, impassioned, flowery, poetic, biblical words. Go on making your declarations."

"Go on mocking me for it," Kitt whispered back. He leaned forward, pressing into her, their hands trapped on his chest, and he kissed her, long and slow and deep, not giving a damn that it hurt his left hand, not giving a damn that the kiss mashed his teeth against the raw cut inside his mouth, not giving a damn about who was watching or who saw them through the pink blooms. He was tired of living in the shadow, tired of hiding a basic human need, his human need that was far more basic than revenge.

Mae relaxed into him for a moment, her arm slipping beneath his jacket and around him. When he lifted his head, she drew her hand away from his and adjusted his sling. "You still smell of chicken shit," she said, laughing, "but it's a better scent than Negroni's cologne."

Kitt laughed too and began look about the garden at party guests.

They wandered past small groups of smartly dressed people

who stood beside hazy swathes of tall grasses and vivid spring blooms, long borders of herbs flanked by pathways and background plants with soft colours and no formal shape. A few people did a double-take at their dusty and blood-dappled and bandaged state, and at the dark-suited men and police following them. They crossed through a dividing hedge, leaving the loose informal garden design, moving into a more structured garden, where the tulip-surrounded windmill stood beside a narrow canal dotted with pink and white and purple hyacinth. The windmill, far smaller than the one they had seen this morning, had a small paved patio at the front.

Kitt snagged a glass of water from a passing server who swallowed nervously and tottered off. He downed the water and glanced at Mae. "There's Vlaming," she said, watching the man come out of the white framed door beneath the white windmill blades.

Vlaming walked toward them and stopped in front of Kitt. "What have I done, Leslie?" he said.

"You robbed your own family. And my name is Hamish Kitt."

Vlaming nodded, his blue eyes bright with tears. "I got people killed, Hamish. I can give back deh money, but not deh lives. My aunt can forgive deh money, but not deh lives." He turned to the police and nodded. Then he looked back to the windmill.

Mae followed his line of sight. "Oh, my sweet mother," she said.

Glass in hand, Kitt watched three people come out of the little windmill house.

Mae's eyes darted from Chanel-dressed nonagenarian Polly Dankwaerts taking a seat at a wooden garden table, to Giacomo Negroni who held a chair for the head of the Gallia Family, a woman who had learned English from American GIs during WWII, and liked to cheat at Monopoly.

Nearly ninety, Fiorella Gullo wore a smart, charcoal grey pencil skirt, a lavender twinset with a string of black pearls, and cap-toed black brogues with a heel.

She waved at them.

"THEY SAID we could see her now." When she didn't respond, Kitt put his hand on Mae's shoulder, giving it a small shake to rouse her from her fatigue and vacant staring.

She looked up at him from the padded garden chair, bright, late morning sunlight spilling over her, the air sweet with the smell of lavender at the edge of the windmill. "I think," she said climbing to her feet, "that this is called lucid dreaming. It all feels so real and yet I am fast asleep."

"You are awake, Mae."

"Then I'm going to pretend I'm not, the way you wanted to pretend I wasn't with you in Amsterdam yesterday. Was that yesterday? I'm going to keep on faking it, except I don't have the energy. How are you still standing?"

"Practice. Give me your hand."

She put her hand in his. Kitt nodded at the Dutch police officer at the door of the windmill house. She stood aside and let them pass.

"*Beddita!* I wonder if you come, if I see you. So, you know, huh?" The small woman got out of her chair, her arms encircling Mae, squeezing her tightly.

Still numbed by the shock, Mae automatically let go of Kitt's hand and hugged Fiorella back.

The slight woman turned to Kitt, grabbing his face and covering it with kisses.

Kitt withstood the onslaught of affection. "They say you're the head of the Gallia Family."

Fiorella let him go and glanced at the armed police standing outside the door. She returned to her seat at the table in a small kitchen inside the little windmill house. "Not anymore. Some people screw me, try to squeeze me out. Now I squeeze back. This business had gone to shit. Family don't matter no more. Today, I am a *snitch*. Bianco can kiss my ass."

"He calls you *Picciridda*," Kitt said taking a seat across from her.

"Little girl. The man has no respect for anything but money, an' that is the problem. What you do to your hand, Soldier?"

"Mae cut off my finger with a pair of gardening shears."

"You so funny, Major." Fiorella jerked her chin and looked at Mae. "You still love older women, huh?"

"I do, yes."

Mae moved to the table and held on to the back of the chair beside Kitt, the numbness turning stodgy, like old mashed potatoes, the thickness creeping into her chest. She looked at Kitt. He wasn't so much maddeningly detached as he was exhausted and doped, although nothing about how he moved or spoke indicated that he was shattered and chemically affected. "Why?" she said simply, looking at a friend who had been like a mother to her.

"Why not," Fiorella shrugged. "No one suspect the old lady. The old man, sure. An old man can still make a baby, but an old woman is invisible. Good advantage to have. Maybe I am older, maybe I am slower, but I am smart. I know how to play the game. You set the other players against each other, use them to win."

Kitt set his elbow on the table. "Is that what you've done, set players against each other?"

"Sometimes." Fiorella bobbed her head. "Sometimes players work together to beat another player. Sometimes you gotta sit back an' let them think they beat you."

"Why did you want to have me killed?" Mae said with a mashed potato tongue.

"*Beddita*," Fiorella shook her head. "You like my daughter. I love you so much, and you love me. You my family. *Vivi* try to kill you. That made me really sore!" she said like she'd stepped out of an old movie. "You wanna know stuff, huh?" She sat back. "Mae, sit down. I will tell you everything." She waved her hand at the Dutch police officer at the door, the little aquamarine ring on her narrow finger catching the light. "Hey, you, buddy, bring us some tea!"

"*No!* No tea." Mae shook her head. "Please."

"Oh!" Fiorella nodded her mouth round. "Yeah. I know. Okay. No. No tea."

Mae gripped the chair harder. "Did you arrange the tea, did you send it to—"

"No, no." Fiorella shook her finger. "That was no me. That was the Enrico people. They are very angry at you. They are, what is the word...*retaliating*. I thought this man who died with the tea last night was a pest to you, Mae, he make your life hard, but I did no send him tea. Enrico did. That is a cross my heart an' hope to die promise."

Her head congested with disbelief and ongoing shock, Mae pulled out the chair and sat.

"I will be honest. I am a little angry. My goddaughter also drank that tea, but turns out she was a greedy li'l brat like Vivi, and these thing happen sometimes, you know?"

Kitt's brows arched. "Tanja Goedenacht was your goddaughter?"

"She is Tania *Buonanotte*, my goddaughter like Vivi Gallia. They are *cuscini*, cousins. Vivi has many cousins."

"Oh, Jaysus."

"It is the greed, you know," Fiorella sighed. "Greed ruins it all. I kept it small. Small is simple, safe, money flow, lotsa money flow, an' the family happy. But somebody always want more because more is better. *Avariza,* greed. Vivi push her way in, an' kept what she was doing from me, the trafficking, the refugees. Missy got too big for her britches, an' go to prison, an' Martini is pushing up daisies. Now look at the mess those two screwups made. Like little kids, they leave it to mama to clean up."

Kitt leaned forward slightly. "And what are you cleaning up for Polly Dankwaerts?"

"Eh," Fiorella gestured with her thumb and forefinger, "Martini and Vivi mix up Polly in this. An' then her greedy *niputi,* nephew, get mixed up in too. He doesn't know Tania is working for us until Martini and Bianco come to him an' say 'Hey, buddy, I know you've been stealing from your Aunt Polly. This is how you can fix it. I know you a big investor in a couple freeports. Gimme your passkey. We're gonna give it to pretty redhead who make us a lotta dough'. *Pfft.* That redhead."

"Ruby Bleuville." Kitt said, matter-of-factly. "Tania said the freeport passkey came from Martini."

"Martini pass the key to Ruby. It is better to blame the dead. That is what is easy. Blame it on Ruby Bleuville. Blame it on Martini. Blame it on Caspar. Blame it on the dead. They cannot protest their innocence or corroborate a liar's lie. It works. The Yeoh Triad and Enrico Cartel embrace this idea."

Mae swallowed, trying to clear ears that were clogged with the paste that filled her pores and throat. "Is Caspar alive?" she said with a paste-coated tongue, a hammering head, and a knot in her chest.

Fiorella glanced at Kitt and slid black pearls between her fingers before she exhaled. "Caspar, ah, well... He is good friends wit Martini an' Bianco. Caspar shoulda stayed dead an' live wit all his money an' play in his gardens in Malta and Croatia, but he come back from the dead an' call himself 'Bruno Sciacca'. He buy a big old house, like Polly's, 'bout an hour from here, and fix up the gardens nice. Then Caspar get this idea. He convince Martini and Bianco there is money to make in giant greenhouse farming. He was right, it is a good way to clean money. They build a couple *enorme* greenhouses, really big—you saw this morning, huh? 'Bruno Sciacca' run the Big Bertha farm for us; it make good money for us and the Enrico Cartel, but 'Bruno' got ideas, an' show-off the greenhouse in the *National Geographic*. The Enrico and Yeoh don't like the attention." Fiorella sighed heavily.

A high-pitched ringing filled Mae's pounding head. "Where is he?" she whispered, her hands quivering on the tabletop. "W-where is he?"

Fiorella pressed her lips together. "*Beddita*, he is dead again. For good. I wash my hands of him. He die yesterday. A big Chinese guy," she chuckled, "his name is Man. He snuff Caspar in sex shop Bianco own in Amsterdam. Yeoh an' Enrico ask, I say okay. They use Man. Vivi use him too. You pay, he kill an' clean. He speaks such nice Italian."

The world around her paused, as if frozen, and she was trapped beneath a crust of paste that had turned to ice. Yesterday, she had looked at Caspar's mashed, bloodied, bearded, plastic-wrapped face and hadn't known him. She had never known him. He had never been. At once, the frozen world cracked open, everything unclogged, life rushing back to speed. Mae let out a shuddering cry and inhaled sharply. She looked at Kitt, tears streaming down her face, her nose running. He gave her a soft smile and blinked back the moisture that burned weary blue-grey eyes full of warmth and relief.

"No, no, no," Fiorella waved her slender hands. "You don't cry for that man no more. No. No. He hurt you so much. You don't cry for him." She pulled a little lace-edged cotton handkerchief from her bra and pushed it toward Mae.

"I'm not crying for him," Mae sniffled and half-sobbed, looking at Kitt. "I'm *not* crying for him."

Kitt held her gaze, lifted her hand, kissed the middle of her palm, and pushed the handkerchief into her fingers.

Mae blew her nose. "There's a picture of you with him not so long ago.

"Somebody watching him, huh?" Fiorella gave a nod. "That is not a surprise. He wanna show off the greenhouse an' garden, 'specially the poison one. His *National Geographic* publicity expose the Cartel an' Triad. They don't like that. I don't like that he and Martini use his friend Torrisi an' my Polly to move people, the *clandestini*." For a moment, Fiorella's mouth was a grim line. "I see all the greedy hands start to grab at the same time. The Yeoh Triad, the Enrico Cartel, an' this family fighting already. Everybody wanna take over business, moving the people 'roun the world. They do not see they are heading for a war an' they do not want to listen to the old lady-*picciridda*. Wars are shitty. Wars make refugees. Polly was a refugee. Lotsa people dying. Children, babies drowning. I don't like that. You can move an' clean money an' not make desperate people *schivao*—slaves. War is bad. You can profit from war without making slaves. Me an' my *fidanzata* Polly survive the big war. You know, in the war, she ate tulip bulbs so she wouldn't starve."

Mae blinked. "Polly Dankwaerts is your *fiancée*?"

"You are never too old for love. Remember that." Fiorella grinned a little shyly. "I ask her to marry me. She wanna but she is a little bit mad at me now. I am today engaged and arrested. Maybe I get a conviction, but *non andro in prigione*—I will not go in prison." She shrugged, the corners of her mouth pulling down. "No. For that, I am too old. Berlusconi, not as old as me an' they give him tree years, but he no go in prison. He work in old people's home in Milano. You see. I will get the same. I will go cook pasta *per i vecchi*

—for the old wit no teeth, an' I do that already. Or maybe the Yeoh or Enrico people will kill me. *Me ne frega.* Now, kiss me, an' go home wit the Major. Him and me, we know: the people who kill for you are the people who love you the most."

CHAPTER TWENTY-FOUR

Three days later, they were home. Life had returned to something familiar with familiar habits.

Sweat-drenched from his run, Kitt unhooked the dog's lead and hung it from coat rack beside the door, just above the chair where he put his sports bag. Felix shot into the sitting room and scurried about in front of Bryce—and The Consortium's silver-haired Special Operations Deputy Director, Barbara Cubby.

Seated on the button-back Chesterfield, Cubby, clearly not a dog person, rolled her eyes at the animal's excited spinning and rushing about in a short circle.

"How's the hand, Kitty?" Bryce said, sipping coffee and biting into a chocolate biscuit that Mae always seemed to have on hand in case the Welshman dropped in.

"Healing nicely. Good morning, Deputy Director Cubby."

"Major," she said, eyeing the dog the way one did a crusty-nosed two-year-old child with a cold. "Forgive the intrusion at home."

"Not at all. I appreciate you stopping by to inquire about my health."

"Please sit, Major." Cubby gestured to the empty leather club chair.

"Forgive me, ma'am," he glanced down at his damp grey tee, "I'm a bit sweaty."

She nodded. "Your butler's assumption was correct. I did some reading about what caused your injury, Major. Reports state the gympie-gympie is a plant so diabolically painful it can, and has driven men to suicide—or to cut off their own limbs. I believe diluted hydrochloric acid followed by wax strips is the standard treatment for gympie-gympie stings."

"Unfortunately, the standard treatment wasn't available in the Chateau Silicië poison Garden. I had to improvise."

"What did the doctors say about your finger?" Cubby chose a biscuit from the plate on the tea tray Mae had set up.

"That Valentine did a remarkably tidy job of severing it cleanly."

Bryce make a face, biscuit at his mouth.

Cubby wrinkled her button nose. "The alligator notwithstanding, that was quite a garden, useful in a way in as much as Tox-Lab was able to establish that the poison that killed Roger Llewelyn came from a dwarf specimen of the *Cerbera odallam*, more commonly known as a 'suicide tree'. There's one growing in the greenhouse poison garden. A seed from the tree was ground up into the chai Hilary Wint presented to Llewelyn. We passed that information on to the Americans. The same toxin was found in Ruby Bleuville and Milton Foley. Curiously, Morland's stroke was just that. A stroke, nothing fishy about it." She paused to sip coffee.

"Johnson found Hilary in the Bahamas," Bryce lifted a biscuit. "She said two men came and told her that they fed her father to a shark and if she didn't want to be an orphan, she would do exactly what they said. She's in protective custody."

"We have a bit of news the Italians and the Dutch have passed along," Cubby said. "The Hedison's product appraiser who flagged the Dankwaerts jewellery pieces as fakes was able to identify the blond Dutchman who tried to sell the gems on behalf of his 'Aunt Polly', as Gert Hugo, the manager of a sex shop in Amsterdam, where, I believe, you found the body of Valentine's husband."

The healing skin beneath his bandaged left hand itched. Kitt wiggled three and a half fingers to stop the sensation. "So, Vlaming was fleecing his Aunt Polly while Gert was robbing him."

"In addition," Cubby licked cocoa crumbs from her finger, "Jill Charteris was an associate of Ruby Bleuville. The two women worked together appraising artwork held in freeports in the US State of Delaware—and Singapore, where you nearly died late last year. Charteris filed a complaint against Bleuville. She was also listed to give evidence in a case involving Fedelio Columbo, the Brazilian artist who laundered money for the Enrico Cartel."

"Good morning, sir." Mae entered with a carafe of coffee and biscuits wrapped up for a delighted Bryce. She wore her standard uniform navy-blue shirt dress, white apron tight and Doc Marten Mary-Janes. Bryce, bless him, had clearly rung ahead to let her know he would be stopping by with a guest in an official capacity. Felix trotted to her, rising up on his hind legs to paw at her. Gently, she pushed him down. "Would you like your coffee, now?" she said.

"No, thank you, Valentine. I'll have it with my breakfast, after I shower."

"As you wish." She poured more coffee into Bryce's mug.

Kitt turned to his unexpected early morning visitors, watching Felix poke his nose behind Cubby's knee and begin to lick.

She shooed the dog away.

"I'm sorry," Kitt said. "The dog has slight anxiety issues we have yet to work out, not a surprise since the poor animal's been bounced from place to place these last few months. Valentine, the dog, please."

Mae clicked her tongue and the dog followed her to the kitchen.

Cubby watched the kitchen door for a moment "Your injury places you on second reserve. You're fine to continue in SOST, but once you've healed, I'd like you reassigned from training, Major."

"To where?"

Cubby didn't say anything, she merely looked at him for a moment as if mulling over how to phrase something.

Bryce slouched in his club chair. "Go ahead and ask him. I told you exactly what he's going to say."

"For fifty pounds, Sergeant," Cubby's brown eyes cut to Bryce, "they have to be Kitt's *exact* words"

"My exact words?" Kitt said.

"The deputy director has something she would like to ask you."

"Ma'am?" Kitt said, and waited. Cubby asked her question, which wasn't as much a question as it was a story laced with insults, praise, a little damnation, rationalisations, and a hint of supplication. "Why not you, ma'am?"

"My area of speciality is lacking, meaning I am not quite fit for purpose. You are. I would prefer to keep it that way."

After a long moment where Bryce sipped coffee and chewed a biscuit, Kitt gave his answer.

Cubby tucked the curved edges of her silvery bob behind both ears and handed Bryce a fifty-pound note. Then she rose and brushed a crumb of chocolate biscuit from her red skirt. "Please thank your butler for her sterling service, Major. We'll let you get to your breakfast and see ourselves out. Let's go, Sergeant." She paused at the door Bryce had opened for her. "I still expect your report on my desk by the end of the week," she said.

"Yes, ma'am." Kitt sat on the sofa the SOD Deputy Director had vacated and watched them leave. He wiped a bead of sweat from his forehead and left a handprint of moisture on the sofa's armrest when he rose to answer the door buzzer. Rather than Bryce grinning at him on the little security monitor screen, Mae's brother scowled at the camera. Kitt buzzed him in.

Ten seconds later, Sean shoved open the flat's door Kitt left cracked open. "Here's yer bleedin' document, the one you asked me to ask me friend to finagle for ya." The blue-eyed man thrust out an envelope.

"You're so Irish when you say *finagle*."

"Get stuffed, brother-in-law."

Kitt dabbed sweat from his chin and wiped his hand on his jogging shorts. He opened the envelope and slid out the paper inside. It was gold edged, *Vicariato Del Citta' Del Vaticano* across the top, with *Parrocchia della Bascilia Papale di San Pietro in Vaticano Certificato di Matrimonio* centred below that, a red seal on the lower left. "Thank you." He said, his throat tight. "Thank you."

Sean held out his hand. "You're welcome. It's my penance for keeping secrets from her and *for* you. I've made peace wit me sister, now I make it wit you. Peace to ya, brother."

Kitt took the man's hand and shook it. Then Sean jerked him forward into a slapping, bear hug. "You hurt her and I'll kill ya."

"I wouldn't have it any other way." Kitt slapped back.

Felix in her arms, Mae watched them from the open kitchen door. Why was it the men in her life, the ones she cared for, always threatened to kill each other?

Her brother let Kitt go, waved at her, and left, singing, "*In da naaaaame ov luuuuuuuv...*" at the top of his voice like a demented Bono.

She set the dog on his feet, turned about and tied on an apron.

"What was that death threat all about?" she said, Felix scampering to paw at Kitt as he entered the kitchen.

He handed her the envelope and picked up the dog, cuddling him close, watching her pull out the thick certificate. "I think it may be time you met my parents," he said.

Mae looked down at the official document. "It's lovely."

He smiled at her. "Yes. It's only a piece of paper. I know you didn't need it, but I did. I didn't do it for you, Mae. It matters to me. It's a gift to me, like your love."

Mae chewed her top lip for a second. "I really, really want to mock you for that last bit. I mean *really*. But look at me."

He did. Two fat tears rolled down her face. His face was wet too. "It means we're legal, my love." He sniffled. "Our marriage legally registered and recognised. Your brother did the paperwork, had a friend at Vatican City help. It's not as uncommon as people think, usually it's military, happens on battlefields, and well, love is…"

"A battlefield?"

He kissed the top of the dog's head. "I was going to say something that knows no bounds."

"Of course you were." She wiped away her tears. "Of course you were."

"Have you forgiven your brother for keeping things about Caspar from you?"

"Let's say it's a work in progress. But he's my brother, the only family I've got."

"You have me—my brother, sister an—"

"Your parents?"

"Yes. And Felix. We're your family."

She moved and lay a hand on his cheek. "Go shower. I'll put the coffee on. When you come back, you can tell me why Bryce and that woman were here."

Five and a half minutes later, Kitt ambled into the kitchen, in his dressing gown, in need of feeding, left hand bandaged. He smelled clean, of orange, bergamot and a whisper of spicy nutmeg that blended with the aroma of coffee. The scent suited him.

"There's something we need to talk about," he said, moving behind her to kiss her neck.

"That phrase always sounds so ominous."

"Yes, it does." He nosed into her hair. Felix nosed the back of his knee.

Mae giggled and squirmed away all goose pimply, kicking a tennis ball across the white tiles where a man had once bled to death. "So, who was she and what did she want?"

The dog chased the ball and caught it, growling as he bit into it.

Kitt watched the dog for a second, then set his eyes on his wife. "That was the Consortium's SOD Deputy Director Barbara Cubby and Bryce. I've been asked to step into the position."

"What position?" She moved to the cooker, switched on the gas, and set a frying pan on the hob.

"Director of Special Operations Division, Llewelyn's job."

Mae looked at him quizzically. "What did you say?"

"I said I'd have to discuss it with my wife."

She leaned against the worktop beside the cooker and glanced at Felix chewing on a yellow tennis ball. "And then what happened?"

"Bryce laughed, Cubby handed him fifty quid, and...I'd say you were gazing at me adoringly, but you're not. Why are you looking at me that way, with that indefinable expression?"

"A few reasons really." She switched off the gas and slid the frying pan from the hob. "Before Llewelyn died, he said something about retiring and naming his successor. I'm quite sure he was about to say his successor was you." She reached for her coffee cup and had a sip. "At the time, I thought he was goading me, but he wasn't. He expected you would step into the role, as if you'd been planning to, which I don't think you were. I don't think you ever considered it, although you are now."

"Am I?"

"You must be if you said it was something we need to talk about."

"Oh, sod, it, I am."

Mae chuckled. "If you decide that you don't want this job—"

"I never said I *wanted* the job. My stepping into that role, hanging on to that life, it isn't safe. I cannot, and will not, continue to bring that life upon you. I have yet to find a way to keep you safe and that job is not it. I hate hiding. I don't want to send you someplace where I only see you now and again, but that is all I can think of. That is not a life for you. *This* not a life for you."

"You don't get to make that decision for me." She laughed and shook her head. "Caspar chose for me. I had no say. What he did decided the course of my life, but it brought me to you. I will not decide the course of yours. You will not decide the course of mine. I want to be part of your life and not have you resent me for something you have to give up to be with me."

"I wouldn't resent you," Kitt said, expecting her to give him the look, the one he loved, the one that told him he was full of shite. But she didn't have to because he knew he was full of shite. Yes. Eventually, he would resent her.

"Your parents," she said. "I've wondered about them."

"We'll meet them soon. They live in," he gave a small laugh, "New Mexico."

"I mean, I wonder how you keep them safe. Your sister, too. Simon can take care of himself, but how do you keep your parents safe?"

"I don't see them often," he said with a more than a touch of remorse. "I don't live with them. I don't sleep with them."

"And they understand?

"Yes."

Mae set her coffee cup on the butcherblock worktop. "The other day, well, night actually, I mentioned that I have a way that this might work for us, that might keep us all safe. Perhaps I have a very good way."

"I cannot wait to hear it." Kitt leaned against the edge of butcherblock and looked at his dog gnawing on a bright yellow tennis ball.

Mae crossed her arms. "Just listen. You have to do what's best for you, for your psyche. It's a strange, selfless virtue to risk your life for others, and I know this isn't something you merely choose to do, it is something you *have* to do. You believe you are giving back to humanity and I have teased you for that."

"Mercilessly." He sipped coffee.

Mae smiled. "You once said that you have a highly developed social conscience, being born into a world with more wealth and comfort that you could ever need means you have a moral responsibility, an obligation to look after and give to those less fortunate and share your wealth in more than a philanthropic capacity. What was it, you believe in community, service, social justice? I know who you are. I know how you are. I know the restlessness typically begins at three months. The inactivity burrows beneath your skin, and it becomes evident, in subtle ways, that the sedentariness of work that doesn't challenge you turns you soft in mind and body. I've lived with you long enough to know the pattern. The occasional pulse in your jaw, the long sigh when you finish your scrambled eggs."

He set his cup down on the worktop a little hastily. Coffee splashed up and over the rim. "Are you—are you *encouraging* me to take on the role?"

"I'm encouraging you to be true to yourself." Mae handed him a tea-towel to mop up the spill. "Being true to yourself in this case

339

means regular hours, close to home, all the intrigue and manoeu-vring, with only the occasional instance of an international crime syndicate trying to kill you."

"Only the occasional?"

"You'll need an assistant. If you pick up the dog poo, I'll do the paperwork."

"I'd have Bryce for that."

"Yes, Bryce, your trusted Moneypenny-type is already sorted, but you are in need of a floor manager, one you can trust, one who would never, *ever* serve you tea."

"Goodness me, you *are* encouraging me to take on the role."

"I'm saying," she looked at him with one eye narrowed thought-fully, "that it's a not perfect solution. We make up stories to fit the image of ourselves and the image of the messy, horrible, beautiful, imperfect world around us. I love you, Hamish. You turn me inside out and upside-down. You want me to stay. I want to stay. I know I am a husk, hollow without you. Th—"

"A husk?" Kitt lifted a brow. "That's a bit dramatic for you."

"Yes, surprising, isn't it?" She poured more coffee in her cup. "This may surprise you as well. Here is my idea. Instead of hiding, I say we live in the open, like ordinary people, because we are ordi-nary people—you just happen to kill. If the idea of safety is such a concern, if you're worried someone might try to poison my coffee beans, or the Chelsea bun I send to work with you, I think I have something of a safeguard for myself, and it might allay your fears for my safety, maybe even yours."

Felix growled and shook the living hell out of the tennis ball, bright yellow fuzz hanging from what had once been a sphere.

"You know I keep a journal, but at this point in time it's maybe less of a journal and more of a...book."

"You've written a book?" He handed back the tea-towel.

Mae topped up his coffee. "It began as something to help me

process the things I've been through. I started last year, I wrote about killing Sal Tornatore with a toilet brush in this kitchen, finding Russo the baker's hand toasting in an oven in Sicily, to you declaring your unspoken love for me right here in this kitchen. Then it became part of the job I had when I thought you were dead and I was observing Taittinger and his wine-collecting, cultural artefact-stealing friends, but the journal became a narrative. Now it's a book."

"When have you had time to write a book?"

"What do you think I did in the empty hours when you were away?"

"Empty hours. I like that."

"I thought you would."

"I believed, in all those *empty hours*, you were renovating and cursing my name."

She shrugged and nodded. "Those days you were gone were devoid of any joy, and in my joyless evenings, when I finished renovating and cursing your name, I wrote. Then after you returned home, in the mornings, when you went to your office, I wrote. Do you see what I am suggesting, the safeguard I have, should I need it?"

He nodded thoughtfully. "I supposed you want to take the story to the *New York Times,* the *Washington Post, The Sunday Times*?"

"It's what happens in spy films and spy novels all the time. Someone goes to the press, feeds classified documents to a reporter. The reporter ends up dead, but the newspaper exposes the corruption deep within a black-ops government agency. But no, I don't want to be an unnamed source. I want to tell the story myself."

"How, take it online, send it out on social media?"

"I was thinking of having it published as a sort of memoir."

"Do you know how hard it is to get published?"

"I'd self-publish it."

He laughed. "Oh, yes, the world will rush to read your *self-published* memoir."

She paid his mocking no mind. "I imagine it would be like Lieutenant Colonel Anthony Shaffer's *Operation Dark Heart: Spycraft and Special Ops on the Frontlines of Afghanistan and the Path to Victory*, only without all the politics, the hollering about classified documents, government attempts at censorship, and my suing the Crown for the right to print an un-redacted document."

"Christ. You read too many spy novels." He had a gulp of coffee, his favourite Tanzanian brew, and wondered if she'd spiked it with something because what she was saying made...sense.

"Shaffer's book isn't a spy novel. It's a *memoir*, and the attempts to keep secret some of the information he included attracted attention, which led to an increase in book sales. Have you ever heard of the Streisand Effect, the phenomenon where an attempt to hide or censor information has the opposite effect of spreading the information widely?"

"Is that what you're hoping for?"

Felix rushed out of the kitchen and back in again, the remnants of the fuzzy, floppy tennis ball in his mouth. Mae looked at the dog and grinned and he zoomed out of the kitchen. "I'm hoping for a satisfying resolution to this strange little love story of ours, which, I suppose is a more like a novel or screenplay rather than a memoir," she said.

"A screenplay? Really, Mae?" Kitt drank the rest of coffee that wasn't drug-spiked.

"It's not that far-fetched. Think about it, it's got everything; suspense, action, thrills, murder, mystery, spies."

"And true love, don't forget true love. This has also been a love story."

"Somebody often dies in a love story."

"We're both still alive, but I see your point. Perhaps you could stretch it out to a fourth book and give it a happy ending. Everyone loves a happy ending."

"I think it works better as a trilogy."

"How then would you conclude this trilogy?"

She lit the hob and placed the frying pan on it. "With scrambled eggs, Hamish."

"And that, my love is the happy ending. If someone was writing a book about your life, this would complete the story or narrative arc."

"It's not an arc, it's a feckin' circle. Here we are, where we started, in the kitchen, frying pan on the cooker, a cup of coffee in your hand as you wait for me to scramble your eggs."

"That was then. This is now. This is forever."

"I prefer *forever* to *until death*."

"As do I. It's far more romantic. Here we are now, in the kitchen, in service to each other, forever." He set his empty mug on the worktop, and the earnestness she'd grown accustomed to, the sincerity that made his cool, blue-grey eyes glow with heat whenever he bared his feelings, appeared, his gaze as hot and bright blue as the flame on the gas cooker. "I love you," he said.

She looked at him, expectantly, waiting for him to continue, waiting for genuine, sentimental declarations that didn't ensue and she frowned. "*I love you*, is that all I get?"

Head cocked slightly, the left corner of his mouth rising. "It's not impassioned, flowery, or poetic, but it is simple. To the point."

"So it is." She cracked three eggs into a bowl. "Would you see to the toast?"

Kitt plunged whole-wheat bread into the toaster and watched her whisk whites and yolks together, watched her pour them into a pan with a knob of butter that melted, watched her push the yellow liquid about until the pan was filled with pale and fluffy scrambled eggs, and he grinned, but the smile was short-lived. "I have no idea what I am going to do for a living."

"So you're *not* going to take the job?"

"It does come with a rather nice Mercedes, but there's so much paperwork, Mae."

"In that case, how do you feel about renovations and restorations? I'm thinking of buying a place in Oxfordshire or Surrey. One of them is a ramshackle estate with a ramshackle cottage that has a stone fence and an orchard right at the front."

"This scares the hell out of me, but I think we ought to discuss my future, *our* future over breakfast. Are those ready?"

She spooned fluffy yellow onto a blue and white Minton plate with a gilt edge. She handed him the dish. Kitt stared down at the mouth-watering, pale-gold, perfect, tiny bites of joy, and grinned again. Could it be that simple? Her idea, *insurance*, the stuff of clichéd, idiotic spy film and fiction, might just work.

"You know, Hamish," Mae said, the toast popping up, "murder, spies, mystery, romance, dead bodies, weird weapons, henchmen, villains, it's all enough to destroy a couple, but our relationship has always been built on the solid foundation of a good breakfast."

ACKNOWLEDGMENTS

I am indebted to Suzanne and Henny for their assistance with Dutch language and culture. Many thanks to Fiona Gregory and Dr Illias Zontirios for the toxicological expertise (and hot dance moves). Thank you my Liebchen, Kriss Wagner Plumer, for showing me true friendship by reading my first (truly horrible) book and sticking it out as I became a better writer. Blessings upon Anne-Marie Scoones for reading the messy draft. I am grateful to Rebekah Turner for all the tireless-nothing-is-too-hard cover love, coffee, and writer bitching sessions. My sincere thanks to Angelo Thompson for the time he read *Goldfinger* to me on a road trip, to Elle Gardner for knowing regret is unprofessional, to Lisa Barry for always being excited about writing. A special thank you to Megan Whalen Turner for telling me stories, encouraging me to as well, and wanting to stuff me into the boot of her car after 40 (*40!*) years of friendship. Many thanks to my big little love Belinda for editing what I never knew was going to be a series.

Finally, to my big, bearded Sicilian—thank you for your enduring patient love and support, and emboldening me to make enough money to buy the really good coffee.

ABOUT THE AUTHOR

All my books present women over the age of forty as lead characters. I am so interested in dispelling the myths and 'Hollywood' stereotypes of older women you often see (or don't see) in fiction and film I did a doctorate on the subject! You can call me Dr Sandra.

Although I live in Australia, please note I use both UK and US English spelling depending on the characters and setting of the book. Any mistakes in Italian, the Sicilian dialect, and Dutch are mine. My US-based novels, *A Basic Renovation*, *For Your Eyes Only*, *Driving in Neutral*, and *Next to You*, are romantic comedies and romantic-comedy-mysteries published through Escape, a Harper Collins imprint. My UK-set books that are part of the *In Service* series, *At Your Service*, *Forever in Your Service*, *True to Your Service* and the short story, *Your Sterling Service*, are cosy and gritty romantic spy mystery-thrillers.

My books are available as ebook and paperbacks via www.sandraantonelli.com and all other e-tailers.

I have been persuaded to write another book for the In Service series. Since it takes me about a year to write a book, I'll aim for a 2021 release. The fourth book is tentatively titled *Your Uncommon Service*.

www.ingramcontent.com/pod-product-compliance
Lightning Source LLC
Chambersburg PA
CBHW070051120726
47909CB00002B/350